SUGAR'S DANCE

Katie Mettner

For Dad

Some of my best memories are of us together at the library. Thanks for sharing your love of reading, your appreciation of Hootie and your love of coffee! Let's meet at Bob's. The coffee's on me!

Sugar Lips

For Mom

Thanks for the winter of 1989 and for everything you gave up to be there for me. Thanks for never saying I told you so and for encouraging me to take all those stairs to that little upstairs ballroom all those years ago. This one's for you!

Katie

Katie Mettner

D

Your unwavering belief in me is the reason Sugar can be the person she is in these pages; you have given me the courage to share her with the world. When we met in November 1999, I didn't believe in soulmates. I do now. You are mine and I love you.

KT

ACKNOWLEDGMENTS

A special thank you to Dennis O'Hara of Northern Images Photography for the front cover photo. The Lord blessed you with an amazing eye for His creation, thanks for sharing it with all of us!

To my sister Jen, my editing goddess, thanks for correcting all those missing, misspelled and misused words on a tight timeline. The title is *perfect*, thanks for helping me see that. I think we make a great team! I owe you five boxes of Kleenex and an endless supply of Starbucks next time I see you! I love you Sis!

To Jessie, my first reader, who welcomed Sugar into her heart and her home. Thanks for being my best cheerleader, my best critic and my best friend. Your job was to keep it real and keep me honest. You're good at your job, but you're an even better friend!

Kisber, thanks for taking trips to obscure places to answer my weird questions and for not rolling your eyes at me. I'm lucky to call you my sister!

To Andrew, you are my inspiration. The paper is my canvas and the words are my paint. I hope I learned my lessons well. Thanks for teaching me perseverance and strength, you've got it down. I love you!

A very special thank you to the guys who keep me dancing. I'm certain you don't get paid enough to put up with me! Thanks for the long hours and the frustrating setbacks, but most of all thanks for those first few fist pumps at the end of the parallel bars. The Lord blessed you with the gift of compassion and patience, thanks for sharing it with me.

To Patrick of the Red Star for taking the time on a busy Saturday to help me bring Sugar's birthday to life. I couldn't have done it without you!

To my 3 E.'s. I saved you for last because you are my greatest achievements in life. Thanks for not laughing at me when I said I was writing a book, for the cheerleading sessions every morning, the extra computer time every night and for not caring that I was the only mom at the park with a notebook! Dream big, love often and dance like nobody's watching! I love you!

Irish Slang Terms

Acting the Maggot - Fooling and messing around.
Bang on - Correct. Accurate
Bazzer -A haircut
Black Stuff- Guinness
Codding ya - To pull someone's leg
Craic – Fun
Crann- Gaelic word for tree
Delira and Excira - Delighted and Excited
Dekko- Look at or inspect
Deadly - Fantastic, Wonderful
Donkey's years - For a very, very long time
Eejit - Complete fool
Fair play! - Well done
Fluthered - Very drunk
Get Outta That Garden - Affectionate phrase generally thrown into a conversation to encourage laughter
Gruiag- Gaelic word for hair
Holy Show- Disgusting
How's she cutting? - 'Hi'
Howya - 'Hi'
Knackered - Very tired or broken beyond repair
Langer - A cork name for a disliked person (male)
Melter- Pain in the ass
Mi Daza- Means excellent, brilliant, fantastic. Pronounced (mee-dah-za)
Mineral- A soft drink
Mi Mot – Girlfriend. Pronounced (mee-moe)
Now you're sucking diesel -You have solved or understand a problem. Now you're talking. Now you're doing well
Oul Doll - Girlfriend (Pronounced: Owl-Doll)
Thick - Extremely stupid
Throw shapes - To show off
Touched - Someone who hasn't their full mental capacities

Sugar's Dance

One

Coffee. In my humble opinion it is the lifeblood of all that is right in the world. Without coffee I'm not sure there would be much point in getting up in the morning. My name is Tula DuBois, Sugar, to everyone I know, and coffee makes my world go around. For some women it's doughnuts, cake or sex, but for me it's coffee. My father always said, "Sugar, if you can eat it, you can drink coffee with it." I have found that to be true. Hot, iced, black, sugared, creamed, frothed or anything in-between it can be done. I cut my teeth on coffee and chances are it really did stunt my growth, but that's a small price to pay for the rich rewards on a cold morning. I live in a log cabin lodge on the edge of Lake Superior where I spend nine months of the year trying to stay warm.

I come from French Canadian descent, my father being a true Quebecois. My mother was English Canadian and pretty much just put up with my father's insistence that he was more Canadian than she. When I was about a year old we moved from Quebec to Duluth so my father could craft custom cabinets for businesses and homes on the lake. He bought this old lodge, which he named Sugar's, and where I have lived for twenty-six out of my twenty-seven years of life. I live where people only dream to live and I love every minute of it.

There was no place else I would rather be at seven thirty on a Tuesday morning than sitting on my porch swing overlooking my little part of Lake Superior. Watching the sunrise with a cup of coffee in my hand and listening to the sound of the waves lapping on the bay and the cardinals singing in the trees. I love this time of year. Being early November there was a soft sheen of frost on everything and the freshness of the air almost took your breath away. I was wrapped up in my parka and doing nothing but enjoying my coffee and trying not to let too many thoughts intrude on the beauty of it all. This was my time and it was quiet. I had spent the last month getting the lodge buttoned up for the winter and by the feel of this morning, snow wasn't far off. Seemed like just yesterday the lodge was bustling with people as they came and went for the weddings I host in the garden. I'm booked solid from May through the Indian summer of October and this year was no different. My day job is teaching ballroom dance to old people looking to stay young, young couples starting out their life together and just about anyone in-between who wants to learn.

1

My lessons are also how I book my weddings. Couples come in for their lessons, fall in love with the lodge and book a dream wedding in the garden. I offer the use of my ballroom for receptions and pontoon boat for pictures on the lake. The new couple gets a weekend in the honeymoon cabin complete with champagne, roses and breakfast in bed. To say it keeps me very busy wouldn't begin to cover it, so by November I'm always looking forward to a quiet winter. My winters are filled with dance lessons and MAMBOS Foundation work minus the pressure and constant running. It was the time I enjoyed the most. It was time for my family and for kicking back with a good book, but this year I was finding it hard to work up my usual excitement about a long winter in the woods.

I thought back over the summer and all the changes that had taken place in my life. I had spent the last few months with one of my wedding couples, Margie and Nathan. They had come to stay with me for a few months before their wedding enjoying what the lodge had to offer, solitude. They were a fun energetic couple and enjoyed participating in all the dance classes and they stuck around on the weekends to help with the weddings. We spent the evenings around the campfire, Nathan playing his guitar and Margie and I singing old goofy camp songs while relaxing with a beer. It was the first time I had ever had a couple stay with me for so long before their wedding and it couldn't have come at a better time in my life. Their company was just what I needed this summer and I was very sad to see them go last week. They had become good friends and I missed them already. I hadn't heard from them since they left and wasn't having any success in getting in contact with them. They had seemed distracted right before they left and I was beginning to worry that something was wrong. Margie's father became ill right before the wedding and couldn't come up to give her away. I'd been telling myself that she wasn't returning her calls because she was too busy running the business. That was getting harder to swallow as each day passed. I know one of the two of them would have gotten back to me by now. She asked me to call her immediately when the wedding photos and video came in and I called, texted, called, emailed and called and had gotten no response. Something was off. I remembered the look on Margie's face when she told me her father wasn't coming. It was a look of relief if I had ever seen one. Something told me that her father was a hard man to love. I told myself that if this went on much longer I would ask my brother Jesse to look into it for me.

I pushed the swing with my toes and sipped my coffee. God bless coffee. The air was much cooler this morning than it was yesterday and I could feel the seasons changing around me. The crispness of fall and its burst of color being replaced by stark, blank trees devoid of leaves, nothing more than empty branches swaying in the bitter wind. The temperature, though in the mid forties, was raw. The old saying goes if you don't like the weather in Wisconsin stick around, it'll change. And it was true. The weather often changed on a dime and there wasn't a damn thing you could do about it. I was feeling that way about my life lately. It was changing and there wasn't a damn thing I could do about it. My business was running smoothly and I was quite content with what I had accomplished with the lodge. I had built the wedding business to where I'm booked every weekend and I hold a strong footing in the local ballroom dance scene. The foundation I run in memory of my dance partner is stronger than ever and soon will need someone to run it full time. My life is full, but for some reason I still feel alone. Loneliness and old memories had started resurfacing, but they weren't welcomed memories and I fought to keep them from taking over my life.

I laid my head back on the swing and heard nothing but the lap of the waves on the lake and the cry of the gulls as they flew overhead. The day stretched before me and I had yet to decide how I would fill it. Normally things fell into place, but with my lack of sleep lately all I really wanted to do was go back to bed. I knew that was a bad idea, the nightmares would just become daymares. Activities that don't require my body to move are fast becoming my favorite and even dancing was becoming a chore the less and less sleep I got.

I got up off the swing taking a deep breath ready to face the day when I heard the crush of tires over gravel. I jumped down the steps to the main parking area wondering who it could be. I had no deliveries lined up for the day and it was too early for students. So I was standing there, one hand on my hip the other holding my coffee when I saw the front grill of the Duluth PD squad car. I dropped my coffee cup and it hit the blacktop splashing hot liquid on my leg, but I didn't cry out. I was rooted in place watching the car pull into the turn around area. The back door opened and I saw my brother step out of the back of the car. I let out the breath I didn't know I was holding as he leaned into the driver's side door and said something to the driver. He backed out of the window and the driver turned the squad and pulled back down my driveway. Jesse was standing there, dressed in clothes that appeared slept in, holding a briefcase in one hand and a drink carrier from Starbucks in the other. He strolled over to me eating up the space between us quickly.

He pulled up short when he saw the coffee cup on the ground. "Jeez Sugar I didn't know you would be so excited to see me."

I threw my arms around his neck and hugged him so tight he almost dropped the coffee and then I punched him, hard.

"Owww! What did I do to deserve that?" He hollered.

"You showed up in my driveway in a squad car at seven thirty in the morning and scared me half to death!" I probably shouldn't yell.

He smiled and set his stuff down on the steps. "Sorry Sugar, I tried to call, but you didn't answer. I figured you were out doing your communing with nature thing, so I decided to stop over."

3

"I'm not communing with nature," I said putting it in quotations like he did. "I think I forgot my phone on my night stand though." I crossed my arms over my chest while I waited for my heart to start beating normally again instead of the scared to death tapping it was doing in my chest right now.

"I didn't mean to scare you, Sug," his voice lowered, "I just wanted to see you." He pulled me back into him and I laid my head on his shoulder.

Jesse is a detective for the Lake Superior Drug and Gang Task Force. My biggest fear is that someday seeing a police cruiser pulling into my driveway will mean he's gone.

"Starbucks?" I whispered into his chest and he sighed. Jesse only brought Starbucks when he needed forgiveness for something. I looked up at him, but I didn't see the usual sheepish grin on his face when I called his bluff. Instead I saw fatigue and something else, fear. I stepped away from him and grabbed the coffee. "Let's go inside. I need to change my pants and shoes and the coffee cake should be done." And that got a slight tip to the corner of his mouth.

He pumped a fist. "Sugar DuBois coffee cake is on the menu."

He turned and grabbed his briefcase trudging up the stairs to the house. I trailed behind him shaking my head. Jesse wasn't my brother by blood, but I had known him most of my life. He and his mother nursed me back to health after an accident that killed my parents and his brother, my dance partner. Without them I would not be here today, that much I knew. He is five years older than me and a few heads taller with sandy brown hair and blue eyes. Jesse is a hard working, serious detective, but when he isn't working he reminds me of a big golden retriever puppy always eager for the next adventure. That wasn't the aura he was giving off today. It was a much more subdued Jesse holding the door for me. His shoulders were slumped and his face was lined.

I patted his cheek, "Go take the cake out of the oven while I change. I will be right there."

He headed for the kitchen and I headed to my bedroom for a change of clothes. I threw my parka on the bed and replaced it with my fleece sweatshirt then sat down on the bed and changed out of the wet coffee stained pants and pulled on a warm pair of Champion sweatpants and stuffed my feet into my favorite pair of Crocs. I threw the wet clothes in the tub for later and went in search of my next cup of coffee.

TWO

I found Jesse in the kitchen standing over the coffee cake and I swear I could see some drool coming out the corner of his mouth.

"Tell me its pumpkin cream cheese." he said, his voice hushed.

I lifted an eyebrow, "Its pumpkin cream cheese."

"There is a God." He said and he grabbed his coffee and sat down at the table while I busied myself with the coffee cake, plates and forks.

My kitchen was old country kitchen meets modern day commercial kitchen. The rough hewn logs flanked us on three sides with a break for a pair of patio doors that opened out onto a deck where I kept my commercial gas grill and my one luxury in life, my hot tub. Right past the patio doors was an opening to the mudroom that used to be covered in sawdust when my father would come in from working in the shop. In the middle of the kitchen was a large country style table with old mismatched farm chairs that lined both sides and both ends. There was room for ten, but rarely did I ever have that many people in my kitchen at once. The floor was hardwood with more scuffs and scrapes than a shed pair of deer antlers, but I didn't care. Each one of those scrapes and scuffs told a story and it wasn't something I was willing to change for the sake of beauty. There was a large pantry opposite the patio doors near the commercial size fridge that held all my deliveries in the summer for a full week and in the winter usually held much, much less. I had a dual range with a griddle and though it might seem too big for one person it was used to its greatest potential every weekend. I had a large country style kitchen sink and an under counter dishwasher. My cupboards were original and another thing I couldn't part with when I redid the kitchen. The cupboards hold the memories. The cupboards are my mom and where she had her being. The cupboards are years of hot chocolate, Campbell's soup and Lucky Charms. The cupboards are my dad too. He picked every piece of wood that had gone into them and loved every knot and imperfection. They were made from pine that matched the wood of the lodge and there were plenty of them. My mother was a baker, so she needed constant space for storing everything from soup to nuts. Dad had even built her two old fashioned pie safes that she used up until the day she died. The oldest one resides in my bedroom, storing books and pictures, and the other one sits in the kitchen, holding all the pies at Thanksgiving and the cookies at Christmas. The room was lit by an old fashioned deer antler chandelier that I didn't even really like, but couldn't take down. Every time I looked at it I remembered the complete fit my mother threw when my dad brought it home. Words like "tacky", "horrific" and "not in my kitchen" were thrown around, but in the end my dad hung it up and it's been there lighting the kitchen every day for the last fifteen years and probably will be for the next fifteen. I had added extra inset lighting over the sink and workspace, but there wasn't a day that went by that the chandelier didn't shine bright upon the table.

I brought the coffee cake and silverware to the table and sat down. Jesse helped himself to a piece of cake and took a drink of his coffee.

He smiled across the table at me, "I'm telling you Sugar, you could sell this stuff."

"Then it wouldn't be any fun anymore. Remember how much my mom used to love to make pies? Then she started making them for the restaurant and bar and it became a chore." My mother made the best pies in the Duluth area and sold them to the local pub when I was a little girl. I spent so much time with her in this kitchen rolling out dough and peeling apples that I was pretty sure it was the reason I hated making pies now.

Jesse stabbed himself another piece of coffee cake and I sat down across the table from him. "So there has been something I have been meaning to tell you for awhile Sugar." He said sheepishly.

I laid my fork down. "Okay, I'm all ears."

Jesse smiled. "I'm seeing someone."

I leaned back in my chair. Well I'll be. Jesse rarely dated and when he did he never followed it up with a second date. He was married to his job and I was usually his date for all the functions that required a woman's presence.

"That's great Jesse. Do I know her?"

He swallowed nervously, "You could say that."

I waited.

"Julie."

My hand stilled on my coffee cup, "Julie? You mean Julie Morris? Like my best friend Julie?"

"Yeah."

"Really?" My tone was disbelieving.

Jesse cringed a little at the tone of my voice and looked at me under his lashes. "We've been seeing each other now for about eight months and it's pretty serious."

My mouth dropped open. "Eight months?" Where have I been that I didn't see this? Falling apart slowly, a small voice said. "I can't believe you are just telling me now." I said softly.

"I've **been** busy with a big case Sugar. It didn't seem like the right time to tell you." He busied himself with his breakfast not making eye contact.

I took a drink of my coffee, "I think it is more likely that you didn't want me to know you were moving on."

Jesse flinched, "That's not it at all Sugar. I just, I don't know. Anyone can see that you are having a hard time right now and I didn't think it was the right time."

I guess all this time I hadn't really been fooling anyone. I took a look at Jesse again with fresh eyes. He was tired, but there was brightness to his eyes that I hadn't seen in a long time. He looked happy, finally happy. And then I thought back over the past few months. The hushed phone calls when I walked in the room, the obvious avoidance of each other at family gatherings and the time at the campfire on the fourth of July when I came out of the lodge and found Jesse planting a kiss on Julie. He claimed it was too much alcohol and I fell for it. I'm such a dolt.

"I can't believe you guys didn't tell me. I mean eight months..." And I was hurt, really hurt, that neither of them wanted me to know.

"Don't be mad Sis."

"I'm not mad, I'm hurt. Julie is my best friend. She's like a sister to me, and you..." I trailed off.

"We didn't do it to hurt you Sugar. I don't know, I guess we thought we were doing the right thing. We agreed that we weren't going to tell anyone because you know if things don't work out then everything is awkward, but as time went I knew I needed to tell you."

"But?" I waited for him to finish.

"But I don't know. You have been so busy this summer." He looked down. Busy coming unhinged is what he didn't say.

"Julie has been busy running the foundation over the summer Jess and had I known I could have helped more. I don't know how, but I would have figured something out. She's done amazing things this year for MAMBOS, but I would have lightened the load had I known." And I would have and I probably should have seen it, but I was too wrapped up in my own world.

"You were a big part of the work the foundation did this year too Sugar." Jess threw back.

Julie and I had spent countless hours campaigning and raising awareness for organ and tissue donation. We were fortunate enough to have gained national attention and we had contributions of time and talent pouring into the foundation. Julie and I both work part-time so that we don't have to pay a salaried position and all the money can go back to the families we help, but I was seeing more and more that we couldn't do it alone anymore. Julie is also a police officer, but she works as a victim counselor for the Superior Police Department and now with her seeing Jesse I couldn't ask her to give up anymore of her personal time for MAMBOS.

Jesse finished his coffee cake and I sat there quietly picking at mine not sure how I should feel. I was happy for Jess and Julie, they made a great couple, but I was really upset with myself for not catching on.

"Wow." I heard myself say it and that was exactly how I felt.

Jess was sitting quietly not sure what to say next.

I stood up and went over to him putting my arms around his neck, "I'm happy for you Jess. Julie is a wonderful person and you know how much she means to me. I'm hurt that you didn't tell me, but I'm mad at myself for not putting it together. There were enough signs there. I just... things haven't been good." And obviously that didn't really begin to cover it.

I let him go and walked over to the patio doors that opened onto my deck where my grill and hot tub sat. They looked lonely now, the usual summer sunshine missing and the cold brown leaves swirling around their bases was like a song telling them that the quiet time was upon us.

"About that Sugar, how are you?" Jesse asked me cautiously not wanting to get into something he couldn't get back out of. I didn't turn to look at him hoping that if he couldn't see my face he might believe the lie that was about to come out.

"I'm fine."

"Really? You don't look fine, you look like hell. You look like you haven't slept in weeks."

"Boy, you really know how to make a gal feel special." And he was right, but I wasn't about to admit that.

Jesse came up behind me and put his hands on my shoulders. "I talked to mom yesterday." And I blew out a sigh, here we go.

"She said she hasn't heard from you since she left. I told her you were busy getting the lodge locked down for winter, but that didn't go far. She's worried about you."

Jesse's mom Sharon had gotten married in September and she and her new husband Lenny had gone off to Florida to spend the winter on an extended honeymoon. She didn't want to go and I had to convince her to. She was a mother at heart and I think she knew that I was going to need her. I was silent for longer than I should have been.

"I've tried to call her Jess, but every time I pick up the phone I, I just can't." I heard my voice break and I held back the tears that were always ready to fall. Jess turned me and wrapped me in a hug. I laid my head on his chest and he rested his chin on the top of my head. We stood there like that for a long time not talking. I was soaking up strength from him so I could get through the rest of the day.

"It's been ten years Sugar. Mom and I are really worried about you. It is hard for us, but..." His voice trailed off and he rubbed my back.

"I've been having a hard time lately, I can't tell you why. I feel like Saturday is a big black hole and until I get past that I can't think about anything else. I wouldn't have made it without you two, I know that and for the last ten years I thought I had it all put where it was supposed to be and then suddenly I don't. I can't remember the reason why I'm here doing any of this. All I can think of is that her son, your brother, died and I lived. How do you put that someplace and leave it there? Sharon's happy now with Len and maybe it's time for her to put this chapter of her life behind her and move on."

Jesse pulled away and held me at arm's length, anger flooding his face. "What on God's green earth are you talking about? You mean you want her to forget about you? Is that what you're saying? That she should say "Oh well, I don't love you anymore. Glad to know you!"

"No, but, I don't know, can we change the subject?" And I really wanted to change the subject before I started crying and he saw just how bad I really was.

Jesse shook his head, "No, we can't. Mom needs to hear your voice. She worries about you out here all alone and I passed worried a few months ago."

I leaned back into him. It felt good to be protected for a few moments. I wanted to tell him about the nightmares and I wanted him to help me, but I couldn't take the chance.

"I'm gonna be fine. I really need you to believe that." And I would be, someday.

Jesse sighed. "I'm going to tell you something I have never told anyone before Sugar. The night the accident happened you know I was a rookie cop. I was off duty, sitting in the police station listening to the scanner and yucking it up with the boys. When the call came across the scanner the room hushed like it always did when we heard the word fatality. Only we heard several fatalities and life threatening injuries. Then the chief came in and the room went completely silent. The only reason the chief would be there was if it was really bad. I was expecting him to tell us that we needed to head out and help with traffic control or something mundane like that, but instead he took me aside and told me that the officer on the scene radioed him that he knew the people in the accident. He told me that the only man who had ever shown me the love of a father, the man I thought would someday take me and my son for a ride in his Mustang was gone. The woman who loved everyone in the whole world and healed my broken heart one day at a time after my father left was gone and that the brother I thought was going to stand by my side when I married the woman of my dreams was not going to make it." He stopped and I didn't move for fear he wouldn't finish the story.

"And I can remember looking at the chief and asking what about Sugar, what about Sugar? He said "Sugar's alive and talking. She's badly injured, but they think she's going to make it." And then he put his arm around me and put me in his car and personally drove me to the hospital. During that excruciating slow drive to the hospital I cried. I cried like I had never cried before and have never cried again. When he pulled up alongside the ER doors he turned to me and told me that I needed to channel all my energy into one thought. He said you still have Sugar, keep it together for Sugar. I walked in the doors of the ER and found mom in the waiting room. She was sitting in a chair in her nursing uniform and when she saw me walk in she fell apart, right there in the waiting room and I pulled her into me. She begged me to tell her what I knew and I quietly told her about the accident. She fought back out of my arms and swiped at her tears and said, "We need to keep it together Jess. Let's assess the injuries and then we can make the decisions that need to be made." And like that she was back into nurse mode and I was back into cop mode and we waited in the waiting room for them to come find us. As we stood there it became glaringly clear to us how little control any of us had over anything in life. There we stood a nurse and a cop, two people who help others every day, and suddenly we were that family. We were that family that the nurses and the police try to help. The doctor came and pulled us into a family room and laid it out for us. Your mom and dad were gone and Brent was not going to make it. His brain injury was too severe and there was no brain activity. Then he said that the young girl in the car was alive and talking and had major injuries, but would survive. He wanted us to help them contact family since she was a minor. Mom shook her head and said we were her only family now and he took us to you."

I nodded against his chest. "I remember that. You in your blues and mom in her whites, and the drugs or the lights made it seem so surreal. I remember Sharon sat right down next to the stretcher and said, "Honey, we will get through this together." She had just lost her son and she was ready to love me."

"She already loved you. You were like a daughter to her even though you already had parents that loved you. So you say that you wouldn't have made it without us, but the reality is that had we lost both you and Brent, God only knows where mom and I would have ended up. You gave us that reason to keep fighting. You gave us that reason to wake up in the morning and lay back down at night. I'm scared for you Sugar and I don't know what to do anymore."

I knew they had pulled me through my recovery, but I didn't know that the opposite had been true. "I'm sorry Jesse. I'm not trying to be this way on purpose. I just can't help it. I don't know what to do anymore either." I said softly.

Jesse cleared his throat, "You know Julie helps accident victims' deal with the aftermath of emotions. You guys are best friends and I think you should talk to her, maybe she could help you."

"No!" I pushed my hand up against his chest and bit my tongue to keep from saying anything more. "No. I will be fine. I will work it out, I promise."

I heard him sigh, "Julie is safe Sugar. Julie has no ulterior motive to being in your life other than as your friend. She loves you and she's scared for you. She can see what's going on. She told me the last time she saw you it was all she could do to keep from shaking you until you talked to her. You try to walk around and pretend like everything is normal, but it's obviously not and you're the only one who isn't in agreement on that. We're afraid you aren't too far from falling apart again Sugar. You being in the hospital is not going to help anyone."

I cut him off, "I don't want to talk about it Jesse. I'm not going to end up in the hospital, I promise you that. If I call Sharon will you leave it alone?"

He sighed again. "For now."

I sat back down pushing the coffee cake away, what little appetite I had was gone. I took a few more sips of my coffee. "Cinnamon dolce latte, you really must be feeling guilty." I looked over my cup at Jesse and he was trying for nonchalant, but it wasn't working. I stood up and carried the plates to the sink.

"Sugar, there's something else I need to talk to you about. The real reason I'm here today." I turned slowly and I saw his cop face shutter down. "Let's go in by the fireplace and talk." Jesse said grabbing his briefcase and walking out of the kitchen. I lingered in the kitchen for a moment because the look on his face told me that what he was about to tell me was going to change my life forever.

THREE

The great room was directly off the kitchen and had a completely different feel from the kitchen. There was nothing modern about this room. This room was all rustic log cabin and it always made me feel enveloped when I was in it. It was filled with overstuffed couches and chairs arranged around the huge brick fireplace my father had built out of rocks from the lake.

The coffee table was a boat made from old hewn boards from a crumbling building on the property. The top was an inset carving of the Edmund Fitzgerald sailing past lighthouse pier on Lake Superior. My father told me it was how he pictured it as it headed out on its last journey, as the crewmen and the captain steered the boat out into the open water not knowing that as they left the safety of the harbor behind they would never see that light shining on them again. He had covered the carving with glass, so the effect was that of depth and distance. It was really an amazing piece and it made me a little melancholy each time I saw it.

Looking up at the ceilings you saw them stretch to heights that weren't conducive to easy cleaning and there was a long wood beam which ran the length of the lodge. It was made from an old red oak log that had been submerged in Lake Superior for who knows how long. My father had it dredged up and brought to the lodge. He spent hours on top of a ladder carving in "Sugar's Est. 1982" with the French fleur de lis on each side. As a kid I could never figure out why he put the log up first and then carved it sitting on a ladder. As an adult I understood why. As I began carving myself I understood you need to walk past something one, two or sometimes even a hundred times before the picture takes form in your mind. Sometimes you have to see where something belongs before you can decide what it will become.

I remember sitting on the big sofa watching him carve. He was up on a huge stepladder and my mother was always fretting, "James you are going to fall!" and he would say, "Bon, relax, I'm fine up here" and he was. He spent half his life on a ladder. We would talk as he whittled at the wood and he would ask me about my day or tell me stories about growing up in Quebec. I really didn't care what it was that we talked about, I just loved being with him. Every time I look at that beam now there's an ache in my chest. My father has been gone for ten years, but it felt like ten minutes I missed him so much.

I sat down on the puffy green and red sofa and punched the on button on the remote for the fireplace. God bless gas fireplaces. Jesse sat down opposite me in an overstuffed, old fashioned log chair.

"Okay, so what else haven't you been telling me?" I asked him taking further stock of his character. His clothes were rumpled and his hair was too long, weeks overdue for a cut. He reached down and pulled a manilla folder out of his briefcase and laid it on his lap.

He folded his hands on top of it and looked at me. "You know what I do at work right Sugar?"

"Of course Jesse, you're a detective with the drug task force."

I saw him nod his head, almost. "One of our cases has become," Jesse stopped for a beat as though searching for the right word, "complicated."

"I'm sorry Jesse. Do you need me to take over MAMBOS so Julie can help?"

He sat back and crossed his legs. He was attempting to look relaxed, but there was an underlying energy that told me otherwise. "No I don't need you to take over MAMBOS and Julie doesn't know anything about this. I'd like to keep it that way."

"Jesse you're scaring me. You don't talk to me about your cases." And I was pretty sure that I didn't want to hear about this one.

"Sugar, I want you to understand before I tell you what I'm about to tell you that I did this because I thought it was the best option at the time. I did this because I love you." And my heart started skipping every other beat.

"Margie and Nathan have been staying here at the lodge as protected witnesses of the state of Texas."

"Excuse me?"

"Margie and Nathan have been –"

"I heard what you said!" And I probably shouldn't yell.

"Sugar, I'm going to ask that you let me tell you what's going on and then you can yell at me afterwards. Okay?" He said it with a smile on his face, but I could see this was no laughing matter.

I folded my arms over my chest. "Fine."

"Margie's father is a very wealthy peanut farmer from Mexico. He has been shipping peanuts across the border. As it turns out he is using the peanuts as a way to ship high quality marijuana out of Mexico. The drugs are being shipped up here with the peanuts and being distributed throughout the upper Midwest by gangs and dealers. We had three teenagers die this past spring, all good kids who came from families who never suspected them to be in gangs or involved in drugs. None of them appeared to be a typical drug overdose either. They had a small amount of marijuana on them, but no cocaine or meth, nothing that would kill them. We couldn't tag them as gang related because there was no trauma to their bodies. It was like they just simply died. They were young and healthy and I had a gut feeling something was off. I had autopsies performed before releasing the bodies to the families and when we got the results we found they only had a small amount of marijuana in their system. It turns out they died of anaphylactic shock. We went back and interviewed the families and found out that all three of the victims had anaphylactic peanut allergies." He stopped for a beat or two.

"Harsh," I said. "I had no idea that could happen."

"Me either. I did some internet research and it turns out that some people with peanut allergies can have reactions if they eat or inhale something that was even grown in a field that peanuts had previously been grown in. I talked to a local doctor and he told me if the marijuana had been grown in a field with or had any contact with peanuts it could cause an allergic reaction for someone highly allergic. We put word out to our narcs that we needed to know where these drugs came from and that led us to Edward "Peanut" McElevain, Margie's father." He paused and gave me a minute to absorb it all.

"So what do Margie and Nathan have to do with any of this?" I asked him quietly.

"Margie and Nathan run the US side of the business selling the peanuts to companies and stores worldwide. Margie had been at the plantation one day and overheard her father talking on the phone discussing ways to get around her and get the drugs shipped past them. She never let on that she had heard him, but when she went back to Texas she started digging around and finally found evidence of the drug running. Unfortunately that wasn't all she found. She also found evidence of gun running. Bad stuff Sugar. Guns being put in the hands of rebels in Mexico and gangs in the US, guns that are killing our border patrol guys and innocent citizens that get in the way." And I let out a breath suddenly afraid for my friends as Jess continued.

"Margie and Nathan have spent the last five years trying to improve the conditions for the plantation workers and pay sustainable wages. They were angry at her father, but more than anything they were very much afraid. They knew if they turned deaf ears to it ultimately they would either get dragged into the fray if her father was arrested or he would pin it on them and walk away. They got in contact with an investigator in Temple Texas to report what they knew and asked for help and protection. That agent, Agent Walsh, had already been in contact with me because of the deaths here. I had worked through my contacts to try to get a lead on McElevain and it turns out Agent Walsh has been working at trying to stop McElevain for years. He met with Margie and Nathan and they decided to turn states witnesses to get her father put away for the deaths of the three kids here in Duluth."

"Can Margie do that if she is a citizen of Mexico?"

Jess held up a finger, "Ahhhh, but Margie is actually a citizen of the US. She was born in Texas when her mother left her father for a period of time." Jesse paused for a moment.

"Go on." And I was suddenly feeling sick to my stomach.

"After Agent Walsh met with Margie and Nathan he got back in contact with me and I flew down there to meet with all three of them. We decided our best shot at arresting him was to get him to Duluth and into our jurisdiction where we could charge him with murder, it might be second degree, but three counts would put him away. Agent Walsh has nothing to directly link McElevain to any illegal activities in Texas. All he has is Margie and Nathan's testimony and three deaths on the other side of the country. So we brought them up here for the wedding hoping to get her father to come up to give her away. We knew that if he was up here he would check in on his operations and we hoped to make an arrest."

"But her father never came to the wedding," I said, "He called and told her he had fallen ill and his brother showed up to give her away."

"It became clear to us at that point that he had figured out Margie's game and knew it was a set up." Jesse said quietly.

"So wait a minute! The Duluth Police Department put them up in my cabin for months and no one ever told me! Jesse Paul Bowers are Margie and Nathan even a couple? Did you lie about the whole thing to me so they could stay here? Was the whole thing just a ruse?" I was on my feet now with my finger inches from his nose. I stepped back and let my hands drop. "No. You know what. I'm done here. Stop, I don't want to hear anymore Jess."

"Sugar you spent the summer with them you already know the answer to that question. No I didn't lie to you about them as a couple -- you know Nathan would do anything for Margie."

I held my hand up and picked up my coffee cup, "Jess, they're gone now so I don't care to hear anything more about your complications. I have things to do." I turned to the kitchen and heard him sigh.

"Sugar they've disappeared and we can't locate them." Jesse's words came out on a sigh, but it raised all the hair on the back of my neck. I sat back down, hard. Jesse reached out and grabbed my hands.

"How do you know they disappeared?" My voice sounded a bit raspy.

"After McElevain didn't show for the wedding we gave Margie and Nathan information as a wedding gift on how we would get them out of here. We knew that we weren't the only ones doing surveillance on the house. They were to be picked up by a cab that would be driven by an undercover agent and they would be transferred to a safe house outside of Duluth. We knew that McElevain would not attempt to take custody of them here because there were too many undercovers around the lodge. We were hoping that we could get him to try to take custody of them on the road, so we had our guy driving them with back up in a second unmarked car. Things didn't go as planned. McElevain's men created a diversion involving the second unmarked and got the cab with Margie and Nathan stopped, taking down our guys before the second unmarked could get to them. By the time the backup car got onsite McElevain's guys were gone with Margie and Nathan. We know that her father is looking for something they hid, so he hasn't killed them." What he didn't say was that they weren't in a hole somewhere being tortured.

I heard myself sigh again. "I can't believe this Jess. I don't want to believe this." I said letting my hand drop to the couch.

"Sugar you have to understand we did everything the way it should have been done. We had to try and protect everyone involved. We can't always predict how crazy, desperate people are going to react."

"I wondered why she wasn't returning my calls." I said nervously picking at the hole at the bottom of my sweatshirt.

"Sugar, I want you to listen to me. I screwed up. When the idea was brought up of putting them somewhere that was easy to cover, but would make them look like a couple ready to say their vows the lodge came to mind and I put it in motion. I was starting to see you walk down that same path you went down before and I was, and still am, deathly afraid that you wouldn't make it back this time. I thought if I put them here then you would have something else to focus on and I could keep a closer eye on you without you knowing it." The pain in his eyes told me he wasn't so cool with the decisions he had made. I stared at him in stony silence.

"I can't believe you have had me under surveillance."

"We had to protect all of you somehow Sugar. You have a lot of property where a man can hide and still keep tabs on what is going on. We have swept the house for bugs, which is why we are talking here and not at my office."

"Did you find any?" I asked.

"Bugs?"

I nodded.

"Yeah we did and they weren't ours." He let that sink in for a beat. "I believe now more than ever that you need someone here to keep a closer eye on you. I can't be worried about you and do my job at the same time."

"I don't like the idea of guys running around my property Jess. That's a serious invasion of my privacy!"

Jesse rolled his eyes, "We are running surveillance on you in shifts and we are holed up in places where no one would ever find us. Have you seen anyone?" I decided that was a rhetorical question. I was fighting the coffee and bile back and trying to make sense of what he was telling me.

"Wait a minute. What do you mean keep a closer eye on me?"

"We know that McElevain is here and we know that he has a lot of people helping him. He has his daughter and I'm sure he intends to work hard at getting her to tell him where the information is that she had. If he can't get it from her then I suspect he will start playing hardball and attempt to get it from you."

"What kind of information?"

"Papers, tapes, **pictures**, cell phone logs and contracts for guns."

"And why don't you have this information? If she was a state witness why didn't she put it in your hands and let you deal with it? None of this even makes any sense to me."

"Agent Walsh and I have seen the evidence and there is a lot of it, but Margie and Nathan refused to actually put it in our hands until we either had her father or she and Nathan were dead. They told me that they knew their father had employees, as they called them, everywhere including inside the police departments. If they turned over the documents then they would chance McElevain finding out and leaving the country for parts unknown."

"So what is that we are looking for? A box full of papers?"

"She told us they would hide the paperwork in a public location we could access. She knew her father would assume it was here on the property and she didn't want to chance him finding it. She hid it somewhere, I'm thinking in a public locker or lock box, and told me the key to open it would be here on the property."

"Did she at least tell you where the box is? Can't you go find it and have the locker cut open or something?" It was almost surreal that I was even having this conversation.

Jess shook his head, "I talked to Margie at Mom's wedding and she was scared. She told me she thought someone inside our organization was reporting back to her father. She refused to tell me where the box was and said she would tell me once they were in the safe house and her father couldn't get them. We had them moved there right after the wedding, but of course we never got that information before they were taken."

"So... do you think there is someone on the inside?" I asked. He didn't answer me as he sat there extremely interested in his shoelaces.

"Jesse?"

His head snapped up. "It doesn't feel right Sugar. I would trust the guys on my team with my life, but I do think there is someone close to us that is feeding him information. It happens all the time and we are always on guard, but this time, I don't know. It certainly doesn't feel right."

"Well do what you need to do Jess and search what you need to search but I can take care of myself."

"Sure you can take care of yourself Sugar, all what, one hundred and ten pounds of you? I'm sure that will deter anyone who wants to come in here and have a look around your place." And **it was one hundred** and fifteen pounds, but I didn't feel like correcting him.

"I have my Glock and I know how to use it." I said firmly.

"You and your Glock aren't going to be running around playing **Commando. Mom would literally have my head if she found out about** this, not to mention if anything happens to you while I'm in charge of this operation."

I had to smile. I simply had to. He was still afraid of his mommy. Well, I guess I might be a little afraid of her too.

He brushed his hand over his face again and let out a sigh, "Sugar you know I could never live with myself if something happened to you because I put you in this situation. I couldn't live with myself if you got hurt."

I had my arms folded across my chest and was slouched down in my chair.

"Please Sugar, work with me here. Please."

I could see the lines the fatigue had drawn on his face and the shake of his hand as he rubbed his eyes. I felt bad for putting him through this even though it wasn't my fault.

"Okay," I whispered, "What do you want me to do?"

"Agent Walsh **will be arriving from Texas this afternoon and he** will be staying here at the lodge with you. He will be your full time bodyguard."

I jumped up and almost fell over the arm of the couch, "*No, no, no, no, no!*" And I probably shouldn't yell.

Jesse had me by the shoulders steadying me. He sucked in a few breaths and did his own deep breathing, "Tula, you have to be reasonable."

"Oh that's low, Jesse, real low." I growled at him and wrenched my arms away from him. I walked over to the stained glass window that looked over the front yard. "You only call me by my real name when you want to invoke guilt!" I yelled at him not knowing he was standing over my shoulder.

"Is it working?" I gave him my death glare. Jesse turned me around and I looked in his eyes. There was no more cop face. There was only fear. He was scared and that made me feel like throwing up. Jesse doesn't get scared. Jesse doesn't show fear. Jesse is my rock.

"I got you involved in this and I can't change that," he said, "but I can keep you safe if you let me. Please Sugar."

I didn't like any of this. I didn't like my place in the world being turned upside down and I really didn't like the idea of having a man living here watching everything I do.

"I don't think I need a 24/7 bodyguard. He isn't after me and you have guys on the property all the time."

"What it comes down to Sugar is that you own this property and now McElevain will come after you to get what he wants. You do need a 24/7 bodyguard because things are heating up. I'm hoping to have this wrapped up in a week, but it is very necessary and it is going to happen."

"Fine." I said defeated, obviously not going to win this fight.

Jesse let out a sigh of obvious relief. "The name thing works every time!"

"Don't flatter yourself. That had nothing to do with it. It has everything to do with the fear I glimpse in your eyes when you think I'm not looking."

Jess's lips formed a tight line and he quickly moved on. "Agent Walsh is former border patrol. His cover story is that he is coming in to work some routines with the famous Tula DuBois."

"Oh please. I'm about as famous outside of Duluth as the owner of the local cafe. Can he dance?" I asked.

Jesse looked at me like I was speaking a foreign language. "I don't know, I didn't ask."

Typical. Heaven forbid a man would actually find out if the cover story you were throwing out there was actually going to work.

"Here's kind of the part you aren't going to like." He said stepping further away from me.

"Are you daft? I don't like any part of this!" I yelled my hands flailing around and I quickly stuck them in my pockets.

"For the next week or so I want you to keep a low profile. Don't go outside without Agent Walsh and you will have to stop communing with nature for a few days until this gets straightened out. I want you to cancel your parties and lessons for the next week at least so that we have no civilians here that we can't protect."

"Well wouldn't that be convenient for you Jess. Too bad it's my business. I won't cancel my lessons. Your Agent Walsh is going to have deal with that."

"Sugar I'm not asking. I will do it myself if you won't. I want no one else involved in this and I want no one else to get hurt."

I thought over my schedule for this week, "I have nothing going on but one lesson on Thursday that I can't cancel, but I promise to get them out in under an hour Thursday morning. That's the best I can do."

"Fair enough Sugar, but it will be Agent Walsh's final decision. He will be following your every move and together you will be searching the property for the key. I want you to give him access to any area of the lodge that Margie and Nathan could have been in."

"Well that was only the whole thing Jess."

I had a sudden feeling in the pit of my stomach and it wasn't one I liked. I suspected I already knew the answer to my next question, but decided to make him say it out loud.

"We have a problem Jesse. The **cabin has been winterized already and** Agent Walsh won't be able to stay in it."

"Good. I don't want him in the cabin. I want him here in the house with you." And I knew that would be the answer. Damn him!

"He can stay in the guest room you keep for mom and me. It's across from your room and I want him close."

"How about if he stays in one of **the rooms upstairs? We use them** for dressing before weddings. They already have beds." I raised my eyes, **hopeful.**

Jesse smiled and patted my hand like I was a child, "If that is where you want to tell people he's staying it's okay with me, but he will be staying in the guest room across the hall." Case closed. He looked at me under his eyebrows. "**And Sugar, Agent Walsh is coming in to help us,** so please don't be difficult."

"What is that supposed to mean? I'm not difficult!" Usually.

Jesse shook his head at me, "Sugar you are more set in your ways **than a sixty-year-old** spinster."

Okay, so sometimes I'm difficult, but only when it comes to matters that I don't like. Like a man sleeping across the hall from me!

"His plane is scheduled to arrive around **three at the airport and** he will be taking a cab here." Jesse made quotation marks around the word cab. "Someone will contact you when he lands. He will be flying in **under the name Donovan MacNamara and that will be the name he uses while here. When he gets** here go over the story together." He handed me a manilla folder with several sheets of paper in it. "This is his dossier. When you finish reading it please put it in the fire. I don't want his file **here if someone was to break in and find it, but I do want both of you** telling the same story no matter who is asking." Right, got it, James Bond **007 and all that stuff.**

"Is it going to self destruct too?" I smirked at him and he rolled his eyes.

"What did you tell him about me?" I asked.

"Only the basics." And **that could cover a lot.**

I held up the dossier, "Did he get one of these too?"

Jess shook his head, "No. I'm leaving it up to you to fill him in on the story. Tell him what you want him to know and make sure you don't **leave anything out that could affect** how he protects you." And he looked at me under his brow and I knew what he was getting at. **He pulled on his coat and pulled me to him in a familiar hug.**

"Think about what I said. I know Julie could help you if you'd let her." He kissed my forehead and grabbed **his briefcase. He stepped onto the porch and held the screen door between us.** "If you do what Agent **Walsh says we can hopefully bring this to a close before anyone else gets** hurt. And call Mom."

"Okay, okay. Hey, does mom know about Julie?"

Jesse nodded. Wow, nothing like being the last to know. He waved from the parking area as the cruiser pulled in to pick him up. I closed the big wooden door that kept out the cold in the winter and the heat in the summer and fought the urge to run and hide under the covers of my bed. I've lived alone in this lodge for years and have never been afraid of my surroundings, but I was suddenly very afraid of the things and people I couldn't control.

I went to the locked gun cabinet in the closet under the stairs and pulled out my Glock. I checked to make sure that it was loaded before I locked the cabinet and closed the closet door. Better safe than sorry was my opinion. The gun would be in whatever room I was in from now on, if not to fight off the bad guys then to fight off the good guys.

My mind was jumbled with images and information and I didn't even know where to start to sort it all out. I decided the dossier was the first step so I got my coffee and headed to my office to get acquainted with Agent Walsh.

FOUR

I flipped on the lights to my office always finding comfort in this small space. I had it decorated with trophies and pictures of my dance competitions with Brent as well as family pictures of me and my parents. I sat down in my soft leather chair and set my coffee on my desk. I had found the desk in the shed in need of a new finish. I had stripped it down and underneath all the old varnish was a light cherry wood that when sanded smooth was gorgeous. I had added a few coats of polyurethane and it was the perfect fit for the room. The top of the desk was covered in paper, calenders, dance brochures, order forms, old coffee cups, you name it. It also held my computer as well as printers, fax and phone. I took a few minutes to tidy the top of the desk, but it didn't look any different when I got done so I decided it was a lost cause for now.

I knew I was only putting off the inevitable, so I took a deep breath and opened the dossier.

> Donavan Walsh.
> DOB: August 8, 1980
> Current Employment: Drug Task Force Agent, Temple, Texas. Lead investigator, six years
> Personal History: Born in the US. Resident of Dublin Ireland, 17 years.
> Marital Status: Single.
> Education: Criminal justice degree.
> Height: 6'1".
> Weight: 192 pounds.
> General: Blond hair, hazel eyes.

I was looking for the part that said Dance Experience. I prayed that he had some and it had simply been inadvertently forgotten on the dossier since it didn't exactly seem thorough. Yeah right, a little voice said, like that's gonna happen. I flipped the page and found a picture attached to the back. I leaned forward and studied the 5 x 7 photo of a man smiling back at me. It was obviously taken for a badge or ID, but there was depth and glint to his hazel eyes. His eyes were the most striking part of his face. His chin was squared off and when smiling he looked inviting, but I pictured when he was angry he would be a force to reckon with. In this picture he was smiling though and his eyes softened the look. His face was framed by blond hair spilling around his ears and falling across his forehead. His hair was actually strawberry blond, but I was guessing he didn't like putting that down on paper.

I set the file on the desk and leaned back sipping my coffee. I was trying to put my thoughts together, but so much had happened this morning. My friends were in danger and needed help and I had to figure out how to put all the rest in the background and focus on that. If I could help Jesse get the key and then get them back safely then I could sort out the rest of my life.

I picked up the dossier and giving it one last look walked into the living room and threw it into the fire. I stood and watched until it was nothing but ash. I was hanging on by an emotional thread and had no idea where my life was going and I couldn't help but feel Agent Walsh was going to complicate matters.

I stood in the doorway of the extra bedroom. I'd had my housekeeper for the lodge freshen up the room before she left for the winter. All I needed to do was vacuum and dust and the room would be ready for my new "partner". This room was mine growing up. It was directly across the hall from my parent's suite when I was a kid. It always made me feel safe to be so close to them. I had repainted it a few years ago the color of ecru and had added a soft coffee brown chenille spread and several throw pillows to the double bed. The desk against the wall held a laptop computer and phone and a flat screen TV hung from the ceiling over the bed. The large window was covered in a sheer curtain the color of butter and a venetian blind to keep the summer sun out. The hardwood floor had several throw rugs placed near the bed and desk, the color of chocolate. Together the room felt inviting and relaxing. There was a guest bath next door and that too was cleaned and ready. Once the cabin closed down for the winter I always had this room ready for anyone that needed it. Often times Sharon and Len would stay for the weekend or Jesse would come out and stay when he needed to get away from work for awhile. Now that he tells me about Julie I guess I know why the room is still clean. After the accident I moved into my parent's suite. There was an attached bathroom and the room was bigger and looked out over the lake. Mostly I moved in there because it made me feel closer to my parents, and I never left.

I busied myself with vacuuming and dusting and making sure that Agent Walsh would have access to whatever he needed. I prayed and hoped the case would be cleared up quickly because the thought of having a full-time bodyguard made me break out in hives. It has been years since I have even been out on a date with a man much less lived with one. I sighed. I didn't especially like my life right now, but I didn't want to complicate it anymore than it already was. The anniversary of my parent's death was only a few days away, four to be exact, and I had to get through that without falling apart. That wasn't likely to happen this year. The past years the anniversary has come and gone without any problems, but not this year. Maybe it was that the foundation dinner was the same night or maybe it was that my emotions couldn't take the limbo of not accepting it any longer, but whatever it was I knew I needed to figure it out soon before I lost everything in my life.

I gave the room one last glance and went into the kitchen. I had skipped breakfast and my stomach was reminding me that I hadn't fed it recently. I made a ham and cheese sandwich on rye and stood at the counter to eat it. I brushed the crumbs off my shirt, putting my plate in the dishwasher and drank some milk from the carton. My mom hated it when I did that. See there was another thing I was going to have quit doing with a house guest. No more drinking out of the jug.

I looked up at the clock. It was noon. I couldn't help but feel like I was counting down the last hours until my life as I knew it would no longer exist. I searched through the fridge looking for something to feed my guest tonight. I may not be happy about sharing my home with him, but I would be "nice" as Jesse had so tactfully put it. I guess it wasn't this guy's fault we were being thrown together anymore than it was mine. I grabbed the slow cooker out of the cupboard and plugged it in. I found all the makings for my Chicago kraut dogs. I put the package of brats in the bottom of the slow cooker, added a package of sauerkraut and sliced several Gala apples over the top. I added a pinch of brown sugar to the apples and covered the whole thing in beer. I put the lid on and set it at low. Never mind that I didn't know if he liked brats or sauerkraut, but I did and I figured comfort food would be a safe bet.

Comfort food for me involved a wide spectrum of things. None of it was particularly healthy for me. When I'm alone I call coffee and cake dinner. Fortunately I have a great metabolism so my indulgences don't immediately head to my hips. I've thought it out and decided that coffee and cake meet several of the food groups. You have dairy, protein and carbohydrates in the cake. If you make it my carrot cake then you have veggies too and what more do you need? It's an overall super food I've decided. Of course, if I stray too long from the well rounded eating habit the guilt of my mother comes down upon me and I resolve to eat more vegetables and less cake.

Cake was sounding good right now and I decided that my Irish crème bundt cake would be the perfect dessert. It might be a little cliché, but hey chances are he will like it. I took a few minutes to throw that together pouring in a little extra Irish cream liqueur. God bless liquid courage. I slid the cake into the oven, grabbed my portable timer and headed in to do what I do best in stressful situations, dance.

I was finishing putting together a routine for one of my young couples that would be competing for the first time after Christmas and I was happy with how it had come together. Becca and Aaron were only fifteen and would be attending their first competition in January. I couldn't wait to get them into the studio Thursday to have them try out the routine. They were naturals at dancing and they were fun, which was another reason I didn't want to cancel their lesson. I needed fun right now.

The timer went off and I ran back to the kitchen and pulled the cake out of the oven to cool then I grabbed my coffee stained clothes from my room and threw them in the wash. I was heading back to shower when my phone rang. I debated for a few rings if I should even answer it. I let out a sigh and picked it up.

"Hello, Sugar's Dance, this is Sugar".

"Hello Miss Sugar. I am calling to notify you that I will be dropping off Mr. MacNamara at your property in approximately thirty minutes."

Mr. MacNamara, wonderful, I thanked him for calling and hung up. I took a quick shower, toweled off and blew dry my hair. My hair is the color of ginger and frames my face when I let it fall loose. I usually wear it up in a ponytail or a braid so it stays out of my face when I'm dancing. Nothing like having your hair in your face to blind you at the wrong moment. I checked out the rest of myself in the mirror. I stood a regal five feet four inches tall and it makes pulling off the tall lanky dancer look extremely difficult. My eyes are ocean blue, one shade lighter than my mother's and one shade darker than my father's. My nose is small, pixyish, as Brent would call it, so I certainly couldn't complain about that. God blessed me with a great nose. My lips, however, not so much. You couldn't call them pixyish. In fact, my lips are downright voluptuous. Everyone always tells me they'd kill for lips like mine. I'm no Tina Turner, but with a little bright red lipstick I might be able to pull it off. I did the Tina pucker in the mirror, but fell short. My eyes traveled further south stopping at my chest. My lips may be voluptuous, but that was the only part on me you could call that. I guess when the good Lord was handing out boobs I was still in the lip line. Pixyish might be a good word to describe them, if pixies had boobs. God bless Victoria Secret.

I went into my bedroom and dug around my closet looking for my most comfortable clothes. The kind of clothes that when you put them on you feel like you did when you were a kid in your flannel jammies. I threw on my favorite flannel lined jeans and a long sleeved turtleneck and tied on a pair of dance sneakers. I wasn't planning to dance, but they were comfortable.

I glanced at the clock, ten minutes to spare. I felt like someone awaiting sentencing. My palms were sweaty, my heart was beating double time in my chest and I thought I might be about to pass out. I didn't really want to look too deeply into my hysterical reaction to having a man in the house. Each step I took down the hall felt like I was walking to my death. I sat on the couch with my head between my knees taking deep breaths and telling myself to get a grip. This isn't going to be so bad and it's not forever. It's all about Margie and Nathan, it's all about Margie and Nathan. I almost had myself convinced when the doorbell rang.

I got up and went to the door, peeking through the small stained glass window. It was the man from the dossier. I took a deep breath and pulled the door open.

"Hello you must be Donovan." I said in my best hostess voice.

He smiled at me holding up his badge, "Guilty as charged. Are you Tula?" He had a strong Irish brogue that surprised me after living in the US for so many years. I opened the screen door.

"Yes, Tula DuBois, nice to meet you."

He took my outstretched hand, "Donavan MacNamara."

I felt an instant energy between us as he shook my hand and I quickly pulled back. That song by Taylor Swift ran through my head about sparks flying and I backed up as he stepped through my door with his duffle bag thrown over his shoulder. He closed the heavy door behind him. He set his bag on the floor and took in the main room of the lodge.

"Mi Daza." He said.

And I didn't know what that meant, but he said it in a tone of voice that instantly eased some of my anxiety.

"I don't know what that means, but thank you, I think."

"It means fantastic, excellent." And I smiled against my will and reached for the black leather jacket he was shrugging off. He tossed it over the bag and looked around.

I crossed my arms over my chest. "The lodge has been in the family for a lot of years." He turned and smiled down at me mainly because if it was possible he was taller than Jesse. There was a swirl to his eyes that made it hard to decide if they were hazel or green.

"It's is a fantastic property, a nightmare for security, but a fantastic property." He said and I noticed his brogue became softer.

"Would you like something to drink Mr." I hesitated, "What do I call you?"

"You can call me Don." I started to giggle and clapped my mouth over my hand. I probably didn't want to make him angry straight out of the gate.

He leaned up against the back of the couch. "What?" He had both arms folded across his chest.

"Sorry, but you don't strike me as a Don. It doesn't" I ran my hand up and down in front of him like an idiot ".....fit."

I tried to stop the giggling that kept bubbling up from within me. I had a feeling it had more to do with fear of having this man in my house than it had to do with his name.

He crossed his ankles and studied me. "Really? What fits then?" He stood waiting for an answer.

I could tell I was already in way over my head and he had only been here for five minutes. I wasn't sure if he thought I was flirting with him or if he thought I was simply crazy.

"Van." I said and he arched an eyebrow.

He uncrossed his arms and nodded. "My grandmother used to call me Van. She was the only one who ever did."

"Good, then Van it is." He looked me up and then down with his eyes much like I had just done to him with my hands.

He recrossed his arms over his chest. "So, Tula that's an interesting name."

In my family the word interesting didn't always mean a good thing. When someone used the word interesting it usually meant the complete opposite.

"If you have a problem with Tula you can call me Sugar like everyone else does." I held my chin level challenging him to come out and say what he really meant.

"No, no, I like the name, really." He had his arms out waving now. "Is it a family name?"

I relaxed a little and shook my head. "My mother named me after Cyd Charisse. She was a famous dancer from the early 1950s." His face was blank.

"She danced with Gene Kelly and Fred Astaire in Singing in the Rain and Brigadoon." I waved my hand indicating it didn't matter. "Her real name was Tula Finklea and she was my mother's favorite actress." And it seemed easier to end it there.

He pushed off the couch smiling. "So is it alright if I call you Tula then?" I nodded and felt color rising on my cheeks. I must have been looking at him funny because he began to shift under my gaze.

"What?" He brushed at his shirt as if he had something on it. I had to ask even if he considered it rude.

"Nothing, I'm a little surprised that you have such a heavy Irish brogue. I was expecting, you know, something more southern."

His eyes sparkled almost as if they reflected his every emotion. "I lived in Ireland for sixteen years and no matter how hard I practice a southern drawl I can't seem to get rid of it. I figured since I am supposed to be an Irish dance instructor it was going to work in my favor this time."

27

He winked at me and my heart skipped a beat. Get a grip Sugar.

"Right, okay, makes perfect sense." I reached down to pick up his bag planning to show him his room. He took one stride and had his hand over mine.

"I'll get that." He picked up the bag like it was a toy and I stepped back taking a deep breath.

I led him to his room and stepped inside, flipping on the light by the door.

"I hope you find the room comfortable. If there is anything you need please let me know." He stepped into the room and tossed the duffle bag on the bed.

The room was actually quite large, but with him in it everything suddenly felt much smaller. He was walking around the room looking at the windows and checking out the desk. I couldn't help but notice the way he moved. He moved very softly and each motion was smooth blending into the next. His upper body was long and thin and his legs were powerful. He moved like a dancer I suddenly realized. It was ridiculous, since he wasn't one, but he had the ability to make every movement fluid. My curiosity made me look forward to getting him into the ballroom to see if my impression was correct.

"It looks great. I think I will be quite comfortable." His words snapped me out of my trance and I quickly looked away. "Is there an internet connection here somewhere?" he asked.

I showed him where the hookups were and how to work the entertainment system and then I backed towards the door slowly.

"Your bathroom is next door and you will find everything you need in the closet. If you want to give me your winter gear I can stow it with my stuff near the back door."

"Winter gear?" He looked at me quizzically.

"You know your parka, gloves, hats, boots."

He shifted uncomfortably. "I didn't bring any of that."

I tried to stop the smile, but it broke out anyway, "You do realize that it gets cold here, right?"

"It's only November. I know this is the tip of the end of the world, but I didn't think I would need any of that for the short while I was here."

I rolled my eyes. "The tip of the end of the world?" I said. A tenderfoot obviously.

"When you leave home and it is baking and you are wearing shorts and a tank top and you land here and it's colder than the toilet seat in an igloo, it's the tip of the end of the world." And cue the giggles again. I had to cover my mouth with my hand.

"What are you laughing at?" He moved in close and I could smell the Irish Spring he had used in the shower. A hint of it floated past me and it was all I could concentrate on.

"It's not that cold! Don't they have winter in Ireland?" I stuttered.

28

Sugar's Dance

"Not like here. There is very little snow and the coldest it gets is about thirty degrees in the winter. Generally we could play sports year round. Besides I haven't lived in Ireland in over a decade and Texas is warm, very warm." He looked wistful.

"I guess we had better make some time tomorrow to go pick up a few essentials then. I don't want the Irish Texan freezing on my watch."

"No, we can't have that." He smirked at me and his eyes were swirling green.

I left him to set up his little mobile home away from home and went in search of my next cup of coffee.

FIVE

I was in the kitchen finishing up dinner listening to Taylor Swift when I heard Van come in. I turned the music down and offered him a beer. He had his laptop with him and set it all down at the table motioning for me to join him.

"I need to talk to you. I know that Jesse has given you the basics about why I am here and what my role will be. What I need you to tell me is if there is anything I don't know about you or your business that is going to impact how I protect you." He opened up his laptop and clicked a few buttons.

That statement made me curious. Maybe Jesse really only had told him the basics? That would seem strange, but I was going to test the water before I offered too much up front.

"Well, I don't know what Jesse told you about me, so I'm not sure what to tell you. I have most of the lodge locked down for the winter and only have a few dance students coming in and out. There will only be one lesson this week. I won't have any deliveries for several months now so as far as my business goes things are quiet." I looked at his face to see if he was satisfied with the answer and I could tell he wasn't.

"Okay, how about your personal life. Jesse told me you are a loner out here, but sometimes big brothers don't know everything. Are there any boyfriends coming in and out or you going out and about at night?"

I almost laughed out loud. Hardly to any of the above. "No, you won't have to be the third wheel on any dates if that is what you're worried about. There are no men in my life currently."

He raised any eyebrow, knowingly or unknowingly.

"My social life in the winter does not include too many evening activities unless they are held here in the ballroom. I have nothing on the calendar anytime soon that we should have to worry about other than the dinner Saturday night."

He was tapping on his laptop and looked at me over the top. "Jesse mentioned that. I hope I'm here for that. It sounds like a party." And he smiled lightly and I almost believed him. "Okay, anything else?" He asked.

I searched his face for any indication that he knew more than he was letting on. I know he'd already been through my bathroom and that was a dead giveaway, but I decided I would call his bluff before I told him more than he had already figured out.

"Nope." Liar, liar pants on fire.

"Good, then I need you to help me with the weak points of the lodge. I have gone through the bedrooms down here putting motion sensors on the windows in your rooms and mine. I have motion sensors on the front door and the sliding doors here in the kitchen. I need to get one on the door from the garage as well. Where else do I need to look at as an intrusion factor? What about the basement?"

It seemed too good to be true that he wasn't going to ask more personal questions, but for now it looked like I was off the hook. I thought about his question for a few moments before answering him.

"The basement is going to be hard to penetrate. It's old rock and there are ventilation vents, but no real windows. No one is going to get in through those. The ballroom and my office are pretty well secured. The windows in the ballroom have Plexiglas between two decorative panes. They don't open because the temperature and humidity has to remain stable for the floor. My office doesn't have a window and there are only two small ventilation windows not even big enough for a small child to get through in each bathroom. There is an emergency door in the ballroom that opens onto the blacktop parking area. We would hear the alarm go off if that was opened and chances are one of Jesse's guys would see someone at that door."

He nodded typing into the computer and I continued.

"That side of the lodge can be locked down separately from the main room as well, so even if someone could get in through one of those rooms we're going to hear them when they hit the locked doors to the main room. The upstairs could be a bigger problem. The rooms have large windows in each one and of course the rooms open to the staircase in the main room. I don't use them in the winter, but I can't lock them down other than putting in the storm windows and locking the panes, but that isn't likely to stop anyone. The windows are pretty high up, but I suppose someone could get in them if they were determined. They wouldn't be able to do it without being seen though." I fell quiet. I hated this. I hated going through my home pointing out all the ways someone could get in to hurt me.

Van closed the top on his laptop and looked at me giving me a reassuring smile. "I'm going to put some motion sensors on the windows upstairs. I have a remote set up that will tell me if any of the sensors have been breached. It won't tell me if anyone is in the house, but at least we will know if someone attempted to get in."

"Can I ask you something?"

"Sure."

"What's your opinion on this McElevain guy? Is all of this really necessary?"

"What has Jesse told you about McElevain?" He asked me brow raised.

"He told me that he is running marijuana and guns out of his Mexican plantation and that Margie found evidence of it and turned state witness. He told me that the three kids died and they linked it to this Peanut guy and he told me that I had to be nice to you because you were here to help." And I threw that last part in because I figured it wouldn't hurt for him to know I was doing this under duress.

"What he told you then in a very nice way was that McElevain is ruthless. I'm talking about ruthless in a way that you have probably never experienced up here at the tip of the end of the world. He doesn't care who he hurts or who dies as long as he continues to put money in his pocket. He doesn't care who goes down in front of him as long as he is standing at the end of the day. He ruthless to the point that he will take his own daughter and torture her as a means to an end. He wouldn't think twice about taking you and doing the same thing if he thought you had what he wanted. We aren't talking about a little bit of marijuana here Tula. We are talking about enough marijuana to fill train cars. We are talking about enough guns and drugs to keep gangs and drug dealers in business forever, which means more people die and more families are ripped apart. He has been on my radar for a lot of years and he has been able to stay in business because we could never pin anything on him that was on US soil. Now that we can we aren't going to take the chance that he slips through our fingers."

"I, he didn't tell me any of that. I thought it was..." I thought it was Jesse overreacting.

"It's extremely important that you do what I say because I'm the good guy here Tula. If McElevain got his hands on you I can promise it would be a living hell and you wouldn't come out of it alive." He stood up then and moved over until he was standing above me, "And I've only been here for a few hours, but I already know that you are too good natured to be anything but nice and I'm going to have a very hard time keeping my mind on the job at hand when you are in the room." And he turned and picked up his computer heading for the kitchen door.

"When I get done I need some of whatever is in that pot." He pointed at the Crock Pot his eyes a deep hazel. They drew me in and I could tell by the look he was giving me that he was going to keep me safe from McElevain. Keeping me safe from him was going to be up to me.

"Sure, whenever you're ready." I stammered out.

He left the kitchen and I sat there staring after him his words echoing in my ears knowing it would be a very bad idea to chase after him and make him promise to keep me safe.

I heard Van calling me from the main room. I was in the office working on the final list of sponsors for the MAMBOS Foundation dinner Saturday night. From the looks of the list Julie emailed me half of the greater Duluth area was contributing in some way. I was also checking with the jeweler about the bracelet I had commissioned praying that he would have it done in time for Saturday.

"Down here!" I yelled. I glanced at the clock and realized it was six already.

I heard his footsteps in the hallway as he worked his way towards me. I was still behind the desk when he filled the doorway. He stepped into the office. My office was small and he filled it. He sat in the chair opposite my desk. I busied myself saving my document and logging out of the foundation website. He was looking at me with a peculiar look on his face.

"What?" I asked. The way he was looking at me was making me want to check to see if I had something on my face.

He tipped his chin towards me, "Is that Aleinware?"

My face was blank.

"Your laptop, is it Aleinware?" He motioned at the back of my computer.

"I guess that might be what it's called." And I knew that was what it was called, but I wondered what his fascination was.

"I didn't have you pegged as a gamer." He said the fingers of one hand drumming on his knee.

I chuckled, "I'm not. I bought this because it had a great sound system in it and a blue ray player. Sometimes I use different programs for teaching and it comes in handy when I can project it up on the ballroom wall. When we have weddings in the garden I can hook my outdoor system to the computer and I have full access to anything I need. Oh and it looks cool." And that got a smile out of him. "Are you a fan?" I asked him. "I can't say I know too many people who can name my computer off the top of their heads." I said.

He sat back in his chair and steepled his fingers, "I have had a few come in from different operations that we have closed down. The computer is amazing. I would love to own one, but I can't justify the price."

I wasn't sure what he was getting at, but I didn't like the innuendos. "Well I use it for business so I can." I said it in a cool voice hoping that he would let it go.

He put his hands up palms waving at me. "Absolutely, I meant for me it isn't worth it. In your situation it's a valuable tool, which is the point behind any good computer."

I stood up putting my glasses on the blotter and stepped around the desk. He stood as well and the smell of his Irish Spring hit me and I stifled a smile.

"What?" He was standing only inches from me now and the heat radiated off his body.

"Nothing." It was all I could do not to lean into him. There was something alluring about Irish Spring on him. It was clean and spicy.

"You are looking at me like *I* might be an alien. What gives?" He kept smiling.

I pondered whether or not I should even ask and obviously it took me too long to decide.

"Again I say what?" He had his arms crossed over his chest now and I leaned my back pockets on my desk.

"I was sitting here wondering if they really have Irish Spring in Ireland. It seems so..."

The corners of his mouth tipped up ever so slightly, "Cliché?" And I nodded.

"No, we don't have Irish Spring in Ireland. When I came to the US the guys I worked with thought it hilarious to buy me a case of the stuff for Christmas one year. My grandmother always taught me not to waste so I used it and by then I really liked it, so I kept using it."

"It's spicy and clean and..." I shut my mouth to keep the word sexy from coming out. "Anyway, let's go eat." I motioned to the door and he ran his eyes down me and back up to catch my eyes before he turned and exited the room. I blew out a breath, shut down the lights and followed him out.

When we reached the main room I showed him how to lock the doors to the ballroom area and gave him a spare key. I led him into the kitchen, gave him a beer and told him to sit down. I didn't want him in the kitchen with me working. That seemed too close.

I put the onion rings in the fryer for a quick few minutes while I got the condiments out on the table for the brats. I drained the onion rings and put them in a bowl on the table. He reached forward snagging one, only to drop it when the hot grease burned his finger.

"Damn, those are hot." He grabbed his cold beer wrapping his hand around the bottle. He held the bottle up to his face and turned it reading the label, "Leinenkugel's?" Only it came out sounding like Len-e-co-gals.

I snorted. "Line-en-coo-gil's, but if you call it that everyone will know you aren't from around here. It's simply a Leinies. The brewery is south of here a few hours. It was started by Jacob Leinenkugel and now his great-great grandson Jake Leinenkugel runs it. They make different kinds of beer and that is a seasonal beer, Fireside Nut Brown. You can only get it a few months out of the year." I put together two brats heaping extra sauerkraut on my plate and brought them to the table.

"It's good beer. I thought it was going to be a girly beer when you handed it to me. I was pleasantly surprised."

I raised a brow, "A girly beer? Really? Isn't that a little sexist?"

He shrugged his shoulder, "Nope. I've learned that there are definitely girly beers."

"Well I'm a girl, so I guess it might fit in that category."

He shook his head, "No it doesn't. What do I taste? Hazelnut and chocolate maybe?"

"And a little hint of caramel." I said.

"Well I like it, so it's not a girly beer." He said smiling.

"Good to know. It's one of my favorites along with Summer Shandy in the summer, which would probably be a girly beer in your opinion, and some home brewed beer from right across the bridge, Big Boat Oatmeal Stout, which definitely is not a girly beer."

"I like a girl who can appreciate a good beer." He said and I sat down not making eye contact.

He eyed his plate curiously. "This looks interesting."

That was all he said. Again, interesting isn't always a good thing.

"I call them Chicago Kraut dogs."

He picked his up and took a bite. I could see by the way his eyes popped open that he wasn't expecting what he got. I took a bite of mine, sauerkraut falling back onto the plate.

"These are amazing. I've had a lot of brats in my day, but nothing like this." He took another bite obviously enjoying it. "How do you get the sauerkraut so mellow? It's usually all you taste." He took another bite.

"I use apples and brown sugar. It tames it down so you can taste a little bit of everything."

He raised an eyebrow. "So how do you keep it all so juicy?"

"You don't precook the brat. You pile the kraut and everything else on top and pour a can of beer over the top. Then you let it simmer for four or five hours on low. Even if you don't cook this is one of those things that anyone can make."

He put the last bite of it in his mouth chewing slowly as if savoring the last bite. "Beer huh? Let me guess a Leinies?" And I smiled.

"Do you cook like this all the time?" He asked eyeing the pot.

"I have a few favorites I pull out now and then. I only cook for parties or if friends are over. When I'm alone I just eat cake." He looked up and laughed softly. "Do you want another?" I asked and his face perked up and it was my turn to laugh. I grabbed his plate and made him another bringing it back to the table. We hadn't gone over the cover story yet and now seemed like a good time. "So, I was ordered by Jesse to go over the cover story with you once you arrived."

"He did, did he?" He shrugged a shoulder. "Okay, should be pretty easy. You read the dossier right? Any questions?"

He was an interesting guy. Not at all what I expected from a cop. He was nonchalant and hadn't gotten too worked up about anything so far.

"One." I set my brat down.

"Shoot."

"Do you dance?" He assessed me while he chewed and I was afraid of what he was actually going to say when he spoke.

"I don't, but I'm sure you are going to change that."

I did a mental eye roll and a grimace at the same time. It's awfully hard to make someone a dancer in a few short lessons much less pull off a teacher look. The whole thing was giving me heartburn.

"Lucky for you we won't start until tomorrow." I said.

He gave me the brow wipe sign and grinned. I couldn't tell if he was being sarcastic or if he was dead serious, but his eyes shone brightly under the lights of the chandelier.

"So, since the dossier only covered the last ten years of your life I should probably know the basics of your early life so I can answer any questions that come up." I said.

"I guess I could say the same about you." He said.

My heart was beating faster at the thought of telling him about my past.

"You first." He said and I lost my appetite. I set my brat down on the plate and pushed it away.

I laid my napkin on the table and measured my words. "Well I'm sure Jesse told you that my parents were killed in a car accident ten years ago along with his brother."

His head snapped up and his eyes stopped swirling. "No, he didn't tell me that. He didn't tell me anything other than that you were his sister and a dance instructor. Oh and he mentioned that if I let anything happen to you I would find myself at the bottom of Lake Superior."

I laughed out loud. That sounded like Jesse. I wasn't sure why he hadn't told him anything about me, but I wasn't going to look a gift horse in the mouth.

"He's a little overprotective."

He eyed me, "I'm not going to test him to find out."

Note made.

I shifted uncomfortably in my chair. "As I said my parents and his brother, Brent, were killed in a car accident in Duluth ten years ago. His brother was my dance partner and we had been dancing together for ten years when he died. I'm not really Jesse's sister by blood, but we have known each other almost our whole lives. After the accident Jesse and his mom Sharon stayed with me here in the lodge. I went to college in Superior and got my business degree and Jesse started a job on the Duluth force." I motioned around the kitchen. "I got a large settlement from the accident and while I was in college I was able to turn the lodge into my home and business by adding the ballroom and modernizing the kitchen and cottage. I knew it would afford me a place to live and a thriving business."

He looked at me over his beer, "So you own this lodge?"

I nodded.

"Free and clear?" And I could tell he was surprised. Most people were. I nodded again.

"Must have been some settlement." He finished off his beer setting it down on the table.

"Nine million." I said and I saw his eyes go wide. I smiled to myself reaching over to close his mouth.

"Sorry your mouth was hanging open."

He laughed and I noticed that it rumbled in his chest more than you heard it out loud.

"The company of the semi truck that hit them settled so that it wouldn't go to trial. Sharon and Jesse got a settlement too and I'm grateful that Sharon doesn't have to work anymore. What I didn't need for the lodge and a small retirement account for myself I used to start a foundation in Brent's name."

I saw a light come on, "Jesse mentioned something about accompanying you to a dinner Saturday night."

"Right the MAMBOS Foundation dinner is Saturday night and I guess you will have the unfortunate task of being my date." And the way I was feeling about Saturday night it was going to be a train wreck and now he would be audience to it.

"I'm not thinking that task will be unfortunate at all. I'm thinking it's going to be delira and excira." And once again I had no idea what he was talking about.

"It means delightful and exciting." He said laughing. "But what is mambos?" He asked looking puzzled.

"It's an acronym for Miracles Are Made By Organ Sharing. It is a foundation that benefits patients and families before, during and after organ transplant. Brent was an organ donor and I have seen the wonderful things that organ donation does for families. It's my other passion." MAMBOS and dancing are pretty much life, but I didn't think he needed to know that.

"I totally wasn't expecting any of that. You are an interesting woman." There was that interesting word again. He really had to stop using that word.

"So were your parents organ donors too?"

I shook my head, "No. There is no real great way to say it, but they were beyond that when they got them out. As it turned out my mother had metastatic thyroid cancer anyway and had been given only a few months to live. I didn't know that at the time though. My parents had told Dr. Mueller that they were going to tell me after the big competition because my mom wanted to see me dance in the big leagues before she died." I stopped and I got up to put our plates in the sink trying to avoid his gaze. "I knew something was wrong though. She was losing weight and she kept telling me that she had stopped tasting her wares and I believed her."

"You were a kid Tula. Kids aren't supposed to doubt what their parents tell them."

I shrugged, "Maybe, but I feel like I probably should have seen it. I was so busy with school and dancing that I bought it because it was an easy answer. The accident was a blessing in disguise for my parents. If my father had to watch my mother die a slow death and continue on after she left us, I don't know that he would have made it." I stopped then looked over my shoulder.

"Okay, enough about me, your turn." And soon, before you have me telling you the rest of my life story.

He rubbed his hands over his belly shifting back in the chair and letting his hands rest on his thighs. "My mother and father met while my father was on leave from the Irish Army. My mother was American and after a wild weekend together she walked away pregnant and he walked away. I was born nine months later. My father was killed in the service and never met me or even knew I existed for that matter. When I was about one my mother decided that I was cramping her style and my grandmother would be better suited to raise me, so she shipped me over to Ireland. I should probably thank her for that. My grandmother was a wonderful woman. She was only forty when I came to live with her. Since I never knew my mother I always felt like my grandmother was my mother. When I was finally old enough she told me the truth, but she took care of me when I was sick, fixed my broken bones and was in the stands yelling during all my football games, so as far as I'm concerned she was my mother. She was a wonderful cook and loved everything about life. She was still so young and had already raised a child, but she never made me feel like a burden to her. She was always a lady and I never had to worry about waking up in the morning and finding her in bed with the mailman or" he waved his hand around, "well you know. Anyway, by the time I reached high school she was able to go and do more, but it wasn't long after that she was diagnosed with breast cancer. She passed away when I was seventeen and burying her was the hardest thing I have ever had to do." He stopped abruptly and I turned from the sink.

"I'm glad you had someone so wonderful in your life. She was obviously a special lady."

"Yeah she was." He said.

"What about in Texas? Where do you live there?" I tried to sound casual and not too nosy.

"It's just me and Lillie in Texas. We have a small two bedroom apartment, nothing special. I look at it as someplace to go home to at the end of the day."

Lillie. The dossier said he was single.

"Lillie? Jesse didn't tell me he would be taking you away from family." Smooth Sugar, not.

He grinned and pulled his wallet out of his pocket. "Lillie's my sister." He flipped his wallet open and I walked over to the table my eyebrows high. Smiling back at me was a beautiful young girl. She and her brother had the same eyes, but that was where it ended.

"Your sister?" I'm sure I sounded shocked. I certainly wasn't expecting that.

He nodded. "My grandmother never made it a secret who my real mother was. When I left Ireland I took some time to investigate where she was. I wasn't interested in seeing her, but I wanted to at least, I don't know, I guess I wanted to know where she was. When I found her I found this little scrap of a girl, only five years old, but acting like the adult in the house. She wasn't being cared for by her mother. She simply existed off the kindness of neighbors. Loretta was as lousy at raising her as she was at raising me, but I guess she didn't have anyone to pass Lillie off on. She was never home, never had food for Lillie and really didn't care what happened to her. I had money from my grandmother's life insurance and sale of the house so I got an apartment and made a deal with my," he hesitated not wanting to call her his mother, "with Loretta. If she signed over custody of Lillie to me then I would make sure that she didn't get arrested for drugs and child abandonment. She signed the papers, I took custody of Lillie, and we never looked back."

And I knew my face showed the shock I felt. "But you couldn't have been more than eighteen!"

He shook his head, "I was almost nineteen, but it didn't matter, Lillie was important. I had to give her a chance at a decent life like my grandmother gave me. There was no way once I knew I had a sister that I was going to let her live like that. Loretta ended up dying of a drug overdose a year later. It was a good thing I took Lillie when I did." He fell silent and I was barely breathing. He left me wanting to know how he did it.

"Can I ask you something?"

"Sure."

"How did you do it? How did you raise a child while working and going to school at such a young age?"

"It wasn't easy. I managed to work our schedules close to the same so that I could be home with her after school until she went to bed.

39

Then I had sitters that would stay at night with her while I worked, usually college friends I knew I could trust. Once I finished the academy I got a job with the border patrol and was able to work days so we had our nights together. Once I got transferred to the task force it got easier. I had to worry less about getting shot every day and leaving her without anyone. As she got older she became more independent and I felt better about leaving her home alone after school for a few hours until I got off work. I found after school programs she could go to and sitters when I needed them. There was a great lady in the apartment building that would check on her for me. We grew up together really. I went from being a kid who didn't know where he was going to a brother and father to this little girl. I got really good at playing tea party and braiding hair." I laughed at the thought and he smiled. "She's going to the University of Illinois Chicago studying to become a pharmacist. She got a full scholarship there. She started this fall and I miss her already. The apartment is empty without her. I wish she hadn't picked a school so far from Texas, but she got a full scholarship and couldn't turn that down."

"You must have done something right. She sounds like a great kid."

He smiled and his eyes twinkled again reminding me of a kaleidoscope. "She's all I have for a family and I wasn't going to let her suffer at the hands of that woman. I was already working the border patrol trying to stop drugs from coming into the country, but after her death I transferred to the task force. I wasn't successful at stopping them from coming in, but at least on the task force I felt like I could shut them down once they got here."

This man was so far from what I had pictured in my mind this afternoon. There was obviously a side to him that was gentle and tender if he raised a young girl for so many years.

"Why are you smiling?" He asked me.

"I was thinking that your grandmother did a great job raising you. She would be proud."

He held my gaze and I felt like he was seeing all my demons.

I cleared my throat. "Maybe when you are done here you can stop in Chicago and see Lillie. I bet she would love that." I said.

"I already plan to drive down there from here and then pick up a flight back to Temple. I never thought I would miss someone so much, but it has been hard adjusting to the bachelor life again."

"Well you're only thirty. Give yourself a little time and I bet it will seem natural again before you know it." His eyebrow went up and I stammered, "Sorry your date of birth was in the dossier."

Recognition crossed his face, "Oh yes, the dossier. You have to forgive me. I didn't get a dossier on you so I'm afraid I'm at a disadvantage." And I'm going to skip right over the comment.

"I'm sure there are plenty of ladies back in Temple that will be happy to hear that you are on the market again." I said changing the subject.

He shrugged that one off and didn't comment. I brought the cake to the table and his eyes lit up at the sight of it. He dug in, forking a piece into his mouth. He chewed and then stopped, his fork hovering over his plate.

"What? Is something wrong?" I took a bite of mine and it tasted the same as it always did.

The corners of his mouth tipped up. "Irish crème cake. I haven't had this since my grandmother made a version of it. Thank you."

I gave him a shy smile pleased that I made his first night here welcoming. He returned the smile and we finished our cake quietly. God bless old memories.

SIX

I stood at the archway of the main room watching him inspect the pictures on the mantle. There was one of my mother and father at their wedding, one of them holding me on my first day home, me about five years old dancing on my dad's feet and the last photo was of me and Brent. We had just finished our last competition and were holding our trophy. My mom and dad were on one side and Sharon and Jesse were on the other. We were on top of the world that night. We had no idea how fragile life really was. I pushed off the door frame and cleared my throat. Van turned at the sound of my voice.

"Howya." And I guess that means how are you.

"Fine thanks. Coffee's going; I'm making Thai coffee, it takes longer, but it's worth the wait."

"I've never had it. It sounds interesting."

It's a good thing I'm secure because his constant use of the word interesting was decidedly unsettling.

He turned back to the photos. "I see where you get your beauty from."

He was holding the picture of my mother and father on their wedding day.

I sat down on the big couch. "My mom Bonny and my dad James. They were very much in love. She was so beautiful."

"I can see why your father was smitten." And that was a good way to describe it.

"We both had him wrapped around our little fingers. There wasn't anything he wouldn't have done for her. They had a true love story." I realized I had put my foot in my mouth. "I'm sorry. I'm being insensitive."

"No." He shook his head and set the picture back down. "There was no love between my parents, only lust, but I understand the difference. I know that true love exists, but it wasn't in the cards for them. Don't apologize for speaking the truth."

We held each other's gaze for a moment and then he turned back to the mantle. He came to the picture of me dancing on my father's feet.

"I love this picture. It tells a story." I sat quietly waiting for his version. He picked up the picture. "If you look closely there are two mugs in the background" he looked at me with a raised eyebrow "coffee I

42

presume." I laughed, so far so good. He continued, "So a song comes on the old transistor radio and his beautiful little girl looks up at him with her blue eyes and says, "Daddy dance with me" and since he can't resist her for anything he stands her on his feet and they dance around the room. The little girl laughs with unbiased glee and dad tucks the memory away forever."

My chest ached at the memory.

"Was I close?" He set the picture back down on the mantle.

I nodded. "Right on. We were dancing to Gordon Lightfoot's 'The Wreck of the Edmund Fitzgerald'."

"You can remember the song that was playing?"

"After I lost my parent's it seemed like every memory was intensified. If I could remember it then I could remember every detail. Maybe it was because I didn't want to forget anything."

He came over and sat down in the big chair. "There's a song called 'The Wreck of the Edmund Fitzgerald'?"

I stared at him. "You're kidding me, right?" I searched his face as he stared at me. Obviously not.

"I'm from Ireland." Which I guess was reason enough for him. I motioned at the coffee table and indicated the large ship carved into the table with my hands.

"The Edmund Fitzgerald." He sat in the chair looking at the ship carved into the wood.

"It's huge."

"Yeah, that's a good way to put it. Her nickname was Mighty Fitz and she was over seven hundred feet long. They make them much bigger now if you can believe it. When she left the harbor full she clocked in at twenty-nine thousand tons. On November 10, 1975, she got stuck in a storm off White Fish Bay; reports say the waves were thirty-five feet high. The ship broke in two on the surface and sank taking all twenty-nine crew members aboard down with her. The lake never gives up her victims and to this day none of the victims have been recovered."

"November tenth, that anniversary is coming up quickly." I nodded not making eye contact.

"You know your history. I guess I didn't realize that Lake Superior was that unforgiving." He ran his hand over the glass like the water would ripple under his hand.

"The lake makes us and the lake breaks us, simple as that. People think it's just a lake, but those of us who live here know otherwise. Lake Superior can be as dangerous as any ocean, maybe even more so considering that the temperature of the water never gets above fifty degrees and is closer to thirty degrees in the winter. You aren't going to last long in the water if you're in it. Anyway, Gordon Lightfoot wrote the song in tribute to all the sailors that have lost their lives to the lake over the years. It was quite a hit in 1976."

"1976, we weren't even alive then."

I shrugged. "Nope, but it plays around here to this day." I quietly sang the last verse.

"The church bell chimed 'til it rang twenty-nine times for each man on the Edmund Fitzgerald. The legend lives on from the Chippewa on down of the big lake they call Gitche Gumee. Superior never gives up her dead when the gales of November come early."

We sat quietly as he really studied the ship in the coffee table.

I tossed up a hand, "It was probably not the best song to dance to, but when you're five I guess you really don't care."

He got up and walked back to the mantle taking down the picture of Brent and me.

"This tells a story too."

I nodded. "That was taken about two weeks before the accident. We had won the competition and named regional junior champions and we were moving on to nationals. It would have been our first shot at the big stuff. We were on top of the world."

He turned then his green eyes bright, "You were stunning." And I could feel myself blushing.

"How close were you to Brent?" Van turned his back to me and tried to sound nonchalant, but it came out strained, forced.

"Brent and I met when we were five. My mother saw that I had potential after watching me dance along with the old videos and decided to try me in tap dance. I hated it! It was awful all that jumping around and banging your feet." I saw his shoulders shake. "Brent hated it as much as I did so we usually spent the whole hour messing around and not paying attention. We came to class one day and my teacher asked us if we would like to go learn a new dance with a new teacher. We jumped at the chance to get out of tap for a day. It turned out there was a ballroom competition in town and one of the couples was friends with our teacher. So they taught us the waltz. We were hooked. We both begged our parents to let us keep doing ballroom instead of tap and a partnership was born."

I smiled remembering back to that day in the car and how I talked a mile a minute.

"My mother was ecstatic of course. Brent's dad on the other hand, not so much."

Van turned around brow raised. "Didn't like his boy doing girlie stuff?"

He didn't know the half of it. "He had the misconception that ballroom dancing was a girlie thing when in fact ballroom dancers are very athletic."

"So how did they convince him?"

"I don't know. I think Sharon lied to him. Paul was, to put it nicely, a bum. He spent most of their money on booze and what money Sharon made he didn't like spent on the boys. The boys had a rough life up until he left."

"He left?" I could tell he was surprised to hear that.

I nodded. "Right, one day he never came home from work. He drove off and six months later Sharon got divorce papers in the mail. She was all too happy to sign them. It was really hard on Jesse. Brent was only seven, but Jesse was twelve when his dad left and he felt like he had to be the man of the house take care of his mom and Brent. He was their protector. He struggled for a long time after Brent died thinking that he should have been there or done something." I guess he and I were alike in a lot of ways.

Van set the picture back down, "I haven't known him long, but I can see that in him. Especially when it comes to you."

A long silence stretched between us. He was looking at me like he knew the secrets I was hiding and it made me squirm in my chair.

"Uh yeah, right, well Sharon couldn't afford for Brent to dance anymore after the divorce and she called my mom to tell her. Brent and I were only seven, but my parents wanted us to keep dancing, so my dad paid for Brent to keep taking lessons by putting in new cabinets in the dance studio. I didn't know any of this until after the accident when Sharon told me. Turns out that Dad would help Sharon with bills and small jobs that came up around the house. When the will was read Dad had also taken out a small insurance policy on himself for Sharon and the boys. Jess took the money and bought a house that he could fix up using the skills he learned from my dad. It's a great little place."

"Sounds to me like your dad was a great guy."

"I might be biased, but I think so. He was the closest thing to a father Brent and Jesse ever had. My dad was a good man and cared deeply about other's feelings. If he could do one little thing to brighten someone's day or help them out of a tough situation he always tried."

I trailed off with the memories of my father hitting me fresh. The hours that we spent together in his Mustang going back and forth to dance lessons, the trips on the lake fishing and our time together carving.

Van noticed my silence. "So that brings me back to my question. How close were you to Brent?"

I wasn't sure that I could put into words what Brent and I were to each other. "Brent and I were best friends. We did everything together. We were inseparable. We were like twins separated at birth. We were soulmates. We needed each other to breathe. Not in a romantic way, just in the very essence of life way. When he died it felt like I died and for a long time I wanted to." I trailed off and stood. "I'll get some coffee." My voice was choked and I hurried into the kitchen to escape the look in his eyes.

SEVEN

I was standing in the doorway to the kitchen. It had been another rough night. After excusing myself and going to my room I watched all the late night TV shows knowing that as soon as I fell asleep the nightmares would return. I spent the night tossing and turning and was never more grateful to see the sun come up over the lake. I had spent a long time in the shower and getting ready for the day trying to put off the inevitable. I knew that today I had to dance with this man. This man who had shown up at my door and managed to get me to open up to him in ways I have never done with anyone else before. I also knew that I was going to have to tell him the rest of my story before he found out from someone else because somehow I knew that it would hurt him too much to not hear it from me. I wasn't emotionally ready to do that yet though. For the first time in ten years I was just Tula DuBois again. I wasn't Sugar to him, I was Tula and whether it was right or not I wanted to see what that was like. He either hadn't done any research on me or else he was a very good liar. The vibe I got was that he was taking what I said at face value. Seemed like that was the way he did things. Ask a question, get an answer and move on. I suppose if he had any inkling that I was lying he would switch into cop mode and grill me for all he was worth, but for now he seemed satisfied with my story.

He had his back turned to me and I was enjoying the view of his well filled out Levis as he dug through my cupboard. He was trying to decide what kind of coffee to make and it seemed as though the decision was overwhelming him this morning. He had thrown on a crewneck maroon sweatshirt and I couldn't see the front, but it probably said something like "Howdy" or "Howyall". The back was stretched across his broad shoulders and it tapered to his narrow waist and I need to stop this line of thought! His hair was shiny from the shower and I could smell his ever present Irish Spring. To say he took a bath in it was literal, but I couldn't figure out how the smell managed to linger all day.

"Need help with anything?" He jumped and turned around at the same time throwing his hand over his heart. I noticed the shirt said Texas A&M. Darn.

"Cripes, could you not do that! How long have you been standing there?" Long enough.

"A while." I walked over to the counter and gazed up at what had him stymied.

"So you found the coffee cupboard."

I had one cupboard reserved for my coffee. It was sorted by region or country and by what kind was used in specific makers. I snuck a peek at him and noticed his eyes were slightly glazed over. I could feel the corners of my mouth turn up and looked back down before he could even consider the idea that I was laughing at him.

"You think this is funny, don't you?" He motioned at the cupboard.

"Who me, no, no, I have no idea what you are talking about." And I did think it was funny, but then I haven't slept much lately and I was feeling punch drunk. And it was taking much too long to get a cup of coffee.

"It is obvious to me," he said holding onto the cupboard door and looking down at me from his towering perch above me, "that you are an addict."

"You are telling me nothing I don't already know. Now either pick a coffee and make it or move over so I can." I put my hand on my hip and waited.

A slow smile spread across his face and he stepped back, hands up, palms out in front of him. "By all means, please, make the coffee. I don't want you to start with the DTs."

Ha, very funny. He wasn't, but he thought he was. Okay, so he was cute and he was funny, but I still didn't appreciate it. I reached up to grab a coffee and stopped my hand in midair.

"So do you want regular old everyday American coffee or something more adventurous?"

"Regular old American? You make that sound like a bad thing." I shook my head.

"No, not a bad thing. I'm wondering if you are a put more goo than coffee in your coffee kind of coffee drinker or if you like it black, strong and pure." And I was feeling the need for black, strong and pure. Pure caffeine. I knew it was going to be the only way to survive the day.

"Well, you look like you could use black, strong and pure. No offense, but you look like you should be going to bed rather than getting up."

He was sitting at the table eyeing me in my baggy workout pants and three quarter zip Columbia sweatshirt. I had my feet stuffed into my dance sneakers and my hair was in a ponytail gathered at the nape of my neck. I didn't think I looked too bad, but then I was probably trying to fool myself. It obviously wasn't working on him.

"Boy you sure can build up a girl's ego." I was holding the door to the cupboard open using it to prop me up.

"You ain't seen nothing yet." Oh boy. Time to step out of the rattlesnake cage.

I grabbed the coffee filters skipping right over that comment, "So we have Guatemalan, Zambian, Costa Rican or German coffee."

I knew he was laughing at me behind my back, but I refused to look at him. I pulled out the twelve cup Cuisinart, docked my iPod in the dock and let the soft strains of Allison Krauss fill the kitchen.

I turned around and glared at him, "I hear nothing but your laughter."

He was looking smug.

I rolled my eyes, "Fine, German it is."

I grabbed the container of coffee down and busied myself filling the pot and adding the coffee before moving the button to bold and switching it on. I could hear him reading the paper at the table behind me and I moved to the fridge grabbing the eggs and letting the door slam shut. I cracked the eggs in the bowl and began to whip them before pouring them in the frying pan. I chopped green peppers and onions all the while feeling like two eyes were drilling a hole in my back. I refused to turn around. I added ham, peppers, cheese and onions and covered it for a few minutes before adding the hash browns.

I could smell the coffee and grabbed a couple of mugs down filling them with the fresh dark brew. I brought a cup to the table for him and he took it from me brushing my hand with his. I pulled my hand back quickly and moved back to the stove to busy myself with the eggs.

He took a sip of his coffee and put his cup down on the table. "This is good." He said it like he was surprised.

"It's one of my favorites. German coffee is ground almost into a fine powder and it makes for an even brew. The coffee is very mild and doesn't have that bitter aftertaste that some coffees do. It's pure."

"I have to say I am impressed, though slightly disturbed, by your coffee collection."

"What can I say? For some it's wine, for me its coffee."

I pulled the omelette off the burner and cut it in half sliding it onto two plates. I added fresh fruit and carried the plates to the table.

He looked at me over his paper as I set his plate down. "This smells great, thanks for going to the bother." His eyes sparkled at me over the paper.

"No bother, we gotta eat we have a busy day today."

He folded up his newspaper and picked up his fork. We ate in silence listening to the music floating through the air. I had it on my "relax" playlist, but it wasn't helping.

"You are an anomaly Tula." He said between bites.

I looked up surprised at his words.

"Excuse me?"

"An anomaly; a contradiction."

"I know what anomaly means. I'm curious why you say that."

He had finished his omelette and was leaning back in his chair sipping his coffee. "I've been here, what about eighteen hours and I have heard Annie Lennox, Taylor Swift, Ace of Base, Billy Joel, Goo Goo Dolls, Michael Bublé, Bruno Mars, Lady Antebellum, Garth Brooks, Allison Krauss, Green Day, Lady Gaga, Enrique and some dude playing the piano."

"George Winston."

He arched an eyebrow at me.

"So you know your music. I still don't see your point." I put my fork down and copied his posture.

"Your choice of music alone is, confusing."

"I didn't think I was going to have to justify my music choices for this arrangement." I took a sip of my coffee begging the Lord to give me strength.

"I never said you did. "

See this is the reason I don't date. Men drive me crazy. They can't seem to carry on a normal conversation in a normal manner.

"It was just an observation really, but I wouldn't mind getting to know you better since we will be spending a lot of time together."

He took a drink of his coffee his green eyes glinting at me from above the rim. I didn't answer him. I took another bite of my omelette buying myself time. I wouldn't mind getting to know him better either, but I wasn't sure how much I could share without treading into dangerous territory. Test the waters Sugar and see where it leads a small voice said.

"I'm a dancer." That was obvious.

His eyes traveled across me again. "Yes. I can see that." He was assessing me with his eyes, again. I probably should have been put off by the way he looked at me, but for some reason I couldn't seem to get too worked up about it. "So that's the whole answer. You're a dancer?"

I sighed putting down my fork. I guess going for the obvious wasn't going to work. I got up and went to the fridge getting out the orange juice and bringing it back to the table with two glasses. I poured myself one taking a sip hoping that the phone would ring or the house would burn down, but neither happened.

"Music to me is about the rhythm. It's about what my feet want to do when the first few bars play. It's about if it makes me happy, sad, angry or lonely. It's about whether I want to throw caution to the wind and swing or if I want to be pulled up tight and waltzed around the floor. For me music will take my mind off the bad stuff, let me be creative or relax me after a long day. It's about what memories it brings back and what memories it makes. If I couldn't dance music would simply be notes, but when I dance it becomes my soul." I clamped my mouth shut and my words hung in the air. I took a drink of the orange juice, the tartness a harsh opposite of the coffee.

He was looking at me pensively. "I never thought **of music that** way. Music to me is the lyrics. It's about what the lyrics tell me about life."

"I don't listen to the lyrics. If I did I never would have been able to dance again." And that was the truth. Too many songs brought back too many memories and my heart broke every time. I indicated the iPod with my fork. "You don't need lyrics to dance. All you need is music. Music and dancing go hand in hand, without music there is no dance. Just like ballroom dancing is a partnership, you can't do it alone, so whether it's Tony Bennett, Dean Martin, Harry Connick or Michael Bublé doing the big band or Madonna, Lady Gaga, or Goo Goo Dolls with the electric guitars and heavy bass, it's really all the same. I concentrate on the rhythm first and then all the rest follows." I trailed off and Van sat quietly studying me. It was making me uncomfortable. I finished the last of my omelette and took our plates to the sink.

"Now that I have told you my theory on dance I think it's time to get to know you better. Grab your coffee, it's time to dance."

I grabbed my travel mug filling it with coffee. I snapped the lid on. I felt him come up behind me, his breath warm on my neck.

"More coffee?" He asked.

I was gonna need it.

I lead the way down the long hallway to the ballroom doors and was about to pull open the doors when Van stepped in front of me.

"Let me."

I rolled my eyes. "Okay James Bond, go for it."

A very small smile formed at the corners of his mouth and he pulled on the left hand door, to no avail.

He looked at me, "Got a key?" I smiled reaching down and pulling the pin.

He pulled the doors open and flipped the lights on doing a quick assessment of the room. He hadn't made his way down this far yet in his assessment yesterday concentrating on the bedrooms and main areas of the lodge. Van stepped in through the opening and stopped doing a three sixty taking in the room.

"This is....savage."

I assumed this was like bad is good type thing. This room was my dream. I designed it and furnished it with great care. The ballroom was contemporary meets old world. The doors were maple and had the fleur-de-lis on each one with ornate waves. They opened out into the hallway and when you step in the room you are greeted by a long Canadian maple hardwood runner that leads you to the dance floor. The dance floor is a Canadian maple floor that floats above a padded underfloor. The entire wall that runs the length of the ballroom to the back is mirrored. I have sheer curtains that I use to cover them if the occasion calls for a more subdued atmosphere, but the way the mirrors reflect the light and the dancers is a unique visual.

The sound system is state of the art with surround sound placed throughout the ballroom; some were hidden in large cherry planters and covered with silk trees and some were hidden in half pillars that ran the height of the ballroom. On each side of the runner the floor was covered in tufted wool carpet decorated with falling leaves. There were a dozen round wrought iron tables on each side complemented by wrought iron chairs with flowing scarves that matched the sheers on the mirrors. The look on his face told me this was not what he was expecting.

He shook his head and I saw his eyes switch over to cop mode. He went over to the windows and checked the emergency door. He filtered the venetian blinds to let in light, but not give anyone a good view of who was inside the room. I turned on the stereo system and cued up a playlist on my iPod. He sauntered over to where I was standing.

"Satisfied?" I asked.

He nodded. "For now."

"Good, then let's dance." I said.

I had the playlist set up to go through some of my favorite dances. My all time favorite dance was the waltz, any waltz, Viennese, country or traditional followed by swing dancing and Latin dances like the cha-cha, rumba and samba. At the bottom of the list were my two least favorite dances, the foxtrot and mambo. Don't get me wrong the foxtrot isn't a bad dance, if you don't mind being bored to death. That was how I felt about it anyway, serious yawner.

The mambo was a dance that was not possible for someone my size to pull off. I just looked plain old ridiculous. Van had kicked his shoes off and was standing in his stocking feet as the first bars of "Walking on Broken Glass" filtered into the ballroom and I met him in the middle of the ballroom.

He pulled me into him and began the cha-cha. I followed his lead surprised that he was as advanced as he was considering his "I don't dance" statement last night. Before I had a chance to gain my bearings the song changed to "Open Arms" and he pulled me to him and began waltzing around the ballroom. His form was excellent and he was obviously lying about his dance experience. His waltzing also told me that I was correct in my assessment of him yesterday. He was a dancer and that was only going to make my life easier.

He started to laugh. "Sorry my feet started to move and I couldn't stop it." I hit the pause button on the sound system and planted my feet.

"I thought you didn't dance."

"I said I didn't dance, not that I couldn't dance." He winked knowing he had me flustered.

"Alright then show me what you can do."

We continued working our way through the dances as the music changed. He was pretty damn good at the rumba, using more hips than I wanted to think about and he made me actually like the foxtrot. Then Michael Bublé filled the room singing about home and how he needed to go there.

Van pulled me to him and whispered in my ear. "I know this one, it's a belly rubber."

I pushed against his chest until he released me reluctantly. "Wrong. It's a nightclub two step." And I showed him the steps.

"I like my way better." And he pulled me back into him for the last few bars. The tempo picked up with "Just The Way You Are" and I was grateful to know it was the last song. I needed to regroup and was having a hard time doing that in his arms. He worked me through what he knew of the west coast swing and I added a few new moves. I was happy when the song faded away and I left him standing in the middle of the ballroom walking over to the sound system to shut it down. I felt him come up behind me and put his hands on my waist.

He bent down near my ear and in his thick Irish brogue he whispered, "You are," I held my breath. "amazing."

Lesson over.

EIGHT

I was sitting on the steps in the garage with my chin in my hand. We were supposed to be going out to the cottage to look for the key, but we were waylaid. Van was standing at the hood of the car arms hanging limp at his side and he was nearly drooling. I remembered back to when I was a kid and the boys would play with those little Matchbox cars that they made to look like real ones. He had that look in his eye.

"It's a '64 two door hardtop." I wasn't sure that it got through.

"It's a '64 two door hardtop." I heard him whisper.

It was nice to see someone else appreciate the car as much as I do, but I wasn't expecting this kind of reaction. He walked around the car, twice, trailing his hands along the body as though it were an apparition. Finally he pulled the driver's door open and sat down in the driver's side.

I stood up and went around to the passenger door pulling it open. The smell of the cherry pipe tobacco hit me strong as it always did. My father hadn't been in this car for ten years, but the smell of his tobacco was always there. I would often sit in the car just to feel close to him.

"It was my dad's." I said softly.

His hands were on the steering wheel and he pulled them off and put them in his lap.

He looked over at me. "Sorry, I should have asked."

I put my hand on his arm. "No, it's okay. It's nice to see someone else get as excited about it as he did. He loved this car. I remember the day we brought it home. He was over the moon. He ran in the house and grabbed my mother spinning her around the kitchen."

"Is it all original?"

I nodded. "Original white and red paint job and only forty-five thousand miles."

He had his hands back on the steering wheel and I laid my head back on the headrest.

"How long have you had it?" He asked and I thought back.

"For about fifteen years. I think Uncle Cutter died in 1996."

"Uncle Cutter?"

"He wasn't really my uncle. I don't have any aunts or uncles because my parents were both only children. He was the man that my dad worked with for years and I always called him Uncle Cutter. His real name was Cutsworth Franzin, but everyone called him Cutter."

"So Uncle Cutter simply gave it to him?" He asked disbelievingly.

I still had my eyes closed leaning against the headrest inhaling the scent of the tobacco. I could see my father and Uncle Cutter sitting on the old porch sharing a beer after finishing work.

"My dad took care of Cutter and his wife Lauren for the last year of Cutter's life. He had cancer and couldn't do anything around the house. Lauren was busy taking him to the doctor and taking care of him. She was getting on in years too and wasn't able to do much around the yard. My dad would go over on the weekends and mow the lawn or go over after a storm and plow them out so Cutter could get to his chemotherapy appointments. I think he was the father my dad needed and Lauren was always mothering us. When Cutter passed away Lauren took my dad to the garage and asked him if he would help her get rid of the car. My dad being my dad readily agreed to get the car ready for sale. He and I went over one weekend and we detailed it, not that it needed much work, but we washed and waxed it. It hadn't been driven in a few years with Cutter being sick so dad asked Lauren if he could run it up the highway to make sure there were no problems. Lauren smiled and sent us on our way with a couple of Cokes and told us to have fun."

I stopped talking. The memory of that first ride was still fresh in my mind. I could almost taste the cold Coke on my tongue and hear the music filtering through the open windows as my dad took us down I-35.

"My dad and I were singing with the windows open to Hootie and The Blowfish and before we knew it we were in Moose Lake and of course the car was behaving like the pretty little thing she is. Smooth as butter, not even a grumble."

I looked over at Van sure I was boring him to death, but he was listening intently waiting for the end. A smile touched the corner of his lips and I wondered if he was thinking about what it would have been like to have a father.

"We rode the car back into the driveway at Lauren's and my dad and I got out and gave her the keys. Dad said, "Lauren, the car's ready and you will get a good price for her". But Lauren smiled and handed my dad an envelope telling him to read it. She pulled me inside and together we stood inside the door watching him. The envelope was addressed to my dad in Cutter's handwriting. I watched my father, the man who I thought was tough as nails, crumble to the ground as he read this letter. I wanted to race out there and pick him up, but Lauren held me back. Dad sat on the ground and cried until I couldn't take it any longer. I broke free and ran out to the car. I was only twelve, but I put my arms around him and held him. He slowly stopped crying and looked up at me." I brushed a tear that was running down my cheek away. "I will never forget this smile that formed on his face and he looked at me and he said, "Sugar, Uncle Cutter wants us to have the car." Now my dad was an incredibly proud man who worked hard for everything he had and this car was an amazing gift for him. When Lauren passed away he led her funeral procession in the car."

I opened the glove compartment and pulled out an envelope. It was dog eared and worn, but the letter was still inside. I had read the letter so many times I could recite it by heart.

"I know this letter by heart. I won't bore you with the details, but Uncle Cutter's words have formed who I have become these last few years. He told my dad not to take any minute of any day for granted. That you should get up and watch the sunrise and then watch it set holding the one you love. He said that following your dreams and taking chances is as important as playing it safe. He said that this car represented what life is. Life is a car that can break down, but with determination you can get it up and running again. I kinda took it to mean that when life breaks down and you have to slap the hazards on at least you know that in the back of your mind you can turn them off eventually and get back on the road to finish the trip." And I was not at all making any sense.

I looked over at him, "I'm sorry. I'm not making any sense here at all am I?"

"Wrong, everything you said made complete sense to me, but I get the impression that you might be in the breakdown lane right now." He stared at me intently.

I shrugged my shoulder and kept going because I didn't know how to answer that. "Jess loves this car. After Paul left my dad was pretty much the only father he had and I often traded my seat in the Mustang so Jesse could go out with Dad and be alone. Someday when Jesse has a son I will give him the car for safe keeping."

"Really?" He looked shocked.

I nodded, "Yeah, I'm the last of the DuBois line and I want the story of my father to continue to be told and that means that the next person that should drive this is Jesse making the memories with his son."

"Lucky devil." He said and I laughed.

"Are you really the last in your family?"

"My parents were both born later in life and were only children. My grandparents were in their seventies by the time mom and dad even got married and by the time I was ten they were all gone. There weren't a lot to start with, but now it's only me."

"Well maybe you will have a son someday and you can tell him all about the car."

No, chances are I wouldn't have a son someday. Chances are the car would go to Jesse. I didn't think I needed to share that with him.

His words intruded on my thoughts, "So if you have this sweet car sitting in your garage what's with the Sorento? I didn't have you pegged as a foreign car lover." He tossed his thumb in the direction of my SUV parked in the garage stall next to us.

I rolled my eyes at him. "I'm not a foreign car lover. The **Sorento is made in the US and its all wheel drive, secure in the snow and gives me** room to haul cargo and students. It's my common sense vehicle. I got a **great deal on it from one of my students who works for Kia Duluth. The Mustang stays in the garage for** the winter." I said matter of fact.

"Well let me tell you if I had this car, it's all I would drive." He said **rubbing the steering wheel. "Wait, so you only drive this in the nice** weather?"

"Yes, only I don't drive it. I can't drive a manual." The look **on his face was one of disbelief.**

"So you have never driven this car?"

Oh I've driven it, but not in the last ten years.

"I can teach you to drive a stick, it isn't that hard."

It is when you can't bend your ankle.

"Jess tried to teach me once and told me I was hopeless." I said **forcing a laugh.**

The thought crossed my mind that maybe I should try again. I knew how to drive a stick and the last time I tried it was less than a year after the accident. Things didn't go so well, but a lot of time has **passed since then and maybe my leg is stronger now, maybe I will have better control. I made a mental note to give it a shot, the next time I was alone.**

"So can I drive it or have we hit that gotta keep her in the garage date?"

He was like a kid in a candy store and I could see that driving it would make his day. I held up a finger and got out of the car shutting the door behind me. I walked to the garage door peeking out at the expanse of blue sky. I came back around and tucked my head in the open window.

"Tell you what, when we get done in the cottage we can take it into Duluth. It might be the last time to drive her for the year."

He pumped his fist and let out a hoot. I couldn't help but laugh at his knee jerk reaction. The man was a surprise around every corner. He got out of the car and shut the door, carefully, coming around to the hood where I was lounging. He grabbed my hand and pulled me to the side door of the garage.

"Let's get this done, I wanna ride."

We walked down the trail to the cottage like it was any other day, but I knew that Van was being watchful of the slightest movement. I had my arms wrapped around myself hating that my usual happy walk to the cottage was now steeped in fear. I hated feeling like my every move was being tracked either by the good guys or the bad.

Van nonchalantly put an arm around my shoulders and pulled me close to him as we made our way down the well worn path. There were woods on both sides of us that in the summer were filled with leaves and flowers and birds singing, but today it was stark and the cold wind blew the trees making them bend to its power. I shivered a little and was happy to see the cottage peek out at us from behind the bare trees.

The cottage was rustic hewn logs, like the main lodge, and when you opened the door you expected it to be rustic and old fashioned. That was the image I wanted to portray to stay with the theme of the property, but the reality is that nowadays even honeymooners want every luxury. The inside of the cabin was modern with every comfort of home including a corner whirlpool tub and small kitchenette with wine cooler. The center of the room was filled with a wrought iron king size four poster bed with iridescent sheers that hung from the bed draped like netting creating a cozy space. The bed was covered in a thick down comforter with throw pillows filling the middle. I usually had fresh rose petals strewn across the bed, but since Margie and Nathan had stayed here for so long the rose petals had long since been vacuumed up. There was a state of the art entertainment system in the corner opposite the bed that included full DVD and CD options as well as wireless internet. Even honeymooners needed to stay current with their Facebook and Twitter.

I keyed open the door and Van stepped in first taking a quick circuit through the main room and bathroom before giving me the all clear. I had shut and locked the door behind me and even though I wanted to throw open the shades and curtains I left them closed. Van was standing in the middle of the room visually inspecting it with his eyes getting a feel for the room.

"Not what you were expecting?" I asked.

"That seems to be the theme of this property." He said as he walked around the room taking in the main living area and then back into the bathroom.

I sat down on the edge of the bed and let out a sigh. This cabin was small, but the number of hiding areas was not and the idea of searching the whole place for a small key was somewhat daunting. Van came back out of the bathroom resting his hand on the door jam.

"This is going to take a while isn't it?"

"Yup."

"Okay, let's go at this from their point of view." He said and I waited wondering what his opinion of their point of view would be.

"If I were going to hide something that I might need to get quickly I'm not going to put it somewhere that is going to take me more than a couple seconds to get too, right?"

I nodded. Made sense to me.

He walked into the main room and stopped in front of me. "So, you take the bed, search the wood areas, any crevices that the key could be set down in and I will take the tables. If we don't find anything then we will move to the next logical spot."

And so we began a methodical search of the room. The bed was large and I had to stand on the mattress to reach the top of it.
I ran my hand along the edges of each rail that held the sheers and down the outside of each poster feeling for anything that could be taped to the metal. I felt down along the inside of the mattress along the bottom of the frame, but the contortions I had to get into in order to do it told me it wasn't likely to be there. I lay on the floor under the bed with a flashlight searching the bottom of the frame. I let out a breath knowing that I wasn't going to find it on the bed, but for the sake of completeness I flipped over the wooden stairs that the lovers used to climb in. Nope, no key. I got up off the floor and plunked back down on the bed.

Van had finished his assessment of the small night table next to the bed and the kitchen area. He was standing with his back to me staring at the large armoire near the whirlpool. It held extra towels and sheets and had room for guest's clothing. The doors were hand carved from pine and were the main focus of the room. He walked over to the armoire and ran his hands over the doors. I knew what he was thinking.

"Did your dad do these?"

I smiled coming up behind him, "No I did."

He turned quickly not realizing I was so close and bumped into me. He reached out and grabbed my arms to steady me coming in close enough to smell the scent of his aftershave and my heart began to beat a little faster. Something about this man and Irish Spring made my heart race every time. I was trying to convince myself it was the soap and not the man, but that little voice was busy snickering about that. I stepped back and he released me.

"Sorry, you took me by surprise." he said.

I stepped around him wanting to put some space between us. I told myself that my reaction to him was due to the circumstances, but I couldn't say that if the circumstances were different that I wouldn't react the same way.

"You carved this?" He asked and I nodded. It was a scene of the Duluth Harbor from atop Enger Tower.

"The ship doesn't look like the Edmund Fitzgerald."

"It's not. It's the Vista Star. It's a tour boat that takes visitors on sightseeing cruises on the lake. They also rent the boats for private events and school groups, things like that." The ship was about to pass under the lift bridge as three eagles circled over the boat. To the left and right of the boat were the lighthouse piers as the boat began to glide off into open water. He ran his hands over the three eagles. He said nothing, but I knew he understood their significance.

"I carved it one winter when I needed something to do." And it sounded lame to my ears too.

"Needed something to do?" He looked over at me. "This is art; this isn't needing something to do."

"For me it was needing something to do. It turned out better than I expected so I decided to use it here in the cottage."

He was quiet for a while inspecting the armoire for a hidden key and I sat back down on the bed to avoid bumping into him. Something told me that the further I stayed from this man the safer I would be. I sat staring at the armoire knowing something wasn't right and yet I couldn't put my finger on what it was. Whatever it was, it was off enough that my eye was registering it without my mind being able to decipher it. Maybe I'm just tired. No, I am tired there's no maybe about it. I rubbed my eyes and closed them for a moment.

"Tula? Are you okay?" I wanted to say yes, but nothing came out. I felt the bed shift, but my eyes wouldn't open. I felt Van pull me into his chest and lay my head on his shoulder. I should have stopped him. I should have opened my eyes and got up and walked out of the cottage, but I couldn't. My body was tired, but my mind was exhausted. I drifted off into a dreamless sleep feeling protected in the arms of someone I found myself trusting without knowing.

NINE

I woke with a start forgetting where I was. I sat up quickly and Van put his hand on my arm.

"You okay?"

I looked around and slowly ran my hand down my face. "I fell asleep." It was more of a statement then a question.

"Yup. You fell asleep. Guess my company has that affect on people. It seemed like you really needed it though, so I let you sleep."

"I've had a rough couple of nights."

Couple? How about couple dozen. I checked the time on the bedside clock. It was a little past noon, which meant I had only been asleep for an hour. Not that it really mattered how long I had actually been sleeping. I had been sleeping in the honeymoon cottage with him! A little voice in the back of my mind reminded me that I had slept for a whole hour with no dreams in his arms. I was busy convincing myself it was coincidence.

"I was laying here watching you sleep and my mind started to drift. If Margie and Nathan stayed here for the last two months of the season and you were already booked what did you do with the other guests who normally would have had their weekend here? I'm only asking because it might be important to the case if you moved Margie and Nathan somewhere else those weekends."

"I tossed that around, but I decided I didn't want to have to move them each time and clean and all that, it would be a nightmare, so I told a little fib."

He smiled, "A little fib?"

"Well I called the last four brides for the year and told them there had been damage to the cabin from a storm, I mean it could happen, and would they agree to a night at the Radisson with a limo ride into Duluth after the reception. I tossed in breakfast in bed and they all readily agreed."

"Smooth." He said.

"What can I say? The reality of it is that with what Nathan and Margie were paying me," I stopped and started to wonder who it was that was paying me. I raised an eyebrow at Van.

"No they were paying you. We would have put them in the cheaper safe house." He winked at me and I was relieved that I wasn't making a profit off the DPD.

I wiped my brow, "Okay good, because suddenly I was feeling like I took Jesse's bonus. Anyway, what they paid me to stay here for the two months more than made up for what it cost me for those four couples to stay at the hotel. It worked out really well and it's something that I can do in the future if the need arises. The Radisson was all too happy to oblige, so everyone got something out of the deal."

"Sounds like you have a real head for business."

I shrugged my shoulder, "Everyone here works together and helps each other out. We may look like a big city, but we still have a small town attitude." I cleared my throat and jumped down off the stairs to the floor. "Are you hungry?"

He moved off the bed and stopped leaning one hand on the poster frame letting his eyes wander their way from my face to my feet and back.

"Yeah." His eyes were smoky and I wasn't sure if he was flirting or purposely trying to make me uncomfortable. Either way he seemed to be enjoying himself. Best to go with nonchalant.

"Good. I'll make lunch and then we can take the Mustang for a ride."

A smile slowly formed on his face.

"What are you smiling about?" I asked him.

"Well so far today I have gotten to dance with a beautiful woman and hold sleeping beauty in my arms. Now I get to have lunch with a local celebrity and drive an incredibly cool car around town with a sexy as hell woman in the passenger seat." He grabbed my hand pulling me towards the door, "I don't know that life can get much better than this."

Yeesh and I had to ask. I was trying hard not to concentrate on the sexy as hell woman part as he busied himself with opening the door and doing his 007 moves with his gun. I was hoping that talking about the car would distract him, but apparently it only served to give him another reason to flirt.

He motioned me out the door and I turned and locked it pocketing the key. We walked back down the path and again he had his arm around my shoulder keeping me close to him as we walked. His eyes shifted back and forth between the trees watching for the slightest movement and listening for any noise out of place. We heard the crunching of the leaves and saw the movement between two trees at the same time. He pushed me behind him and drew his gun aiming it at the tree as a small deer stepped from behind the tree into the open. He dropped his arm and clicked the safety back on and I stifled a laugh.

"He looks dangerous. You gonna let him go?" And I shouldn't mess with him, but I couldn't help it.

"Funny." He didn't sound amused.

We finished our walk to the garage and went inside. He radioed the man in the woods to inform him that we were not longer in the cabin and then he checked his remote attached to his belt.

"Looks like it's been quiet, which I expected. I really think they are going to let us do the legwork for them." he said, pocketing the remote and holding the door open for me.

We stepped into the mudroom and took off our coats before moving into the kitchen. He excused himself and went through the lodge checking to make sure everything was still secure and then went to his room to check messages. I waited for him to leave and then spent several minutes banging my head against the refrigerator door. I still could not believe I fell asleep in the cabin with a man I hardly knew. This whole no sleep thing was starting to affect my brain and I felt like I was losing control. You slept for over an hour without any nightmares and you feel better a little voice said. I told it to shut up and stuck my head in the fridge. BLTs were on tap and I grabbed the bacon, lettuce and tomatoes before dipping my head back in for some fruit.

"I'll have what you're having." I jumped not realizing he was right behind me and cracked my head on the top of the fridge.

"Ouch!" I jumped out of the fridge rubbing my head.

He leaned over and gave my temple a kiss. "Better?"

No, not better, scary. I didn't like the way my heart picked up every time he got near me. I gave him an under the eyebrow look and stuck my head back in the fridge pulling out the fruit salad and Top the Tator. I threw some onion buns on the grill to warm them and busied myself with washing lettuce and slicing the tomato.

Van was sitting at the table nursing a Diet Coke, or a "mineral" as he called it and was smiling at me in a way that made me wonder what he was thinking. I grabbed a bag of chips from the cupboard and took them to the table with the fruit salad and Top the Tator. I was working myself into a frenzy trying to avoid his wandering eyes, but it wasn't working. I grabbed the buns off the grill and without turning asked, "BLTs, what's your poison? I held up mayo or Miracle Whip.

"Pardon me. Do you have any Grey Poupon?" He asked me in a horrible fake English accent. I couldn't help but laugh at him it was so awful.

"But of course!" I reached back into the fridge for the mustard and finished the sandwiches. I set his plate down at the table and pulled out my chair.

"This looks fantastic, but yours is missing something."

I looked down at my sandwich. "What?"

"You can't have a BLT without the T then it's just a BL and that doesn't work." He was smiling as he took a bite of his sandwich.

"It's the way I like it, but thank you for your concern. Tomatoes are icky. Never met one I liked yet."

He took a swig of his soda, "Icky huh? Wait a minute you ate like a half a bottle of ketchup last night on your onion rings."

"What's your point?" I took a bite of my sandwich enjoying the onion bun. I would have eaten the bun alone if I didn't have company, but it seemed a little too weird with someone watching.

"My point is that ketchup is tomatoes, goofball. You just told me you didn't like them."

"I like ketchup, I don't like fresh tomatoes. I want the spices and the onion and the sugar all mixed up in them before you are going to get me to eat tomatoes."

What can I say? A girl has to have standards.

He wiped his hands on his napkin, "You are an interesting woman Tula DuBois."

He really had to stop using that word!

"So can I ask you another question?" He asked between bites and I shrugged my shoulder, which I guess he took as permission. "Is your fridge always this stocked?"

I took a bite of my sandwich chewing slowly and washing it down with my soda.

"Isn't yours?" I took another bite.

"Lillie always kept the fridge stocked. She started doing the cooking as soon as she realized that my repertoire was TV dinners and macaroni and cheese. She used to make me take her to the store and wait in the car because I got in her way." He set his sandwich on his plate and leaned in over it like he was going to tell me a secret, "This one time she was about nine and I took her to the market for groceries. She was standing there looking through the glass at the meat counter and the butcher asked her if she wanted the usual. We knew him well and he always got a kick out of this little kid doing the shopping. So anyway, here's this huge butcher standing there with his white apron all stained with old blood and she starts giving him the business! I will never forget for the rest of my life the image of her standing there on her tip toes telling him how she wanted two pork chops and they had better be the same thickness because last time he gave her two different thicknesses and one was dry by the time the other was done."

"I think I would really like this girl. I love an independent woman who stands up for herself." I said.

"You remind me a little of her. You both have that get out of my way I can do this myself kind of attitude. I admire that in a woman. But I digress, so to answer your question I'm a bachelor now. All I have is beer in my fridge and you still didn't answer mine."

Like a dog with a bone this man. "I keep my fridge stocked for the most part. I never know when I'm going to have company drop in, hungry students or unplanned houseguests." I put extra emphasis on the later and he gave me a half a smile.

"Not that I'm complaining or anything." he said.

Good. They say the way to a man's heart is through his stomach, but this time I'm hoping that if I keep him well fed he will stop looking at me like I'm lunch.

TEN

I took a few minutes after lunch to change clothes deciding that jeans and a sweater would be better attire for an afternoon of shopping. I didn't want to look too deeply into why I suddenly cared what I was wearing when normally any old thing would do. I pulled the rubber band out of my hair and let it fall free around my shoulders tucking it behind my ears. I added some lip gloss and mascara hoping it would give me the courage I didn't feel. Looking good is half the battle right? Yeah right, in this case looking good was probably only going to encourage the "sexy as hell" part. He didn't seem the type to be easily put off if he wanted something bad enough and that was the reason I was emptying the bottle of Tums in the medicine cabinet.

I shut the medicine cabinet door and looked at myself in the mirror. You need a plan Sugar, what's your plan for the afternoon? I decided my plan was going to be keeping the topic of conversation focused on him. My first question being where in the hell did you learn to dance? After we left the ballroom this morning he showed me his "beloved dance shoes". They were an old, ratty beat up pair of jazz shoes that looked as old as he was, but he insisted that they were the only thing that made him feel like he was dancing in his stocking feet. Personally, I don't want to feel like I'm dancing in my stocking feet, but to each their own. I dragged him back to the ballroom and dug out a new pair of jazz boots that I had gotten in to let him try. We gave them a whirl around the dance floor and he readily agreed that they were much more comfortable and I told him that at least they made him look like a respectable dance instructor. I didn't get him to agree to throw out the old ones, but I did get him to agree to wear the new ones Saturday night.

I gave myself one last look over in the mirror making sure my jeans fell right across both legs. I took a deep breath, grabbed my parka and bag and met Van in the mudroom. He was standing there foot tapping obviously ready long ago. I grabbed the keys to the Mustang off the board and threw my parka on. He turned to grab the keys from me and I let out a sigh, obviously he hadn't seen the need to change his clothes.

"Why the sigh?" He asked it like he was used to the female persuasion sighing at him.

"Are you going out in that?" I indicated his sweatshirt and he looked down at himself confused.

"What's wrong with this? It's just a sweatshirt."

Really? Way to think this out Bond.

"It says Texas A &M."

"Yes, it does, you can read, very good." He patted my shoulder.

I rolled my eyes at him. "You're from Ireland remember? Not Texas. Don't you have something more Irishy than that?"

He arched an eyebrow, "Irishy?" He snapped his fingers and gave me the "I'm bummed" look. "Sorry, my silk shamrock boxers are in the wash." And then he smirked at me and I was pretty sure I was going to start flailing my hands around and yelling.

"Listen, we are about to go to a town where every other person we see I will know! Can't you cooperate and put on something more Irishy? Good god man, play the part!" And here came the hand flailing. Why must men be so obtuse?

He rocked back on his heels and stuffed his hands in his pockets. "You know we do have stores in Ireland that sell clothes without shamrocks."

I let out an exasperated sigh, "How many people do you see walking down the middle of Dublin wearing Texas A&M sweatshirts?" I asked it between clenched teeth trying to keep my hands from flailing around, too much.

He seemed to be considering that for a minute and then he stepped up and grabbed the front of my parka in his hand.

"You know Jesse was right. I guess I should have taken him seriously." He said it in the tone of voice that made me want to punch him.

"Excuse me? Right about what?" I hissed back.

"He told me not to get you excited because you start to yell and," he flailed his free arm around like I did, "stuff."

"Fine then you can't say you weren't warned, now let me go and put on something that doesn't indicate in any way that you are not a dance instructor from Ireland." I said it with a bravado I didn't feel.

He pulled me up to within inches of his face. "Okay, but just for the record he didn't tell me how cute you would be during all that yelling and flailing." And then he planted a kiss square on my lips and released me taking off for his bedroom.

I stood there counting to one hundred trying to get my fury at him under control. I wasn't even that mad at him about the whole hand flailing thing because, well, frankly everything he said was true. I'm a hand talker, always have been. I was mostly frustrated about the cute thing and that whole sexy as hell thing earlier not to mention the whole kiss thing. He was just flirting, but to someone whose last date was half a decade ago I was a little out of practice and experiencing a lot of uncomfortable emotions. I needed to focus on the prize and that was getting Margie and Nathan back. This is simple all I need to do is not let his comments get me flustered. It seemed simple enough, but I was so tired that I wasn't firing on all cylinders and I had a feeling that it was going to be much harder than it sounds. I prayed that Saturday would come and go quickly assuring myself that the dreams would fade then and I would sleep.

I took a few deep breaths as I heard him coming back down the hallway and plastered a smile on my face. He pulled up next to me in a new sweatshirt. It was a grey hoodie with a large shamrock on the front and the words Kiss Me I'm Irish.

He leaned in, a little too close for comfort. "Better?"

He was enjoying this too much and I fought the urge to lean all the way into him. "It's perfect."

No way was I giving him the satisfaction of seeing he had me flustered. I grabbed his hand and pulled him down the stairs to the waiting Mustang. I threw him the keys and climbed into the passenger side. He opened the driver's side door and gently sat down in the car, almost like if he was too rough it would break. He put the key in the ignition and turned it over. The engine roared to life and he was a little boy again. His eyes were rolled back in his head and he was rolling his head around on the headrest like he was having a seizure. Having experienced this same response with every male who ever drove the car I sat quietly waiting for him to come back to this world. He snapped out of his trance and rubbed his hands over the wheel.

He looked over at me. "Ready?"

"Yup, I've been ready for about five minutes now."

He grinned at me and I had to wait some more while he adjusted the mirrors and readied himself for the maiden voyage. Finally I opened the garage door and he backed it out getting a feel for the car. I closed the door while he turned the car towards the drive that ran along the lake. The wind would occasionally gust and rattle the few leaves left in the trees before they would flutter down to join the others blanketing the ground. There was a thick layer of maple and oak leaves below the empty trees that had now lost their color and turned brown. I could picture them covered in snow the tips reaching up through the whiteness like lifeless limbs. I sighed. Winter would be here soon there was no denying it.

I snuck a glance at Van. He had thrown on his leather jacket over his sweatshirt leaving it unbuttoned and to an untrained eye he appeared causal and comfortable. To the trained eye he looked cold. I pushed the levers around on the heater waiting for some warm air to fill the car.

"You want to know where I learned to dance?" he said offhand.

I turned in my seat. "Now you're a mind reader too?"

He accelerating the car out of the driveway onto Moccasin Mike Road.

"Nope, but I figured you've been dying to ask since we were in the ballroom."

I snorted, "Don't flatter yourself." Apparently there is nothing wrong with his ego. He stopped at the stop sign looking for traffic before pulling right onto Second Street heading into Superior.

"So you don't want to know?" No, I wanted to know, but I hated that he could tell how much.

"Well, whatever, if you want you tell me that's fine." I said waving my hand like it didn't matter much.

He laughed out loud and shook his head. "Nice try at nonchalant." I bit my tongue to keep from saying something less nonchalant. "Okay." I tossed my hands around in the air letting them fall onto my lap, "Please honor me by telling me how you learned to dance."

"See that wasn't so hard."

I rolled my eyes at him my sarcasm lost.

He had one arm on the wheel and the other draped across the gear shift. "My grandmother."

That was it. Two words. Men can be so informative sometimes.

"So your grandmother taught you to dance?"

"Yup."

He slowed as he entered the city limits of Superior and got into the left hand lane. I twisted in my seat until I had my left leg up on the seat and my back pressed up against the door.

"Sorry if I find it hard to believe that your grandmother taught you everything you know. You were formally trained by someone."

"Yeah, I was, but my grandmother actually taught me. She was still pretty young when I came to live with her and would go dancing all the time. She would take me with her and at first I would sit at the table and color or play games while she danced. As I got older she started showing me some basic steps at home and then would give me a chance to practice out on the floor. I enjoyed it so much that I took private lessons for several years before she got sick. When I moved to the US all I brought with me was her collection of LPs and her record player. I didn't have much time when Lillie was younger to go out and dance, so we used to listen to the old records and I would teach her at home.

It was good way to spend time getting to know each other. As she got older we would go to street dances and bars that would let her in with me. Once she got into high school she would get a group of friends together and we would spend an afternoon learning a dance in the high school gym. She is actually quite good now. All the boys wanted to dance with her at the prom."

"And I bet that you were there to make sure that dancing was all they were doing." His smile was answer enough.

"You know when you talk about her your whole face shows me how proud she makes you. You love her deeply don't you?"

"She has been my life for the last twelve years. I know she's my sister, but we have more of a father-daughter relationship." He said stopping at the lights near Barker Island.

"I can imagine that it would be difficult not to. She counted on you to be her life and take care of her the way a father would." I trailed off.

His body language had changed and he seemed melancholy. He obviously was missing this girl that he had raised for so many years. He was still so young and I was in awe of his dedication to her.

"I want you to know that I really am impressed with your devotion to her. You don't see too many people stepping up and doing the right thing anymore." And he shrugged his shoulder and I could tell he was uncomfortable with the praise.

"I'm also impressed and enormously relieved with your dancing ability. I wasn't sure how I was going to teach you enough in a few short days to pass you off as a teacher."

He looked at me under an eyebrow. "I wouldn't have agreed to the story if I couldn't dance."

Good point, guess I should have thought of that.

"I enjoy dancing and you're right it is very athletic. I used to do it in the off season to stay in shape for football. I never told anyone though because, as you said, most guys think it's a sissy thing."

I guess he was listening last night. I sat back in the seat enjoying our conversation.

"Turn left here and follow it down to the next set of lights." I said giving him directions to the first store.

He nodded, "I do know that I can't hold a candle to you, however, and I'm actually looking forward to learning a few things."

He said it in a voice that made me unsure if he was talking about dancing. I could feel color creeping up into my cheeks as he pulled his eyes off the road long enough to give me soft smile. We wove our through Superior and I pointed out the college as we stopped at the lights along the way.

"What's with all the yellow bees on the street?" He asked me as we headed down Belknap Street.

"They're yellowjackets. The University of Superior's mascot is the yellowjacket. They painted them on the street in front of the college. Can't say you won't find your way to the school."

He looked over at me smiling and I knew exactly what he was thinking. I was thinking it too.

"So where am I headed?"

"Next set of stop lights go straight and then take a left at those up there." I said pointing at the next street over near the Super One.

The best place to head for gear to keep him going here at the tip of the end of the world was Northwest Outlet. As usual it was busy, as we pulled in and parked. We worked our way into the back and found a black North Face parka and several Carhart flannel shirts. We stopped in the front for a pair of Columbia cold weather boots before checking out. There was no way his government issue Under Armour Valsetz trail boots would stand a chance of keeping his feet warm in this climate. We picked up a pair of Columbia driving gloves and a thicker pair of fleece waterproof gloves for longer outings.

We paid for our purchases and he traded his leather jacket for the parka in the car, stowing the rest in the trunk. We roared across the Bong Bridge in the Mustang and worked our way through the hills of Duluth to Miller Hill Mall for some Under Armour Coldgear for layering. Van was thoroughly enjoying driving the car and it was nice to take it out for a final spin before the long cold months of winter set in. It took us longer at the mall than I had planned after stopping to talk to at least ten people and I could tell Van was getting anxious to be done shopping.

We climbed back in the car and I looked over at him with sleepy eyes, "I have a problem."

He was buckling in, "What?" He looked at me a little concerned.

"I need some coffee." I said my words slurring.

He looked at his James Bond watch, "Good god, it's been four hours since you had a cup! It's an emergency! If I had a siren I'd slap it on until we found the nearest Starbucks!"

And I stared at him because it wasn't a joke. I've been in need that bad before and it's possible that Jesse may have used the sirens once or twice.

"Starbucks?" He asked sheepishly and I nodded.

He shifted the car into gear and took off for the nearest port in the storm, but I had a feeling he didn't mind being seen driving the Mustang. We swung out of Starbucks and headed back down the hills to make a stop on Superior Street at the Electric Fetus. I had ordered a new speaker for the ballroom and I was hoping it was in. My friend Mike was my sound man for the lodge and his day job was selling old LPS and new CDs, not to mention other interesting and obscure items, in this old brick building in downtown Duluth. Van looked at me eyebrows raised when he parked in front of the store and I smiled and climbed out. He held the door for me and we stepped into the warmth of the building not realizing how cold it had gotten until we felt the warmth of the store. It smelled like soap and incense and old records and it was welcoming and made you want to stand around and listen to music for hours. We stopped short at the t-shirt rack and I picked him out a t-shirt and a stocking cap that said Electric Fetus giving it to him as a welcome to Duluth gift.

"Now you have official Duluth clothing." He immediately stuck the hat on being that it was "freezing" in this town. Mike was in the back looking for the speaker, so we perused some old 33s while we waited.

"No way." I could hear the excitement in Van's voice and I walked over to where he was standing. He was holding an old 33 album in his hand.

"Find something?" He was looking at the album the way you do a long lost friend.

"Sam Cooke, 1957. I haven't seen this album since my grandmother had it years ago. I actually wore it out listening to it." Apparently he hadn't heard of CDs.

"You can get that on CD now you know."

"I'm well aware of that, but it's not the same. I gotta have this album."

I looked at the price tag on the album and snorted. "A buck ninety nine. Do you think you can swing it?"

He gave me the ha-ha funny look and tucked it under his arm just as Mike came back out with my speaker. Mike approved of Van's album choice and they chatted about growing up listening to 33s and the difference between the old music and today's. I rolled my eyes. They sounded like two old grandpas in their rocking chairs. I finally managed to get Mike to ring up our purchases so we could get on our way back to Superior before the sunset.

We took an extra minute to zip up knowing the cold would hit us after being in the warm store for so long. We stepped out the door and it was obvious that the temperature had dropped while we were inside as it was downright bitter now. I quickly unlocked the back door to the Mustang and set the speaker on the seat not wanting to take a chance it would get knocked around in the trunk. Van slid his album behind the speaker box. I was surprised he didn't seatbelt it in.

"What?" He asked.

I smiled. "Nothing."

I was happy that he was happy.

"Well, you are officially ready for a stay at the tip of the end of the world." I said as I pulled my seatbelt on and finished off my café mocha, which was surprisingly still hot.

"I look good don't I?" He said huffing on his fingers and rubbing them on his chest.

Oh brother. His ego was not going to fit in the car soon. Unfortunately, he was right. With the black parka, black stocking beanie and his sunglasses he looked good. He looked like he belonged in an ad for L.L. Bean or Lands End. My mind was wondering places it didn't belong and I dragged it back to reality.

"I'd say yes, but I'm afraid then I would have to get out and walk so your ego had room to ride."

He laughed from deep down and his smile reached his eyes crinkling the corners ever so much. He had his hands wrapped around the wheel and his sunglasses on following the signs to I-35. I was looking out the window at the lake as we drove trying to figure out how I was going to make it to Sunday morning.

"Whass keepin' yeh?" He asked as I twisted my coffee cup in my hand and glanced in his direction. This whole Irish thing was going to take some time to get used too.

"Do you have cliff notes for these Irish sayings?" He looked over at me and I noticed that the sun shining through the window was reflecting off his sunglasses giving me a reverse view of the lake.

"It means, why are you so distracted? I feel like you are only half with me. We are driving around in this incredibly cool car and there isn't even any music playing."

He was right, I was distracted. Not only was my gut twisted up about Saturday night, but I was trying to figure out what I had missed in the cabin this morning. My brain seemed to have checked out and I couldn't make it dredge up what was out of place. I reached over and snapped the radio on, not caring what was playing. I turned my head back to the lake mentally taking myself through the cabin. I could feel his gaze burning a hole in me. I looked over.

He had his glasses pushed down his nose and was looking at me with disdain. "Really? Public radio?"

I did a little fiddling and found Enrique yelling that he liked it, whatever that meant, but with Enrique I think I knew.

"Better?" I asked and he nodded. I got him turned around and we merged onto I-35 as my phone rang. I looked at the read out. Julie.

"I need to take this do you know where you are going?"

"You betcha." I smiled at his attempt to copy a northern Minnesotan.

"Hi Julie."

"Hi Sugar, are you driving?" I could hear the scanner in the background telling me she was at her desk in the station.

"Nope, I have a chauffeur today."

"Hey yeah, Jesse told me that you had a guest teacher this week."

I had no idea how much information Jesse had given her about the real reason Van was here.

"Great dancer. He really knows his stuff." I said smiling at his reaction.

I paused and Julie asked, "Is he hot?" And I knew right then that she didn't have a clue why he was here.

"Guess you will have to stop over and see for yourself."

She laughed and assured me she would. I listened while she filled me on new information regarding the foundation dinner. She told me quietly that a storm was being predicted for Friday night. I tensed in my seat. I didn't need a snowstorm to hit this weekend for a myriad of reasons, the least of which being the foundation dinner. She told me it was too early to be sure yet, but she was being assured that it if it snowed everything would be cleared by Saturday night. That only added to my anxiety. I was still hoping to make Saturday night go away. I hung up the phone taking a minute to put the information in my phone for later before I forgot.

I looked up and my heart sped up to cardiac arrest rhythm and sweat broke out on my forehead. Van was bopping to the radio in his seat, sunglasses still covering his eyes.

"You're going the wrong way!" I shouldn't yell.

He looked over at me obviously not disturbed by my shouting. "Relax Tula, who's doing the driving here?"

I shook my head frantically. "No, no you don't understand. This is the wrong way. You have to pull over and turn around."

Van pulled his sunglasses off and looked at me one eyebrow raised. "Did you forget something?"

I felt the car slow and I fumbled for the door handle.

"Turn around, please turn around." I was still fumbling with the door and my breathing was becoming faster and shallower.

Van was looking at me with concern. "I can't, there is no place to turn around."

I could see the high bridge in front of us and I was pretty sure that I was going to throw up, hyperventilate and pass out.

"Pull over." I said between clenched teeth. I was fumbling for the door lock trying to get it open. I wasn't sure what I was going to do once I got it open, but I had to get out of the car.

Van slowed the car further and looked over at me. "Tula, stop." His voice was level, but firm. My hand stilled on the door. "I am going to pull over, but do not open the door, I don't want you to get hurt."

I nodded eyes glued to the bridge, chest heaving, tears forming at the back of my eyes. Van pulled the Mustang over to the shoulder and stopped putting it in park and throwing on the hazard lights.

I couldn't pull my eyes away from the bridge knowing that at the top was a memory I didn't want to relive.

"Tula," I felt Van's warm hand on my arm. "What is going on? You look brutal, are you not feeling well?"

I shook my head and was grateful when my hair fell down hiding my face. I felt him reach out and tuck it back behind my ear.

"I, I can't go over this bridge. I'm getting out." I put my hand on the door and he stopped me.

"Where are you going to go?" Anywhere but here was all my mind was screaming. "We came over the other bridge on the way over, it's just another bridge."

"It's not just another bridge!" It came out as a choked shriek. I turned my head and leaned my forehead against the cool window closing my eyes trying to take deep breaths.

"I can't go over this bridge." My voice was quiet and I heard Van blow out a breath. He turned me in my seat so he could look in my eyes. "Is this where the accident happened?"

I nodded, not able to speak.

"So you drive out of your way every time you have to cross the lake in order to avoid this bridge?"

I nodded again.

"Are you going to do that for the rest of your life?" The question was quiet, but I could read the undertones.

"That was the plan."

He took my hand gently, tentatively. "Maybe we should drive over the bridge."

I jumped back against the door banging my elbow on the door handle. I cried out and Van grabbed my elbow holding both arms until I was still. My breathing was ragged. He looked down at his hands holding my wrists and his fingers traced the scar that ran up my arm. It was faint, but he'd finally noticed it. Realization dawned in his eyes and he let out a breath like he had been punched.

"Tula, were you in the car that night?"

A tear escaped down my cheek and he wiped it away knowing the answer. "I was the lucky one."

I know I should have told him the rest, but my mind was not having any of it. My mind was still screaming and my heart was nearly pounding out of my chest. His jaw worked as he ran his finger up and down the scar.

"Do you trust me?"

I nodded. I had only known him twenty four hours, but for some reason I trusted him with my life.

"Okay, we are going to do this. I'm going to drive up and over the bridge and you are going to hold my hand as tight as you can. Ground yourself on me and remember that nothing up there is going to hurt you, I won't let it. Okay?" He smiled at me again and my heart slowed a fraction.

I stared at him unable to answer. He put the Mustang in gear and moved back into the lane of traffic. I had one hand in his and the other grasping the door. He crossed the apron of concrete onto the bridge and my heart stopped beating. I could hear him talking to me and telling me I was alright. I could see the lake below me the waves rippling in the light breeze and the sun glinting off the top of the cargo ship filled with ore heading out onto the lake on its next journey. It registered in my mind how serene it was, but I still couldn't breathe. I couldn't speak. We reached the top of the bridge and I wanted desperately to close my eyes, but I couldn't do that either. I still wasn't breathing and I could see Van out of the corner of my eye watching me closely. I was starting to see spots and yet I couldn't make myself take a breath. I couldn't make my body do anything. I couldn't remember where we were on the bridge when the truck hit us. There were no details of any of that in my mind. All

I had was the sound of metal crunching and then me crying and screaming for my parents to talk to me and then nothing but the sound of the snow hitting the car. Tears were streaming down my face and I still couldn't breathe.

I heard Van's voice. "Take a deep breath Tula. Now." He shook my hand snapping me out of my trance and I sucked in air relieving the burning in my lungs and the stars disappeared.

"There ya go babe, now you're sucking diesel."

He kept talking to me until we made it over the bridge and he pulled off into the parking lot of the Best Western. He killed the engine on the Mustang and sat quietly holding my hand while my breathing slowed.

"You did it." He said softly.

"I did it." And I don't ever want to do it again. "You think I'm silly don't you?" I said quietly. For some reason it mattered to me what he thought.

"No, I don't think you're silly. The look on your face was all I needed to see that was completely real for you. I would never discount that as silliness." He reached up and brushed off a couple more tears that had slid down my cheek. "Have you heard of posttraumatic stress disorder?"

I shrugged.

"Do you think you might have a touch of that when it comes to the bridge?"

"Probably more than a touch." I said.

He gave a soft laugh and opened his door coming around to the passenger side of the car. He pulled open the door and unsnapped my seatbelt pulling me out of the car and straight into his arms. I threw my arms around him and held on breathing in the scent of him mixed with the fresh lake air. I stood there listening to his heartbeat the way I used to hear my Dad's or Brent's when we danced together. I willed my heart to slow down to match his rhythm. He stroked my hair quietly knowing words were not what I needed. I don't know how long we stood there, but I felt safe in his arms and I could feel myself relax as each minute passed.

"Can I ask you something?" I felt his words as much as I heard them.

I gave a nod.

"When your phone rang did I actually hear it singing about hot coffee?"

I giggled, I couldn't help it. He always seemed to know how to make me feel better.

"'Hot Coffee' by Carl Anderson. The only problem is when my phone rings I always get a hankering for coffee."

I felt his chest rumble as he laughed. He slowly pulled away and looked into my eyes, "You took a huge step today. I know it wasn't easy,

75

but remember that it can only have as much hold on you as you let it. You walked away from that accident, don't let it control you now." He looked like he wanted to say something else, but stopped. "Let's get you home." He held the door open for me and I climbed back in the car. My pulse was jumping, but it wasn't because of the bridge anymore, but because the smell of him lingered on my chest and I liked it too much.

ELEVEN

Van was driving through Superior headed back to the lodge and I was trying to come to terms with having just done something that I never thought I would ever be able to do. The old saying, what doesn't kill you makes you stronger, kept running through my mind when his words broke into my thoughts.

"I'm hungry. Do you want to stop and get something to eat?"

He was looking at me trying to gauge if that was a good idea.

I gave him a smile. "I'm starving. Whatta ya hungry for?"

"I could go for a burger." My kind of man.

"I know just the place."

I gave him directions to head up the highway and take the usual road that led to the lodge. I punched up the volume on the radio as Billy Joel came on. We reached the road and he turned right slowing down on the gravel road with the car.

"See that dirt road up there?"

He squinted. "Possibly."

"Take it."

I could see the question in his eyes, but he did as I told him. We drove further back into the woods, the path worn smooth by the many cars in and out. The sides of the path were jutted from snowplows coming and going year after year and there were several spots where cars had worn thin the brush from getting stuck. It looked to the casual observer that the only place this would lead was to parking your car in the lake, but I told him to hook a quick right and he saw the sign.

Van arched an eyebrow. "The Dew Drop Inn?"

"They have great burgers."

"Seems a little," he paused, "off the beaten path."

"You should probably get used to that, everything at the tip of the end of the world is off the beaten path." I flashed him a full on smile and he shook his head. I'm pretty sure I frustrate the hell out of him.

We pulled up into the parking area and got out of the car. Van trailed behind me his hand at the small of my back. Dewey was behind the bar wiping down glasses when we walked in. The light was dim and it took a minute for my eyes to adjust. There were a few regulars nursing a beer and watching ESPN, but it was mostly quiet as I knew it would be on a Wednesday.

Dewey looked up, "Sugar! Long time no see." Dewey came around the bar and I gave him a quick hug.

"Hi Dewey, I know it's been ages. I've been busy with the lodge." He noticed Van and took a step back. "Dew, I'd like you to meet Van MacNamara."

Van stepped forward and stuck his hand out to shake. Dewey sized him up and reluctantly gave it a shake while looking at me.

"Don't think in the fifteen years I've known you Sugar that you've ever brought a man in to eat."

I could see Van stifling a grin. "Cripes Dew, you're making me sound downright pathetic. Maybe you could stop doing that? Van is here from Ireland to work a few routines with me." And Dew was sizing up Van as friend or foe.

Dewey gave Van a look over, "All the way from Ireland to dance with Sugar, huh?"

Van laid on the accent. "Yes sir. Ms. DuBois's reputation is global and I jumped at the opportunity to learn some new moves from her. Are you aware that she knows more about the waltz than half the professional dancers in my country?"

I rolled my eyes. Good gravy if he laid it on any thicker he was going to need a knife.

Dew broke into a smile that over took his face, "She knows more about dance in her little finger than most people will ever know so I believe ya, lad."

Dew looked over at me, "The usual?"

"That would be great Dew, thanks." Dewey headed to the kitchen and I led Van to a booth towards the back. I didn't see much point in adding to the town fodder by sitting out in the open. But sitting in the back will probably only fuel the flames harder a little voice said. I did a mental eye roll at myself this time.

"Nice place." Van had his hand at the small of my back and he waited for me to sit before going around the booth and sliding in, facing the door. The booth was made from old brown naugahyde on the top and the bottom and the table was laminate wood grain with old cigarette burns pot mocking the top. It always felt like home when I slid into one of these booths. It meant good company and great food.

"What's the usual?" He asked as he scooted into the booth and pulled his beanie off.

I could tell him, but decided that wouldn't be as much fun. His hair was all askew and reminded me of a little kid after they came in from recess on a winter's day.

I gave him a sly smile. "You'll find out."

Dewey brought us two beers and a bowl of chips and dip. The chips were fresh out of the fryer and Dewey's homemade salsa smelled hot and spicy. We both dug in. Van was busy explaining some of the finer points of Irish slang when I reached for my beer. I took a long swig and nearly choked.

"Good gravy, Dewey, this beer is rancid!" I yelled towards the kitchen and Van was turning red trying hard not to laugh at me.

"What? Did you try yours?" I took a bite of a chip to get the taste out of my mouth.

Van picked up his glass and took a longer swig. He set the glass back down and in his thick Irish brogue yelled, "Dewey, my lad, you are a good man."

I saw Dew wave from the kitchen. I was obviously missing something. Van nodded his head at my glass.

"The beer isn't rancid its black stuff. Guinness."

I gave a shiver. "I've heard of that and no offense and all, but it's awful."

Van laughed. "Guinness beer is like....your Thai coffee, it's an acquired taste."

I was about to say something smart when Dew arrived with our burgers. My mouth was watering and I checked to make sure there was no drool.

"Two Sugar burgers with a side of rings and for the tender bud a Diet Coke." Funny. "Anything else I can get ya?" Dew had set the plates in front of us and Van held up his empty beer glass. Dewey reached out for it, but Van didn't let it go.

"What's the usual? She won't tell me."

I saw Dew's face light up and knew we were in for a conversation.

"It's a delight to the taste buds is what it is." He said and Van raised a brow at me. "It's a piece of meatloaf fried on the grill and smothered in caramelized onion on a light onion roll. I never would have thought of this, but Sugar came up with it one night for a casual party. Everyone was talking about it, so I convinced her to give me the recipe and promised to name the burger after her if it went on the menu. I sold fifty of them the first week and so the Sugar Burger was born."

Van didn't seem too surprised by the explanation. "She does seem to know her way around a kitchen."

Dew laughed. "I would hire her any day, but she'll have nothing to do with it."

He winked at me and stepped behind the bar to refill Van's beer. Van picked up his sandwich and took a bite. I could see his eyes roll back into his head as juice and onions slid down his hand.

Dewey came back with his beer and set it on the napkin.

"Anything else I can get you Sugar?"

I smiled up at him, "Thanks Dew, we're good."

I saw him head out the back door with the garbage, but I was pretty certain he'd be sneaking a cigarette while he was out there much to the chagrin of Ivy. We ate in silence for a few minutes.

"This is deadly. How do you make the meatloaf so moist?"

"Coffee." He laughed putting his hand in front of his mouth, "Seriously?" I nodded.

"What makes the onions so sweet?"

I gave him an under the eyebrow look and he gave his head an almost imperceptible nod.

"Sugar."

I took a bite of my sandwich. We ate quietly enjoying our burgers and each other's company, but I was still trying to focus my mind on what I had missed earlier at the cabin.

"These onion rings are deadly. Does he make them himself?"

I laughed before I could stop myself. "No, he sells so many of these that he would spend the whole day doing nothing but slicing rings. He buys them in a little town about ninety minutes south of here in Rice Lake. It's a great little city. They are like the biggest onion ring facility in probably the whole country, maybe, I don't know, but they sell a lot of onion rings. We used to go down and buy cases of them, but now that he can get them delivered we don't have to drive there anymore."

Van's eyebrows went up, "Really? I guess I don't think about Wisconsin as a big player for anything other than cheese."

"That's okay I mean let's face it we are the cheeseheads. I used to ride along with Dew and his wife when they would go pick up the onion rings and we always stopped at Dana's Beer Cheese. It's this little bar restaurant type place, a little hole in the wall really, but they make the best beer cheese soup served hot with popcorn on the top."

He had his nose curled slightly and I laughed. "No, it's really good!"

"I guess I will have to take your word for it."

I guess so.

"I can't say I have been around the US too much. I've made it to Chicago with Lillie, but that is about as far north as I have come. I can say I was in awe of the landscape as I flew in yesterday. Even though it was the end of fall there was still so much green. It reminded me a lot of the hills of Ireland as I flew over."

"Wisconsin and Minnesota are beautiful pretty much year round whether its fall with all the color, winter with the stark white contrasting the green pines or the summer sun on the lakes there is usually a season to please everyone. We have a lot to offer with industry and culture. We have a lot of colleges in the state with theater, music and art. My favorite place to go is Eau Claire where they host the Viennese Ball at the University every April. I take some of my students every year and it's an absolute party."

"Now that I can picture." And I wasn't sure if he was making fun of me or not. "I don't mind theatre, but what about, you know more fun stuff. What do you northerners do for fun?"

"Probably the better question is what don't we do for fun. We have fairs, music festivals, rodeos and air shows in the summer not to mention baseball. Depending on which side of the bridge you are standing on you can either root for the Milwaukee Brewers or the Minnesota Twins, but be careful to remember which side you are on when you open your mouth if you are going to talk trash. Same thing can be said about the Green Bay Packers and the Minnesota Vikings. Winter leads us to snowmobile racing, cross country skiing, ice fishing contests and, of course, hockey. We adapt to any season and find fun in just about everything."

"I do know that you have a heck of a football team. The few times I've seen the Cowboys play the Green Bay Packers the fans are all wearing cheese hats and clanking beer glasses."

"Well I'm sure you have figured out that the Pack, which by the way is what you should call them if you don't want to sound like a foreigner around here, are highly celebrated. There are some years where we don't have a heck of a football team, but it doesn't matter, there is no greater fan than a Packer fan, in my opinion."

"Do you own a cheesehead?" And I smiled giving a slight lift to my shoulder not willing to admit that there might be one in the back of my closet.

"I shouldn't bore you with all of this." I said wiping my mouth with my napkin and tucking it back in my lap.

He shook his head, "No, no, I'm enjoying myself, really. I love to hear about other places. I have no home really. Home for me has always been Ireland. Texas is where I live, but I haven't found it to be home. Now that Lillie is off to college I find myself wondering where home should be. Don't get me wrong, I have great friends and I love my work, but Texas isn't green enough for me to ever want to stay there forever. I would probably have left already, but I stayed for Lillie."

"My guess is that you still have plenty of time left to find home."

"Yeah, I guess I do."

We fell silent and finished our food both lost in our own thoughts.

"Earth to Tula." Van was waving a hand in front of my face and I put my burger down.

"Sorry."

"Everything okay?" He looked concern again like maybe I was going to have another meltdown.

"Yeah, yeah I'm fine. I've been thinking that we need to go back to the cabin when we get home."

His food was gone and his beer was empty and he sat with his elbows on the table fingers steepled.

"Okay, can you tell me why?"

I shook my head. "No I can't to be honest, but something is off."

I eyed the last onion ring and he pushed the plate over. "It's all yours. If I didn't know better I would think you like onions more than coffee."

I smiled and took a bite of the ring. A girl can have secrets too.

TWELVE

He pulled the Mustang down the long driveway to the lodge. I was hoping we would find everything the way we had left it. Nothing appeared out of place, but if there is one thing all of this has taught me is that nothing is ever as it seems. I remoted the garage door up and we pulled in. Everything looked secure, so I closed the door as Van got out his little remote for the house.

"The remote has not been activated, so no one tried to get in any of the covered areas."

He pushed the door open and went in, gun drawn. He did a quick walkthrough as I waited by the door to the kitchen. He came back from the ballroom with his gun holstered and nodded for me to come in. I pushed through the door with his bags of clothes and took them to his bedroom setting them on the bed. I turned to leave and bumped directly into him. He grabbed me by the arms to steady me and I could feel the heat radiating off him. His chest was all hard muscle and his hands were firm, but gentle.

I stepped back. "Sorry, didn't know you were there."

And he didn't let me go right away rather he held onto my arms and finally asked.

"Ready?"

And I nodded because words would not come out. We replayed the same scene as earlier on our way to the cabin. I unlocked the door and stopped short in the doorway. The room had obviously been searched by someone other than us. The bedding was rumpled and the drawers were hanging open. I wrapped my arms around myself and sucked in a breath. Van stepped in front of me, his gun drawn and did a quick circuit of the cabin. He came back out and sat next to me on the bed.

"Bathroom window. I radioed our guy on the property and from his vantage point he can't see the bathroom. I guess we let that one slip past us." He sounded angry at himself for not doing a better job of securing the perimeter as they say. I hoped that McElevain didn't get the key.

"It's going to be hard for me to figure this out now. Everything is out of order."

He took my hand pulling me off the bed. "Then let's put it all back in order so it looks like it did this morning and start over."

We busied ourselves with righting the tables and chairs, straightening the bedding and reloading the armoire and closing the doors. I couldn't help but think it may all be in vain if McElevain had already found the key, but I knew I had to try for Margie. A half an hour later we had the cabin looking like it always did and I sat back down on the bed. Van closed his phone after reporting the latest events to Jess and sat next to me on the bed. His thigh was tight against mine and he put his chin in his hand resting his elbow on his knee. He was copying my posture and it made me smile.

"What are we looking for?" He asked.

"Honestly, I don't know. I have been in this cabin so many times, but something is different. I need to sit and stare until I figure it out."

He nodded and laid back spread eagle on the bed. I gave him an eye. "Sorry, the burger made me tired."

More likely it was the two glasses of black stuff. My eyes ran across the surfaces of the tables, but nothing seemed out of place. I walked around letting my hand skim across surfaces and touch linens. My eyes kept going back to the armoire. I had spent hours carving the doors, painstakingly carving in each window on the boat, each grid on the bridge. Instead of concentrating on it I tried to let my mind wander over it.

I walked over to the armoire and ran my hands across the carved wood with my eyes closed. I could feel Van came up behind me standing a few feet away, waiting. My mind wandered back to so many years ago when I spent every night working on these doors. Every night I cried and every night I dreamt. Every night for three months I bloodied my fingers chipping away at this wood as the dreams chipped away at my sanity.

After I finished the doors I set them in the corner and my life fell apart. I went to school, I went to family functions and I pretended like everything was normal, but it wasn't. I didn't sleep. I lost twenty pounds, twenty pounds I didn't have to lose and one day I fell down at school and couldn't get up. I laid there my whole being so exhausted that I couldn't even talk. I couldn't tell them not to call the ambulance. I couldn't tell them not to take me to the hospital. I couldn't tell them not to call my "mom". I laid there and cried until I simply passed out.

I remember being in the hospital and a lot of whispering. I remember the doctors coming in and saying words like "dehydrated" and "exhausted". I remember other doctors coming in talking about "antidepressants" and "counseling". I remember that Sharon never left my side and Jess came and went between shifts spelling Sharon long enough for her to get a shower or a hot meal. But more than anything I remember laying there at night when Sharon thought I was asleep and listening to her sob and talk to Brent and my mom and dad. I remember her pleading with them and God to help me. Asking for their help in this world where she couldn't. I remember thinking how bad my heart hurt and I knew that hers must be hurting just as much. I remembered all the love and all the patience she had shown me over that last year and I remember feeling horrible for putting her through this. I remember that was the first time I had a feeling about someone else in a very long time. I remember sleeping for four or five more days straight and each night listening to Sharon pray and I knew that I had to find a place to put the pain and the memories that were haunting me.

I refused the antidepressants and I refused the counseling. I asked for a physical therapist and I ate all the food I could get my hands on. I transferred to a rehab center where I worked myself into the ground all day so I would sleep all night and the dreams faded. I worked with the trainer who strengthened my weakened muscles and showed me that I hadn't lost my ability to dance. He didn't have a clue how to dance, but he learned, quickly, as he saw how important it was for my recovery. I remember the day we pulled back up to the lodge and I got out and I sucked in a breath of the sweet air that had been home for my whole life. I walked down to the dock and out onto it, my legs steady and my steps sure. I remember that life felt worth living again and I remember the look on Sharon's face when I was able to laugh at the dinner table again and shop the way a young girl should, without a care in the world. But mostly I remember the look on her face when Jesse pulled me out onto the floor at a friend's wedding and tentatively took me through the first few steps of the waltz and I was able to do the steps that no one thought I ever would again. I remember that the doors went into the storage unit and I didn't look at them again for three more years until one day the image of them returned to my mind and I went out to the old dusty shed and pulled them out of the corner. I remember showing them to the carpenter and I remember the look on his face when he saw them. I remember how he ran his hands over them like I was doing now and saying it would be a shame not to use them and to leave it to him. I remember walking into the cottage with my eyes closed as he led me by my hand and him telling me to open and I remember that little piece of my heart falling into place when I saw them. I jumped as I felt a hand on my cheek and I realized it was Van.

"Tula. Are you okay?" His voice was deep.

I nodded and my voice came out sounding distant, "Yeah, I'm okay. There are so many memories in these doors that sometimes it catches me by surprise."

It was then that I realized that he was wiping away the tears that were falling down my face and I brushed my face against my shoulder wiping them away. And he was silent and I was grateful. I still had my eyes closed and I still had my hands on the doors running them up and down the wood one section at a time when I felt it. At the bottom of the door where the waves lapped up against the hull of the ship there was a new wave, a wave that I never carved.

I popped my eyes open and got down on my knees running my hand over and over the area. The new wood had been carved to match the other waves and then glued on. I looked back at Van.

"Do you have a knife?"

He handed me his Leatherman and stepped back giving me space. I carefully shimmied the blade under the wave prying it back being careful not to mark up the wood. The glue gave and the small piece of wood dropped to the carpet. We both stared at it. Van reached down and picked it up. He flipped it over and inside was a small bronze key. It was big enough to fit a small padlock or lock box. Van pulled me to my feet and took his Leatherman.

His voice was soft, but jubilant, "I don't know how you picked that out, but you were bang on."

He tossed the key up and caught it pocketing it in one smooth motion. Then he pulled me into a hug and whispered in my ear. "I think you just saved two peoples' lives."

THIRTEEN

I couldn't sleep, well I could sleep, but I couldn't take the dreams anymore. Last night after we found the key I had gone down to the ballroom and worked on the routine for Becca and Aaron while Van did some preliminary groundwork on where the papers might be stashed. I had stayed in the ballroom for hours partially to avoid him and partially to get so tired that I could fall asleep and not dream, but neither worked. I was in the ballroom and Rascal Flatts came on with "I'm Movin' On" and my feet began to waltz, right there with no one else. It was me and the music.

Each step was measured, each step was soft and each step was putting me in a world where there was no pain. It put me back in that little top floor dance studio in Duluth where I danced my first waltz with my best friend. It put me back in that ballroom in St. Paul where Brent and I had taken home the waltzing trophy. It put me back in the place that made me happy. Each step reminded me that there was always a place to escape when I couldn't take anymore of the world around me. There was always that place that I could go to where my heart didn't ache and I didn't have to struggle to keep the tears at bay. I danced with a smile on my face because I saw the brown eyes of my best friend with each turn and I heard him laugh as he led me through turn after turn until I was so dizzy that I could barely stand. And then I heard, "I've lived in this place and I know all the faces, each one is different, but they are always the same." And his hand was in mine and he was turning me as he sang, "They mean me no harm, but it's time that I face it, they will never allow me to change. But I never dreamed home would end up where I don't belong. I'm moving on."

I kept my eyes closed because I could feel the tears on my face and I couldn't stand to see the look of pity in someone else's eyes. I finished the dance and when the music died he pulled me to him whispering. "I've never seen anything more beautiful than you waltzing like that and I've never seen anything as heartbreaking as the sad smile on your face." And that was all he said before wiping away the tears and leading me out of the ballroom.

He had his arm tucked around me and his hand resting on my hip and my head on his shoulder as he led me to my room. He told me to get some sleep because tomorrow was going to be a busy day. He had also said that I should call him if I needed anything, almost like he knew I was going to. I heard him go back down to the ballroom and lock everything up and then I heard him for a very long time in his room tossing and turning and I wanted to call him, but I knew I couldn't. So I laid there until I couldn't lay there any longer and then I got up slipping on my clothes.

I needed to be alone, but not in this room and not in this house. I grabbed my Glock and snuck past his door, praying he wouldn't wake up. I stuffed my arms into my parka and grabbed my hat and gloves and cracked open the garage door stepping out and quietly clicking it closed behind me. I walked down the ramp and opened the side door a crack doing the James Bond routine looking right and left before stepping out. I didn't need a flashlight. The moon shone bright casting pale light along the trail that I had walked so many times my feet knew every rock, every root and every indention in the path. I made my way to the old shed next to the fire pit where I kept wood and kindling. The area was a hot spot of activity in the summer where the coals from the night before rarely were cold before another fire was started. My family and friends gathered here like moths to a flame and we sat on the old stumps around the fire roasting marshmallows and singing campfire songs. This morning it was barren, no flicker of the campfire, no laughing and no singing. The stumps sat around the ring like sentries watching over their master. The tops of the stumps had been rubbed smooth from years of jeans pockets rubbing them soft. I opened the door of the shed and tossed a couple of logs in the fire pit and got some kindling to start a small fire. In no time it was going strong and I felt like I had succeeded in keeping whatever was lurking in the dark at bay.

It was likely I was going to catch hell for being out here without reporting it to the proper authorities, but I really didn't care. Let Jesse sweat it out in some cubbyhole or get a call waking him up. I didn't care how hard he had to scramble to cover my back. He dumped all this in my lap and I didn't feel the least bit guilty about coming out here and living my life. I found that I still had to concede I was a little bit scared.

I grabbed my carving tools from the shed and rolled them out in front of the stump I was sitting on. I laid my Glock next to the tools and picked up my palm spoon. I began to slowly spoon out the beginning of a design on the stump I was sitting on. It didn't take but a few more minutes and I felt him advancing on me like a wolf stalking his prey. He was quiet and I felt him more than I heard him. I didn't turn keeping the rhythm of my carving and trying to ignore the intrusion. I glanced down at my legs relieved that I had put on my flannel lined jeans and mukluks before coming out.

He sat a few stumps down and stuck his hands in his pockets. The stump he chose was Jesse's. Jesse always sat there because he said he could see every angle of the property from it. He said it was the cop in him that made him prefer that spot. I guess I believed him now. The cop sitting across from me didn't look very happy. His hair was mussed from sleep and he wore a pair of Joe Boxer sleep pants and his new parka pulled up around him like it was a negative twenty eight instead of a positive twenty eight. With the fire going the area was toasty and I had long since ditched my hat and gloves. I watched him reach into his pocket and pull out his skull cap tugging it down over his ears.

"How's she cutting?" His heavy brogue still full from sleep.

I looked up, "Not bad, probably could stand a sharpening though."

He laughed softly then, "No I mean hi."

Oh right, that Irish thing.

"Hi."

"How are you?"

"Tired."

"Yeah, me too." He said wistfully, "Why aren't you in bed if you're tired?"

"Can't sleep." And I left it at that.

He was silent staring into the fire.

I stopped carving for a second and looked up. "You can go back to bed I'll be fine out here."

He stuck his hands out towards the fire and rubbed them together, "No, one phone call with someone yelling in my ear that I'm incapable, inept and incompetent as a bodyguard is enough for me."

"Sorry." I wasn't, but it seemed like the right thing to say. "I needed some time to think."

"Can't do that inside?"

"Nope." And there was silence again.

There was the crackle of the fire and the howl of a wolf or the hoot of an owl high above in the trees, but no words. I had to bite my lip to keep from filling it. He had a way of making me want to tell him everything in case he could make the pain go away. Don't ask me why.

"Come here often?" he asked stuffing his hands back in his pockets and stomping his feet on the ground.

"Yeah."

Spring, summer, fall and winter. It didn't matter to me. This was my place. I went back to my carving, but with him staring at me it was getting harder to concentrate. He looked down at his own stump then and ran his fingers along the carvings. He got up and did a three sixty around the fire pit stopping by each stump and sitting bending over and looking at the carvings. The carvings began at the seat and worked their way down the stump to the ground. I carved them while sitting on the stump so that when you looked down the designs were right side up.

"I've never seen anything like this before."

I shrugged my shoulder, "It's just some doodling."

He rolled his eyes at me and went to sit back down on Jesse's stump.

"Mind if we play Guess that Crann?"

89

Whatever he said sounded like "crohn" and I didn't have a clue what it was.

"Excuse me?" I asked tiredly.

"That's the Gaelic word for tree, a crann. So mind if I play?"

I shrugged my shoulder again.

"This one is Jesse's." He said quite confidently.

I nodded. There were so many things carved into Jesse's crann. There were police cars, American flags, fish, a bottle of Leinies and a Harley Davidson motorcycle to represent some of his favorite things. There was plenty of space left on his to add everything he had yet to experience.

Van pointed at the one I was on, "I'm assuming that one is yours."

"Yeah."

"Not much on that one." He said flippantly.

"Nope."

My crann was pretty paltry compared to the others that sat around the rest of the ring. I never seemed to want to work on mine preferring to work on the ones I loved and leaving mine at a standstill much like my life. There were three eagles and a lone dancer. That was all. I was adding the Mustang today the memories fresh in my mind from yesterday.

He pointed at the one next to me. "Your Dad's?" He raised a brow when he said it and he pointed to the one on the other side of me, "Your Mom's." Not a question this time. I nodded again.

The two cranns that sat on each side of me were finished. There was only one other one that was finished. The rest had a row or two carved to start with and then I left room on each crann to add new events that transpired in the lives of those who sat on them. My dad's was covered top to bottom with all the things I could remember about him. Coffee cups on cabinets, a little girl holding her father's hand and all the things that you remember about a father who was gone before he had a chance to see you graduate or walk you down the aisle.

My mother's was filled with birds, which was her other passion besides baking and her family. There wasn't a day that she didn't go bird watching that I could remember. I had carved an image of her standing in the woods with binoculars tight to her face and her head heavenward in search of the next bird in her book. It was how I pictured her now, in the woods watching over all of us.

He put his hand on the crann to his left, "Sharon's?"

I nodded. Hers had rows of carvings starting with her swimming in an olympic pool like she used to do when she was on the swim team, her nursing career, holding her boy's hands and eight butterflies, one big one and seven smaller. The next row I had finished carving this summer, it was her wedding picture, all of us around her and Lenny.

He put his hand on the crann to the right, "Brent's."

I nodded. Brent's was filled with dancers and musical notes. There were cheeseburgers and pizzas and a can of Pepsi. There was a picture of him and Jesse from behind as they walked through the trees together and at the very top, well or bottom depending on how you looked at it, were the names of the people who received his organs that went around in a never ending circle with his.

He pointed to the one to the left of Sharon and raised a brow in question.

"Lenny's, he was an Olympic skier so I did a skiing theme and carved in his medals from each Olympic and the years. He's a great guy. He fills the hole that my dad left when he died and I'm okay with that. He loves us and would do anything for us and he loves Sharon to death. She married Paul very young because she got pregnant with Jesse and that was what you did back then, but she never loved him and he never loved her. She has lost so much in her life. She met Lenny at a nursing convention she was attending for MAMBOS. He was a nurse coordinator in the hospital and they hit it off immediately. She told me that he asked her out for a drink after her speech so he could learn more about MAMBOS and how the hospital could get involved, but really he wanted to have a drink with her and get to know her better. They talked all night about every part of their lives. She talked about Paul leaving her, raising the boys on her own and then losing Brent. She told him about Jesse and me and everything that she did with MAMBOS. He told her about how he was an Olympic skier until a knee injury ended his career and then he joined the real world, went to college and got his nursing degree. He loved being a nurse coordinator and was working with the transplant department at the hospital in St. Paul. By the end of the evening, or early the next day if you believe them, he took her back to her room and told her that Paul was a fool. Then he kissed her and handed her his number and told her that if she ever wanted to jump back in the pool he would be there to catch her." I chuckled a little, "Whenever he tells that story he blushes because he thinks it was so cheesy, but I think it was sweet. Sharon came home and told me about him and I could tell that she really wanted to call him, but you know she'd been out of the dating game for a long time. Well I decided that if she wasn't going to call him I was, so I called the hospital where he worked over in St. Paul and asked to speak to him. I told him that I was the Marketing Director of MAMBOS and I was hoping that he could come over to Duluth and help me with some coordinating efforts we had underway in the Twin Cities. I introduced myself as Tula and of course he had no idea who I was because Sharon always calls me Sugar."

He was smiling.

"What?" I asked as the smile took over his face.

"Nothing, I'm picturing you playing matchmaker. Go on."

"So long story short I got him to come over and set up a sunset dinner cruise on the Vista Fleet. I called him shortly before at his hotel and told him that I was sending over my second in command because I had fallen ill. Well needless to say it worked because a little over a year later they were married here at the lodge on a beautiful fall day."

I fell quiet then and went back to carving. There were several more cranns sitting around the fire, one that was carved with the MAMBOS insignia and one with dancers in different positions so that as you went around the crann it looked like they were dancing. Of course it helped if the light from the campfire played just right on them and if you had a Leinies or two in you.

The MAMBOS crann was always the one that Julie sat on. The more she came to the campfires the more personal little touches I would add like her favorite saying which was "never forget that someone somewhere will listen", a police badge and a kitten. The kitten, Moe, was her first arrest of her career. He was robbing the garbage can of one cranky old man so Julie scooped him up, put him in her squad and he never left. He is over eight years old now, but he's about the same size. I've never seen anything like it really. He's the tiniest little thing ever, but he rules the roost. She never talks about her family so I can only add things that we experienced together.

I guess I was going to have to move hers next to Jesse's now. I always knew the day would come that Brent wasn't next to Jess, but I never dreamed that position would be taken by Julie. It still threw me for a loop when I thought about it. It wasn't that it was a bad thing. I was glad that Jesse and Julie were together, but I wondered how the family dynamics would change. She always liked coming to the lodge because she said it was the closest thing she has ever had to a family and I was always happy that she enjoyed it here. Maybe she would be official family some day, but I was afraid that if things didn't work out that we would lose her for good. That was scary because she was my best friend and she belonged here.

Maybe I was finally seeing with my eyes what my heart had been telling me for a long time. Seemed like time and life were moving on more and more and I either needed to figure out a way to catch up or I was going to be left in the dust of the past ten years. Van sat absorbed watching me carve out the hood and the grille of the Mustang. I changed tools frequently and soon it began to take shape as I started on the wheels.

"I'm missing something here, aren't I?" He asked it as he looked around him, up through the bare trees and then down the paths that lead to the lake and the cottage and back towards the house.

Is it a cop thing? Do they all have this intuition that tells them that things aren't always what they appear to be on the surface? Jesse and Julie were that way too. It was like they never let their brains rest. I didn't answer him as I finished the last hubcap completing the carving. I laid my tools down brushing off the shavings and blowing out the chips of wood from the smaller spaces. It was good. It matched the car on my dad's crann. I laid my tools down on the ground and stared into the fire not wanting to look at him. He was being a good egg sitting out here in the cold even though I knew he would rather be tucked up in a warm bed slumbering. The sky was starting to lighten as the hour moved closer to seven and once the daylight broke then I had to leave here and go back to the reality of what my life was right now.

"I'm going to go out on a limb here," he said, "and guessing that this space holds some special significance in relation to your parents?"

I kept staring at the fire and hoped that I could explain to him what this place was. Jesse, Sharon and Julie come out here all the time too, sometimes together, sometimes alone and it has become our place to be in that space where everything is safe and you can say anything you want and only the trees and God are here to listen.

I finally looked up at him, "My grandpa always told me that you don't have to go to church to talk to God. You can sit in the woods on an old tree stump and do the same thing you can do in a pew. He told me it isn't about the physical place, it's about the relationship you have with Him."

"Sounds like your grandpa was a wise man." He kicked at a pebble lying at his feet and then straightened his legs out crossing his ankles.

"I didn't know him well, but the memory of his words stayed with me. He always had this kind of strong quiet faith and one day I asked him how come he talked about God so much when he didn't even go to church. He sat me on his lap and he said, *"But the hour is coming, and now is, when the true worshipers will worship the Father in spirit and truth; for the Father is seeking such to worship Him."* I later found out that was from *John 4*. He told me that true worship is how you live your life and how you spread the word of the Lord and how you do His work, not that you sit in a pew every Sunday."

"So you don't go to church?" he asked.

I raised my palms and motioned around, "This is my church. This is where I feel close to God. This is where I can come and be with the people that I love and ask Him to forgive me for not being the kind of person that He wants me to be. I can't be that right now, but I keep coming out here anyway hoping someday that will change."

"I think that about anyone who knows you might disagree with that."

I shook my head, "I'm still mad at Him and He knows that. I can agree to be friends with Him, but I haven't figured out how to love Him again." And that was like asking for a lightening bolt to drop out the sky and strike me dead. Thankfully it didn't happen. Van let out a breath and I wondered what he was thinking and then I wondered why I cared.

"That is one of the most frank admittances of imperfection I have ever heard. You are a surprise around every corner, Tula. The fact that you still come out here and you still talk to Him and you still believe in that higher power is admirable considering what you have been through. I'm inclined to believe that He loves you for your honesty because I don't believe He gets that from a lot of his worshippers." And he was probably right.

"Do you go to your parent's grave and talk to them? I would go and talk to my grandma before I moved here and I always found it comforting. I always felt like she was helping me see the answers. Maybe that would help." I didn't say anything and he looked around then searching for something he thought he would find then turned back to me. "We are at their grave, aren't we?"

I shook my head, "Yeah."

"I don't see any markers."

"There are none. They are in the wind Van. When the accident happened I was obviously not up to funerals and wouldn't be for many weeks. My parent's were cremated and Sharon also had Brent cremated. The funeral home was able to do the wakes later when I could attend and then they gave us the urns with the ashes."

He nodded.

"Well winter turned to spring and the urns sat, two in my house and one at Sharon's and it didn't feel right. It didn't feel right that they were separated in death when they were together so much in life. So one day she and Jesse came over and asked me what I thought about letting them be back together in a place where they were the happiest and I was relieved. So the next windy day we came out here and had a private ceremony and let them be in the wind together again." He didn't say anything as he sat staring into the fire.

"I'm sorry if that was too much information."

He cracked a smile, "No, not at all, I understand more and more why you love this property so much. They really are here in spirit for you."

I nodded, "They really are and some days the only place I can come is here because it's the only place where my heart will stop hurting for them. It's the only place that, I don't know…" He was waiting for me to finish but I couldn't. I had no words to explain how it made me feel.

He stood up and walked over to me sitting down on my dad's crann taking my cold hand in his, "I got lost in this whole world and forgot who I am. I thought if I could touch this place or feel it, this brokenness inside me might start healing. Out here it's like I'm someone else. I thought that maybe I could find myself." He sang the words softly and I leaned my head on his shoulder.

"'The House That Built Me', Miranda Lambert. Two step." I whispered.

He put his arm around my shoulder, "The words to that song came to mind when I saw you sitting here as I walked up. Does it sum up the "I don't know" part of how you are feeling?"

"Yeah, yeah it does." And I knew I needed to get up because falling asleep on his shoulder again would cause me nothing but pain later on.

I stood up and rolled my carving tools up tucking them back into the shed. I grabbed the bucket of water that I always kept next to the pit for putting down the fire. I went to throw it on the fire and nothing came out. I looked down and laughed at my stupidity. It was frozen. The nights were getting cold enough now that any unmoving water was going to freeze over long before morning.

Van moved next to me and peered in the bucket, "Guess you are gonna have to get outta that garden." I looked at him expectantly.

"It means give it up." He laughed. I laughed too admitting that he was probably right. I grabbed some sand out of the shed and tossed it over the fire.

He slipped his arm around me, "There are enough guys watching this place that any potential fire is going to be put out quickly."

Oh yeah, I forgot. We walked along the path towards the house and I stopped, changing directions and pulling him down through some trees to the edge of the woods. In front of us the sun was rising over the lake and the colors were in layers, orange, yellow, pink, blue, white, purple and black. The sun was a giant ball of color reflecting off the blue of the water and the green of the coniferous trees. Every time I saw the sunrise over the lake I saw something I hadn't seen before. Like an eagle flying outlined by the sky or a cloud shaped in some unusual way. Today it was a group of Canadian geese flying past us honking their goodbyes as they headed to warmer waters. I loved the sunrise and tried to come out and watch it as much as I could. It reminded that I was alive for another day.

I felt Van take my hand, "I think this is pretty close to heaven."

"About as close as you can get and still be alive if you ask me." I whispered.

"In Ireland we call this éirí gréine, the sunrise."

We stood there like that for a very long time until the sun had said its official good morning and then Van turned me back to him.

"Let's go inside. It's getting early and I have a feeling you could use some coffee."

I smiled, it's getting early, that was the way I felt too and I could definitely use some coffee.

FOURTEEN

Van pulled me into the garage and pulled his boots off waiting for me to do the same. I wasn't taking my boots off in front of him so I made up an excuse that I was going to get something out of the Sorento. He took the remote out of his pocket and busied himself with looking for security breaches as I stepped to the back of the SUV and opened the hatch. I grabbed my emergency shoes out of the back and quickly changed out of my boots. I grabbed some paperwork out of the back before slamming the hatch and joining him back on the ramp where he had the door open and waiting. He looked at me a question in his eye, but didn't say anything motioning me in the door and closing it behind him.

"I'm going to go take a shower. You want to start the coffee?" He asked me.

I told him I would get it started and it would be ready when he was done. After he left I puttered around the kitchen making the coffee and putting together in my mind dinner for tonight. It wasn't going well and I was thinking maybe a burger at Fitger's Brewhouse would fit in perfectly and with it being a college crowd on a Thursday night I might not know anyone there. That was a comforting thought. Going somewhere where no one knew me and where I wouldn't have to explain Van. Just a girl out for a burger with a guy. Simple. Even though I knew it was far from simple and every minute I spent with him only re-enforced that feeling. I slid the twist bread into the oven to bake and inhaled the scent of the rich french roast that filled the kitchen telling me it was done. I filled my cup and took a long swig as the steam warmed my nose and the hot liquid burned my tongue.

I carried it to my room wrapping both hands around the mug to warm them. A shower sounded like a great idea plus it would put a little distance between the two of us. I could hear the water running in his bathroom as I strode past. The steamy air that was coming out from under the door smelled like his Irish Spring and my mind began to conjure up the image of him in the shower. When my minds eye hit his backside my cell phone rang making me jump and spill hot coffee on my hand. Damn it! What was wrong with me -- it was like I was fifteen again! I didn't need to look at the caller ID to see who it was and I wasn't sure I wanted to talk to him, but I also knew that if I didn't answer he would keep calling until I did. I stomped my foot and answered the phone with my teeth clenched.

"Good morning Jess."

"Good morning? Is it? It's been a really long morning already Sugar." His voice held that contained anger that he saves for the truly daft.

"No Jess it's been a really long night." And that was the truth. There seemed to be very little differentiation for me now. There was silence on the line.

"I really wish you could stay in the house Sugar. Any place outside is going to be hard to keep you safe and it doesn't help when you light a fire to guide the bad guys in."

I started to giggle the image of someone striking a match and holding it up as the flame catches while a group of burglars come to life and follow the flame. It was official I needed more sleep.

"It's not like I haven't seen you out there with your head in your hands several times over the last few weeks." And he was silent and I felt bad for saying it in a nasty tone. This all sucked and I hated that we couldn't use each other for support right now. Right now it seemed like we were all fighting with our own demons and were too tired to fight off anyone else's.

"I'm sorry it won't happen again." He said it quietly, but I knew he was hurt and it was my fault.

"Jess, no, listen. I didn't mean it like that. You know you are welcome out there anytime. I'm frustrated and I'm tired and I'm sitting on the edge of a very bad fall."

"I know Sugar. I guess you probably understand why my head was in my hands." And it felt like he was blaming me even though I knew he wasn't.

"I promise not to go back out there, but don't accuse Van of not doing his job again. I left without telling him. You need to put that blame on me, not him."

He sighed an exasperated I can't believe I have to deal with someone like you sigh, "I owe him an apology. I need to remember that you can't predict the unpredictable."

He repeated his usual saying about me as a mantra. He would always tell people "Well you can't predict the unpredictable what did you expect?" It was always a funny loving thing, but today it felt more pointed. I told him good bye and turned my phone off. I didn't want to be reachable today. I stripped off my smoky clothes and stood under the shower letting the steam build up in the bathroom so that when I got out the mirror was fogged over and I couldn't see my reflection. I dried off and put on a clean pair of jeans and an old UMD Bulldogs sweatshirt before stuffing my feet in a pair of old Reebok sneakers that had seen better days. Wiping the steam off the mirror with a towel I grabbed a brush and pulled my hair up into a ponytail leaving it to dry on its own. There wasn't much left to do and it was only seven thirty. I put on my poker face and headed back out to the kitchen for another cup of leaded plasma.

I strolled into the kitchen feeling a little bit more relaxed. The bean juice was flowing through my veins and I half believed I could take on the world. I could smell the apple strudel twist bread in the oven and saw Van sitting at the table taking apart my Tribune in short order.

"Hey." I said and he looked up from the paper and let his eyes meander first down and then back up my being like he was memorizing every shape. I snatched the hot pad out of the drawer and pulled the twist bread out of the oven plunking it on the top of the range and leaving the oven door cracked to let the heat escape into the room, not that it wasn't warm enough in here already with him ogling me like he was.

"So what's the look you are going for today?" He asked a hint of laughter in his voice.

I did a spin ending with my backside to him. "The college kid look. Is it working?"

He shifted uncomfortably in his seat, "Uh yeah, it's working."

Good. There was a little bit of satisfaction in the idea that I was making him uncomfortable. I don't know why, but there was. Maybe I'm not as impervious to the male persuasion as I would like to think. Even though his comment made my heart speed up to double time and my palms sweaty it also made me a little bouncy inside to feel that again. I knew I would never let it go anywhere, but for the first time in a very long time it didn't petrify me. I cut up the bread and grabbed the butter out of the fridge shutting the door with my foot and carrying it all to the table.

"So what's on the agenda for today?"

Van folded up the paper and set it next to his plate. "We are going to take the key and start looking for places that she might have stashed the papers. I'm counting on you to help me with that." He grabbed a piece of bread and buttered it before taking a bite.

"Your cooking is going to make me fat." He said.

"No, your eating is going to make you fat!" And he laughed then because I was right and he didn't care.

I grabbed a piece of my own, "I've been thinking about it, but I didn't get a good look at the key are there any markings on it?"

He shook his head, "No, it's just a plain brass key, the size that would fit about any box or padlock ever made." And that was so encouraging.

"I was hoping it would say Master on it or something that would give us a starting point. This is not going to be easy it could be anywhere." I went over downtown Duluth in my mind. "Okay, I think that we can assume that it has to be either in Superior or in the vicinity of downtown Duluth."

"Why?" He asked.

"Because Nathan was afraid of the hills and I don't mean that he didn't like them, I mean he was deathly afraid of them. They never went to Duluth alone, ever, but they went to Superior a lot."

"Alone?"

"Yeah they would take my Sorento and go drive around and check out the lake, but they never crossed the bridge alone."

The Sorento! I threw my finger up and ran to the mudroom grabbing the keys to the Sorento and throwing open the garage door.

"Tula?" He asked standing in the doorway.

I beeped open the car and opened the hatch pulling up the seats that I kept down and opening all the little hatches and spots where things could be stashed. He was behind me then as I searched under the front seats.

"What are you looking for?" He finally asked.

"The papers! They drove my car all the time, I thought maybe they stashed it in the car somewhere and I didn't know it." But they hadn't.

"Good thought, but I take it by the look on your face that didn't work out in our favor."

I shook my head and he helped me close the car back up and slung his arm around my shoulder, "Good try though, way to think it through."

He kissed my temple and it seemed too friendly for bodyguard to guarded. We went back into the kitchen and resumed our seats at the table.

I drummed my fingers on the table, "The airport? Could they have stashed the stuff at the airport when they flew in?" I grabbed my phone, "Hang on let me ask Jess how they got here. I'm pretty sure the story they told me wasn't quite accurate."

He tried to hide the smile, but I saw it anyway. I regrettably turned my phone back on and hit autodial for Jesse.

He picked up on the second ring, "Lo"

"Hey Jess did I wake you?" And I was secretly smiling inside at the thought.

"Yeah, what do you want?"

"Is that anyway to talk to your sister?" And I was egging him on because it felt like he deserved it.

"It is when it's eight in the morning and I've been up all night. What do you want?" Touchy, jeez.

"How did Margie and Nathan get to Duluth?"

The line was silent for a minute and I could almost see him shaking his head trying to wake up enough to have this conversation.

"They flew to a private airport in the Cities and then took a private plane to Sky Harbor. We tried to keep them out of the main terminals so that they couldn't be tracked as easily. Isn't Van there?"

"Yeah, why?"

"Because he knows all this information. Good bye."

The line went dead in my ear and I carefully set the phone down on the table to avoid smashing it like I wanted to.

"So you think you could have told me you knew?" I asked him between clenched teeth.

"You didn't ask." He said.

"For Pete's sake! You are all driving me to distraction!" I got up to keep from choking him. I was agitated and frustrated and probably had too much caffeine flowing through my veins. I paced the floor in the kitchen with half a mind to say to hell with all of you and take a plane to somewhere warm and sunny.

"Were they picked up from the Sky Harbor immediately?" I asked.

He shook his head, "No, they were never alone. They flew here with an agent and went from the plane directly to the waiting car to here. They weren't alone until they were dropped off here."

"Great. This whole thing sucks."

"Look at it as a means to an end. A puzzle that once we find the last two or three pieces we can finish putting it together and then – voila-- you get to see the whole picture."

I paced around the floor some more trying to run the summer through my mind starting with the beginning. "The only time they went to Duluth was if they were with me. They didn't know where they were going so I would let them ride along if I was going into town and they would go off on their own while I did my shopping or whatever."

"So that narrows it down to all of Duluth and all of Superior." He said this while trying not to laugh.

"No, not all of Duluth. Like I said, Nathan was scared of the hills, so we pretty much stayed around Superior Street. He never even wanted to go to the mall. Margie and I went to the mall, but she was never alone long enough to stash something without me knowing. The mall doesn't have public lockers anyway. I think we can safely assume it is in downtown Duluth or Superior."

"Okay, that narrows it some. Tell me where you think they might have put it." He had his pad out and was making columns.

"Well I was thinking a gym, you know, you could go in and put something in a locker and no one is the wiser, but the problem is that the gyms around here are the twenty-four hour ones like Snap and Anytime. So if you want to get in you need a membership card. It's staffed, but only a few hours a week, so it would be risky to put it there and then have your trial membership run out and not be able to get back in. The only place I think we should check is the DECC. It's a long shot, but they have a huge locker room. I don't know if the public has access, but for the sake of thoroughness we should probably check. They would have avoided the university because they didn't have ID and that would have gotten too complicated."

"Okay. So that takes care of gyms. Any other ideas?" He asked as he was writing down DECC in the go to column.

"Post offices maybe. I'm thinking that they could have rented a p.o. box and then stuck the papers in there. The keys usually say U.S.P.S. on them somewhere though. You sure there is nothing on it?"

I looked over at him and he took it out of his pocket and handed it over. Yup, nothing on it. "Okay, so it's a pretty safe bet it isn't from the post office, but there is a place in Superior called Goin' Postal and they have private mailboxes so that's a possibility. The only thing is they are closed on Sunday."

"Do you know where it is?"

"Yeah and it's easy to get to, and since it's in Superior they could have gone there alone."

"Okay. Any other ideas?" He asked tapping his pencil on the pad.

"Bank boxes are the only other thing I can think of. It could be a key to a bank box somewhere."

"Why do you think that?" He asked his head cocked.

"I mean think about it, you have something you really need to protect so where do you go? A bank, and it wouldn't look funny if she went in with a bunch of paperwork and stuff because that's commonplace. Granted banks are closed on the weekends, but I'm still leaning towards it because you are going to have to really work to find it. Does that make sense?"

He was smiling, "It makes sense alright. It usually takes me weeks to teach a guy what you just did in three minutes. You have a mind for this kind of stuff."

I shrugged, "I read a lot." Because I had nothing else to do with my nights. And where did that come from. Sometimes stream of consciousness isn't what it's cracked up to be.

"Here's the kicker. There are only about forty banks around here." I plunked back down in the chair.

"Well let's think it out. Did you ever take her to a bank? Did she ever do any banking here? She had to have an account if she was paying living expenses."

I snapped my fingers, "Yes! She had an account at Wells Fargo." I was getting excited because narrowing down the search would certainly help with the timeline.

"You have to have an account in order to have a safe deposit box right?" I asked him and he nodded.

"There is a Wells Fargo down on Superior Street. If I dropped them off I usually left them at Fitger's and they would walk the lake walk and shop and be tourists for a while. The Wells Fargo would only be a ten minute walk from Fitger's. I suppose they could have gone to the Miller Hill Wells Fargo in a cab, but that would have meant them going up the hills and Nathan wouldn't do that. He also wouldn't have let Margie go alone." A thought crossed my mind. "Did you guys have us under surveillance when we went out places?"

He shook his head, "No. We didn't have the manpower to follow you around nor did we feel the need. There was no direct police surveillance on the lodge until the last few weeks before the wedding. Up until that time we had it on good authority that her father believed her to be up here to get away. His comings and goings were being tracked and we were confident that he didn't suspect anything. That all changed when he boarded a plane for Duluth."

"Okay, well there goes that thought. Then my best guess is the Wells Fargo on Superior Street." I finally said.

"Think back and tell me if there was ever a time that you took her to Duluth that she had a bag with her or satchel. Something she could have had the stuff stashed in." He waited while I thought about it.

"She always carried this big purse and I always wondered why. I always teased her that you could fit a small child in it." And I guess now I knew why.

He nodded then, "So what I have here is Goin' Postal in Superior, Wells Fargo and the DECC. That's a good start, no sense chasing rainbows if we don't have to. We will start with what makes the most sense and then if we don't find anything we can branch out." He pulled me up out of my chair, "So, are you ready to go?" He asked.

"I have a lesson this morning. What time is it?" I looked over at the clock, it was almost nine. "I have a lesson from nine to ten and then we can leave after that. I'm sure you can find something to do for an hour right?"

He nodded, "Sure, I'll watch you."

FIFTEEN

Becca and Aaron were right on time for their lesson and I took them down to the ballroom hoping that Van wouldn't make good on his promise to watch. So far so good, he was in his room trying to get some information from his boss in Texas. Becca and Aaron were nervously chatting with me about school and the upcoming Thanksgiving break. Mostly they were waiting to find out what song and dance they would be doing in what would be their first competition. It was a low key competition in St. Paul, but it would get their feet wet and it would give them the chance to see if they were ready for the bigger stuff. I always choose the music and dance for each couple because often times the dances they think they are their best at aren't even their strongest. Becca and Aaron reminded me a lot of Brent and me when we were that age. They were both naturals in ballroom and had a love for it that you usually don't find in fifteen year old kids. They breathed dancing and they were fun to work with. Their parents are as devoted as ours were and since they had study hour from nine to ten their parents allowed them to come over for a lesson and then go back to school. Overall they were my favorite young couple to work with because they had the potential to become great dancers. Becca was perfectly suited for ballroom having the ability to take any dance and make it her own with her fluid movements and her obvious joy to be on the floor. Aaron was a gangly teen who was incredibly quick on his feet and had a sharp mind. He could watch me do a move once, know it and never forget it. Besides that he was beyond smitten with Becca and never minded spending a lot of time with her in his arms. The kids were lacing up their practice shoes and doing some stretch lunges on the floor.

"So you guys ready to find out what your dance is going to be?" To say that they were eager would be saying that Lake Superior is chilly.

"Aaron and I have a bet going Ms. Sugar," Becca said, "He's betting east coast swing and I'm betting heavily on the waltz, since you love that dance."

I smiled because she had me pegged, but they would both lose the bet. "Nope on both accounts, you will be doing the rumba." Their eyebrows went up and Aaron began to blush a little at the idea of a dance that was danced close to the belt with a lot of hip.

"Have you ever noticed that when you two start a rumba that everyone else fades off and gives you the floor?" I asked them.
They both shook their heads no.

"Well I've had a lot of experience with knowing what comes natural to a couple and knowing what is work. For you guys the rumba is natural, so you are going to go out there and have all the fun you can have in the length of a song and be confident that you are doing your best dance." They looked at each other and smiled a little, both getting used to the idea.

"Ready to know the song?" I asked.

They both nodded obviously a little wary of what I would pick. I hit play on the remote and joined them on the floor. The first bar of "Falling For You" by Colbie Caillat rang out across the ballroom and their faces broke into full on smiles and they gave each other a high five. I was laughing at them and I remembered why I enjoyed working with the young couples so much. They made me laugh and right now that was something more precious to me than I realized.

"I have a great routine planned for you guys, so let's get started." I walked them through the routine with the music off and then with the music on. It became obvious very quickly that they were going to have a hard time dancing to the song because the lyrics were making them think a little too much about each other and not enough on the dance itself. I knew that would happen and that was why I picked the song. You have to feel the music, you have to love the music and you have to be able to apply the music to how you are feeling in that moment. I was pretty certain watching them that I had nailed it. I let the smile that played at the edge of my lips take over my face and turned the music down.

"Guys, I'm going to do something I never do. Aaron, I feel like you have a dance in your mind that you want to let loose for this song, so let me see it. Instead of me telling you what to do I want you to show me what you are feeling. Remember the moves that you have to have in the routine and show me how you want to dance this. Aaron that means the responsibility for that is on your shoulders. Are you okay with that?" And I knew he would be. I could tell in the way he was moving to the music.

"Yes Ms. Sugar." He said his eyes locking with Becca's.
I started the music back at the beginning and walked the perimeter of the dance floor with a legal pad writing down the moves as he put them in so that they had a routine to practice when they got done dancing their hearts out. I watched them and it was hard to remember being that young with no greater care in the world than finishing one dance and moving on to another. Aaron used Cuban breaks at the end of the dance leading Becca into the shoulder to shoulder. The final time she came up to his left shoulder, he dipped her and planted a kiss on her lips as the final note died. There was clapping from the door and I joined Van in his applause as Aaron stood Becca back on her feet. The young dancers were both flushed

and blushing. Van came over and stood next to me on the edge of the dance floor.

"You've done amazing things with them, they're fantastic."

"That's natural talent my friend. I just get to enjoy it."

He rolled his eyes at me and said whatever like he didn't believe me. I introduced Van to the kids as my guest dance partner from Ireland and Aaron was quite excited to have a guy in the room. He began to ask him some questions about how a guy was really supposed to do some of the rumba moves and I could see the idea forming in Van's head before Aaron finished his sentence.

"Well from what I could see you had it down, but if you really want a second opinion I can show you." He said tongue in cheek.

Aaron told him he really wanted him to and he looked over at Becca who was also nodding. "Come on Ms. Sugar we never get to see you dance. You are always walking around telling everybody else what to do." Becca said pinning her eyes on me. Van's eyebrows went up and I knew I'd been had.

"Come on, Becca, now you're just playing me, I dance all the time."

"I know, but I mean we want to see you really dance. We want to see you dance with somebody as good as you are." And then I saw Van's brows go even higher.

I shook my head seeing that I wasn't going to win this war. "Okay, okay. We'll dance, but first we finish the routine so you guys can get practicing it over the next week." I busied myself putting the information into my computer and getting the kid's input on what worked and what they wanted to change. I sent it to the printer and went and grabbed it from my office. I stepped in the door and took a couple of calming breaths. Dancing the rumba to "Falling For You" was not going to help me get him off my mind. There were some dances that were too much of an invasion of personal space. And I wasn't sure I was ready for that. I was starting to feel like karma was getting me for thinking it was a good idea to make the kids feel the music. I knew I made the right choice though. The dance Aaron let come through was beautiful and was truly an excellent example of why they are so good at the rumba.

I strolled back to the ballroom taking my sweet time, gave them each a copy of the routine. I told them it was a good beginning but if they made any changes they needed to write the moves down in order on the sheet. I have to inform the judges of the number of bronze, silver and gold moves they would be doing in their routine. They assured me that they would. They had their street shoes on already and Van was on the floor in his stocking feet, again, lounging against the mirror waiting for me.

Becca nodded at the floor, "Your turn Ms. Sugar, show us what you are feeling when you dance to this song." And I groaned. I didn't need to hear her say that. Van came up behind me and pulled me onto the dance floor. Aaron hit play and the music started. Van pulled me into him and said, "Yeah, show me what you are feeling when you dance to this song, Tula."

"Well since there are two very impressionable young adults in the room that would probably not be a very good idea Mr. MacNamara or Walsh or Bond or whatever the heck I'm supposed to call you." I whispered, flirting the way he was.

Then he leaned in closer to my ear and said, "Call me Lucky and don't worry I know I'm not as good as you are, but I'm going to pretend for this one." He looked at me with eyes the color of emeralds and began to move me through some beginner moves before moving into some progressive walks and then pulling me back into Cuban breaks every so often. I was watching the kids holding hands not looking at each other as their eyes focused on the dance floor.

Van was thoroughly enjoying making me flustered in front of them and began to join in on the lyrics, "As I'm standing here and you hold my hand. Pull me towards you and we start to dance. All around us I see nobody. Here in silence it's just you and me. I'm trying not to tell you, but I want to. I'm scared of what you'll say." At that moment he threw in a few moves that were not on the rumba syllabus and probably were not exactly PG 13 either. The last chorus of the song was spent with him doing Cuban breaks, or rocking back and forth on each foot to the beat of the music while plastered up against your partner.

"Do you know anything other than Cuban breaks?" I asked looking at him under my lashes.

"Yeah, but I like this move. It keeps you close to me." He responded.

Way too close. He must have decided he liked Aaron's version of the dance because he sent me into some shoulder to shoulders, dipping and kissing me as the last note of the song rang out. Only this was no teenage kiss, this was a take your breath away kiss. The song finished and I may have lingered longer than I planned in his arms as Becca and Aaron hooted and whistled. He stood me back up on my feet and I hurriedly shut down the music before anyone got any ideas of more dancing. My heart was racing and it wasn't because I had been dancing.

I heard Van ask Aaron if that had helped and Aaron blushed profusely, "Yes, sir, Mr. MacNamara. That was very helpful."

I stifled a laugh with my hand because I was pretty sure that Aaron had gotten a lesson that he never expected when he got out of bed this morning.

SIXTEEN

It was my turn to drive. I had the Sorento fired up and the heat going waiting for Van to finish his phone call with his boss. I had my iPod plugged in and was jamming to Lady Gaga. I had my sunglasses over my eyes and my fingers drumming on the wheel as I cooled my heels. It was ten thirty and I really wanted to get this over with and get home. I honked the horn and he held up a finger and I rolled my eyes. They talk about women and the phone. The music switched to "Need You Now" by Lady Antebellum and the rumba in the ballroom came back to me. I eyed the man standing on the ramp leading to my door and smiled unwillingly. The man had hips that were made to rumba and god knows what else. It was the god knows what else that I was trying really hard not to think about. He was walking towards me now tucking his phone in the case and pulling the door open. He slid into the seat and took a look around him.

A slow smile developed on his face, "I officially see why you drive this. It's pretty much your dream come true. How many speakers in this thing?"

I punched the built in garage door opener and the door rolled up. "Ten, Infinity surround sound." I hit the door closed and pulled up and out of the drive as the next song led us into Black Eyed Peas and "Hey Mama". Not exactly the best song for conversation I realized pretty quickly, but it was a rocking samba and I danced in my seat as I drove. There was something about the song that made me dance no matter where I was.

He dropped his glasses down his nose, "This is the stuff I wouldn't let Lillie listen to when she was a kid." He was smirking.

I shook it a little harder. "Loosen up Daddy, you know there are only so many songs that you can do a kicking samba to and this is one of them."

"I'm thinking "Hey Soul Sister"." He said.

"Excellent choice, but it's still not as good. Ignore the lyrics and feel the beat." I reached over to adjust the bass and his shoulder started to go to the beat of the music. I notched one corner of my mouth up. Nothing like getting an Irishman to samba. Whenever I taught the samba I usually had to turn the lights low or no one wanted to dance. It was one of those dances that required very little inhibition. I was on my way to Goin' Postal, but first I was getting a coffee. I wasn't doing this without coffee. I swung through McDonald's and picked up a caramel mocha looking at Van for interest. He waved his hand at me so I grabbed mine and swung onto Tower Avenue that led me straight to the postal station. I pulled into a parking spot on the street and shut down the SUV jumping out of the car. He was next to me before I had the door closed and I wondered again how he moved so quickly.

He put his arm around me and whispered in my ear, "Got the key?" I nodded. "I'm going to distract the guy at the counter with questions about international shipping while you see if it will work in any of the boxes. He kissed my temple then and pulled the door open for me. I was praying that he was going for the young couple in love look, but I couldn't be sure. He sauntered over to the counter and struck up a conversation about shipping to Ireland. I glanced over at the counter. With the size of the computer screen blocking out the boxes I didn't think distraction was going to be necessary, but I'd let him play cop anyway. I stepped over to the boxes pulling the key out and trying to insert it in a couple keyholes. The key was way too small. It was tiny compared to the size of these boxes that looked like they needed something the size of a house key to open them. I pocketed the key and went over to Van sticking my hand in the back pocket of his jeans making him jump before he recovered.

The fact I knew no one in the place gave me the courage to flirt a little with him, "Hey baby, did you get the info you needed?" I asked him, my lashes fluttering softly. He reached around and stuck his hand in my back pocket and it was my turn to jump regaining my composure and trying not to look like I was being chased by a pack of hungry wolves.

"Yes I did fine thing, you done?" He said laying on the accent obviously knowing what I was up to.

"I'm done here." I said leaving the here open for interpretation. He thanked the attendant for the information and turned me towards the door, but he didn't take his hand out of my pocket and that kept mine locked in his as well. We walked out the door to the car and I beeped open the car with my free hand.

He finally extricated his hand from my pants pocket and leaned in pushing me up against the car door. "Probably shouldn't tempt me like that again unless you intend to give me full access." He stalked around the back of the SUV and I closed my eyes and sucked in a breath. Don't jump in the fire if you don't want to get burned, Sugar.

I opened the door to the SUV and sat down in the seat putting a light lift to my voice, "Check that one off, the key was way too small for those types of boxes." I started the car and avoided looking at him.

"Okay, where to next then baby?" He asked. And the baby came out sounding very sultry and very natural.

"Wells Fargo." I turned the music back on and Five For Fighting blew us back into our seats with "'65 Mustang".

Van pumped a fist, "No way!" He reached over, cranked it up higher, and started singing. "She's my time machine. She's my rolling memory. She's my family. And I love her so. She knows my secrets well. But her back seat won't ever tell. She's no Jezebel, no, my '65 Mustang rides along every mile's another song and what I don't remember, she never forgets. That little girl ain't let me down yet." There was some dash drumming and I joined him on the next verse singing until we hit the final verse and I turned down the volume. I was grinning large because that song was one of my favorites.

"Your voice is amazing. Did you train somewhere?" I had been meaning to ask him, but the moment never came up.

"No, I've always loved singing, but then I love music. My grandma always had music playing. I think she always felt kind of bad that I never knew my father, so one day she broke out some old recordings and it was him singing. I figured out pretty quickly where I got my talent from. It made me a firm believer in the idea that we all get something from our parents, some little hidden talent. Mine's singing just like yours is carving." He trailed off then.

"I like to hear you sing. It makes me feel good and it gives me hope. I need that right now."

"Hope for what mi mot?" He asked softly.

"Hope that maybe someday things can be different." And I left it at that because I knew that someday things had to be different, they had to be.

He reached over and rubbed my shoulder with his hand like it was something he did every day. I was across the Bong Bridge and was heading down I-35 to the Mesaba Avenue exit. I found a place to park on the street not far from Wells Fargo, put the car in park and shut down the engine.

I turned to him, "So are we going in playing good cop bad cop?"

He laughed then, genuinely, "I don't think good cop bad cop is going to work here. I have a gut feeling you are going to know half the people in there." And he was right.

"Probably. Will they give you the information then if you ask nicely?"

He shook his head, "Not unless I have a signed search warrant from a judge."

"So in other words it's Sugar to the rescue again?" And I got no response, just a smile.

I grabbed my purse off the backseat and opened my door as I tried to quickly come up with a story that would make sense. I came around the front of the car and stepped onto the sidewalk where he joined me putting his hand in my back pocket. I growled at him and he slowly pulled it out.

"Sorry, I had to make sure everything was still where it was supposed to be." And I punched him, hard.

We stepped into the lobby of the bank and stood in front of the beautiful cherry wood desk. There were offices to the right and left of me down the hall and the large plate glass window looked out over Superior Street. I sidled up to the desk and put an arm up on it as Van stood behind me. I could tell by the look on his face he was expecting a performance.

"Hello, welcome to Wells Fargo Bank. Can I help you?" The young lady asked me from her perch. She was obviously new since I had banked here for half my life. I looked at the name plate on the desk.

"Hi Jamie, I'm here regarding a safe deposit box." I said in my sweetest voice.

"Of course may I have your name?" She had her hands poised over the computer.

"Tula DuBois." I said and heard Van snicker behind me. She began typing into the computer and surprise, surprise I had an account.

"Yes, Ms. DuBois, I have several accounts under that name, which would you be inquiring about." She said it in her best business voice.

"The one with about ten grand in it, give or take a few thousand." I said. She did some more typing and it was getting a little uncomfortable.

"I'm sorry, but there are no accounts that match that dollar amount. They all have considerably more in them. Could you be wrong Ms. DuBois?" She asked nervously.

I leaned in over the counter and went for the "I'm telling you a secret" act. "See, here's the thing, it's probably under my parent's name and not mine."

"I see, Ms. DuBois. If you would like to have one of them come down here with you then I would be more than happy to make the box available to you. However, if you are not on the account then I simply can't give you that access without one of them present."

"I see, but I have the key." I didn't want to play the last card until I had to.

"Like I said, I still need the presence of an account holder in order to open the box." I tried really hard not to roll my eyes.

"I understand where you are coming from Jamie, but see here's the thing." I leaned in further, "My parents both passed away suddenly in an automobile accident." She gave me that look that I had experienced too many times and I felt Van's hand on my shoulder. She held up a finger and picked up the phone speaking to someone and then hanging up.

She stood and she led us in the door of an empty room. "Eli will be right with you, Ms. DuBois." She said closing the door behind her.

Van pulled me into him, "You don't have to do this, Tula. We can figure out some other way." He never got to finish his thought because the door opened and a nice looking man in a business suit stepped in clicking it closed behind him.

"Hello Sugar. How are things going in the land of weddings and ballrooms?" Eli reached over and shook my hand and then Van's as I introduced them.

"Hi Eli, things are great, better than ever. Busy every weekend and can't ask for more than that." And I was happy to see Eli because he already knew my story.

"So Jamie said you were here about a safe deposit box?" He said sitting down behind the desk.

I nodded, "Well I'm not really sure. I came across this key not too long ago and it seemed like something that might fit a bank box or something of the like. I thought I would bring it down since I know my parents have an account here and see if they also had a safe deposit box."

Eli pulled up the account on the computer, "That account still has the ten thousand in it, well almost fifteen thousand now with the interest, but there has been no withdrawals from it in ten years Sugar."

"And that means?" I asked nervously.

"That means yearly safe deposit charges are not coming out of the account, so chances are they don't have one here." He said folding his hands and giving me the look that I hated.

I pulled the key out of my pocket, "Can you look at it for me and tell me for sure Eli? I'm really at a loss as to what it could be." I reached out and handed him the key and he turned it over in his palm.

"No, this is not a key to one of our boxes. It would have numbers on it indicating the box number, Sugar. This is small, almost like a padlock key." He extended his hand with the key and I took it back, pressing it into my palm.

"Okay, well thanks for checking for me. It was tucked in some important papers so I thought it might hold some significance." And it sounded lame to my ears too.

"I'm glad you stopped in anyway Sugar. I was planning on calling you. This account has been sitting here for the last ten years and I was hoping to convince you to get it closed and the money moved somewhere that would be better for your portfolio." He was stepping carefully now and I knew why. Even though I did all my banking here I refused to close that account. It felt like if I closed it I lost the last of what I have left of them. It was stupid, but no one ever said grief always made sense.

"Listen Eli, I know it's time to do that, I really do, but right now I can't." My voice broke and I cleared my throat. "I will bring by the paperwork to get that all done in the next few months okay?" Eli and Van stood at the same time. Van came up behind my chair and Eli came around the desk and gave me a gentle hug.

"Whenever you're ready, Sugar." He said his goodbyes then and left.

I followed him out quickly trying to keep the tears at bay hoping the fresh air would stop the stinging in my eyes. Van had his hand at my back and it was warm, the only part of me that was. I had my head down looking at my feet as we left. The sun was still shining when we stepped outside, but it didn't make me feel any warmer. I walked head down to the car and Van stayed with me rubbing my back. I unlocked the Sorento and he stuck me in the backseat and then climbed in next to me. The windows were tinted dark and no one could see in except through the windshield.

I was about to ask him why were in the backseat when he pulled me into him, "I thought maybe you could use a hug and I didn't want to make it a public event." he whispered.

I pretty much lost it, the tears I had been keeping at bay now fell. I had always been a crier. I was Hallmark's dream come true. Give me a sappy card, I'd cry. Watch a sad movie, I'd cry. Sad song, yup, I'd cry. I usually cried harder at the weddings than the brides did. I can't help it, it's who I am. Unfortunately I also knew more tears would be coming in the days ahead. They were always there ready to fall. I didn't even need a sappy movie or a sad song anymore. All I needed to do was wake up in the morning or think about going to sleep at night. Van was rubbing my shoulder and kissing the top of my head much like I pictured him doing for Lillie when her heart was broken.

"I'm sorry." I finally said.

"For what?" He asked laying his cheek on the top of my head.

I let out a shaky breath, "For being a sap. I'm even worse than usual lately."

"You don't need to apologize for who you are, Tula. It was heartbreaking to sit in there and watch you. All I wanted to do was take away some of the pain in your eyes and then I wanted to punch that guys' lights out for putting it there."

I laughed his words making my heart a little bit lighter, "It's not Eli's fault -- he's just doing his job. I know I need to do something with that account."

"So why are you leaving fifteen thousand dollars sit in an account untouched? If I may ask."

"Because it was my dad's dream money and now that he's not here to fulfil that dream I don't know what to do with it."

"His dream money?" He was still rubbing my back and I wanted to fall asleep and stay in his arms where I knew the dreams would stay away and I could rest.

"One of the last jobs he did was redoing the inside of the bank. He took the money they paid him and he put it in an account there. I don't have any idea what he planned to do with it. I would ask him, but he would just smile and say you'll see. It was only a few months before Mom got sick and before the accident. I guess I never will know. It's dumb I know, but I keep thinking if I leave it there maybe someday I will find some little thing that tells me what he wanted to do with it." I willed the tears to stop choking me.

"Maybe if you really let yourself think about it you will know what it was he was planning." He said stroking my arm now shifting under me so he was leaning up against the car door.

I let my mind drift back to all those hours that I used to spend with him and I could feel the smile playing across my face. "You know he always joked that he was going to build my mom an aviary and fill it with all the birds she never got to see. He also had these grandiose dreams about building a cottage on the property someday for friends to come and stay." I shrugged my shoulder. "Guess I already made that dream a reality."

"And I bet if you really thought about it you could come up with a dozen more things that he mentioned he wanted to do." Van said softly.

I sat up and wiped my tears, smiling, "Yeah I could. My dad was always coming up with some kind of big project that he was going to do when he retired. He was very creative and he was always looking to that next project before he even finished the last."

"So maybe the next thing you should think about is what he would want you to do with the money. What would make him happy? I'm pretty sure that he would want you to be happy." He rubbed a knuckle along my jaw.

"I know that he would. I'll have to think about that over the next few months. I like the idea of doing something with it in their names." I felt a smile on my face for the first time in a long time and my heart didn't feel quite so heavy.

"This is the first time I've seen you smile so freely. I really like your smile." He was still rubbing my face and the atmosphere was beginning to change to something much more electric and I knew it was time to retreat. The fire in his eyes was much more than I could handle without getting burned right now.

"I could use a beer." I said.

He dropped his hand and nodded, "I'm with you. How about some food to go with it since it's only noon."

"It's five o'clock somewhere." I playfully reminded him climbing out of the backseat and into the driver's seat. I looked in the rearview mirror. "Are you joining me?" I asked him as he sat rooted in the back.

"No, I think I'm going to stay right here for now if that's okay with you." And he had a funny look on his face.

I put the car in gear, "Okay, I guess I can play chauffeur. To the Brewhouse Henry!" I said in my best servant voice. "I need a good burger and a great beer." But that wasn't entirely accurate. Mouthwatering burgers and fantastic beer would start to cover it a little better.

"I'm not really in the mood for a burger." He said and I glanced up into the rearview mirror and he was watching me closely.

"No problem they have a full menu. I'm pretty sure you can find something you'll like." And I convinced myself he was talking about food. **God bless denial.**

SEVENTEEN

I parked at Fitger's and headed directly into the Brewhouse not wanting to hang around outside where people could see us. The Brewhouse wasn't too busy and I was glad there were no familiar faces. I asked the hostess if we could sit upstairs and she grabbed two menus and led us up, Van taking the tail. She seated us in a booth snug against the wall. I noticed Van hesitate for a minute before picking the side facing the stairway we had come up. He turned himself sideways in the booth and looked out straight over the bar area. I ordered two glasses of Tugboat Irish Stout and she handed us the menus and left for the bar.

"Afraid to be seen with me?" He asked his brow raised.

"Nope, I'm pretty much afraid to be seen at all." I said honestly.

"No need to be oul doll I got you covered." He said winking at me.

I noticed his cockeyed position, "So keeping an eye on both stairways then?" I asked copying his accent.

"I like to think of it as being aware of my surroundings." He picked up his menu, "So what's good here?"

"Oh let's see, just about everything."

"Have you tried just about everything?" He asked looking over the menu.

"I've been here a few times." And that would be like saying only one ship has sunk in Lake Superior. "They have the best black bean chicken quesadillas. The artichoke chicken sandwich is incredible and the Lake Superior smoked fish wrap is like nothing you have ever tasted." He curled up his nose a little bit and I laughed

"No, it's good. I mean really good."

The waitress appeared with our beer and took our order. I was taking the fish wrap with no tomatoes, heavy emphasis on no tomatoes, and Van went with the black bean quesadillas since he had it on good authority that they were the best. Then he winked at the waitress who blushed and stammered off to put in our order.

"You do have a way with the ladies." I said shaking my head and I suspected the feeling I was experiencing might possibly be jealousy.

He looked at me sipping his beer with that half a grin on his face. "It's the accent. There was a study done once and the results showed that women thought the Irish accent was the sexiest." And I guess I had to give him that.

"So what do you think?" I asked motioning towards the beer.

"It's interesting." I let out a sigh. I guess I was going to have to tell him.

"Why the sigh, little fry?"

"You have this really bad habit of using the word interesting." I said, drawing designs in the water droplets of my beer mug.

"Interesting?" He leaned in close to me and whispered, "Is that a swear word here? I read the Northwoods Handbook, but it wasn't in there." He was staring at me intently trying not to crack a smile.

"You are a funny one aren't you? No it's not a swear word around here. See in my family when someone says the word interesting it means they can't think of a better word because they hate it that much."

"That?" He asked me.

I waved my hand, "Whatever it is that you are talking about. For instance when your opening line was "Tula now that's an interesting name", in my family that would actually mean "Tula that's a horrible name, why did your parents saddle you with that."

He was in the midst of swallowing a drink of beer and it came out his nose as he attempted to keep from spitting it out through his mouth. He grabbed a napkin and cleaned himself up.

"Well where I come from interesting means interesting. Like if I said, I find you to be an interesting woman, I would actually mean that you make me think, make me smile and make me wonder what it would be like to kiss your lips. You know, you are interesting." He didn't look away first, I did. "But I will try to keep my use of it to a minimum for you." he added.

I was drinking the beer faster than I should be and the alcohol was hitting my brain with an empty stomach. "So what do you think of the beer?" I asked him again.

"It's interesting." I reached over and punched him, hard.

He was laughing at me and I wasn't so sure that I cared. "It's good, but it tastes like chocolate coffee, is that what they were going for?" he asked.

I nodded, "That's why I love it. If I'm going to drink beer and it can taste like coffee and chocolate I will take it all day long."

He gave me a full on smile, "Of course you would."

The waitress brought our meals and set our plates in front of us. "Did you enjoy the beer?" She asked and I noticed her question was not directed at me. I rolled my eyes, but only a little so no one saw.

"It was great for the sinuses," Van said, "but I'm working so how about a mineral?" The waitress looked at him waiting for him to explain so she didn't have to ask what a mineral was.

"He would like a Diet Coke," I said, "And so would I." Van gave her a brilliant smile and she headed back to the bar. I picked up my fish wrap and inspected it for tomatoes.

"No icky tomatoes?" Van asked scooping his quesadillas up.

"Thank God for small favors." I said taking a bite.

We dug in, talking about Lillie and her plans for her future. I tried to be engaging, but my mind was on other things. The wrap was sitting like lead in my belly and I set it back down on the plate and picked at it while he mowed through his quesadillas and black bean salsa.

"Penny for your thoughts?" He asked and I looked up.

"Oh sorry. I was thinking about Margie and Nathan."

"The waitress is going to be offended if you don't eat that fish wrap." He said motioning to my plate, "I thought you were hungry."

"No you were hungry, I just wanted a beer." He smiled then, but didn't give up.

"I still think you should eat. You don't eat enough."

"What are you my mother now? I have one of those." And he kept eating.

"What if we never find the information, Van? What if we can't find what the key opens and we never save Margie and Nathan? What then? Does this go on forever?"

He set his fork down, "We will find it Tula. This won't go on forever. Too much is at stake for all of us for this to go on forever." He reached over and took my hand, "Just trust in time no matter how long it takes." he sang softly.

"Oh, you are good. "You Can't Hurry Love", The Supremes, East coast swing." I said.

We had started a little game where he sings a lyric from a song and I tell him the song, the artist and the dance. Ever since I told him that I don't listen to the lyrics I think he thinks he's going to stump me. All I said was that I don't focus on the lyrics not that they don't register. I didn't mind though because every time he sang a little verse from a song it made my heart a little lighter for those few minutes. I looked over at him and he was looking at me in a way that made my stomach drop down into my toes. I needed to get away from him and clear my thoughts.

I stood, "I'm going to the restroom." And he stood stepping out of the booth. "Alone." I added.

He put his hand to my back and led me to the back stairway that led to the restrooms on the main floor and I prayed the whole way down he wasn't actually going to go in there with me. He didn't. He leaned up against the door and motioned for me to continue. God bless chivalry. I sat in a stall and took deep breaths telling myself that it was all this craziness in my life that was making me so attracted to him. It was the fact that he was here to be my protector that made me like him so much and once he left, life would be fine. That little voice was laughing so hard in the back of my mind I had to turn the water on high and let it run to drown it out. I was drying my hands when my phone started to ring and I expected it to be him wondering what was taking me so long, but when I looked at the caller ID it displayed private caller.

I stepped out into the hallway and met his eyes as I answered, "Hello." Van was next to me in two steps.

"Ms. DuBois? Lovely to finally hear your voice." My stomach flipped.

"Who is this?" I asked not letting my voice waver.

"Well now, it's Margie's *el padre*." He said in a heavy Spanish accent. At that point Van grabbed me and pulled me into the men's room leaning against the door blocking it from anyone trying to enter.

"Is there something I can do for you?" My voice was steady, but I wanted to vomit.

"Yes, I would really like for you to finish up your date and get back to looking for our treasure."

"I don't know what you are talking about. I'm just showing a friend around town."

He laughed then the kind of laugh that sent a shiver down my spine and made the bile rise in my mouth.

"Where did you get my number?" I asked him, angry that he thought he could use it for his own sick enjoyment.

"From a friend, make sure to thank him for me the next time you see him. Oh and you better stop playing tour guide and start looking for the bounty. Margie doesn't have much time left."

There was silence and I looked at the read out and it was blank. He was gone. I slipped my phone back in my pocket. I looked around me then realizing that mens bathrooms smell rather unpleasant and the beer and fish was turning in my stomach.

"Let me out." I said starting to retch. He stepped aside and I ran out the door and directly to the ladies room where the beer and the fish rolled around in my stomach and the nausea made me cry. I felt him then pushing me down on my butt and putting my head between my legs. He was rubbing my back slowly telling me to take a few deep breaths and I concentrated on his voice and my stomach settled.

"You okay now?" He asked and I nodded.

"Don't let him in, Tula. Don't let the fear get the better of you. He isn't worth it." But he sounded as angry as I felt.

"I don't want to stay here. Please, I want to go to the car." And he pulled me up and took my hand pulling me out of the ladies room. He put his arm around my waist and stopped long enough to throw some money at the waitress. We stepped outside and the fresh lake air and crispness of the fall day hit me. I was able to breathe again. By the time we got to the SUV I was feeling better and could make sense of my thoughts. He stuck me in the driver's side and stood in front of me leaning on the roof of the car with the door open.

"Tell me what he said." He was very much in cop mode now.

"He told me who he was and that he wanted me to finish my date and get back to finding our," which I put in quotation marks, "bounty. He laughed really hard when I told him that you were a friend almost like he knew otherwise. He said that Margie didn't have much time left."

"What was his response when you asked him about your phone number?" He was absently rubbing my upper arm as I talked.

"He said he got it from a friend and I should thank him next time I saw him. I don't know what that means though." And I had thought plenty about it in the last ten minutes.

"It means one of two things. He's either messing with you and he got your number off the million advertisements and flyers everywhere or it means that whoever he has on his payroll you consider a friend." He said still rubbing my arm.

"I am going to sit here and convince myself that it's the first option because the second option is going to make me sick to my stomach again." I swung my feet in the door and pulled it shut. As he walked around the hood of the SUV, I heard him mumbling some Irish words that I had no trouble figuring out the direct American meaning to, no cliff notes needed.

I started up the SUV cranking up the heat to try and get warm, something I didn't think was going to happen and then I laid my head on the steering wheel and tried not to think about the fact someone I considered my friend was selling me down the river for money. I was also trying to hold back the tears that were threatening at the edges because we still had a long way to go today and I needed to hold it together until I was alone. I felt the car shift as he got in the passenger's seat and clicked the door shut.

He was silent and rubbed my back in slow circles, "Let's concentrate on finishing our task and then we can try to figure the rest out, okay?"

I lifted my head up off the steering wheel and put it in gear heading down Superior Street stopping at the light by the Electric Fetus. I noticed Van checking out the rear window, "What's going on back there?" He asked me as the light turned green and I turned left towards the DECC. A block down from the corner was a store with a line out the door.

"They sell K2 there. There is always a line out the door." I said, "To say the least it's been a fiasco for the cops."

"I'm guessing that's cutting into McElevain's business around here too. No wonder he's got his cacks in a wad."

I started to giggle partly because it was funny and partly because the whole thing was craziness on top of craziness. "Undies in a bundle?" I threw back.

"Now you're sucking diesel oul doll!" He was smiling at me and I was trying to remember we weren't on a date.

EIGHTEEN

We pulled up to the DECC parking lot and I shut down the SUV.
I turned to Van, "I'm thinking that we need to check both the men's and the women's locker rooms. If I were Margie I wouldn't necessarily hide it in the women's locker room. I might have had Nathan hide it so that they would have to search both rooms and that would take more time. I've been thinking about it and the locker rooms aren't open to the public, but if Nathan went in dressed as a maintenance man or something of the like he may have been able to talk his way in."

He nodded, "Jess told me not to underestimate you and I'm starting to see why." And then just to fluster me he planted a kiss on my forehead.

"Okay, so what's the plan here?" I asked trying to pretend it didn't happen.

"I'm going in as a cop this time, there is going to be no other way. Hang back and we will see what happens. You may become my "partner" or I might lock in you the ladies restroom. Time will tell." I rolled my eyes at him and he put his hand on my wrist. "Keep your phone connection open so that I can call you if we get separated. Do not, I repeat do not, get too far from me."

"Eye-eye captain." I said, giving a salute.

I reached in my pocket and pulled out the key pressing it to his palm. He got out of the car and waited for me to come around. He pulled me into him again propelling me towards the door at a fast clip. As soon as we got inside he stepped ahead of me and went to the information desk. I hung back hidden from the view of the desk. I stayed close enough to see and hear what he was saying to the attendant at the desk. He pulled out his badge and flipped it open asking them about public locker rooms. I could hear them tell him there were none and the only locker rooms were those used by the UMD Bulldogs and those were not available to the public. I heard Van tell them he didn't care and needed to inspect the locker rooms anyway and he expected their full cooperation with the investigation. I tried not to snort. The man was obviously not from Duluth. You don't go in and be all Walker Texas Ranger around here, it doesn't work that way. Midwesterners are friendly people, but if they feel threatened they aren't going to give you a damn thing. Van was shifting from foot to foot while the information attendant told him that he would have to call the Duluth PD for confirmation of his identification.

I rolled my eyes. I guess I really was going to have to do everything. I pulled my parka off and pulled my UMD sweatshirt over my head glad I put my favorite, white, nearly see through, MAMBOS t-shirt on under it this morning. My bra happened to be hot pink with white hearts and it contrasted through the white softening the brightness, but it would be enough to catch the attendant's eye. I tied the shirt at the bottom in a knot pulling it tight and pushed my Miracle Bra to its limit. I believe it was what you called accentuating the positives. I sauntered over to the desk my chest thrust forward. I leaned on the desk with one hand. Crossing my ankles and leaning in.

"Hey Ben." I said casually. Van's eyes were like saucers and happy was not a word I would use to describe the look on his face.

"Hi Sugar! Long time no see! How are you?" Ben said taking much too long of a glance at my cleavage.

I batted my lashes at him, "Now Ben, you know that's not true. It was only a few weeks ago that we spent the evening doing the hustle." I turned and leaned my other hand on the desk so he had a full fledge view to kingdom come.

"Yeah like I said a long time." Ben responded and I heard Van try not to snort.

I tossed my hand at him like an old southern belle, "You devil! You are free with the flattery." I leaned in close and put my hand aside my mouth and whispered, "He's kinda with me." I tossed my thumb at Van. "He's a friend of Jesse's, helping him on a case, but I know I can trust you to keep this conversation hush-hush right?"

"Of course, Sugar, anything you want, anything you need." And he was like putty in my hands.

"What I need is for you to let my friend take look at what he needs to look at and what I want is for you and me to have a Coke in the bleachers and talk, or something." I added giving him a shy smile.

Ben reached behind him and grabbed a walkie-talkie and a set of keys his eyes never leaving my cleavage, then motioned us down the corridor. I was sure that Van was thoroughly displeased with my approach, but I didn't much care. I hung on Ben's arm pretending to understand everything he was saying about the new arena while Van's eyes bore holes in the back of my head. We rolled up to the locker rooms, Ben let Van in, and grabbed a couple of Cokes. We sat in the bleachers of the arena to wait. Ben was a few years older than me and hung out with Jesse playing softball and hockey. He was a great guy. He was good looking and was an accomplished dancer, but that was about where it ended for me. He has made it quite clear that he enjoys my company more times than I want to count. I felt a little bit bad for leading him on, but was telling myself it was all in the name of helping my friends.

"So did you make the **Michael Bublé concert this summer? I** figured you had front row seats." Ben asked sipping his Coke and invading my personal space.

I scooted down the bench a spot, "No, I didn't. I had a wedding that night." I sighed.

He threw his hand over his heart, "No way! I can't believe it! If I had known I would have come and thrown you in the truck and drove you there myself. You missed a hell of a show."

"So I've heard. Thanks for rubbing it in! When I got up the next morning and read the Tribune I really hated being a responsible businesswoman. I was depressed the whole next week." And I was, seriously depressed.

Ben was laughing and I was really starting to hope Bond would hurry up before he asked me out to dinner or worse. Thankfully my cell phone rang and I was all too happy to answer it. "Are you and Mr. Hockey Head having a good time?" Van asked me in a rather sugary voice. I smiled at the thought this was bothering him that much.

"Hey there, yes I am, but I'd be happy to come and rescue you if that's what you need."

"Yeah that's what I need, rescuing. Please come rescue me o' great woman of the north." Van said sarcastically. I punched it off and smiled at Ben.

"Hey sorry about that Ben, I gotta go help Jesse's friend. I guess he's ready to go." I rolled my eyes and laid my hand on his leg. Ben stood up and helped me over the steps to the aisle. We walked back to the locker room, Ben's arm around my shoulders, where Van was lounging against the wall waiting. I noticed he had my sweatshirt and parka in his hand and I had to repress a smile. He stepped up in front of Ben then and removed his arm from my shoulder.

"Thank you for attending to Tula while I was busy with my dekko. I will take it from here." And he put his hand on my back possessively pushing me towards the front of the DECC.

I heard Ben say, "Tula?" In a questioning voice. Obviously we have never formally been introduced. I waved and thanked him for the Coke and he waved back tentatively saying see you soon. I think I heard Van mumble something that sounded like "not if I have anything to say about it" as he propelled me to the SUV and practically shoved me in the driver's side door. I was getting the impression he was angry. Or jealous a little voice said. He climbed in the passenger side door and slammed it, hard.

He threw my parka and sweatshirt at me. "What the hell happened to hanging back and letting me do the talking?" He demanded motioning to the building.

"Well, sorry, but I saw you having a hard time up there so I figured I'd help out." I was going for the innocent look, but it was hard when my shirt was that low and it was cold in the car.

He was shaking his head, "I didn't need any help. I had the whole thing under control."

"Oh is that what you called that, under control? It looked like you were trying to play Walker Texas Ranger in the middle of downtown Duluth. You gotta have some decorum around here!" He was literally almost ripping the arm rest off the seat he had such a death grip on it. "Could you ease up on my seat there, cowboy? This baby's expensive." I was going for playful, but he wasn't playing.

"What on earth made you think it was a good idea to hussy up and step in?" His jaw was twitching and it was kinda cute.

"Hussy up? Is that what you thought I was doing?" And I was, but this was fun.

"Yeah, hussy up. You know all" he pushed his chest up and around and flipped his hair around like he was a playboy centerfold, "hussied up!"

I was starting to get the impression that this had less to do with the fact that I stepped on his toes and more to do with the fact that he didn't like me coming on to Ben.

"Are you going to tell my daddy on me or something?" I turned and stuck my chest out further.

He leaned over the console, "No, but I am gonna tell Jesse."

And I sucked in a breath. "Low, very low Van. I'm a big girl. Jesse doesn't control my life. I can date whoever the hell I want!" I was meeting him halfway on the console now.

"I never said you couldn't. I'm telling Jesse so he can beat the hell out of that guy!"

I started to laugh then, really hard and he wasn't amused, "Van! That's Jesse's friend, they play softball together! Ben's like a brother to me."

"Ha!" Van shook his head.

"What?"

"What? What? He's like a brother to you? Really? Did you see how he was looking at you? It was the most holy show I've ever seen!"

"What the hell is a holy show?" Couldn't the man speak English?

"It means disgusting, it was disgusting!" He added extra emphasis on the gusting.

I threw my hand up, "Okay, so I think of him as a brother, but I can't speak for him. Is that better?"

"No, that's not better because it is quite obvious to me that he would like to be hustling you into his bed!" Oh my, we were getting into interesting territory weren't we?

"Oh come on Van!" I said trying not to roll my eyes.

"Listen to me Tula. You may have been acting the maggot, but he was buying it hook, line and sinker and he wouldn't have thought twice about acting on it if he had the chance. I'm a man, I've been there!"

"Acting the maggot?" And I made room for a new entry in the cliff notes.

"Yeah, acting the maggot, fooling around, messing around, acting stupid, being a pain in the arse." He glared at me.

"I wasn't acting stupid and I'm not a pain the arse! I knew exactly what I was doing! I was taking one for the team so to speak." And you would think he could show a little appreciation.

"Don't ever do that again, do you understand me? I can't say that if you try that again I won't punch the guy's lights out when his eyes stray to your cleavage." And his were straying there right this very minute.

"Why Mr. Bond you sound a little green eyed." And he looked at me with those eyes that said don't push me or I will show you how green eyed I am. I took a calming breath and pulled on my sweatshirt and parka. I leaned back against the seat, "Did you find anything during your dekko?"

"Fair play!" He said giving me a high five obviously assuming I understood what that meant.

"The answer is no, not that I expected too." He buckled his seat belt.

I pounded my fist on the steering wheel, "Damn it!" I opened my door and got out and slammed it, hard. Then I kicked the tire and said some inappropriate words for a lady and felt a lot better.

Van hung his head out the window, "Could you ease up on that there, cowgirl? This baby's expensive." And he stuck his head back in the window and rolled it up. I dropped my head, took two deep breaths and climbed back in the car.

Van looked over at me, "Frustrated?"

"My life sucks right now. My friends are missing, I can't find the information to help them, I have a maniac calling me for fun, Jesse is yelling at me whenever he feels like it, my best friend is hiding something and I've got a 24/7 bodyguard!" And he sat there and laughed at me.

"I wouldn't make a good cop." I finally said.

"I agree, but not because you don't have the mind for it. Your analyzing skills are quick and accurate. You just have too much heart." He said it like a doctor breaks the news to someone with a deadly disease. He was right. I wasn't cut out for this. I needed results sooner rather than later.

He laid his hand on my shoulder and I jumped, but he didn't pull it away. He sat there until I relaxed. "Maybe we should go have a little fun. I've never seen Lake Superior up close. Do you want to be my tour guide?"

I thought about that one for a minute and decided what the hell -- maybe it would take my mind off the picture of him punching out a guy because he looked at my chest. Or maybe it will only make it all that harder for you to tell yourself you don't need him the little voice said. I growled at it and it fell silent, but not before Van looked at me curiously. I turned right out of the DECC and went down behind the aquarium and past the Coast Guard's cutter. I came around the corner past the William A. Irvin and slowed.

"That boat seems a little out of place." He said as we approached the bow of the ship.

"It is," I slowed down to a stop. You could read the name on the boat and he saw the stairs leading up to the top of the freighter.

"It's a floating museum." I said, "It gives the public a chance to walk through one of the lake freighters so that you can really get a feel for how big they are and how they work. The boat was decommissioned because it became too small and too slow to load without automatic loading equipment. I like the fact that he's here. It's one of those things that you can go through over and over and still see something new you missed the first time. They do the haunted ship every year where they turn it into a nasty scary terror hall at Halloween. I guess it's all the rage."

"You guess? Have you never been?"

"No and I have no interest. Halloween for me is about little ghosts and cute witches, not floating heads and amputated limbs. I try to have a Halloween party at the lodge every year around the campfire. I'm pretty unadventurous I guess."

"You say that like it's a bad thing." He said pinning me with a look.

"I've seen enough carnage for my lifetime." And that was all I could say. I drove around the Irvin and turned right into Canal Park driving past Old Chicago Pizza and the Marketplace with the lift bridge looming ahead. I turned left and pulled into the public parking area near Grandma's Restaurant. The lake spread out before us and I put the SUV into park.

"Where are we?" He had his seatbelt undone and was turning around in his seat taking in the view.

"This is Canal Park. Across the bridge is called Park Point and at the end of the point is where the airport is that Margie and Nathan flew into."

"That is the lift bridge I presume?" He was turned backwards looking out the back of the SUV at the bridge that loomed behind the Lake Superior Maritime Visitor Center.

"That's her. She is a constant here. She goes up and down up to thirty times a day during the busy summer season. It's fun to come down here and stand on the pier and watch the ships come in and out. They blow their horns in these different sequences that mean different things. I can't remember it all now, but they do a sequence to tell them to lift the bridge or one to say hello. It's fun and it draws a lot of tourists down here in the summer. Across the bridge there are beaches and Park Point is usually crammed full in the summer."

"So what happens if you are on that side of the bridge," He pointed to the other shore "when the bridge is up?"

"You wait just like if you are on this side of the bridge. Sometimes you can sit ten or fifteen minutes for the whole sequence."

"How does that work? What if there is an emergency on that side of the point and they need to get to this side or vice versa?"

"That is a problem then." I laughed because he was sitting there, his eye squinched shut like it was difficult to comprehend.

"The locals call it "getting bridged". If you spend enough time here you will start to hear it a lot. Someone was late for work, "sorry I got bridged". Missed church, "sorry father I got bridged". You get the idea."

"The things you don't think about." And that was all he said.

"So I thought maybe you would like to take a walk out on the pier to the lighthouse. There's a great view of the lake out there."

"Sounds good to me." he said, reaching for the doorhandle.

"Wait." I grabbed the sleeve to his parka, "are we going to get in trouble for this?"

"Come again?"

"I mean is Jess gonna have a bird because we are walking around down here? He's probably got a GPS on my car and is watching my every move from a tree house somewhere."

A smirk took form on his face, "Well since you're with me he's probably not in the tree stand."

I laid my head on the steering wheel and tried to keep myself from banging it over and over again. I took a few moments and sat back up.

He was still smiling, "He loves you, that's all."

"Something tells me he also doesn't trust me."

"Cut the guy some slack and let him play detective. It's only for a few days and he's a little unhinged right now. So no, we won't get in trouble I'll make sure of it." And he pulled back his parka so I could see his Glock tucked in his shoulder harness. I pulled back my parka so he could see my Glock tucked in my holster. He grabbed my coat and tugged it back down looking around like he expected something to descend upon us.

"What the hell are you doing with that?" His voice was kinda squeaky.

"I always carry it with me when I go out. Jess makes me. Don't worry, mine's still smaller than yours. I'll let you take the lead." And where was all this flirting coming from?

He wasn't amused, "You do realize that there is a difference between registering a gun and having a permit to carry concealed right?"

"Yes, oh wise one, I do understand that. I also understand that it's not illegal to carry concealed in the state of Wisconsin anymore."

"Do you have a permit?" He asked his teeth still clenched together like they might fall out of his head if he opened his mouth.

"It's on my to do list." I said.

It was his turn to lay his head on the dashboard and bang it a little.

"And besides Mr. Know-It-All, it's not concealed, it's on my hip and you're carrying concealed too!" Enter hand flailing.

"I'm a cop!" He yelled sitting up his face animated now.

"So whoop de do." I said.

He held his hand out to me fingers waving in the breeze and I tickled them with mine. Now he *really* wasn't amused.

"Hand over the gun." He said through clenched teeth.

"No." I might need it to shoot him.

He reached over and took the holster right off my belt clicking the gun out of the holster, "Is it loaded?"

I rolled my eyes at him, "Of course it's loaded, isn't that the point?"

He didn't respond, pulling the clip and put it in his pocket and shoved the gun in the glove compartment slamming it shut.

"Do you know that your gun is pink?" And now he looked kind of amused.

"Pretty isn't she? All the guys at the range thought it was fun to play with my gun all the time cause it was so tiny and snappy, so I had it DuraCoated pink and that took the wind out of their sails. Now no one messes with it."

"I can see why," He said it tongue in cheek, "But new rules from here out. You may have the gun in the house but that is where it stays. Got it?"

I mimicked him and said, "You're just afraid that I'll out shoot you and I'm a girl."

He grabbed the front of my parka and pulled me up to him. "There is no doubt in my mind that you could out shoot me. It wouldn't look good in front of my friends, so that's why I'm going to be the only one with a gun." And he released me and opened his door.

I straightened my parka and followed suit beeping the Sorento locked and he pulled my parka up and zipped it to my chin nearly choking me. His was up around his face and his skull cap covered his ears. "Cold?" I asked as I unzipped my parka.

It was a balmy forty five degrees and I was thinking I should have worn my lighter coat. I could feel a change in the weather though. A storm wasn't far off and I could see it gathering over the lake. This one could get ugly like they were predicting and it wasn't making my day. He took my hand and told me to lead the way. We made our way down to the pier and strolled towards the lighthouse. There weren't too many people about. A few locals were running or power walking through Canal Park, but it was pretty desolate as darkness approached. We took the stairs to the lighthouse and leaned over the concrete abutment that looked out over the lake.

The lake itself was quiet. No boats coming or going and the water tippling a little every so often as the gentle wind blew across it. I pointed out Fitger's where we had come from and the lake walk that led to it.

"We are standing on the north breakwater lighthouse." I pointed straight across at the opposite pier, "That is, of course, the south breakwater lighthouse. You get to it by crossing the lift bridge. The view is pretty much the same except you can see the beach on Park Point better from there." I fell silent then letting him take in the lighthouses and the pier and the lake beyond.

"So do you come here often?" He asked me as he copied my posture, arms folded on the concrete.

"I come down here a couple times a month. Grandma's Sports Bar has an alcohol-free night on Sundays and I bring my young couples down to dance. Then I sneak over to Old Chicago Pizza for a Canadian bacon and black olive pizza with extra cheese."

"No onion?" He looked shocked.

"Not with Canadian bacon and black olives!"

"I meant do you come here" he pointed to the lighthouse, "often."

Oh. "No." And I was pretty sure I wanted to leave it at that.

"How come?" And it was obvious he didn't.

"Because I'm too busy?" It should have come out like a statement instead of a question.

"Too busy for this?" He motioned his arms out in front of him opening them wide. The sun was starting to set and the oranges and reds and yellows mixed and reflected off the water. It was opposite of the sunrise. The black, purple and blue descended on the yellow, orange and red pushing them away until the black of the night met the black of the water.

The streetlights on the pier were coming on as the light dimmed and the lights from the lighthouses added to the colors that played across the water. And like every other time I came out here I began to wonder what it would be like to watch the sunset from a shore on the other side of the lake. A shore I couldn't even see. And then I wondered what it was like to see it from my parent's view and Brent's. Do they get to see this where they are? Is it fair that I do? I felt the tears coming like they always do and I turned and ran down the stairs of the lighthouse not wanting to answer those questions. Not knowing the answers really, knowing only I missed them so much right now. I was running down the pier trying to outrun the tears and the memories of coming here as a little kid. We came every Sunday after church and walked the pier to the lighthouse. I would be up on my dad's shoulders my hair blowing in the wind as he walked along the pier. I would drag my hand along the concrete of the pier all the way to the lighthouse and then feel like a giant as I looked out over the lake safe on his shoulders. My mother would fret about me being so high up and insist on holding onto my coat from behind as I leaned over my dad's head for a better view of the lake. After while she would say, "Well Tula, I think it's about time we get ourselves home for some dinner." And she'd pull me off my dad's shoulders and I would hold her hand and skip all the way back to the car. I was running fast, my eyes closed and my mind in a whole different place. I pitched forward catching my foot on a crack, but was pulled up short by gentle hands on my arms.

"Tula!"

I turned and looked at him then, his voice reminding me that I wasn't alone.

He took my hand and reached up wiping the tears off my face with his other. "Was it something I said?" He asked it in a light teasing voice letting his thumb linger on my cheekbone. I stood there staring at him his voice bringing me back to the present.

"No. I'm sorry that was rude of me to leave you standing there. I usually come out here alone." I hugged my arms around my chest swiping at the tears that still clung to my cheeks.

He pulled me into him and wrapped his arms around my waist, "Do you usually run away like that when you are alone?" And I didn't answer him only because the answer was yes and that wasn't something I felt like sharing.

He let me go then, "Let's go back up I was enjoying the luí na gréine."

"The sunset?" I asked wiping my tears.

"Yeah, the sunset, luí na gréine, and it's beautiful, but not nearly as beautiful as you." He said smiling softly at me and taking my hand.

I didn't make eye contact and he led me back to the steps. I climbed them again and moved back to where we had been standing. I leaned my head on his shoulder and watched the sun set in the sky trying to keep the tears from falling.

"This place reminds me of the time I took my Grandma to the Irish seashore right before she died. The doctors had told her that the cancer was back and they gave her a few months to live. She knew she wouldn't be able to make it out to the beach if she didn't do it soon, so one day I came home from school and she had the car packed. She put me in the driver's seat and told me to take her to the shore. We drove out and got there as the sun was setting. I stood there with her, like I'm standing here with you now, and we watched luí na gréine. We sat there in the dark, with nothing but the twinkle of the stars, and I asked her what she was afraid of. She told me that the only thing she was afraid of was leaving me alone. My grandmother had a strong faith and she wasn't afraid of dying, but she was afraid of leaving me alone. I was a seventeen year old kid who was about to lose the last of his family, or so I thought, but I lied to her and told her that I would be fine and that she didn't need to be afraid for me. I told her that all the things that she had taught me were in my heart and I would miss her desperately every day, but that she didn't need to be afraid. I wanted her to have the peace that came with knowing that she did her job and I was going to go on and be strong, but I was actually dying inside. I didn't know how I was going to get up the next morning or the next or the next. Those days were filled with so much anguish for me, but standing there watching that sunset with her was peaceful and it let my soul rest. So peaceful that we got up the next morning and watched the sunrise from the same exact spot. Like if we were there to see it then that meant that there was another day coming. She died two weeks later and to be honest that sunset and that sunrise are what I think about when I remember her." He was quiet then and I slipped my hand in his.

"I'm glad you had that time with her." My voice broke and I shrugged.

"It is obvious to me that you treasure the sunrise, but something about this is too final for you isn't it?" He asked turning his body into me to block the wind.

"The sunrise reminds me that I made it through another night." I said.

"But the sunset makes you afraid of what the night will bring?" He asked softly.

I wasn't going to answer that. "It's beautiful, don't get me wrong, it's something that I used to live for, but now it makes my stomach hurt to be here. There are over three hundred and fifty boats on the bottom of this lake, big boats and little boats and with those boats so many lives. The words that come to mind when I look out there are mercy and peace. It reminds me about being absolved of your sins in case you don't make it to the sunrise. It makes me think about being at the mercy of God and trying to find peace in all of it. I haven't found peace, I haven't gotten through the mercy yet, I don't think."

"Or maybe out there is where you find God's mercy, get absolved of your sins and find peace."

"Maybe. I wish that when I come up here and I look out that I could think about the memories and smile instead of cry. I haven't figured out how to do that yet. I never had that chance to say all those things that you would say if you knew your time together was ending. One minute we were driving the same road we had driven a thousand times and the next minute they were gone, just gone. Wiped off the earth with no warning. I haven't figured out how to find peace with that, but I'm sure you have probably figured that out by now." I laughed a sad laugh.

He tucked his hands around me and softly sang, "Have no fear for giving in. Have no fear for giving over. You better know that in the end it's better to say too much than never to say what you need to say again. Even if your hands are shaking and your faith is broken even as the eyes are closing. Do it with a heart wide open."

"'Say', John Mayer, rumba." I said, almost to myself.

"Maybe you should say those final things you never said to your parents. Maybe you should say them out loud to the wind and the water. Maybe that would allow you to come out here and see this as everything that it can be instead of everything that it was."

"I want them to be proud of me and what I've done with my life. I want them to see that I didn't take my second chance and waste it. I want them to see that I fought back and everything they taught me is in here." I patted my chest. "I want them to know that I loved them and I want them to know I still miss them every day and I haven't forgotten them. I want them to know I'm mad at them for leaving me alone and I'm not mad at them for being together. I want to thank them for everything they ever did for me and for sending Jesse and Sharon to watch over me. I want to hug them one more time and I want them to tell me that they are okay. I want to know they are okay. I need to know they are okay." I slid down the abutment and sank down until my pockets touched the cold concrete.

He slid down next to me and put his arm around me, kissing my temple. "They are trying to tell you its okay, baby. Stand up and look out there and tell me they aren't trying to tell you they are okay."

He pulled me up to look out over the lake and he stood behind me holding me and rocking me back and forth in his arms. The sun was now nearly set and you could hear the cry of the gulls as they flew across the sky. I knew he was right. I knew they were okay and I knew they wanted me to be and I almost felt like I might be someday.

He leaned down then, "You are so beautiful right now." And he touched his lips to mine, gently, almost like they were just hovering. I knew I couldn't encourage it, but I couldn't pull away. This was a very, very bad idea, but it didn't feel that way. It felt natural and it stirred something in me I had forgotten was even there.

For a few seconds those thoughts went through my mind, and then he was pushing me down and yelling for me to take cover. I heard a pinging off the metal of the lighthouse and instinctively reached for my gun, knowing the sound was bullets ricocheting all around us. My hand met air and I suddenly remembered he had taken my gun. I rolled behind the lighthouse and he was yelling into the phone for backup.

"Tula! Where is it coming from?" He was yelling and I pointed at the south pier lighthouse. I could see the burst of fire from his gun as he shot at us.

I was as flat up against the lighthouse as I could get. "The south pier!"

The lighthouse was going to protect us here, but God help anyone on the pier! Van yelled into the phone and flipped it shut. He inched around the lighthouse gun drawn aiming at the lighthouse unloading his clip. More bullets rained down on us and then the world was silent again. Van was reloading and I saw the light glint off the goon's gun as he made a break over the side of the pier.

"There he goes!" I shouted at Van as the gunman swung over the side of the pier and disappeared.

Van reared up and took aim, but he was gone over the rail before he could get a shot off. I heard a boat motor take and then off they went in a blur of churning, white water as they headed for the open lake. Van shot off a few more rounds knowing his nine mm wasn't going to reach them, but it helped his frustration. We heard sirens in the distance and I sat on my butt my head between my knees taking deep calming breaths.

"He was a crappy shot." I said it flippantly hoping to break the tension.

"He wasn't trying to kill us. He only wanted to scare us. If he wanted to kill us we would be dead." he said frankly.

His cell phone chirped and he answered it the conversation consisting of lots of yes and no answers. He flipped the phone shut again and sat down on the concrete stretching his legs out in front of him. It was dark now and I felt like if we sat there up against the black of the lighthouse no one would notice us again until morning.

He pulled me to him. "Bird?" I asked.

He shook his head up and down, "Absolute canary." And I smiled. God bless predictability.

NINETEEN

We sat at the lighthouse until we heard feet pounding on the pier and I knew that we were going to have to face the music. We stood up as two Duluth PD guys and Jesse came up the stairs.

"Hey Jesse," I said throwing on the charm, "You should have seen the sunset."

His lips were nearly sucked inside his head he was trying so hard not to yell. I was kinda wondering if he was going to bite off his tongue. He pointed to the stairs and Van and I went down flanked by the other officers in front and I could see the lights of the cop cars spinning and the team on the south pier as they started their investigation.

"He's gone," I said, "had a boat waiting and they took off for greener pastures." I was directing my words at Jess and he came up between Van and I and slung an arm around each of us.

"I'm going to do you a favor and not talk right now. Get in the back of the squad and when I am certain I don't need anymore information out of you I will have you taken to the lodge. I will bring your car back after the investigation is complete. Do you understand what I want you to do?" He growled at me.

I rolled my eyes, "Yes, Officer Bowers I understand fully what you want me to do. Are you going to handcuff me too?" And my tone was not joking.

"If you don't do as I say, yes I will handcuff you, so don't push me." I just rolled my eyes harder and the two officers taking charge of me had to duck their heads so Jess didn't see them smirking.

I was led to the waiting squad while Van and Jesse talked. It was like watching a silent cartoon back in the old days. All the hand motioning and exaggerated facial movements told the story. Van was not doing nearly as much motioning as Jess who was flailing his arms around almost enough to be in my league. And then they started pointing at the squad I was sitting in both of them ramping up their yelling to be heard over the other. I was sinking further and further down in the seat and the cop in the front seat didn't even try to make conversation. I heard "trying to get her killed" and Van threw his hands up and walked away. I decided he was either really brave or really stupid because no one walks away from Jesse. He strode over to the car and got in the back seat slamming the door shut.

"Pete take us to the lodge. Now." Van **ordered.**

"I have not been authorized to do that Agent Walsh." The officer said **rather meekly.**

"I'm authorizing you. Drive." Van pointed at the road and held the guys eyes **in the rearview mirror.**

"Yes, Agent Walsh." The officer finally said and he put the car in **reverse and pulled out and** headed for the lodge. **I turned in the rearview mirror and** saw Jesse standing there his hand on his hip and I couldn't resist giving **him a little finger** wave as we drove away.

"He's gonna have an aneurysm." I finally said.

"He needs to get over himself and getting a fecking clue about..." Van **punched the seat and sat rigid.**

"Fecking clue about what?" I asked him.

"Nothing. Never mind it's not important." He said still staring **straight ahead.**

"Did he give you a hard time about not doing your job again?" **And I already knew the answer to that.**

"To put it mildly." He **ground out. And my phone rang. I** figured it was Jesse so I let it go to voicemail.

"Aren't you going to answer that?" **he finally asked.**

"Nope. I don't want to deal with him when he's like this. Better to let him cool down."

But the phone wouldn't quit ringing. **Finally I blew out a breath** and picked it up glancing at the caller ID, but it wasn't Jesse, it said private **caller.** He looked over at the private caller and swore, "It's him, answer it."

I hit the call button with a shaky finger, "Hello."

"Ms. DuBois **lovely to hear** your voice again, did you enjoy the sunset?" McElevain asked in **a most repulsive voice.**

"I was until you decided it would be a good idea to use **me as** target practice." And I was getting angrier with each word.

"You didn't seem to be getting the message, Ms. DuBois, so I **thought I would reinforce it. We want the information my daughter left at** your lodge and we want it sooner rather than later."

"I don't have the information you think I have!" I yelled into the **phone.**

"Not yet, but I know you are working hard to find it aren't you? Next time my guy won't miss so you might want to think less about your lover and more about staying alive."

"He is not my lover!" I yelled into the phone, but he was gone **already and I threw the phone on the floor of the car and sucked in a deep breath.**

Van reached out and found my hand on the seat and began **rubbing a slow pattern over the top of it.** He leaned over and whispered in my ear, "Don't say anything more until we are alone."

I looked over at him and nodded then leaning my head back against the seat shuddering at the words that played over in my mind. Next time he won't miss. Lovely. When would next time be? That was the question. I was so tired I laid my head back on the seat and fell into a light sleep rocked by the rhythm of the car on the road and Van's hand on mine. When I opened my eyes we were pulling into the driveway and the squad parked us at the front door. Van got out and took the stairs two at a time holding the remote up and checking for breaches. I guess he found none because he came back down and opened the back of the squad and helped me out. I unlocked the front door and stepped inside. He closed it leaning against it heavily and let out a breath eyeing me. He stepped forward and dragged me into him.

"You okay?" His voice was muffled against my hair.

"Oh yeah, Jim dandy. I've been shot at and yelled at and let's not forget threatened. It was a perfect way to top off a very unsuccessful day of bounty hunting."

"I know you are frustrated and scared, but you know what I'm going to remember about today?" He asked me pulling back.

"What?"

"That I got to see the sunrise with you this morning and sunset with you this afternoon and that was great crack."

"Crack?" I was mentally waiting for an entry in my cliff notes.

"Craic," He spelled the word for me, "it means fun. I had a lot of fun today even though we got shot at and yelled at. I would take it all day long if it meant I got to do that again with you."

"Well, I will take it as a compliment that you would take getting shot at just to hang out with little old me." He smiled and planted a kiss on my temple. "And you do know that in the US you probably shouldn't use the word craic when you are talking about fun, right?"

"Yeah, I got that impression when I landed here and asked someone where I could go for some good craic. They sent me down a back alley and I figured out pretty quickly that I need to not be so free with the lingo."

He walked over to the windows pulling the curtains closed and starting the fireplace. I sat down on the couch and he went to the kitchen. I shook my head thinking about a young Donovan all alone looking for great craic. He was right though, today was great craic. I also knew that I had better be careful because he was too easy to lean on and it felt too natural to be in his arms and he was going to be too hard to forget if I let myself get in too deep. I needed to back off and remember he is here to do a job and that job description didn't include fixing my heart. I heard him rustling in the fridge and then heard the clanking of two glass bottles.

He came back in with two Leinies handing me one, "Thought maybe you could use this."

I took the bottle and took a longer swig than I had planned. "Thanks."

"I apologize Tula, I didn't think that McElevain would go after us in such a public arena. It was my plan to kind of walk around a little in public and let him see us out, but I didn't expect him to use us as target practice and I know this guy well. I have dealt with him several times in the past. I'm really starting to believe that he's getting desperate."

"He obviously doesn't care who he hurts. Thank God no one was on the pier besides us. People could have gotten seriously injured or killed." I said trailing off and swigging more beer.

"Tell me what he said on the phone." Van put his hand on my knee and I jerked back.

"He said that I didn't seem to be getting the message that he wants the information that Margie hid so he thought he would send someone to spell it out for us. He told me I needed to be thinking less about my lover and more about staying alive. Oh and he mentioned that next time his guy won't miss." And I took another long swig of my beer hoping it would calm my nerves.

"He's just trying to throw shapes. Don't let him get up here." He tapped my temple with his finger.

"Throw shapes?" And another entry please Alex.

"Showing off, acting mighty." He said.

"Well I guess that fits in this instance. He was angry and he wants whatever it is that he thinks I have that I don't have and I'm not sure that I will ever have and that's obviously going to be a problem because if I don't have it and he doesn't have it then he will think I'm keeping it from him and then he's going to throw shapes in a way that's gonna mean I'm dead." And I took a deep breath.

Van was smiling, "That was an incredible sentence." He finished his beer and took my empty one and went in the kitchen for two more bringing them back and handing me mine.

"My limit's two or I won't be able to walk in a straight line." I said.

"Well is that all it takes to get you fluthered? Good to know." He was smiling that smile that made my stomach clench and I decided that some information should not be shared.

"Jesse's going to explode like the fourth of July, Van. That little spat you had back there, that's nothing. That's like talking when Jess is mad. Wait until you see him full bore mad." I laid my head back against the couch shaking it back and forth at the thought.

"I'll deal with Jesse, babe." And that was all he said.

I drained the rest of my beer as I heard the garage door go up and then back down. I heard Jesse walk in the garage door and followed his footsteps to the fridge where he helped himself to a beer and then stood in the doorway of the great room tossing an object up and catching it in his palm. I was starting to feel the beer mashing around in my brain.

"Hi." I said it like I have every other time he has come into my kitchen and helped himself to a beer.

Without a word he flicked the object in his hand at Van who caught it one handed without dropping his beer. He turned it over and over in his hand his face relaying the anger he was feeling. I might not be a cop, but I could assume it was the GPS they were expecting to find. Jesse came in and sat in the big chair feet up on the coffee table staring at the fireplace, drinking his beer, still no words. I really didn't want him to open his mouth because I could see by the look on his face that he wasn't going to go easy on us. I had a feeling he'd had his butt chewed out and he was looking for one to chew himself.

"So did you kids enjoy your date?" He finally asked his voice sarcastic.

I was not enjoying his tone. "As a matter of fact we did Jess." I folded my arms over my chest the beer giving me the courage to give him a little back.

"You know Tula, what part of don't go outside are you having trouble with? I can explain it for you in simpler terms if you need me too. Don't leave the shelter of a building. Don't go parading around out there!" He was saying it slow like I was a small child and motioning towards the front of the house like he was using sign language.

I stood up mad as hell that he used my real name, again, "You know Jess you don't have any right to talk to me like this and you certainly don't have to be a jerk." My arms were waving and my voice was getting louder, "You've been yelling at me since too early this morning and I've been shot at and embarrassed in front of pretty much the entire Duluth Police Department! I didn't ask for any of this! You put this in my lap at the worst possible time in my life and you can have it back! I quit! I quit the whole damn thing. I'm not a cop, Jess, so quit expecting me to act like one! I love you, but I'm too tired to pretend to like you right now, so you can go to hell Jess because I'm not interested in your game anymore!" And I turned and ran out of the room and headed straight to mine. I could hear Jesse calling my name and then I heard Van tell him to stop and to let me go. Thank you, finally someone was listening to me.

I slammed the door to my bathroom because I knew that the shouting that was about to ensue between them was not something I wanted to hear. I cranked George Winston up and let him fill the room with the soft sounds of "Forest". That was the only thing that was going to help me relax after this day. That and a nice soak in the tub. My bathroom had been gutted a few years ago and turned into a state of the art barrier free bath. The walls were the original log of the lodge, but had been refinished and were a soft golden brown. The sink covered one wall with a dressing area off to the side and was barrier free allowing a wheelchair or bench to be snugged up to the lowered vanity.

The toilet was off to the side between two lowered log walls, not for privacy, but so that the walls could have grab bars secured to them and still fit with the natural log cabin feel of the room. The tub sat in the corner and was a walk in tub shower combination that allowed me to step in, close the door, sit down and then shower or fill the Jacuzzi tub with water and soak. That was my option for today. I stripped off my clothes and climbed in my tub. I closed the door, letting it fill with scalding hot water and I turned the jets on to play the bubbles across my legs. I laid my head back against the tub trying not to cry. I'd been doing way too much of that lately. I stayed in the water listening to my music until I was rosy pink and the water turned cool. I grabbed a towel and let the water drain out of the tub before I opened the door and stepped out. The gritty feeling of the floor was always a reminder to me when I stepped out of the tub to watch my step. The floor had been taken down to the natural hardwood and a coating much like something that you would put over the deck of a swimming pool was poured over it. It allowed the natural beauty of the wood to shine through, but allowed for traction when feet were slippery.

I pulled the bench up to the vanity and dried my hair letting the heat and the noise of the dryer drown out the thoughts in my head. I went to my bedroom and grabbed my Fitger's hoodie and my long fleece sleep pants. They were too big, but I liked that they were roomy and fell evenly across my legs. They were also warm and I wasn't. I felt like I was chilled to the bone and nothing was going to make me warm for a very long time. I looked at my bed longingly. It was only seven o'clock and I'd already been up too many hours. I knew I would fall asleep eventually tonight and dream the horrible dreams. My body was too tired to stop it.

I opened the door to my bedroom listening at the door for voices. I heard none and saw Van's door shut so I knew it was safe to head to the kitchen for a cup of coffee. I was dreaming of some Fitger's Crème Liqueur coffee with a splash of Irish cream. I flipped the lights on in the kitchen as I walked in and jumped backwards, almost falling over, as my mind registered there was a person sitting in my kitchen chair -- and he was damn lucky my gun was still in the car! It was Jesse and he was waiting for me. I chose to ignore him. I wanted my coffee and then I was going to pretend that today didn't happen and that tomorrow and Saturday weren't going to happen either. Then on Sunday morning I was going to get up and I was going to put my life back together and I was going to take a very long vacation somewhere sunny and warm where no one shoots or yells at me. I was thinking about going to Florida. There was a lady down there I knew I really needed to see. I got the coffee out of the cupboard and scooped some into the pot not even asking Jess if he wanted any. I hit brew and stood there waiting for it with my back to the table. All be damned if I was going to apologize. I might feel bad that I had yelled at him, but I didn't say anything that wasn't true and he needed to deal with that.

"Making any of that for your complete jerk of a brother?" His voice was reticent and I turned at the sound of it. He looked about as bad as I felt. His DPD t-shirt was pulled lopsided out of his black cargo pants and his eyes were dull. I couldn't stay angry at him no matter how hard I tried. He was trying to hard to do the right thing and I loved him too much. I held my arms out wiggling my fingers and he came over and stepped into them laying his head over my shoulder.

"I'm sorry for not having better control of my anger. I didn't mean it, Sugar, I'm really frustrated. I need you to tell me you understand that you can't quit this game until the last person crosses the finish line. I have to know you are going to play until this is over."

"I will play until this is over, but then I don't ever want to play again. Do you understand?" And he nodded against my shoulder.

The coffee maker beeped and he reached around and grabbed a couple of mugs and filled them with coffee. I dumped some Irish cream in mine taking a few gulps. "Have you eaten today?"

He sat down at the kitchen table and put his head in his hands. "I think I had breakfast."

I reached in the freezer and grabbed out a container of my beef and wild mushroom stew putting it in the microwave to defrost. "Jess can I ask you something?"

He nodded without taking his head out of his hands. I turned to ask him a question and I heard snoring. He had fallen asleep and I was pretty sure that it was my fault. I had him up early and late and he had so much weighing on his mind. Probably more than I do and I was getting the feeling he wasn't sleeping much. The microwave dinged and I pulled the stew out and stirred it popping it back in to heat and grabbing some bread to toast. When the toast popped up and the stew was hot I brought it over to the table and shook his shoulder. He reached up and had me in a head lock my arm twisted behind my back before I knew what was happening.

"Jess!" I tried to holler at him, but it came out sounding strangled with the death grip he had on my neck.

His eyes got wide and he released me, "I'm sorry." He ran his hands over his face, "Sorry, I'm on edge."

I rubbed my arm, "Apparently. Remind me never to make you mad."

He looked down at the stew and toast, "Where did this come from?"

"You said you hadn't eaten so I made you dinner."

He perked up a little and picked up his fork, "I don't deserve you." And he always knew exactly the right thing to say. I sat down across from him my heart slowing back down to its normal rhythm.

"Van told me that you have a new secret admirer." He spooned in some more stew while eyeing me.

I snickered, "He might possibly be worse than you. It was just Ben. He acted like I was cozying up to Jeffrey Dahmer."

"He wasn't talking about Ben." He had laid his spoon in the bowl.

"Oh. What?" And then it hit me. "McElevain."

Jesse nodded, "Sounds like he has decided to make this a game between you and him. How do you feel about that?"

"How do I feel about that? I feel like throwing up, that's how I feel about that!"

"Van told me that he told you a friend gave him your number, but I want to stress what Van told you. Your number is everywhere and it wouldn't be hard to get it. Don't get too hung up on who it might be okay? Leave that stuff to me and focus on getting ready for Saturday night. If he calls again don't let him make you angry, try to get information out of him. Even something you don't think is important could lead us to where he might have Margie and Nathan."

Oh great, like I wanted to chit chat with the guy. I let out a sigh, "Fine, but I think we should cancel the dinner Saturday night. I don't want to put anyone at risk."

Please, please say we can cancel the dinner Saturday night, but Jesse shook his head. "No, I have a gut feeling that they are going to try to get to you in person Saturday night and I want to give them that opportunity."

"What! What do you mean get to me?" And he wanted to give them the opportunity, fabulous.

"I mean I think they are going to try and contact you in person and apply some face to face pressure. I expect one of his men to show up and try to rattle you. McElevain made his point, if they wanted you dead they would have done it today. You were perfect targets out there and there was no reason for him to miss except that he didn't intend to kill you to begin with." His voice wavered every so slightly and I knew it was a combination of anger and fear at the thought. "He's playing the cat and mouse game, but I suspect that they are going to push harder now. If they can get you to give them the information they want by strong arming you they will. So I want you to be prepared for that and have that in the back of your mind. Van and I will be working the room along with several of the casino security detail. Van will be on you like glue for the night so be prepared for that also. No sneaking away at any point in the night without an escort. Got it?" I nodded my head. Great another thing to look forward to.

"Van has his orders for the rest of the night. He's not to let you outside and he's to make sure you get some sleep. Tomorrow he and I having a meeting with the rest of the team to discuss Saturday's dinner. After what I found on the Sorento tonight I believe now more than ever there is an inside guy. The SUV never left the garage and it was in a place that was not going to be gotten to by a quick walk by. Someone had to crawl under the car to put that GPS on. I am pulling as many people as I can from this operation in hopes of getting McElevain's employee gone, but I can't be certain since I don't know who it is. I think the less people the lodge is exposed to the better. There will be a new squad in the driveway tomorrow while Van is with me. It will be a Superior PD squad. I was going to take him into town, but have decided we are staying on the property. I have the nine to noon shift tomorrow so I will show him the layouts for the casino and go over the plans for Saturday night with him while we watch the property. I want him to study them and really know them before Saturday night. Even though the squad is here and we are on site I need you to make sure you have your Glock with you at all times." Jess pulled it out and handed it to me, "found that in the glove box." And I rolled my eyes, but it reminded me I needed to get my clip back from Van. "And don't let anyone in, even if they say they are a cop. Anyone tries to come in shoot first and then call me. I will get him back here as quick as I can. Are you comfortable with all this?"

"No I'm not comfortable with all this, but I know I don't have a choice. I will be fine tomorrow. I know my way around a gun and I have some work to do anyway. After today I have no intention of hanging around outside anytime soon."

"From what I'm hearing tomorrow is not going to be a day to be hanging around outside." Jess said it as quietly as Julie did when she talked to me about the storm. "Would you like me to send Julie over to be with you? I'm sure she wouldn't mind."

I shook my head, "No, I've been through hundreds of storms in the last ten years. What's one more?" One more too many probably. "Jess I talked to Julie again today and she sounded worse than yesterday. Is everything alright? It seemed like every word was a chore for her." And that wasn't like Julie. She normally was so bubbly and outgoing and always ready for the next challenge.

Jesse looked up at me. "Something's wrong, but I don't know what. She says she's just tired and needs a break, but I'm not so sure. She has been having these spells where she gets so weak she needs to stop what she's doing and lay down or she will pass out. I can't get her to talk to me about it. She keeps saying she's fine, but I can see in her eyes that's a lie. I spend half the night holding her to me because she keeps telling me that she's afraid to lose me. I keep telling her that isn't going to happen, but she can't fall asleep unless I'm there. When she wakes up in the morning she's fine again until the evening and then she collapses."

"Sounds like she is overworked, Jess. Give her until after the dinner Saturday night and then I will take over MAMBOS again and she can have a break. I'd do it now, but I don't really have a clue where she is in execution of the whole thing and would probably muddy the waters."

Jesse dropped his spoon, "No! No, she doesn't need any help, Sugar. Don't worry about it. I've been helping her with the dinner too and we have everything in hand." And that was a very strong reaction to me offering help.

I put my palms up, "Well, okay, if you say so. Maybe you should take her off somewhere when all this settles down. Maybe she needs some time with no responsibilities, even if it's just for a weekend."

"I like the way you think, Sis. I already have a weekend booked in Grand Marais in a couple of weeks. It's going to be me, her and the swing on the front porch of the cabin. No pagers, no cell phones and no communication with the outside world. I plan to drag her to the doctor Monday though and make sure she isn't ill. I don't like the way she looks some days." And I could see that some of the worry I thought had to do with the case was really about how much he loved this woman and how scared he was that she was sick.

"You deserve a break and so does she. Maybe you will find it the perfect place to make things more permanent."

He raised his brows at me, "Maybe I will." And that was all he said. He finished off his stew and pushed the bowl away. "Van told me that you haven't slept but a few hours since he's been here and he's heard you crying at night. Are the nightmares back?" He looked at me over the rim of his cup waiting for the lie he expected to hear.

"Yeah, they are." And that shocked him. He set the cup down sloshing the coffee onto the table.

"What? Did you expect me to lie to you?" I asked him as his face took on a stunned appearance.

He nodded vigorously, "Yes because that's what you always do."

"I figured you were honest with me and you deserved the same."

"So what are you are going to do about them?" And I could tell he was nervous that I was going to say nothing.

"I'm going to get through the next two days on a wing and a prayer and after that I don't know." I took a drink of my coffee.

"Sugar, you have to get some sleep before your body gives out again."

"I'm stronger now than I was then Jesse. I can go a few days with some interrupted sleep and be okay."

"But it's been more than a few days hasn't it, Sugar? What's it been now a few weeks, a few months?" he asked softly.

"A few months off and on, but they have gotten more constant over the past few weeks. I don't really know what to do about them. I want to see if they will fade away after Saturday. If they don't then…" I shrugged my shoulder not sure what then.

He stood up and came around the table putting his hands on my knees, "Then you are going to talk to Julie. I'm going to lock you in a room with her until you tell her everything that is going around in that beautiful head of yours. I know she can help you and it's killing her that you won't let her."

"I'll think about it." And I would, but that didn't mean I was going to agree to it.

He walked to the sink and put his coffee cup on the counter, "I guess that's all I can ask."

He walked back over and kissed me on the forehead, "The offer stands if you decide otherwise. Now, go get some sleep if even for a little bit. You look like hell." I punched him then, hard, but he didn't laugh like he normally does.

He got down on his knees and pulled me into him whispering in my ear, "The look on your face when you think no one's looking scares me to death Sugar. I really need you right now and I can't, no I won't, let the same thing happen this time. I won't let it. So I pray every night that whatever I have to do to get you through this doesn't leave you hating me. But even if it does and you never talk to me again as long as you are happy then it will be worth it."

"Jess, please, stop. Nothing you could ever do is going to make me hate you. I can't even stay mad at you long enough to make a pot of coffee. Hang in there with me for a little while longer. I just need a little while longer." And that was a mantra in my head that played all day long, five more days, a little while longer, four more days, a little while longer, three more days, a little while longer and now I was down to one more day and I still needed longer.

"Okay, a little while longer, but then I'm taking things into my own hands. I love you and I can't watch this much longer." And he walked out of the room convinced that I didn't see the tears in his eyes. I heard him leave through the front door and I went in and closed and locked it again then I went back to the kitchen to finish my coffee, but I wasn't alone. Van was rummaging through the fridge.

"Can I help you?" I asked and he pulled his head out.

"I'm starving." he said.

I motioned for him to sit down and grabbed another container of stew out of the freezer going through the same routine I had done with Jess and brought it to the table.

At least this time I didn't get a head grip as a reward. At least this time I got a genuine thank you.

"Aren't you eating?" he asked me as he dug into the stew.

"I'm not hungry." And I wasn't. I wasn't hungry much at all anymore and I knew that wasn't a good thing. I've walked this road before and I made myself promise that I would eat, tomorrow.

"Coffee really isn't a food group did you know that?" He asked it teasingly but I could read the undertone.

"Depends on who you ask." I said, but I pushed the cup away having had enough anyway.

He got up from his chair and grabbed a spoon out of the drawer and opened the freezer and pulled out my Cold Stone Creamery. He brought it over to the table and put it in front of me picking up my hand and putting the spoon in it.

"Eat." He ordered and sat down in his chair.

"Ice cream? That's your idea of a food group?"

He shrugged his shoulder, "No, but isn't that what women eat when they are stressed out? They grab the Haagen-Daz and eat straight out of the container." He was sorta smiling, the kind of smile that you do when you don't want someone to know you are laughing at them.

"That's the most sexist remark I've ever heard!" And it might be true, but it was still sexist!

I picked up the container and stuck the spoon in, the call of the Heath, almonds and caramel too much to block out even if it proved his point. I had a couple of spoonfuls and then put it back in the freezer throwing the spoon in the sink. "There Mr. Male Chauvinistic Pig, I ate."

But he wasn't smiling. "No, you didn't and you didn't eat much at lunch either."

"Jeez it's like living with Sharon. Sugar, you need to eat more. Sugar, you need to put some meat on your bones."

He stared at me so I rolled my eyes, blew out a breath and got up and made a sandwich. I ate it leaning against the counter putting some distance between us. I grabbed my coffee cup and refilled it with hot joe and rejoined him at the table.

"Better," he said getting up and bringing his bowl over to the sink. "Thanks for dinner, now get some sleep." And he walked out of the kitchen.

Get some sleep. No thanks. That little voice in my head told me that I managed to sleep whenever he was around and maybe I should try that again. I drowned that voice in my coffee.

God bless Fitger's.

TWENTY

It was midnight and I was not asleep. After Van left the kitchen I remembered I still needed my clip back and had knocked on his door. He handed the clip over rather begrudgingly and I noticed he was working on his computer. I asked him how things were going with work and he looked a little sheepish when he figured out I saw his Facebook page. I asked if I could see a few more pictures of Lillie and he grabbed the computer and brought it over to the bed.

He showed me about twenty different albums of her. The first one was when she looked to be about twelve and she and Van were standing before a judge. Turns out it was the day he was officially adopting her and she became Lillie Walsh. She shared his last name now and he told me it was the best day of his life. Then it was her in the marching band playing the saxophone and him and Lillie at her graduation followed by their trip to Ireland. The next shot was of Van hanging upside down kissing the Blarney Stone! I was laughing because all Lillie managed to get in the frame was his shoes and his hands holding onto the iron railing. My guess was she was laughing too hard to keep the camera steady. Then there were pictures of freshman move in day at UIC. Van had had his arm around Lillie and they both looked like they were ready to cry.

He keeps tabs on Lillie through Facebook and it was the only thing that kept him from leaving Texas and moving to Chicago. I asked him if it would be such a bad thing to leave Texas and move to Chicago and that maybe he needed to do that if it meant that he could be near Lillie and worry less. I told him that I happened to know that they probably would find his skills useful and there were plenty of police departments that would take a glance at his resume. He laughed then slipping his arm around me. He told me it wouldn't be a bad thing to leave Texas. He liked the people he worked with well enough, but now that Lillie's wasn't there, there really wasn't any reason for him to stay. Lillie had no intention of moving back to Texas after she graduated. She wanted to experience something different. He told me he was trying to give it some time and some space to let the world settle down around him and then see where it led him. I knew how he felt. That was my plan too. Wait for the world to settle down and then get off the roller coaster and leave the carnival for safer rides.

We were sitting on his bed and he was tired, I could see it in how his shoulders slumped. I told him good night then promising him I had no intention of going outside so he could sleep in peace. He didn't look convinced, but wished me a good night and walked me to the door. He looked like he was thinking about saying something more, but stopped short and I turned to my room clicking the door shut. I had lain there for too many hours thinking about the day and the man in the room across the hall.

I was trying to figure out how it was that he could come into my life on a whim and make so many changes in such a short time. He had me trusting him two minutes in the door, something that never happened in my world. Unless the guy was just a friend and not interested in anything else there was no way I was going to trust him. Maybe that was why I trusted him, he was only here for a short time and I knew his only motive was to keep me safe. That kiss on the pier didn't seem necessary to keep you safe Sugar, the little voice in my head said and I groaned at it.

All of this thinking was keeping me awake, but I knew if I lay there much longer I was going to fall into the night and dream. I thought about taking one of the sleeping pills I had shoved in the back of the medicine cabinet, but I was afraid I wouldn't be able to wake up if the dreams started and that would be worse. I went with plan B, which was dancing until I fell down and then passed out from exhaustion. At least when that happened the dreams would stop for awhile. I snuck out of my bedroom and made my way to the ballroom in the dark.

I had the music on low so that I didn't disturb Van. He had been up early because of me and I wanted him to sleep. He was going to be spending the morning outside tomorrow and I could hear the wind blowing against the window and knew that the storm was rolling in over us like a blanket, but not one that would keep us warm. Hiding under the covers until Sunday seemed like it would be easier all the way around as I stood staring at myself in the mirror. My clothes looked too big on my frame and I knew I had lost too much weight already. I stood on the floor as Hootie sang "Only Want to Be With You" and I leaned up against the mirror with my forehead pressed against the cool metal and the song took me back to that first ride with my dad in the Mustang. We had the windows down and the radio up as we floated down I-35 and we sang at the top of our lungs. My dad loved Hootie and the Blowfish. He would have loved the fact that Hootie was now a single recording artist.

"I only wanna be with you. Yeah I'm tangled up and blue, I only wanna be with you." It took me more than a second to discern it wasn't Hootie singing. I opened my eyes and looked at his reflection in the mirror. He was standing behind me in a ripped up pair of jeans that he had thrown on over his boxers, which hung out between the rips in his jeans and a long sleeved shirt that said "Guinness, don't be afraid of the dark". I kept watch in the mirror not turning around hoping that if I didn't acknowledge him maybe he would go back to bed and leave me to my memories.

"Hey there, fancy meeting you here. Is this the new nightly routine?" He asked lightly. I shook my head no and didn't turn.

"Tula, why aren't you in bed?" He took a few steps forward until he was nearly plastered up against me and reached out with his hand laying it on my shoulder.

"I'm not tired." I said, the words sounding slurred.

I heard him give a snort like laugh, "Sure and I'm not thinking about kissing you right now."

I whipped my head around and he was laughing at me, "See I knew I could make you look at me." And the funny thing was I think he wasn't lying about the kissing part or maybe it was me that was thinking about the kissing part. His hair was curled around his ears and his eyes were soft and I was thinking about that kiss on the pier. Stop it, stop it, stop it, Sugar.

Edwin McCain opened up into "I'll Be" and he pulled me in, turning me into the first steps of a Viennese waltz. My body responded immediately to the music and I felt the breeze blowing across my face as we waltzed. I was floating around the floor my eyes closed as he led me through turns, not talking, just dancing, flowing and moving like two flowers in the wind. I tuned out all the thoughts about how bad of an idea it was to depend on him this much and enjoyed being led through a dance that made me love life. It was a dance that let me forget about the nightmares and the pain that was my life right now. The dance floor was what made me smile when nothing else could by releasing the weight of life from my shoulders. There was something here that gave my soul a break from the demons. A break from having to be something I couldn't figure out how to be and simply be who I was. I was a dancer and I was dancing with someone who loved being here as much as I did. I knew it wasn't a good idea to love how it felt in his arms as he danced me around the floor and I knew it wasn't a good idea to like him as much as I did, but each turn he led me through and each time he pulled me to him to dance me across the floor was filling my tank up for what I had to face over the next few days.

"I'll be your crying shoulder. I'll be love suicide. I'll be better when I'm older. I'll be the greatest fan of your life." He sang to the music softly pulling me to him as the saxophone began its plaintive cries at the end of the song and turned me around in a circle held tight to him.

"Why are you here?" I asked breathlessly.

"Because I want to be." And then his lips were on mine and he was finishing the kiss from the lighthouse and I was reluctantly responding. He broke off the kiss slowly pulling back, his eyes a color I had never seen before.

"And my remote started vibrating off the **night stand** when you breached the door to the hallway."

I looked at the clock, "That was an hour ago."

"I know, but I also knew it was you and I figured you had a good reason. When I didn't hear you come back I decided I needed to come get you."

"I'm fine." And I was trying to tell myself I didn't need him and **that little voice was laughing at me, hard.**

"Go back to bed Van. You have a morning meeting with Jess and you better be on your game. You can't help me here anyway." And I knew **that was a lie because he already had. I tried to stop moving then, but he kept turning me and he laid my head on his chest and stroked my hair. I waited for him to pull away, and I waited and waited and waited.**

I finally looked up again, "Anyone ever tell you you're tenacious?"

He shrugged, "Once or twice. Wanna tell me why you aren't sleeping?"

I shook my head no, afraid if I opened my mouth then the whole story would come spilling out and I would lose what little control I had left.

"Do you always run on this little sleep?" He murmured softly as **the music died off.**

I shook my head no again and shrugged my shoulder keeping my mouth firmly closed.

"It feels like if I let go of you right now you are going to collapse on the floor."

So he didn't let go of me. He put his arm **around my waist and went over to the stereo system and turned it off. We walked slowly over to the light switches shutting them down one by one until all that glowed were the red exit signs. He moved me towards the door of the ballroom stopping long enough to lock the doors and walked me to the kitchen. He never said a word. I guess he sensed I didn't need words right now. He sat me down in a chair and made me some hot milk bringing it to the table in a mug and sat across from me while I drank it, quickly, praying for him to** go back to his room once I finished. I wasn't ready for him to know my secrets yet.

"Ready for bed now?" He asked as he put the mug in the sink.

"No." And the word came out sounding like I was one word away **from crying.**

He pulled me up and into him, "You know it's my job to protect you from things that go bump in the night even if those things aren't in the same world I'm in."

Oh no. "I don't think anything is going to be able to protect me **from the things that go bump in my night Van, but thanks for offering."
The last word came out hesitantly.**

"I'm not offering. I'm ordering." And he took my hand pulling me down to my room where he flipped on the light and searched for the bogeyman before climbing on the bed and patting my spot.

"Don't look so petrified Tula. I won't bite and I will stay on top of the covers. We both need to get some sleep, you more than anyone, and I'm going to make sure that happens."

I flicked the light switch off and quickly kicked off my shoes and made quick work of getting under the covers before he noticed my leg. I laid my head on the pillow and felt him soften next to me as he pulled the spare afghan over himself. He didn't touch me. He laid there and kept his breathing even until he started to sing.

"When you're weary, feeling small, when tears are in your eyes I will dry them all. I'm on your side when times get rough and friends just can't be found, like a bridge over troubled water I will lay me down. Like a bridge over troubled water I will lay me down." He was whisper singing the song and my eyelids were heavy.

"'Bridge Over Troubled Water', Simon and Garfunkel, belly rubber. I love that song. I think of it every time I cross the lake."

"I think of it every time I look at you. It's like you desperately need a bridge right now or you are going to fall into the water and never surface."

I lay still the tears falling down my face silently because I didn't want him to know how true that was.

"When evening falls so hard I will comfort you. I'll take your part when darkness comes and pain is all around. Like a bridge over troubled water I will lay me down." I started to drift off as I listened to him sing and when the darkness absorbed me my heart started racing and I fought to come back awake.

He put his hand on my arm and whispered softly in the night, "You need to relax. You need to sleep. You need to let your body rest mi mot."

"You don't understand." I said the darkness making me feel safe enough to utter those words.

"I know I don't Tula and maybe I never will, but I want you to understand that I will keep you safe tonight."

He began to rub my shoulders gently then and I fought the urge to bolt out of bed and run as far and as fast as I could. The idea of leaning on him was too tempting and too frightening to think about. But I was too tired to run away. I relaxed a little bit and he continued to rub my shoulders gently as my eyelids drifted closed and that darkness swallowed me up again. And it didn't take long before the dreams began like I knew they would and I struggled and fought against them knowing that what came at the end was the part that would leave me crying out and begging for the morning light.

I felt his arms around me then and he was whispering in my ear.

"You are okay love. You are okay." And then he was rubbing my arm in cadence as he sang an Irish lullaby softly in my ear. I couldn't understand the words, so I concentrated on his voice and the dream faded away and finally my mind slept.

TWENTY-ONE

I woke up slowly and I already knew he was gone. The dreams started up as soon as he left, but I didn't know how long ago that was. I glanced at the clock and was shocked to see it was nine thirty. I had to admit to myself that I felt a little bit better and the hours of dream free sleep I got should keep me going for at least today. He was off with Jess and I had a little distance from him this morning. I laid in bed thinking that maybe, just maybe, asking him to stay with me again tonight would be the best bet if it meant I got sleep before tomorrow. If I could swallow my pride maybe I might be able to pull off tomorrow night without looking like a fool. I also knew that I needed to tell him the rest of my story when he came back because there would be no more hiding it when tomorrow rolled around.

I flipped on the Weather Channel and watched the local forecast. They had been calling for snow last night, but by the looks of it that was certain now. I threw back the covers and went to the window pulling back the sheer covering and was surprised to see a pretty good storm underway. Mother Nature was not on our side anymore. I let the curtain drift back down and went into the kitchen.

I found a note from Van. "Coffee's waiting. I'm thinking pizza for dinner, let's order in." I smiled. What a guy, my two favorite things, coffee and pizza. I grabbed my favorite mug and poured myself a cup of rich cinnamon pecan roast and went into the great room. I could hear the storm howling outside and that familiar fear was back in the pit of my stomach. I squelched it, not willing to go down that road. I was happy Van wasn't driving on the roads in the winter weather. It looks like canceling the party for tonight was the right choice. Obviously no one would have come out tonight anyway. That was okay. I was staying out of the ballroom. Seemed like every time I went in there I ended up in his arms and that was not a habit that was smart or easy to break.

I went back to my room and showered getting ready for the day. I spent some extra time blow drying my hair and dug out my Danskin capris and sweatshirt from the back of the closet. Out of respect for the day I left my feet in my fuzzy bunny slippers Jess had given me for Christmas last year. It seemed like a good day to make cookies or decorate a Christmas tree. Since it wasn't even Thanksgiving yet the Christmas tree seemed a little weird so I went with cookies. I mixed up a batch of peanut butter cookies tossing in a cup of the peanuts that Margie had brought me this summer. Take that McElevain I thought as the mixer grabbed them and spun them into the batter. My nerves were jumpy, so I had the iPod in the dock and it was softly playing George Winston's "All the Seasons". God bless George Winston. As the cookies baked I enjoyed the aroma of fresh peanuts wafting through the air and I glanced at the clock. It was nearly eleven.

I walked to the sliding glass door in the kitchen and wrapped my hands around my warm coffee mug. Everything was white, the deck, the grill, the hot tub, the bird feeders and the woods beyond. When I was a little girl the first snow of the season always brought out the snowmobile suit, mittens, hats, scarves and boots. It always brought out the horribly off-kilter snowman that barely made it a day before toppling back over onto the ground. It always brought out the first cups of hot chocolate and marshmallows. It brought nature to life here at the lodge too. I remember spending hours with my dad scouting out the rabbit prints, deer, fox and the occasional bear print. I remember holding my mom's hand as we traipsed through the woods and she pointed out all the different birds that stayed here during the winter and we checked bird feeders and corn plates. The woods almost seemed alive after that first snowfall as the animals moved about looking for food on ground that was now cold and unforgiving.

After the accident the first snowfall always brought anxiety. It always brought back these kinds of memories and I always tried to busy myself so that my heart wouldn't hurt. I usually succeeded, but not today. Today the first snowfall was too much like that night ten years ago and my wall of protection had been all but stripped away. All that was left was the never-ending question of why. Why did I survive? Why am I here? Why did they have to leave me? Those questions have been there for years, but I've been able to answer them with logical thoughts. This year for some reason I couldn't make those logical answers work anymore. I felt like they were only excuses that I had put there to make everything go away, but they weren't the right reasons. My heart feels like it has been pulled out of my chest and trampled on and then put back in dirty and smushed without a chance to recover. Every little thing reminds me of them now. Maybe it was the ten year mark looming and once I made it past tomorrow then everything would go back to normal, but for some reason it didn't feel like that was going to happen. For some reason it felt like this was the end of something and I had to figure out how to begin again. Today I couldn't convince myself that everything was going to be okay and that hot chocolate and marshmallows would fix it all. I couldn't convince myself that I would ever answer the why that never lessoned its mantra in my mind.

As I looked out the door I searched for any sign of movement, but there was none today but for the fall of the snowflakes. It looked peaceful. The gentle falling of the flakes as they built up on the deck blending together and losing their identity to become one flake. Maybe that was what I needed to stop doing. Maybe I needed to stop trying to blend together to make one flake and be who I am. I let the thought wander through my mind as I watched the snow pile up. Who am I and who do I want to be? I know I don't want to be the person I am right now. I know that I don't want to spend every night in fear and every day afraid of the night. I want to be a dancer and want to love it as much as I used to before the accident. I want to be the face behind MAMBOS and I want to keep doing all the things I love and I want all the rest to stop. I want to be a place where my friends come to be with me and not come to make sure I'm okay. I want to be happy as everyone keeps telling me I need to be and I had to figure out how to do that. I knew that answer lay with answering the why. I told myself that if I couldn't answer that question by the end of the weekend I was going to talk to Julie and see if she could help me answer it. It was time. At almost twenty-eight years old I deserved to put this behind me and be free of the torture. I sighed knowing the whole night stretched before me and it wasn't likely to get much easier as the storm went on. At least Van will be back later the small voice said, probably afraid I would tell it to go to hell, which I did. There was already three inches on the ground and there would be many more to come by the looks of it.

I set the timer for the cookies and went to my office to do some radio spots for the dinner tomorrow night updating that, as of now, the dinner was still being held and to listen for further details to come tomorrow. I could smell the cookies all the way in my office and grabbed them out seconds from being burnt. The fragrant steam pouring out of the oven was mesmerizing and I set the pan on the stovetop and left the oven cracked to let the heat and aroma escape into the kitchen. My phone was ringing, vibrating and dancing around on the table. I reached over and grabbed it and stopped dead when I saw private caller. It was him again and I sat down hard in a chair.

"Hello." I was firm, but not harsh.

"Ms. DuBois are you enjoying the beautiful weather? It's a bit chilly, but the snow is quite lovely."

"Snow in November is always lovely, McElevain. How can I help you today?" I was trying to not tell him to feck off as Van would say even though that is all I really wanted to say to him.

"Well let's see. You can tell me that you have found the information that Margie has tucked away."

"Nope. Sorry I can't tell you that. I don't even know what the hell you are talking about or why it's so damn important. I do know that it's really rude to come to someone else's town and call and harass them –

and oh did I mention shooting at them, that's rude too." And I was kinda enjoying telling him off even if I had to be nice.

"Let me make it clear for you then, Ms. DuBois. Some of my paperwork, computer disks, and other important business information got left behind when my daughter and her husband departed from your lodge." And I was so far ahead of him.

"I have cleaned the entire lodge top to bottom, including where they stayed, and I found nothing like that. You know it is possible they took it offsite somewhere."

He chuckled then with a very annoying gurgling at the end, "Anything is possible, but I expect that you are trying your best to locate the information so that we can bring this whole unfortunate fiasco to a close."

"Do you have Margie and Nathan?" It was a stupid question, but Jesse had said anything is better than nothing.

"Of course I have my daughter, Ms. DuBois. You didn't think I was going to leave her in the hands of the Duluth police once I found out what her game was did you? Oh no, I have a special place for her and her hubby. They are enjoying the honeymoon suite right now. I sure hope they don't get too cold now that the snow is here. Let it snow, let it snow, let it snow." And the line went dead.

I slammed the phone down on the tabletop and that's when I heard the side door to the mud room open and close. I wasn't expecting anyone and Jess was going to call when Van was on his way. I grabbed my Glock from the drawer next to the fridge and pulled up alongside of the fridge. My heart was kathudding in my chest doing a double two step and my breathing was ragged. I held my breath watching the doorhandle turn.

"Drop your weapon and put your hands where I can see them." I yelled. Eat your heart out Cagney. The likelihood of me actually shooting anyone was slim. I didn't like blood, but maybe in a pinch I could aim for a kneecap. The door was pushed open and Van stood with his hands on his hips.

"Well, there's something you don't see every day. How about if you put the gun down before you shoot me accidently?" Wouldn't be an accident if I did shoot him. I dropped my gun, my heart coming back down to minor coronary level. I stepped around the fridge. "What are you doing here?"

"I live here, remember." Oh yes, how could I forget?

Van pulled his camouflage sweatshirt off and hung it over the kitchen chair. He went to the fridge and grabbed a Sam Adams, unscrewing the cap with his T shirt bottom. I put the gun back in the drawer and watched him from the corner of my eye take a long swig from his beer and set it down on the table, hard. Seemed a little early to be drinking to me, seemed like maybe he had something on his mind. His eyes were traveling up and down my body, raking me like he was seeing me for the first time. Stating that it was making me uncomfortable didn't begin to cover it. It felt like we were playing a game and I didn't know the rules.

"It's cold out there." He said. And if he got any colder in here the blizzard would be inside.

I busied myself with the cookies, "So how did things go? Any new info on McElevain?" For some reason I sensed it wasn't a good idea right now to mention I spoke with him.

"We know he's here. We know he has guys watching us and that is about all we know."

I got a plate out of the cupboard and put half dozen cookies on it busying myself to avoid looking at him.

"So what are we supposed to do?" Assuming that we made it through tonight without killing each other that is.

"Jess and I both think that there will be some communication made tomorrow night during the dinner like he told you. It will be a good place to have someone approach one of us without being noticed. They can come and go in a place that large and not be remembered by anyone. We have a plan put together we'll need to go over."

"Okay. Well mother nature has plans for tonight so I guess we might as well use the time to have everything set." I said lightly.

His words came out hard, "Yeah, word is the last big storm like this was ten years ago." My steps faltered, but I quickly regained my composure and carried the plate of cookies to the table.

"It is unusual to have a storm like this so early in the year." Play it cool Sugar. "Did you have lunch?" I asked him in my best hostess voice.

"No." I could hear the tone of his voice change to controlled anger and I stiffened.

"Would you like me to make you something?" I flipped the oven door closed and leaned against the handle.

"No." He picked up a cookie and took a bite.

"Oh, well, okay then. I have some work to do in my office, enjoy the cookies and let me know when you are ready to go over those plans." I threw the dish towel on the counter and tried not to run for the kitchen door.

"Jesse's a mess." Three words. I stopped dead in my tracks.

I turned and saw the anger in his eyes and the tight set of his lips. He twirled the bottle of beer around in his hand. I didn't know what to say. I stood there like a deer in headlights hoping this was about the case, but I knew deep down it wasn't. The wind blew snow hard against the pane and I jumped.

"Afraid of storms, Tula?" Van was on his feet and coming towards me looking more dangerous now than I had ever seen him with a gun.

I crossed my arms over my chest and held my ground. He was inches from my face now and I could smell the beer mixed with peanuts on his breath.

"Jesse told me a few things today that I didn't know." Van put one hand on each side of me pressing me up against the countertop.

"Well I'm glad you are getting an education while you're here." My voice was steely cold.

He glared at me. "He was a mess worrying about you with this storm. By the time we were done with our little chat I had him relieved of duty and on his way home to Julie promising him I would stay with you for the night."

"Lucky me."

"Damn it, Tula!" He grabbed my arms and I cried out.

"Sorry, damn, I'm sorry Tula." He let me go and ran his hands through his hair and over his face. I rubbed my arms and looked down at the floor. Realization dawned. When I got dressed this morning I was going to be alone and didn't put the covering over the titanium of my artificial leg. It was obvious below the cuff of my pants and where my foot was stuffed into my slipper. The game was up. I felt his hand on my shoulder and I shrank away.

"Why didn't you tell me?" The hard edge was gone from his voice.

"What was I supposed to say?" I walked over to the sliding door, turning my back to him looking out at the snow coating everything. The image was that of a winter wonderland, but it felt more like an unforgiving hell. "It's not something I talk about."

Van was reflected in the door as he walked over to me and led me away from the window. "Please don't stand in front of the doors and windows. I'm going to go defrost in the shower. When I come out we will talk about this."

He turned, picked up his beer and sauntered out of the kitchen. Goody, something to look forward to.

TWENTY-TWO

I was in my office off the ballroom when Van came out of the shower. I had gone in and used my office phone to call Jesse and report my phone conversation with McElevain. He told me I did a good job and he was sorry and he loved me and he hoped I was okay and not in too much hot water. And I told him I loved him too and it was my fault and to go relax with Julie. I could hear the strain in his voice and I prayed that he could get some rest.

I put the phone down on the desk and could hear Van calling for me, but I wasn't responding. I had no intention of having a little "talk" with that man about anything. He could think what he wants. Maybe he's hurt that you didn't tell him something so fundamental about yourself. I told the little voice in the back of my head to mind its own business. I could hear him moving down the hall, the softness of his footsteps telling me he was in stocking feet.

"I will find you Tula," he called out.

The rest of the sentence hung in the air. I threw my pen down on the blotter and was about to stand when the door opened. Damn. Van stood there, hands on hips, hair freshly washed and glistening red from the unshed water. His eyes were dark shamrock green and his mouth was held in a straight line.

"I have business to do." I took my glasses off and laid them on the blotter.

"Well so do I. Business that could be life or death." I rolled my eyes at him.

I let out an exasperated sigh, "Fine Mr. Bond, let's go talk, but I need coffee first."

He gave me a death glare as I went into the kitchen and threw a K cup in the machine hitting dark brew. I grabbed my bottle of Kahlua out of the cupboard and poured in a generous amount before adding milk and coffee. God bless Kahlua. I took my time heading to the main room. He had the fireplace going and was sitting on the couch waiting for me. I plunked down in the big chair, room for one. The choice wasn't lost on him. I tossed my legs up over the arm of the chair letting the fire warm my foot.

"Comfy?" He asked.

If I looked close I could almost see the steam coming out of his ears. I batted my eyelashes at him and drank from my cup.

"Now I am going to ask you this question again. Why didn't you tell me the truth about the accident?"

I shrugged a shoulder. "You didn't ask." And I don't know why I felt the need to aggravate him.

"Touché Tula." The memory of when he said that to me fresh in my mind.

"And I did tell you. I told you my parents and Brent were killed in an accident. You figured out I was in the accident yourself. Not much left to say." Technically.

"You're right Tula, you did tell me that. Maybe when I said how lucky you were to walk away with nothing but a broken arm you could have interjected the truth."

I stared at him drinking my coffee waiting for the Kahlua to hit my gut. "What do you want me to say, Van?" It came out much higher pitched than I had planned.

"I want you to tell me the truth, damn it! You had plenty of opportunities to fill me in."

I could see in his face that I had pushed him far enough. "Okay fine, you want the truth, here's the truth. I was in the accident that night. We were coming home across the bridge and a semi lost control and slammed us into the median before rolling on top of our car. I lost my parents, I lost my best friend, I lost my right leg and I pretty much lost my entire life! Satisfied?"

I put my cup down on the table fighting back the tears that were coming as the coffee and Kahlua turned in my stomach. I could feel the bile rising and I ran to the bathroom.

As I ran I heard him yell. "No, I'm not satisfied! I looked like a fool in front of Jesse not even knowing one of the basic facts about the person I was protecting! And where are you going?" He yelled as I slammed the door to the bathroom off the mudroom and leaned over the sink the coffee coming back up, still hot. I turned on the water to cover up the sound of my sobbing. I was falling apart, the storm and his anger breaking the last piece holding me together. There wasn't a chance in hell I was going to make it through the rest of the night now that he was angry with me. I was sitting on the toilet with my head on the cool porcelain of the sink splashing cold water on my face trying to get my frayed nerves under control. My stomach hurt and I knew it was because I hadn't eaten anything today. You forgot I tried to tell myself, but I knew that I simply didn't care. I resolved that I was going to make sure that I ate something hoping that it would take away the pain in my stomach. I needed to go back out and face his anger, and I knew I deserved that, but I was hoping that if I stayed in here I might be able to put enough distance between us that he would cool down a little before we talked.

The door opened and I felt his hands pulling my hair back out of my face. He reached around and turned off the water. My head was balanced on the sink and I didn't want to look up. I was a chicken and I didn't want to see the disappointment in his eyes.

"Tula, are you okay?" he asked very cautiously.

I shook my head no and he tucked my hair behind my ears and grabbed the towel handing it to me to wipe my face. I tried to suck up some air quickly to stop the tears that hadn't finished falling.

I kept the towel near my face, "I'm sorry. I'm sure you didn't appreciate looking like a fool in front of my brother. I understand that you are angry with me and I deserve that. I know we need to talk, but right now my gut is twisted in knots and I need to go change my shirt."

He squatted down in front of me, rubbing my shoulder, "I think you need to lay off the coffee. Have you eaten anything today?"

I shook my head no.

"I can see that you have lost weight since I have been here. You can't keep going like this. I think it's all starting to catch up to you. And I'm not angry. I'm frustrated." He pulled me to him and hugged me softly. "It's okay. Okay?"

I nodded again. He led me down the hall to my room and left me at the door. "Get cleaned up and then we will have a nice quiet conversation that doesn't involve yelling."

I went into my bathroom and changed my shirt throwing the wet one in the tub for later and I brushed my teeth getting rid of the taste of coffee and Kahlua that was making my stomach continually turn. I grabbed some more Tums out of the bottle that now resided on my bathroom sink and when I came out he was gone.

I wandered down the hall and found him in the kitchen making a cup of tea. He had a plate of crackers and cheese made sitting on the counter. He handed me the cup of tea and we went back near the fire to sit. The storm outside was raging and even though it wasn't cold in the house the wind made it seem so. I sat down on the couch and he sat next to me, to my right, which wasn't lost on me. I sipped the tea and ate crackers and cheese at his insistence. He told me he wouldn't talk to me until I had something in me so my stomach didn't eat my backbone. That comment got him a little smile. So we sat in silence except for the howl of the wind and the scatter of the snowflakes on the windowpane and stared at the fire. I glanced over and he was much more relaxed than he was a few minutes ago and that made me feel a little better too.

Then he slipped his arm around my shoulder and began to sing softly, "The legend lives on from the Chippewa on down of the big lake they called Gitche Gumee. The lake, it is said, never gives up her dead when the skies of November turn gloomy." My heart did a little flip flop as he sang the song. "When afternoon came it was freezing rain in the face of a hurricane west wind. When suppertime came, the old cook came on deck saying fellas, it's too rough to feed ya. At seven p.m. a main hatchway caved in, he said fellas, it's been good to know ya."

"You learned the song." I said leaning my head against his shoulder.

"I did. It's really a great song, you were right. I love the story that it tells."

"Did you know that he actually changed the lyrics to the song last year? A Canadian film company did a documentary on the ship and they wanted to use Gordon's song in the film. Gordon Lightfoot has rarely given anyone permission to use the song, but he watched their film and he was presented with the evidence that said it wasn't crew error or a main hatch failure and he was so impressed that he allowed them to use the song. Then he also changed the lyrics in the song to better reflect what happened. So now when he sings it at concerts instead of singing at seven p.m. a main hatchway caved in. He changed it to at seven p.m. it grew dark it was then that he said fellas it's been good to know ya."

"The song is really old. Did it matter that much to change the lyrics?"

"It mattered to the family members of the crew. By saying the main hatchway gave in it insinuated that the crew didn't secure it properly and crew error caused the hatches to flood and the boat to sink. The latest research shows it actually could have been a rogue wave that hit the boat and sank her. We won't ever know for sure, but I respect that he felt strong enough about the new evidence to change the song. I've been in a place where people say it was your loved one's fault and that's really hard to swallow. I have great respect for him for doing that."

"You mean people actually thought your father was to blame for the accident?!" He turned and looked at me stunned.

I shrugged my shoulder wishing I hadn't said anything. "It has been my experience that people will believe what they want to believe. I know that my dad was not to blame for what happened. I'm pretty sure that he didn't force the semi to run him into the embankment since I was there, but like anything people will always assume the worst before knowing the facts."

"That's really crappy." he said.

"It's actually the one thing that doesn't bother me anymore. The court documents tell the story and that's all that matters to me." The food and tea had helped my stomach and it wasn't hurting as much.

"Feeling better?" He asked me and I nodded knowing that the time had come to have that nice quiet conversation that didn't involve yelling.

"Will you explain to me then why you didn't tell me? I want to try and understand." And I hated that it mattered to me how much it meant that he did.

"I didn't tell you because for once someone didn't know. I was just Tula DuBois to you, a simple businesswoman from Duluth. I was like every other woman you had ever met. I didn't think it would really matter." My voice was soft and tired. I concentrated on the fireplace watching the flames dance and lick up the bricks as I sipped my tea. "I desperately wanted to be me, the me I used to be, for the first time in a lot of years."

He reached over and took my hand. "I need you to understand that as a cop I'm frustrated about not being told this. It's my job to always be assessing, always determining what the next play on the board is going to be. It wasn't hard to find information about the accident. Have you ever Googled yourself? I had all the old newspaper stories pulled up one minute after Jesse told me. If I can do it, so can McElevain and if he knows about the accident that means that he knows your weakness."

"Honestly, I hadn't carried it all the way through. I just..."

Van looked tired. He ran his hand through his hair and looked at me. "I have to ask you a question." He looked like it wasn't one he really wanted to ask.

"Do you always wear your leg?"

"Of course." I said between gritted teeth.

"Always?" He leaned forward and stared me down. I suddenly felt like I was a suspect in a crime. Heat rose up on my face and sweat trickled down my spine.

"Well, not always," I said in a resigned voice. "I don't wear it at night and I don't wear it, you know, in the shower."
I refused to look down. I held his eyes.

"So if I was McElevain and I wanted to get information out of you when would I drop in?" He asked.

I dropped my head and thunked myself in the forehead.

He pulled my chin back up with his index finger. "I asked you to be totally honest with me the first day I was here and you didn't tell me one of the most important things I needed to know. It opens up a door for someone to use it against you if they get a chance, do you understand that?"

"You're right and I understand that now. I apologize. I knew I needed to tell you. In fact I woke up this morning and knew that today was going to be the day that I wouldn't let anything stop me from telling you. I have tried before, but every time I opened my mouth something kept stopping me. I have a lot of fun with you and I didn't want to ruin that. I know it was selfish not to tell you, but I don't know, I liked having one person in my world not knowing."

"Why would telling me about your leg ruin the fun we have?" He asked quietly.

"Because not everyone understands that having an artificial leg doesn't stop me from doing what I want and they slowly start to treat me differently. They start to think they need to compensate for it somehow. I feel really comfortable with you and I need that right now. I need someone who believes in me right now and my tired brain thought that maybe, just maybe, a complete stranger could do what no one else has been able to do and that's help me move on. It was stupid and I'm sorry. You deserved more respect than that and you shouldn't have had to hear it from Jesse. You deserved to hear it from me."

"As a cop I was really angry when I found out you lied to me because that makes my job harder, but as a man I understand why you didn't tell me. It's not stupid and you're wrong, you aren't like every other woman I have ever met. You are so much more than any other woman I have ever met. The fact that you don't have a leg doesn't change a damn thing for me, Tula. You have more than proven to me that it doesn't stop you from doing anything you want to do and there is no question in my mind that I don't need to compensate for that. I would have treated you differently as a cop, but not as a man. I want that on the record because as a man I think you are amazing and incredibly sexy."

I was pretty sure I was blushing.

He leaned over and kissed me, a gentle kiss, "Yeah, incredibly sexy." he said, nodding.

"You're embarrassing me." I said shyly.

He pulled me into him then and I laid my head on his chest. "Can I ask you something?" I asked him.

"Sure."

"Did you really not know? I mean down deep did you really not suspect anything?"

"In other words did you pull off being normal?" Which he put in quotation marks with his fingers.

"Yeah, I guess."

"You dance like an angel and you move so fluidly that even though I suspected that you had a problem, I never went that far, but I knew something wasn't right. There were signs. Your bathroom alone should have told me. Your leg is hard when I brush up against it when we dance, you drive with your left foot, your ankle doesn't bend and your toes don't move. Those were a couple of big red flags." I had to stifle a laugh at that one because I never thought of that, but he was right, my toes don't move.

"I'm happy that you don't have to wear those baggy pants anymore, these are so much better." He had my pant leg in his hand and was tugging on them with a look in his eye that made my stomach twitchy. "I was trying to respect your privacy as best I could by not asking too many questions, but I figured there was more to the accident than you were letting on. I decided that if it was something that pertained to me protecting you then you would tell me." He stared at the fire for a moment, "Does it make you feel good to know you were able to pull it off for a few days?"

No. When he put it like that it made me feel crappy for deceiving him. I blew out a breath the breeze ruffling my hair, "No it doesn't make me feel good. It makes me feel really bad that I led you on when you were completely honest with me. I wanted to tell you that day in the car, but my brain shut down and wouldn't let it out. I'm ashamed that I'm not a stronger person, but I've been too terrified of everything lately."

"You don't have to be ashamed of being scared. We all get scared sometimes. Look at Jesse, your big brother is so scared right now that he couldn't finish telling me your story without getting out of the tree stand and going for a walk. When he came back I politely pretended that I didn't see his red eyes. See, I've been that big brother and I've been that scared too. That's part of life. He was really upset that he said anything and I had to assure him that I wouldn't be too hard on you."

He laid his hand on my right knee and I tried to jerk it away, but he held it there with his hand. It was resting between the two ears of my socket nestled in against my knee. I took a deep breath not wanting him to see how much his touching my leg bothered me.

His words were tight, "I'm not going to hurt you, Tula. Am I hurting you right now?"

I shook my head no.

"Then why are you fighting me?"

"Because no one touches my leg, no one."

He still didn't move his hand. "Why not?"

"Because the last time I let a man touch my leg things went bad quickly."

"Have I done anything to indicate in anyway that you can't trust me?"

I shook my head no again.

"No, because I'm not here to make you be someone you aren't. I'm here to make sure that when you wake up tomorrow morning you are safe for all these people that love you. When I look at you I see this beautiful woman, all of her, and I really like what I see. I see an amazing dancer who if she let loose would knock my socks off. I see a woman who has taken something as tragic as losing her entire family and turned it into loving a whole new one. I also see a woman who doesn't have a clue how men look at her. I see a woman who thinks that she doesn't deserve to be with a man for some reason that I have yet to understand. I can tell by the way you conduct your life that you don't focus on the fact that you have a disability. It's become part of who you are in your everyday life, that's why I never figured it out, and everyone around you just sees Sugar. They see you as the person, not you as the disability. But it's obvious that when it comes to men all you see is the disability. It's like you can trust that as a cop I'm going to keep you safe from the bad guys, but as a man I'm one of the bad guys."

"I know you aren't going to hurt me up here." I pointed to my head, "but I've been hurt here before. Really bad." And I patted my chest, my voice breaking.

A look crossed his face for a second and it looked like anger. "Maybe someday you can trust me enough to tell me what happened. Maybe someday you can trust that what I'm telling you is the truth. You are an incredible woman and you need to stop hiding and be who you are. It's okay to be alive, it's okay to feel alive and it's okay to just plain feel."

He leaned in then as to prove his point and he kissed me. It was soft and it was gentle and it was everything that I needed to feel right now. He broke away and blew out a breath, "Let yourself be safe with me. I'm safe. I'm not going to hurt you."

And I didn't believe him because the fact that he had to walk out the door when this was over was enough to tell me that caring about him was going to hurt in the end. I laid my head on his shoulder anyway and let my leg relax a little into his hand as he rubbed my thigh.

We sat there like that for a very long time before he asked. "Is there anything else I need to know that you aren't telling me? Anything that could put your life at risk?"

I shook my head. "You know all my secrets now. There is nothing else I can think of that you would have to know about me in order to keep me safe." In the sense of him being a cop. There was a lot more he was going to have to know about me to keep me safe from him as a man.

Van brushed a stray lock of hair off my forehead. "Okay then. I'm going to step outside for a moment because I need to try and forget about how beautiful you look right now and how much I like having you in my arms, so I don't do something unbelievably stupid. Call me if you need me and stay away from the doors and windows."

He got up and strode out of the room. I sat on the couch for a long time staring at the fire. So he thought I was sexy, incredible and beautiful. I hated to admit to myself that I loved the feeling of his lips on mine and that with very little provocation I would be the one doing something incredibly stupid. The phone rang then distracting me from the man who had been holding me in his arms.

God bless Alexander Graham Bell.

TWENTY-THREE

It was four in the afternoon and the storm was going as strong as ever. Julie had called and assured me everything was running on schedule for the dinner tomorrow night and she didn't need any help. I came right out and asked her if she was feeling okay and I heard the hesitation in her voice as she told me she was fine. I told her I didn't believe her and she told me she didn't care because that was like the pot calling the kettle black. I laughed then because she was right. I made her promise to shut down the computer and go be with Jess. I told her that he might act like he was fine, but tonight was going to be as hard on him as it was on me. She told me that he wasn't even trying to act fine. He had come home, crawled into the shower and then into bed and it was her turn to hold him because he was so worked up that he couldn't fall asleep even though he was exhausted. She told me that after a nap and a beer he seemed to be back to himself.

Then she lowered her voice and asked me in her serious counselor tone how I was managing the storm and I lied through my teeth. It was quite a performance I thought, but I didn't want to take the chance that they would decide to come over here. She didn't buy it, I know she didn't, but she had her hands full and I was a little bit grateful that Jesse was having a hard time and she wouldn't want to leave him. She made me promise to call her if I needed anything, which I swore up and down I would and then I hung up quickly before she could change her mind.

I needed to do something to work off my nervous energy so I went into the kitchen and started pulling ingredients out of the fridge. I was having a pizza craving and I could see there would be no deliveries tonight. I plugged my iPod into the dock and turned Brian Setzer up loud enough to drown out the wind. I pulled my commercial mixer forward and threw in flour, sugar, yeast, oil and water and got a crust rising on the oven. I put some homemade sauce in the microwave to defrost and started cutting pepperoni and frying sausage. I felt a presence behind me and knew it was him. The temperature in the room went up a few degrees whenever he was in it. He reached around me and notched the volume on the iPod down a few levels, but I didn't turn.

"Howya?" He grabbed another beer out of the fridge. "Smells good."

"I thought you were working." I said wiping my hands on my apron and going back to the fridge.

"I was, but between the music and the smells coming from the kitchen I couldn't concentrate." He smiled and his hazel eyes turned green again.

"Sorry."

"Not necessary, I like to watch you cook." The words were said in a much too sultry way.

"I decided to make pizza."

His eyes perked up at the word, "You're my dream come true. Will you marry me?"

I rolled my eyes at him and laughed trying to ignore how my heart responded to that question. "Do you like mushrooms?"

He wrinkled his nose. "I'm not a big fan of fungus on my pizza."

I laughed unable to help myself. "I feel the same way. I have sausage and pepperoni. How about onions?"

Van was taking a drink of his beer but agreed with a nod of his head. "Can I help with anything?" he asked, setting his bottle down.

"Nope, I'm good." I was far from good, but I couldn't have him wandering around in the kitchen with me.

"Jess called me and told me that McElevain called. Why didn't you tell me?" He asked it offhandedly, but I could read the undertones.

"I was going to tell you, but then you know, we got distracted. I was planning on telling you over pizza." And I was.

"Is that why you were so upset when I came in? Jess said that he was a melter," he looked at my face, "that means a pain in the arse."

I laughed, "He is that. It's like he enjoys being able to dig at me and try to get in my head. I don't want to talk about him anymore right now. It just adds to the stress." And I went back to the pizza.

"That's the best idea I've heard all day. So seeing as I didn't have the benefit of a dossier do you mind if I ask some questions?"

I didn't turn around to look at him. "You can ask..."

"But you may not answer?" And I decided that was a rhetorical question.

"How do you keep this big place running by yourself?" I washed my hands and dried them on the towel.

"In the summer I'm not alone. I have a lot of help. I have a housekeeper who keeps the lodge cleaned and the honeymoon cabin changed over. I have lawn care and snow care removal. I have a great guy that comes in once a month year round and keeps my ballroom floor serviced and you met Mike from the Electric Fetus, he takes care of my sound needs. I have a small army of kids I hire to help me with wedding set up and tear down. I couldn't do this alone." I set the sausage aside to cool and put the pan in the sink.

"I figured that was the case, but I had to be sure. You do come across as wonder woman." I turned and he winked at me.

"So why does everyone call you Sugar? I finally feel comfortable enough to ask, but it strikes me as something very personal."

I wiped my hands on the dishcloth and went over to the table and sat down. "When I was a little girl my mom used to make pies all the time. She baked everything really, but pies were her specialty. She would make pies for restaurants and bakeries in the area so she could stay home with me while my dad worked."

Van was leaned back in his chair one leg crossed over his knee and he leaned forward. "Your face lights up when you talk about her, did you know that?"

"I didn't know that, but I know my heart lights up when I talk about her and the ache disappears for a few moments." He tentatively put his hand over mine and I didn't pull back.

"So every night when my dad would come home from work he would come in and find my mother and me in the kitchen. He would pick me up and give me a kiss and all he would taste was sugar, because I had been in the kitchen all day with mom. It didn't take long and he started calling me Sugar Lips. My dad called me Sugar Lips till the day he died, but eventually everyone shortened it to Sugar and it stuck. My mother was the only one who ever called me Tula, besides Jesse when he wants to make me feel guilty."

Van feigned shock. "I imagine that hardly ever happens."

"Only about once a week."

"I like the name Tula. Did you know that it means strength? I think that's fitting."

I could feel myself blushing and I ducked my head. "I didn't know that either." I got up and took out the deep dish pan pouring olive oil in the bottom letting it soak into the cast iron. I worked stretching the dough and putting it into the pan for the second rise.

"I couldn't help but notice all the pictures and awards in your office. Why don't you compete anymore?"

I was silent fiddling with the edge of the pizza dough. Admitting the real reason why always felt like admitting defeat. My silence wasn't lost on him.

"I'm sorry, forget I asked." He said softly.

"No, it's okay. I don't compete anymore because," I indicated in the direction of my leg and held up my arm.

Van shook his head. "No one would ever know. When you dance it's like you aren't even connected to reality. You're just, I don't know, it's like you lose yourself."

Dance was my escape, but it didn't mean I could fool everyone. "I've gotten good at optical illusions, but there are certain things I can't do. I can't point toe and I can't do some moves correctly. When you dance as a couple you are judged as a couple and I won't put that on anyone else. I get to go to competitions as an instructor and dance with my male students. It gives me an opportunity to be on the floor, but only the student is getting judged." I could never step out on a dance floor in a competition setting because the pain of not being there with Brent would be too great. I was not going to share that with him. He already had a way of getting too much out of me.

"That leads me to my next question and if you don't want to answer me that's okay I'll understand."

I raised an eyebrow at him. "Okay."

"Was it hard to learn to walk and dance again? You make it looks so natural, but for some reason I have a feeling it was earned."

I blew out a breath blowing my bangs off my forehead.

"Again, you don't have to tell me." He looked almost embarrassed that he asked.

"No, it's okay. I get asked that a lot. It was as much psychological as it was physical. You wake up one morning and you go about your regular routine and the next morning you wake up and half your leg is missing. No matter how many times someone tells you that it was for the best and that you made the right decision you second guess yourself. You play the What If game and you think that maybe you made the absolute wrong decision. You remember during the day why it was a good idea and at night you want to scream because getting to the bathroom is a production and your tired mind forgets that you don't have a leg and you fall down. Half the time it feels like your foot is still there only it's on fire or it has a bad case of pins and needles that you can't get rid of. You kind of go through the days trying to make it from morning to night and hope the next day gets better. But then, slowly, things start to heal and pretty soon you are sitting there putting on that first prosthesis, which is nothing more than a block of wood on a stick. You pull yourself up between those parallel bars and you look at yourself in the mirror at the end of the bars and you are petrified to take that first step. So you take a deep breath and put one foot in front of the other and after the first couple of steps you gain a little confidence. Pretty soon you are at the end of the parallel bars and you are staring at yourself in the mirror and the person you see staring back at you is doing high fives and fist pumps because you just watched yourself do something that you never thought you would ever do again. And then you turn around and never look back."

"It wasn't that easy though, the never looking back part, was it?" he asked.

"No it wasn't. Sometimes it seemed like it was one step forward and two steps back. Sometimes I was in Trey's office two, three or four times a week trying to tweak things so that it felt natural again. It took me a long time to figure out it was never going to feel natural and once I accepted that things got a little easier. The hardest part was learning to trust that I wasn't going to fall. That the leg was going to do its job. It's hard to explain it to someone who hasn't had the experience. Take for example stairs. You know when you go down a stair and you feel the edge of the step under your foot and you roll down to the next?"

"Yeahhhh"

"Well with a prosthetic foot you can't feel that. You can't feel anything. The only thing you feel is what's at the bottom of your limb, not the bottom of your foot, so I have to judge the pressure on my limb to tell me if I have a secure footing, which is a whole different sensation than what you feel on your foot. Does that make sense?"

He nodded.

"It was learning where to put my foot so that I wasn't on the edge of a step or on a ridge or on someone else's foot." He laughed then at the image of me standing on someone's foot without knowing it. "Balance was a whole new thing to learn because the dynamic feet are made to do all the things that your own foot does, but in a much different way. The way your leg sits down into the socket doesn't prevent you from pitching forward or back if you hit an uneven patch of ground. For a long time I had to walk up and down inclines at an angle in order to keep from getting too much forward momentum or throwing my kneecap up against the socket. I guess the hardest part was learning different ways to do the same things I had done before and being patient with how long those things can take."

I shrugged my shoulder. "You get used to it. It becomes who you are. One day you wake up and everything clicks. I have found a few upsides over the years though and they tend to make up for some of the inconveniences."

That got his attention, "Upsides?"

I smiled and leaned up against the cupboard, "Yeah, upsides. Like I only have to shave one leg, my socks last twice as long and I always have a great Halloween costume." He was turning red laughing at me. "Oh and let's not forget that I can stumble around like a fool and no one assumes I'm drunk. One time I got pulled over by a new cop in town and I will be the first to admit I was speeding. So he pulls me over and asks me to get out of the car. I get out of the car and it's late and I'm tired and I had been driving for a long time so my leg was wobbly. So of course he assumes I'd been drinking and he asks me to do the sobriety tests. I blow a zero on the breathalyzer, but I guess he decides that I'm on drugs or something so he wants me to do all the tests. I was trying to tell him that it was probably not going to work, but he was all, "Just do as I tell you miss". Well I can't walk heel-to-toe very well and I immediately fall right over." I shook my head at the memory, "So I was trying to explain to him who I was and that

I really was fine and could I have my ticket and go home. He wasn't having any of it so I finally sat down on the curb to pull my leg off so he would understand and another patrol pulls up, a buddy of Jesse's, and he pulls the guy aside and they have a conversation. The young cop comes back and was like, "Sorry Ms. Sugar I uhh, you can go now." I imitated his voice and Van was laughing and nodding like he'd been there. "So yeah, there are a few upsides." I finished.

"You have a great attitude."

"I didn't at first. I was really a pain in the beginning, but I figured out pretty quickly you aren't going to survive very well in this world without one."

"I agree. Okay, now I promise not to ask any more heavy questions." He leaned back in his chair.

"What's your favorite color?"

"Pink."

"I already know what your favorite drink is, so how about your favorite food." He gave me a smirk.

"Like you don't already know!"

"It's a toss up really. I can't decide if it's onions or Cold Stone." He said grinning.

"Hmm, you're right, that is a tough one. Let's call it a tie." I said.

"Okay, agreed. Now when's your birthday?" I took hold of the freezer door.

"Don't you know you aren't supposed to ask a woman her age?"

"I think that only matters if they are obviously over like sixty or something."

"You just made that up didn't you?"

He nodded giving me a wink.

"December 4, 1983."

"Really you are going to be twenty-eight? You don't look a day over twelve." Liar.

"Okay, this might be dangerous, but favorite song?"

"'Piano Man' by Billy Joel."

"Whoa that was quick. Nice choice, a waltz."

"Very good. Viennese to be exact." And I'm pretty sure he thought I was a dork.

"Favorite movie?"

"That's easy, X-Men." His eyebrows shot up in surprise.

"Really I was expecting like Dirty Dancing or something."

I rolled my eyes. "I was three when that movie came out! It's a good movie, but the X-Men series is far better."

"I suppose if you like all that testosterone in one place." He winked at me.

I didn't think it wise to tell him that was the only place I got testosterone. I was putting the crust in the oven when a large gust of wind came roaring through the trees throwing snow and crusty ice against the sliding glass doors. I jumped, dropping the pan and burning my hand on the oven door. He was at my side in two strides. He stuck my hand under the cold water and bent down to get the pan putting it in the oven and then reached over me to get the towel. I turned my head so he wouldn't see the tears. The storm was literally tearing me apart inside and I wasn't sure how much longer I could hide it. He shut the faucet off and took the towel drying my hand. He brought my hand up and kissed the burn letting his lips linger.

"You look absolutely knackered and it's killing me to watch." His voice was strained and he held my arm between us like I might break if he let me go.

"I don't know what that means." I was still fighting the tears and my voice was full.

"It means tired, broken." he whispered.

It almost seemed like he understood. If things had been different I might have been able to tell him how broken I was. I tried to pull my hand from his when Michael Bublé filled the room with "Lost". His fingers traced the scar on my arm then he pulled me into him tightly, protectively, and began swaying me back and forth. Against my better judgement I laid my head on his shoulder. He smelled like the ever present Irish Spring and his warmth enveloped me. His heartbeat was even, whereas mine was jumping from fear and pain, and something else. Something that only happened when I was near him.

He rested his cheek against mine. "Do you want to talk about it?"

"I can't."

He sang along to the song pulling my hand up into his chest. "Summer turned to winter and the snow it turned to rain and the rain turned into tears upon your face." He was moving me back and forth around the kitchen as he sang in his deep baritone voice.

"Why is that?" he asked softly.

"I just can't. I talked to someone about it once and it didn't work out."

"Then he wasn't the right person." And that wins the award for understatement of the year.

He slowed his steps and began more of a slow dance turning me in a slow circle. "I've only been here a few days and it's everything I can do not to beg you to let me help you. I can understand why Jesse is so worried. If you were my sister," he paused, "I don't know. All I know is that it's killing me to watch."

I took a deep breath. "I need to work this out on my own, once and for all." And it made my heart jump to know that he cared enough to be so bothered by my pain.

172

"I hope you're right Tula. There are so many people that care about you." And I was really starting to feel like he was one of them. There was a thought that didn't help my heart slow its pace.

I tensed up and started to pull away knowing that spending any more time in his arms would be a mistake, but he held me to him whispering in my ear, "Just relax and dance with me." And I was trying to relax, but the way he was rubbing my back was making that nearly impossible. "Relax. Forget about the storm. Relax, you are safe here with me." He was whispering in my ear and I concentrated on his warm breath against my skin. I felt myself begin to relax and my shoulders lost some of their tension. "There ya go oul doll just relax."

The song ended and another started, but I didn't pull away. I knew I should, but for the first time in days my whole being wasn't in tatters. He was singing along quietly with Mr. Bublé, "And in the end when life has got you down you've got someone here that you can wrap your arms around. So hold on to me tight. Hold on to me tonight. We are stronger here together than we could ever be alone. So hold on to me don't you ever let me go."

If only it were that simple, but it was so far from that. I wasn't even dancing anymore. I was just standing there in his arms while he sang. I could listen to him sing all night until I fell asleep in his arms again and made it to tomorrow morning wrapped up safe from the storm, but I would be far from safe when it came to him and I knew it. I finally pulled away knowing I had to get out of his arms.

He looked down and smiled at me tucking a lock of hair behind my ear. "You are stronger than you think Tula."

He leaned down and kissed me not as gently as before letting his lips linger long enough for me to taste the beer on his lips and long enough for me to want to take it further. He pulled back for a second and then kissed me again taking it deeper before he seemed to snap out of his trance and pull away. He managed to take my mind of the storm with that kiss, but the fact that I wanted more sent a new skittering through my stomach.

He hugged me to him and took a couple of deep breaths. "How about a cold beer?"

I cleared my throat not trusting my voice. "Please."

He grabbed one for me and one for him and pulled the caps off. He handed me mine and picked up his line of questioning like nothing ever happened.

"What do you like to do when you aren't dancing? I know you obviously enjoying carving and the campfire, but what else? What can't you wait to do when you turn the lights off in the ballroom?"

"I like kayaking and being on the lake in the summer. In the winter I like snowshoeing. I spend a lot of time listening to new music and in the winter I read, a lot." We sat together at the table sharing a beer and firing questions back and forth. His favorite color is black and his favorite food is pizza.

"So, what is your favorite song?" I eyed him curiously the beer forcing me to relax and forget about the storm.

"'You Send Me' by Sam Cooke."

I clapped my hands together out of surprise. "You lie!"

The corners of his mouth upturned ever so slightly. "I'm not codding ya. It's a hell of a foxtrot." He took a swig of his beer. The Irish are strange, strange people.

I rolled my eyes.

"What?" He had that look in his eye again and I could see that he was enjoying himself.

"The foxtrot? The foxtrot is boring."

His grin was lopsided. "Have you ever done the foxtrot with me to Sam Cooke?" He was flirting and I was unwillingly responding.

I tipped my shoulder and took a swig of my beer.

"Someday you will and then you will have a whole new opinion of the dance, that much I can guarantee." His voice was smoky and I dipped my head to avoid his eyes. I wasn't sure if that was something I should look forward to or not. The moment passed and the beer settled in and my brain allowed my tongue to ask the question that I wasn't sure I wanted to hear the answer to.

"Can I ask you one more question?"

"Sure." He said sitting his beer down.

"Has there ever been anyone, you know, that you were serious about? I'm just curious." Yeah right, just curious. How about dying to know, that might be a better statement.

"I had a girlfriend in high school that was pretty serious until she decided that while I was busy burying my grandmother that she would rather be at the beach with a different rugby player."

I grimaced, "Not cool."

He shook his head, "No, but now I can see that it was meant to be. I needed to come here to the States and that might not have happened if I had stayed with her. But once I took custody of Lillie I didn't have time to date really. I was a full time police officer and a full time dad. When most guys my age were going out to the bars I was helping with homework, going to school plays and falling asleep in bed reading the newest edition of *Parenting Magazine*." He paused and looked like he wanted to say something more.

I held up my hand, "You don't have to continue, I shouldn't have asked."

He twisted his beer bottle around on the table, "No, it's an honest question, but you are the first person I've ever told this to. All I ask is that if you ever meet Lillie you never bring it up."

"Of course. That goes without saying." I said curious at the change in his demeanor.

A shadow crossed his face and I didn't like it. "When Lillie first came to live with me she would act out. She would cry or have nightmares or overreact to the littlest thing. Most nights were spent getting up at least two or three times with her crying one minute and punching and kicking me the next. I didn't know what to do. I went in and talked to the counselor at school and together we decided that we needed to get Lillie into some therapy. She helped me find a counselor and I started taking Lillie there three times a week for "playtime". She would act," he struggled with the next words, "things out with the dolls with the counselor as I watched from behind a mirrored window. If her mother hadn't been dead I would have killed her myself. This little five year old girl had seen things and had things done to her that were so fundamentally disgusting that I didn't know if she would ever recover from that."

He stopped and it was my turn to lay my hand on his. It was his choice if he wanted to continue. I wasn't going to pressure him.

"For a while they talked about putting her in a foster home that was suited to deal with children with her problems, but for some reason Lillie trusted me. Even though I was a man she always ran to me and refused to leave my side, so the counselor felt that the best place for her was with me."

"You have an innate ability to make people feel safe, Van."

He shrugged his shoulder, "She was my sister and I wasn't going to abandon her because things got difficult. While Lillie went to her counselor I went to mine and she taught me how to help her and how to try to move on and live as a family. After a few years the dreams stopped and the visits to the counselor were few and far between. By the time she was eight she was a happy little girl again. She loved school and had lots of friends. So to answer your question, no there hasn't been anyone special in a very long time. Lillie trusted me that she was going to be safe and she needed that stability in order to keep moving forward. I refused to leave her with sitters unless I had to be working and I wasn't going to bring different women to the house because I knew that it could cause her a lot of anxiety. It was just her and me. By the time she was in high school she sat me down and had a very frank, too frank for a fifteen year old if you ask me, discussion about dating."

I smiled because he was blushing.

"She told me it was time to take my dad hat off and put my man hat back on, well you get the point."

"So did you?"

He shook his head, "I dated a little, dinner here or a movie there, but I had a very impressionable young adult living in my home and I felt that I needed to lead by example. You know what I mean?" Yeah, I knew what he meant.

"A father at heart I guess, huh?" I asked.

"Something like that. She meant more to me than anything else at that time. It was my job to make sure that she grew up right and had a good start in life. I shudder to think what my life would have been like if it weren't for my grandmother and it was my way of repaying her. I wanted her to be proud of me." He took a long swig of his beer and set it down.

"I believe that our loved ones watch out for us. Give us strength on the days that we need it and help us through the tough times in our lives. I have seen so much in the last ten years that has told me that guardian angels are real. I'm pretty sure your grandmother is smiling right now because she couldn't be prouder."

"I hope so. I really do." He said giving me a small smile.

I got up and checked the crust and it was perfectly golden brown. I pulled it from the oven and added the rest of the toppings before putting it back in the oven.

"How long until that masterpiece is done?" He asked his eyes roving over me.

"Can't rush perfection." I said more sensually than I had intended.

He looked like he was about to say something when his phone rang. He excused himself taking his beer and his phone to his room and closing the door.

He had easily taken my mind off the storm outside, but the one raging inside me had ratcheted up a few notches with that dancing. I let out a sigh. There was no question in my mind that he was the whole package, intelligent, maddening, frustrating, caring, gentle and sexy as hell. It was the last part that had me the most nervous. I could feel the tension buzzing between us as soon as he walked in the room. When he kissed me it was all I could do to not wrap my arms around his neck and draw him in closer. For some reason my usual hands off sign wasn't flashing on my forehead around him.

I shook my head and tried to focus on other things like walking on hot coals, splinters under my nails or falling from a twelve story building. I checked the pizza and pulled it from the oven. I didn't hear him come in over the music, but felt him behind me as I was trying to reach the plates. I was a little tipsy from the beer and was having a hard time not falling over standing on my tip toes. He pressed up against my back as he reached over my head, steadying me with one hand and pulling the plates down with the other. He set them on the counter and I felt his other hand settle on my waist. I froze, but didn't pull away.

He whispered in my ear, his brogue heavy and his breath warm against my ear. "Let's eat in the main room and watch a picture."

I nodded, afraid to speak. He picked up the plates and the pizza and strode out of the kitchen. I opened the fridge and grabbed another beer.

God Bless Jacob Leinenkugel.

TWENTY-FOUR

After the pizza and movie I went to my room and slowly got ready for bed. Van wanted to stay with me tonight, but I told him no. I didn't want to start using him as my crutch when he wouldn't be here forever. The common sense side of me said let him help one more night so you can be ready for tomorrow, but the woman part of me said that would be a bad idea. I told him that I had to make a phone call and assured him I would be fine. We both knew that I wouldn't be, but he let it go, at least for now. My thoughts turned to how much of a force he had become in my life over these past few days. With one inflection of his voice he could tick me off and with the next turn me on. I wasn't expecting this kind of reaction to a man I didn't know when Jesse plunked him on my front steps. The fact that he was with me all day only added to my inability to think straight when I was around him.

Watching *X-Men* with him was an experience. He spent the first half of the movie snorting at the action scenes as we ate our pizza on the coffee table. He joined me on the couch halfway through the movie pulling me into him resting my head on his shoulder. He rubbed my shoulder absentmindedly holding my other hand in his. I was grateful for the warm body and the distraction from the storm. When the wind howled and I tensed up he would smile down at me and I would slowly relax again. I threw my arm over my eyes embarrassed by the fact that I couldn't stop thinking about him. I didn't know how much longer I could take his presence in the house without doing something stupid and that kiss in the kitchen was not helping. If he ever climbed in my bed again I couldn't say with certainty that I would be able to stop anything from happening. Being that I haven't been with a man in a good lot of years the thought caused my heart to palpitate a whole lot.

I needed to stop thinking about him so I forced my thoughts to move towards that phone call I knew I had to make. I should have made it a long time ago, but I couldn't figure out what to say to the woman who lost her son on a night just like tonight. It seemed to me that a call from me was only going to make that pain worse for her and for a few minutes I almost had myself talked out of calling her. Maybe I should let it go and call her Sunday. Get over the anniversary, get through tomorrow night and then pick up the phone on Sunday and tell her that I'm coming to visit, but I knew that wasn't going to work. I was at a crossing point in my life and to be honest, I needed a mother and I was terribly afraid that she couldn't be that for me. I was afraid she was missing her son too much right now. One night had changed so many lives and I was beginning to think it was costing me mine.

I rested my forehead in my hands and took a few deep breaths. I tried to remember how relaxed I felt in Van's arms willing my heartbeat to slow. I picked up my cell phone hoping the storm would have knocked out coverage, but no luck. I dialed Sharon's number and held my breath as the phone rang. Maybe she wouldn't answer and I could leave a message. I'm a coward, believe me I know that. I heard a connection on the other end.

"Sugar?" It was Sharon.

"Hi Sharon, yeah, it's Sugar." It was so good to hear her voice. It had been too long and I felt sick for not calling sooner. We talked about the weather, how nice it was in Florida and how crappy it was in Duluth.

There was a silence on the other end of the line and then Sharon said, "It's storming? Are you okay?"

Her motherly voice was coming across the line loud and clear. I clung to it. "I'm fine Sharon, really. It's just a storm and I'm not out in it." And I've had one hell of a day and I'm glad you aren't here to see this.

"I got your flowers, Sugar. I didn't think I was going to hear from you." She sounded hurt and I didn't like that. Tears welled in my eyes and I blinked them back.

"I'm sorry Sharon I should have called sooner." My voice was a choked whisper and I couldn't say anything more.

"I knew you would call in your own time hon, but I have been really worried about you. Jesse made me promise not to call, but I almost got on a plane and came home yesterday. I wish I could be there right now for you."

"When night comes I wish you were here too, but during the day I'm glad you are enjoying your time with Len."

"Jesse told me the nightmares are back again." She said softly, but pointedly.

I held my breath. Damn Jesse and his big mouth.

"Maybe someone is trying to tell you that you need to deal with this and put it behind you."

"I have Sharon. I have moved on." Who was I kidding? That was the biggest lie of my life.

Sharon let out a ragged laugh. "No, no you haven't. You haven't even been over that bridge in ten years. You haven't moved anywhere." There was a hardness to her voice that I struggled with. I could feel a tear tracking down my cheek and I fought to keep the rest in check.

"Yes I have." I whispered not sure if she heard me.

"Excuse me?" I knew by the tone of her voice that she had.

I cleared my throat. "I went over the bridge a few days ago. It was completely paralyzing, but I made it."

"You weren't driving, were you?" Her voice had a deep note of concern to it.

I chuckled, "No Sharon, I wasn't driving, one of my friends was. He helped me through it and to be honest I feel like it has lost some of its hold over me."

"I'm proud of you Sug. You've needed to do that for a long time, but I know it still had to be rough." She was quiet and I wouldn't have known she was still on the line except I could hear the TV in the background. I heard her take a deep breath, "Sugar, I need to say this and I want you to listen to me very carefully."

My breath caught in my chest and I felt the tears starting, "I'm listening."

Sharon was quiet for another minute like she was trying to figure out how to word what she was going to say. "Sharon?" I asked my voice cracking, the sound of silence was harder on me than if she let loose and really told me what she was feeling. I can respect honesty, but silence allows you too much time to form your own ideas.

"I'm here, Sugar. I'm working at trying to make sure that I say this in a way that you understand. Each year that goes on is time lost. I love Brent, he was my baby, but now when I think about him I see the seven people he saved that night. He's my hero angel in heaven, but you," she paused and I heard her take a breath and I wondered what I was. I wondered what I was to her even though my heart told me I already knew. "are my angel here on earth. You are who God gave me because he knew that we would need each other more today than we did ten years ago. I want you to understand how much I love you, how much we all love you, and I want you to always remember to keep that foremost in your mind no matter what is going on in your life." And I let out the breath that had burning in my lungs.

"I do know that Sharon."

"I don't know that you do Sugar. Jesse told me that you thought the best thing for me to do was to forget about you and move on with my life now that I'm with Len."

"I swear that boy has diarrhea of the mouth!" I yelled. And I couldn't believe that he would tell her that. "It was a stupid thing to say Sharon. I know that and it wasn't what I meant at all. What I meant was that maybe you guys shouldn't worry so much about me because you are all moving on with your lives and that's okay." And I may never move on with mine, but that shouldn't stop them from being happy.

"I know what you meant, Sugar, because I know you that well. I've been with you for the last ten years and I know I'm not technically your mother, but I feel like it and I feel like that gives me the right to say no I'm not going to stop worrying about you. That's what mothers do. Jesse and I are so proud of you and I know your mom and dad would be too. Your dad would be ecstatic with what you have done with the lodge and your mom," Sharon paused and I could almost see her smiling. "Your mom would be over the moon about the dance studio. You are the place to be for anyone in ballroom. She would eat that up, Sugar! You know how she was." I was smiling through my tears. Yeah, I knew how she was. "Do you understand what I'm saying, Sugar? Do you understand that we are your family now and there is nothing that will change that?"

There was silence for a few beats as I gathered my courage to utter the next sentence. "Do you forgive us, Sharon?" For some reason that was all I could think about. I needed to hear that Sharon and Jesse didn't blame me for what happened.

"Forgive you? Sugar, honey, what are you talking about?"

"For taking Brent from you." I whispered into the phone. It was a question I had never voiced but had lurked in my mind for the past ten years. "If Brent hadn't been with us that night he would be here today." I fiddled with the corner of the pillowcase absently.

"Sugar, it is obvious to me that Brent had a greater purpose in life. If it hadn't been that night, it would have been some other night, some other time, some other way. We can't change the past and we have to live in the present and not worry about the future. How angry do you think Brent would be right now to see you like this?"

"Probably pretty angry. He'd be up in my face telling me to quit being so hard on myself like he always did when I screwed up a move or forgot a step."

"See you already know the answer in your heart, Sugar. I can't forgive you for something that I don't blame you for. Tell me you understand that, Sugar." I knew she was right, but for some reason it didn't make me feel any better.

"Yeah I understand." At least it would make her feel better to hear me say it even if it wasn't true.

"Jesse and I think that you should talk to Julie about how you are feeling. She loves you, Sugar. I know she could help."

"No!" I brought my voice back down to conversation level. "Sorry Sharon. I'm thinking about it, I really am, but I'm only at the thinking stage right now."

"You know not everyone is like Geoff."

Geoff was my one and only lover and the biggest mistake of my life. I had met him through a student and he came into my life on a whirlwind. I let my guard down and told him about the nightmares and the fears one night after having too much to drink. It became apparent that he wasn't interested in having a girlfriend with "baggage". He walked out of my life and I never heard from him again. I can see now that he did me a favor since it obviously was not meant to be. Some of what he said to me that night made sense, but most of it hurt me to the core and I was too afraid to open that side of me up to anyone again. It didn't seem worth the heartache.

"I'll be fine Sharon, I promise. Besides, I don't want any uncomfortable situations now that Jesse and Julie are dating."

Sharon hesitated long enough for me to know that she didn't know I knew.

"I know about Julie. He told me the other day. I was really hurt that he didn't cut me in the loop sooner, but I guess I have to take some of the blame for not being more observant."

"He didn't do it to hurt you, Sugar. He's really worried about you."

"I've gotten that message loud and clear, Sharon." And I had. All that was left was for me to figure out was what to do with it.
"I think Julie is great for him. He already looks so much happier, more alive."

"We all deserve some happiness, Sugar, but you most of all." Sharon said quietly.

I sighed, "I think the anniversary of the accident and the stress of," I hesitated for a moment, "the summer has me a little down. I'll be fine, really."

"Promise me that you will do whatever you have to do to sleep tonight, Sugar. Tomorrow is going to be a big day and you are going to need your rest." And it was almost like Jesse had told her a few other things about my life right now.

"I promise I will sleep tonight. I was kind of thinking about coming to Florida next week. I was kind of thinking that I could really use a mom right now. I was kind of thinking that maybe you could take me shopping." Sharon loved to shop and we had spent many hours together going back and forth to the Twin Cities looking for deals.

"Sugar, I would love to have you come down here. I miss you so much and I need to see with my own two eyes that you are okay. I will get a ticket and have it ready for you at the airport for Tuesday morning. Is that enough time?" And then I thought about Van.

"No, you know what I forgot that I have lessons next week I can't miss. I will have to look at my schedule and hopefully by next weekend I can leave. Is that okay?"

"Anything you want, Sugar, just call and let me know and I will make sure it happens. You won't believe the shopping options down here!"

I laughed then because leave it to Sharon to find all the hotspots. I could hear her sigh quietly on the phone as if hearing my laughter released some hold on her.

"I wish you could come tomorrow night Sharon," I said, "but I understand that you and Len can't make it back. I will make sure we get a tape out to you Monday morning so you can see the awards."

"I'm gonna be there with you in spirit, **Sugar, just like** your **Mom, Dad and Brent. You will only have to look around the room to see how mu**ch you have changed everyone's lives."

"I like to think I just planted the seed, **Sharon. Without the** volunteers and Julie I wouldn't be able to keep MAMBOS going."

"You think whatever you want to think, **Sugar, we all know the truth. I love you sweetie and I will be waiting to hear from you tomorrow** night. I want all the details!"

I told her I loved her too and that I would call her after the dinner regardless of the time. It wasn't going to be the same without her there, **she has been my mother for the last ten years and I needed her now more** than ever, but I was glad that she wasn't coming home. I knew that Jesse wouldn't want her here where she might be in danger. **I laid the phone on my night stand, rolled over and cried until I fell asleep.**

TWENTY-FIVE

Someone was screaming. I guess it was me. It was dark and the wind was blowing hard. I was wrapped up in my blankets, soaked in sweat and disoriented. The storm was blowing outside my window and the room was cold. I sat up in bed my chest heaving. My bedroom door slammed open and Van was outlined in the doorway, gun in hand, no shirt, Under Armour shorts hanging low on his waist.

"Tula?" His voice was low and controlled.

"I'm fine, sorry, I'm fine." My voice trembled.

He lowered the gun and walked into the room and over to my bed. "You don't look fine."

He laid the gun on the night stand and punched the button on the fireplace and the warm glow threw shadows on the walls. I was still wrapped up in my sheets and busied myself with untangling my legs, telling myself I didn't need his help.

"Cold in here, don't you think?" He turned around and smiled at me. I nodded and felt my bravado slip a little. He disappeared into the bathroom and came back with a glass of water.

He handed it to me and I took a sip. "Thanks," I said.

He sat on the edge of my bed, tentatively; one leg curled under him the other touching the floor. "Nightmare?"

I shrugged my shoulder.

"Want to talk about it?"

I shook my head forcefully enough that my hair fell and curled down around my ears. He smiled and brushed it back.

"That seems to be your standard answer." He was being too nice and I was feeling too close to the edge to talk. "This isn't the first time I've heard you crying out you know. It's just the first time you didn't stop."

I shrugged my shoulder again, a sign of noncommittal, not confirming, not denying. I bit down hard on my lip instinctively covering my mouth with my hand to cover the trembling. I tried to take a deep breath, but the tears broke free and slid down my cheeks and my breath caught in my chest. I knew that I wasn't going to keep it together this time. I knew this time I was going to sink.

"God, Tula, please let me help you." He pulled me into him and I didn't care. I needed a buoy, fast. He tucked me into his arms and leaned up against the headboard.

"I keep dreaming Van, I keep dreaming I'm back in the car and I'm screaming at them and they aren't answering me. Everything hurts so bad and I just want someone to talk to me, but then they open their eyes and stare at me, their eyes saying why didn't you come with us?" My words turned into sobs and he rocked me back and forth as I cried. I couldn't stop it. I couldn't change it. It was ten years of guilt and anger pouring out and the dam I had used all these years had been destroyed. Time was standing still and I was there again, in the snow, pinned in the car. I was screaming at my parents and they weren't responding. I was screaming at Brent begging him to talk to me and nothing, just the sound of the snow hitting the car and it was then that I realized I was alone. All alone.

"You're not alone Tula, I'm here." He was rubbing my back and stroking my hair. At some point the sobs that wracked my body diminished and I laid against him completely spent. His chest was soaked from my tears. I brushed at the tears and felt his muscles ripple under my hand and he sucked in a deep breath.

"Your chest is all wet." I said my voice raspy.

"Don't worry about my chest." His voice was distant like he was trying to keep me calm.

I was quiet for a long time. "Thank you for being here."

"I think this is where I'm supposed to be." And it didn't matter to me that he knew all my secrets anymore. It didn't matter to me what he thought or if he judged me. I couldn't do this by myself any longer. I couldn't go on pretending that I was alright. Maybe he felt safe because he wasn't staying or maybe he was really safe. Maybe he was what he was supposed to be and that was here. I felt the warmth of his chest on my cheek and the rhythm of his heart under my hand. I felt myself relax a little. He felt good and he was real. We didn't talk for a long time. We lay there, together, not talking, staring at the fire. Van had me tucked up into him tight, one arm wrapped around me rubbing my shoulder the other was resting at my waist. He kept rubbing my arm and I was finally feeling warm again.

"Tomorrow is the tenth anniversary of the accident." It came out as a quiet whisper. I'm not sure I meant to even say it out loud.

"Does this happen every year?" I shook my head slightly. He didn't say anything more.

I kept listening to his heartbeat and I closed my eyes. Thinking back, going back. "We were all in Duluth and a storm kicked up over the lake. We left the dance studio and headed for home across the high bridge. We never made it." My voice broke and he continued the long slow circles up and down my arm. "By the time we got to the top of the high bridge it was whiteout conditions. My dad never saw the semi. It

spun out in the lane next to us going way too fast and plowed us over."
The pain was so real that it was hard to breathe. "Mom and Dad both died
instantly. I could see Brent slumped over. I was pinned in the jump seat of
the back of the station wagon. I was screaming for my parents or Brent to
talk to me. I couldn't get to them. I couldn't save them. It took Jaws of Life
to get us all out. They rushed Brent and me to the hospital, but the storm
slowed them down. I knew my parents were gone, but I thought Brent
was going to be okay. They had to repair my arm with titanium rods and
my leg was," I stopped and took a breath. He was quietly rubbing my arm,
not wanting to interrupt, "my leg was bad. There was so little left to it. I
begged them not to try to save it. I knew I would never have a chance of
dancing on it again if they did. I had a great doctor that night who actually
listened to me, even though I was so young. I think he knew deep down it
was the right thing to do."

"You do seem to be able to get your point across when you need
to." he said and I laughed softly.

"I remember waking up after the surgery in horrible pain to
Sharon leaning over my bed. She looked like an angel at that moment and
she hugged me softly promising me she would never leave me. I begged
her to let me see Brent and she agreed getting an orderly to push my
stretcher into the ICU. She never told me that he wasn't going to be okay,
but the instant I saw him I knew he was gone. They rolled me in and Jesse
was sitting by his bed blank faced and I knew. Brent was seventeen, but
he looked like a little boy. Very peaceful. Sharon pushed me over to his
bedside. We thought we were going to be together forever." I sucked in a
shaky breath. "Sharon had already signed the paperwork to make Brent
an organ donor and she told me to say goodbye."

"Have you ever thought that when you see them staring at you
they aren't asking why, but rather they are trying to tell you they want
you to be happy and to find peace? Maybe they are trying to tell you to
quit blaming yourself." he said.

"That thought never crossed my mind." And it hadn't, at least not
until he said it out loud.

He shifted under me and lay on his side, propped on his elbow,
head resting on his hand. His other hand was still rubbing my arm as we
faced each other. "I'm sorry this is so hard on you right now. In law
enforcement we call this the lone survivor syndrome. Maybe you should
talk to someone about how you are feeling." His hand came up and
stroked my face catching my tears with his knuckles.

"What is it with everyone? No. Not interested." I looked down at
my hands.

Van was quiet for a moment. "I've only been here for a few days,
but I can see that you have so many people that love you here in your
world and they don't want to see you hurting."

"It's complicated." I said and he let that go with a raised eyebrow. Story for another day.

He reached up and tucked a wayward lock behind my ear. "Jesse told me a few other things today."

"Jesse should learn to talk less."

Van raised an eyebrow. "Afraid he will give away too many secrets?"

"I don't have any secrets." Not many anyway. Not any that really mattered anymore.

"He told me more about the foundation and about the dance lessons for new amputees."

"I don't make that a secret."

"He also told me that he's your only date, though I think he threw that in as a warning." He smiled at me softly. His finger was moving along my hairline continually tucking in the hair that fell free. "Makes me wonder if you live for Tula or if you get up every morning and make your way through the day trying to prove to everyone that you are worthy to have been the one spared that night." His words were quiet, but they hit me like a slap in the face.

My lower lip started trembling again and I couldn't find the words to try to convince him that it wasn't true when I wasn't convinced myself. "I'm trying to figure out the reason why I'm still here. It's been ten years and I don't feel any closer to that answer now then I did then."

"Wanna know what I think?" I didn't respond, couldn't. He brushed away another tear. "I think the reason you're still here is to teach all of us about perseverance and strength."

He slowly peeled the comforter back off my legs. He glanced down at my right leg, resting on top of my left and sucked in a breath. His silence was enough.

I reached for the blanket. "Just..." I choked on the words.

"No. You are not going to hide from me this time." He pulled the comforter from me and ran his hand down my leg tracing the scars. The ones that ran from the knee up and the one that ran just inches below.

"I had no idea." His voice was hushed.

I tried to stop them but the tears were too close to the surface. They slid silently down my cheeks falling onto the pillow. I closed my eyes and it felt like I was suffocating.

"Does it hurt?" He asked softly.

I shook my head no.

"Then why are you crying baby?" His hand traced back up my thigh to my waist where it rested gently. I took in a shaky breath.

"Tula," he said, "look at me."

I let my eyes come open afraid of what I would see, but he was smiling, "You are so incredibly beautiful and stronger than anyone I have ever met."

I shook my head no. I felt so far from strong and beautiful. I felt completely shattered and not sure how I was going to put things back together. I started to move away from him and he pulled me back cocking his head to the side. "You really believe that, don't you?"

I shrugged my shoulder.

"What's that supposed to mean?" His voice was sharp and his eyes were flashing green. I looked away.

"It means that I know I'm not beautiful or strong. Look at me, I'm a mess. I can't keep anything together. I'm sure you didn't sign on to protect an emotional wreck. You don't have to be nice and try to tell me otherwise. I see the scarred up flesh with angry welts. I know what its like to struggle to do the same things everyone else does. I know what it's like to think that you might have a chance at happiness again only to have that snatched away because he can't deal with the reality of who you really are. I know what it's like to be hurt that deeply by another human being." I trailed off putting a hand over my mouth. I could see anger in his eyes as he stared at me the words hanging in the air.

"Any man," he stopped, struggling to get himself under control. "Any man who didn't treat you like the beautiful woman you are doesn't deserve you." He brushed a stray hair behind my ear. "And it is okay to be a mess sometimes. Sometimes it's okay to let someone else lead." He scooted down the bed and began to feather kisses from my thigh down to my knee, tracing each scar with his lips as though that would heal it and make me whole again. He kissed his way back up my thigh stopping at the hem of my shorts.

He pulled me to him and traced my lips with his finger. "It's okay to feel again, Tula." Then his mouth was on mine, kissing me, tentative, testing. I kissed him back and he deepened the kiss tucking me into him, molding me to his body. My thigh was pressed between his and his hand was working its way up my t-shirt. He pulled back and we were both breathing heavy. He kept me locked to him. His hair was tangled and his hazel eyes were all pupil. I could see a war being waged in him. His body was telling him yes and his mind was yelling *NO!* I could hear that voice telling me that he was right and I deserved one night to feel again, to live again. Maybe it was time to listen. I raised my eyes to his and reached up running my finger along his cheekbone.

"This isn't a good idea." Van said, not sounding like he cared.

"Probably not, but I like the way you make me feel." I whispered.

He groaned and brushed his lips against mine again. I quickly deepened the kiss and our tongues touched and I lost all control over my thinking. He rolled over and pinned me to the bed, hands in my hair. He was kissing my eyes and I could feel his breath on my neck as he worked his way to my collarbone. He left a trail of kisses along my collarbone and up to my ear. His hand was resting at the base of my breast rubbing slow circles over my ribcage.

He whispered in my ear, "If you want me to stop tell me now honey. Twenty more seconds and I'll be lost."

I put my mouth gently on his lips whispering against them. "Take it slow."

He let out the breath he was holding and looked at me with eyes of fire. "Mmmmm, gladly."

I woke to sunshine streaming through the window. I rolled over feeling relaxed and mellow. Van and I had spent the night making love. He left me only to find the complimentary condoms I kept in the upstairs room for the forgetful groom. God bless common sense. We finally fell into an exhausted sleep at four as the storm was losing its punch and the wind was quieting. I reached out for him, but the bed was cold and I was alone. I sat up and looked at the clock, nine a.m. I had slept five hours again with no dreams and was starting to feel rested.

Van was leaning on the door frame when I looked up. "Good morning beautiful how was your night? Mine was wonderful with you by my side and when I opened my eyes to see your sweet face, it's a good morning beautiful day." He walked across the room singing in his baritone voice with a cup of coffee in his hand.

"'Good Morning Beautiful', Brad Paisley, rumba. Your voice is amazing." And I love to hear it. He leaned in to kiss me freshly showered and dressed in an Under Armour workout shirt and shorts.

"Going running?" I asked.

He gave me a devilish grin. "No I was hoping we could workout together." He handed me the cup. "That's to keep your strength up." I laughed out loud.

"You have a great laugh." He said and I smiled pulling my coffee cup to my lips. I took a sip and Van leaned over kissing my temple, then my earlobe, neck and collarbone.

"Can we talk?" I asked him and he pulled back, resting on his heels.

"Sure." He smoothed my hair back and it was hard to concentrate with him looking at me with those soft hazel eyes.

"I just want you to know that I don't do," I motioned with my hands, "this, all the time."

The corners of his mouth turned up ever so much. "This being casual sex?" I nodded. He took the cup from my hand setting it on the night stand and pulled me into him. His lips brushed across my ear as he spoke. "I know."

"Was I that bad?" Personally I thought we had it going on, but then with my lack of experience maybe I was way off.

"On the contrary oul doll, you were amazing."

I twisted my neck so I could see him. "Then how could you tell?"

"A man just knows."

He whispered a few ways he knew in my ear and then moved on to other murmuring. He laid me down gently on the bed trailing kisses down my shoulder and across the top of my breasts. I sucked in air as he took my nipple in his mouth. Fire roared through me settling low in my belly.

Slowly he moved his way back up my chest and back to my mouth kissing me. "You taste great." he whispered.

"It's the coffee."

"It's you."

Last night he had been caring and gentle. This morning he was feverish and barely holding back. I could feel the tension buzzing in him as he tried to take the time he thought I needed. I could feel his hardness resting against my thigh. I reached down and ran a fingertip up the side. He groaned and pulled off his shorts so I could touch him, feel him.

"You keep doing that and I won't last long." And to test him I went on a longer exploration. He froze, not breathing, not moving. "You are wicked." And his breathing was shallow and ragged.

I looked up and in one motion he tossed me back on the bed and before I took a breath he was inside me and we were dancing again.

When we were done we laid there for a while tangled together. "You are so beautiful and I love seeing that smile on your face." I looked up and he was smiling at me lazily brushing the hair out of my face and tucking it behind my ears. I could feel the color rising on my cheeks. "I'm going to tell you that every day until you believe it." He brushed a kiss across my lips.

But we both knew that would be hard once he was back in Texas. I pushed the thought from my mind.

"You do things to me, things no one has ever done to me before." He said twining my fingers in his and I grinned, wickedly. "Not those things!" He leaned in for another kiss and I broke it off slowly.

"I hate to bring this up," I said, "but, it's getting late and I'm starving." I heaved myself into a sitting position.

He groaned as his eyes traveled the length of my body coming back to rest on my breasts. "Me too."

"For food." I said slowly.

"Right, I knew that."

He got up off the bed and gave me the come here motion with his finger. I scooted to the edge of the bed and he picked me up under my legs and carried me to the bathroom depositing me on the dressing table bench like I was a small child. He bent down and kissed me thoroughly.

"Shower and dress, I'll go start breakfast."
God bless mornings.

TWENTY-SIX

When I came into the kitchen it was filled with incredible smells. Coffee, eggs, bacon and toast. Van was dressed in his fleece Columbia and Levis, hair wet from the shower, eyes bright.

"Good morning sunshine." He came over to me spatula in hand and kissed me until my toes curled.

"Coffee's ready." I smiled and grabbed a cup taking it to the table.

"Good looking and domestic? Does it ever end?" I asked.

Van laughed. "You are looking at the extent of my cooking repertoire, my dear."

"So I was thinking about what to do today and," he was interrupted by the doorbell playing "Sugar, Sugar" by the Archies and he raised his eyebrow at me.

I laughed and bounced into the main room to see who was at the door. I wasn't surprised to see my guest. He came every year on this day, but this time he had a friend. I threw the door open.

"Jesse!" He pulled the screen door open and I launched myself into his arms.

"Morning Sugar." He said quietly. He pulled back from the hug and held me at arms length. Jesse looked tired, but there was a barely contained energy about him. I darted my eyes to the woman standing next to him and smiled.

"Hi Julie." I walked over and pulled her into a hug. She was almost limp, "Are you okay Julie?" I felt her stiffen a little in my arms.

"Yeah I'm fine, Sugar."

She pulled back out of the hug and her eyes flicked to Jesse for a blink. He didn't look like he believed her either. I was ushering them in and was closing the door when Van came in the room.

"Who's at the door?" And he pulled up short when he saw them.

"It's Jesse and Julie." And Van and Jesse assessed each other, some unspoken communication happening between them. I offered breakfast, but they had already eaten.

"Breakfast?" Jesse whispered in my ear. "It's ten o'clock."

I linked my arm in Julie's and threw over my shoulder, "I slept late." I got Julie a cup of coffee and we both settled at the table.

Jesse came in carrying a vase of flowers and set them on the table. His eyes met mine and I smiled as acknowledgement. He grabbed a cup of coffee and Van brought two plates of bacon, eggs and toast to the table. Van and I dug into our food as Jesse and Julie filled us in on the storm. There had been the usual slide ins and fender benders, but nothing more serious, thankfully. The storm had dumped a foot of snow in downtown Duluth and up to eighteen inches along the lake. The further west and east of Duluth saw less as it moved south towards Wisconsin. My service had already been out and had me plowed out and ready to go. I was happy to hear that. Julie had already checked with the convention center and everything was on schedule for the dinner there as well. She insisted that I didn't need to do anything more than be there at six sharp.

"And to make sure you are on time the limo will pick you up at five thirty, so you don't have to drive out. You can sit back and enjoy the ride."

She was trying to be cheery, but she really didn't look good and it seemed like everything was a struggle for her. I knew right then and there that I needed to figure out a better solution for MAMBOS. She couldn't work full time, do MAMBOS full time and still have a life. I had tried many times to step in and help her with this dinner, but she insisted all I needed to do was the sponsor list and show up.

I looked over at Jesse. "I talked to Sharon last night. She told me that you wouldn't let her call me."

Jesse looked up and I saw him exchange a look with Julie. "I didn't want her to catch you off guard. I know things have been tough lately. "

I looked over at Van remembering how the night started and how it had ended. I let out a sigh and Van smiled at me softly. I looked back at Jesse. "It was great to talk to her." And I left it at that. Van felt the uncomfortable silence and I was grateful when he changed the subject.

"Green carnations?" He looked at Jesse mystified.

Jesse set his cup down. "The seven green carnations represent the seven people that live because of Brent's organs. Green is the accepted color for organ donation."

Van nodded and asked, "And the three white?"

"Those represent Brent, my mom and my dad," I said, "The innocent ones." I picked up my cup suddenly interested in what was at the bottom.

"And the pink rose?"

"The pink represents Sugar." Julie said.

Van raised an eyebrow. "What does pink stand for?"

I sat quietly in my chair hands in my lap. I felt Jesse's arm around my shoulder. "Thank you and I love you." I laid my head on Jesse's shoulder. He kissed my forehead.

"So Julie," I said, "You've been dating my big brother for eight months. How did you manage to keep it a secret from me?"

I saw terror on her face as she tried to come up with an answer.

"It's okay Julie, I'm happy for you, really I am." The look of terror fell away from her face and it was replaced with a huge smile that didn't quite meet her eyes. She pushed her coffee cup away and leaned back in her chair. I think she would have fallen asleep if we hadn't been there and Jesse jumped in almost like he knew this was all too much effort for her.

"You know that Julie and I have known each other for years professionally and through the foundation, but we really got to know each other at the Bowl for Life in March."

"Really? I was there with you that night. I don't remember seeing you two together." Jesse laughed. "That's cause you were too busy tearing up the dance floor all night. I had to find a new bowling partner."

I sighed. I hated bowling. It was a lesson in frustration for me. I tried to bowl with those gutter guards that they give kids, but they said that was unfair since I was over eight.

"Seems like I helped you out for once. I guess I have finally been replaced with a real date." I winked at Jesse and he punched me playfully.

We finished our coffee talking about the UMD Bulldogs and their shot at the Frozen Four his year. I assured everyone that there was no question it was coming back to Duluth. Julie insisted that the Badgers would lock it up, but Jesse and I refused to even consider that. It was the Bulldogs all the way.

I got up to clean the table and Jesse grabbed my hand. "Can we talk?" I looked over at Van and Julie, "Uh sure."

Julie jumped up and came around the table. She laid a hand on Van's shoulder, "We'll clean up, you guys go ahead."

Van shrugged so I followed Jesse out of the kitchen. Something told me this was going to involve uncomfortable topics by the look on Julie's face. Jess stopped and grabbed something out of his coat pocket, turned and took my hand.

"Let's go to the ballroom." I looked up in surprise. I suggested we could go to my office if he wanted privacy. Jesse shook his head, "No, the ballroom will do."

I followed him down the long hallway that led to the ballroom in the back of the lodge. Butterflies were jumping around with the eggs and toast in my stomach. I was praying he wasn't going to bring up the accident, but I knew that prayer was likely to go unanswered. The seriousness in Jesse's eyes and the tension in his hand as he pulled me down the hallway to the ballroom assured me of that. I had to run to keep up as he strode the length of the hallway in a few steps.

We opened the doors of the ballroom and I flipped on the lights. The room was chilly, but everything looked to be as I had left it yesterday. I flicked the thermostat over to add a little heat to the room not wanting to open the windows that faced the woods afraid of giving anyone an easy target. Jesse went over to the sound system and toggled over the on switch. He plugged his iPod into the accessory port and did some fiddling. I was standing there arms crossed not sure what was going on.

He walked over to me and took my hand. "Please forgive me for what I'm about to do, Sugar, but I'm taking matters into my own hands."

I didn't even have time to figure out what that meant before he turned me in a spin and pulled me in to him settling me into a sway as the first few strains of "I Hope You Dance" filled the ballroom. I felt my knees buckle and suddenly I couldn't breathe, couldn't think, couldn't move. Jesse pulled me up and kept dancing. We swayed in place, tears streaming down my face and soaking into his shirt. I crumbled to the floor and put my head in my hands.

Jesse sat beside me and whispered into my ear. "I'm sorry, Sugar. It's time for you to hear the music again, time for you to dance with your heart again." I looked up and into his eyes, eyes that were no longer shuttered. "This is tough love. Julie has taught me to dance again, taught me that it's okay to live again. I want that for you little sis. You need to know that you can do anything and you need to start by listening to this song again."

He pulled me to him and he sang to the music, "May you never take one single breath for granted, Sugar. Whenever one door closes I hope one more opens. Promise me you will give faith a fighting chance and when you get the choice to sit it out or dance, I hope you dance. Living might mean taking chances, but they're worth taking. Loving might be a mistake, but it's worth making. Give the heavens above more than just a passing glance. Dance, Sugar, I hope you dance."

It had been ten years since I had heard that song. It was the last song that Brent and I danced to together. It was a new dance to both of us, the California two step, and we were thrilled to take home the trophy for freestyle that night. It was two weeks before the accident. It was the picture on the fireplace mantle. It was my last incredibly clear memory of him. I could never listen to it again. I wiped my face with my t-shirt and Jesse held me tight against him.

"Van told me about hearing you cry out at night and that he has to stay with you in order for you to sleep. What are you going to do when he leaves?"

I closed my eyes and took a deep breath, "I need you to tell me its okay. I need you to tell me what Brent would want. I need to know you forgive me."

He sucked in a sharp breath and I looked up and saw his eyes harden, "What am I supposed to forgive you for? Being alive?"

Bingo. He and I both knew it the moment he said it. I dropped my head mortified to let him see how true it was. We sat in silence, the song long finished. He was holding me and rocking me back and forth and we cried together. Cried for what we both lost and for what would never be and then he released me, got up and walked away. I wasn't expecting him to walk away. I was expecting him to tell me everything was going to be okay. I couldn't move locked in place by sadness that had come down upon me quicker than I thought possible just a few minutes ago. I heard the song start over and felt Jesse above me.

He knelt down beside me. "I'm going to show you what Brent would have wanted." He pulled me up and there were still fresh tears in his eyes. He hugged me to him and then he started moving me through the steps that Brent and I had taken so many years ago. I wasn't thinking my feet were simply moving to a familiar song as my mind wandered back to times when I danced with my whole being. I reached up and touched Jesse's face. He looked so much like his brother. I wondered every day what Brent would have done, what we would have been, if he had lived. The song ended and he twirled me out and back into him pulling me into an embrace.

He whispered, "There is nothing for me to forgive, Sugar. It's like Mom said. We can't forgive you for something that we don't blame you for."

I looked at him in surprise.

"Yeah, I talked to mom. She called me after she talked to you. I knew you were bad, but I didn't realize how bad. No one blames you for what happened that night Sugar. You had no more control over it than I did. There is nothing for us to forgive. Tell me you understand that no one blames you."

"My head knows that Jesse, but my heart is still working on it."

He led me over to a table and sat me down. "You lost your entire life in one night, Sugar. No matter how much you tell yourself you have moved on there is always a corner of your heart that will remain shattered. There will be those days that you can barely get through because it hurts so much and everything reminds you of what you have lost. Those are the days that it's okay to call a friend and talk or take the day off and do something that you want to do. You go and go and do and do for others and you don't remember that you need to be taking care of yourself."

I folded my hands in my lap. "Van thinks that I'm trying to prove to everyone that I deserve to have been spared that night. Is that what you think?"

Jesse thought that over. "I think that you do amazing things for so many people and you love doing it. But I also think that part of the reason you pile so much on is so that you can pretend parts of you don't exist. So you can pretend that you don't need the fundamental human emotion of love because if you open your heart up it could get hurt again." And he nails it. "The last time this happened you got so exhausted it took you a year to come back to us. I need you right now. I'm being selfish and I'm going to make you stay well for me."

"What do you mean, Jess? Are you sick? What's wrong?" My heart was in my throat and I searched his face for something to clue me in.

"No, I'm not, Sugar. Not at all, but can I ask you something?"

"Yeah, anything." My heart was still pounding hard in my chest.

He looked off behind my shoulder then back to me, "Do you want me to be happy?"

I slammed my hand down on the table anger clogging my throat. "What kind of question is that? Of course I want you to be happy, why on earth would you think otherwise?" Jesse looked past me at some unknown reflection in the mirror. I lowered my voice. "Jesse you know me better than that. I have been prodding you for years to find someone you can share your life with." And I wasn't angry at him. I was angry at myself for letting it come to this.

Jesse nodded. "You mentioned it a few times, Sugar." He smiled at me and I laughed because it seemed that I "mentioned" it every time I saw him.

"I fell in love with Julie years ago Sis, and it took her a while to catch on and to trust me. You've been so," He made a motion with his arms like two snakes twisting on themselves, "twisted up that I just wasn't sure anymore. I'm just not sure anymore." Jesse sat quietly holding my hand.

"I can promise you, Jess, that things are going to get better. Things are already better. I'm trying to learn how to forgive myself. I still need to answer that question of why, but it seems like I can wait a little longer for the answer if I have to."

The corners of his eyes relaxed a little and he leaned back in his chair. "You seemed happier than I have seen you in months when you greeted me this morning."

Van instantly filled my mind, but I decided it would be better to not mention that now. Better not lead him down that path yet. "I finally slept some over the last few nights and I'm feeling better in general because of that." And there was a whole lot of feeling last night, a whole lot. "Now, you still haven't told me why I need to be well for you. Julie looks sick and you look a little tense. Is everything okay with you two? I want you to feel like you can tell me everything that is happening in your life Jesse. Please don't ever be afraid to tell me if something is wrong."

"Julie and I as a couple are wonderful. She is basically living at my house now and I'm trying to convince her to give up her apartment and move in officially, but she is having a hard time with that."

"Then maybe you should back off and not push her." And I should be the one giving advice? Hardly.

"I'm having a hard time backing off. She keeps having these spells and I'm really worried about her being alone right now."

"If someone would have told me I would have taken over this whole dinner tonight. I feel really bad. I want you to know that I will take care of the foundation stuff for the next few months so she can rest and know that I'm trying to find a more permanent solution."

He nodded. "I think that would be good especially considering what I'm about to do."

"What are you about to do, Jesse? Are you going to take a vacation and run away! I think that's a great idea, you both need a long break from life right now." My heart was happy that he was going to get some well deserved time with Julie, but he shook his head and looked very serious.

"No, Sugar, I'm not going to take a vacation, not right now there's too much at stake, but," he reached into his pocket and pulled out a sterling silver engagement ring. The diamond glinted off the lights and danced sparkles of light across the mirrors. "this is the reason I am having a hard time backing off and getting her to see that she isn't going to lose me. I want to make things very permanent. I want to make her my wife." And I was stunned silent. "This is the reason I need you to stay well for me Sis. I wanted to tell you first because you gave me the idea the other night at the table. I thought about what you said and I realized that I didn't need to take her away for me to know that I wanted to make things more permanent. I already wanted things more permanent. I also knew that I needed to make a new memory for this day and I couldn't think of a better way. I'm going to ask Julie to marry me at the MAMBOS dinner tonight."

Tears sprung to my eyes again and one rolled down my cheek. He put the ring back in his pocket and came around the table pulling me into a hug. I whispered in his ear. "My guess is this is what she needs to hear, Jess. Julie is an incredibly lucky woman."

He laughed. "No I think I am an incredibly lucky man."

Someone cleared their throat and we looked up to see Van standing there in the door to the ballroom. He strolled over and Jesse released me from the hug. "I love you, Sugar. This is only the first happy memory for us. We are going to spend the rest of our lives making more. It's time to put the sadness behind us, okay?"

"That's what I've been telling her." Van said putting his arms around my waist. I leaned back into his chest happy to have his arms around me again.

Jesse looked up at Van and then down at me, anger flashing in his eyes. He got in Van's face, "Man, I told you to keep your distance! I told you she was vulnerable and off limits!"

I put my hand against his chest, "Jesse you don't have that kind of control over my life. Relax, he's the reason I'm standing here talking to you. He's the reason that I can see a tomorrow. Please, take the big brother thing and bring it down a few notches."

I tried to give him a reassuring smile and patted his chest softly. Jesse looked down at me then and the anger fell away. Maybe it was what he saw in my eyes.

"Julie's waiting with your coats." Van said, "She said you had some place to be." Reminding him about Julie put the smile back on his face.

He bent down and kissed me on the cheek. "See you tonight at the dinner?" He asked bending one brow like a principal reminding a student about detention.

"Wouldn't miss it for the world, Jess, I'm suddenly looking forward to it. I'm still scared to death and sick to my stomach that McElevain is going to hurt someone, but I'm looking forward to all the rest." I said.

"Sugar, your job tonight is to show up and have fun. Our job tonight is to worry about McElevain. Got it?" Jess said in his most authoritative cop voice.

"Yes Officer Bowers, but something tells me you might be a little distracted tonight." I said.

"Nope, I have everything under control for tonight and even with the added plans everything will go off without a hitch." Jesse said giving me his thousand watt smile and my eyes filled with tears again and I nodded.

Van was obviously sensing something was going on. "Take the rest of the day off, Jess. I promise to call you if anything develops and I will hand deliver Tula to the dinner at six sharp."

Jesse gave a nod and reached out to shake his hand. "Limo will be here at five thirty. Make sure she's in it and make sure she's safe." He walked to the door and stopped short turning around pointing a finger at Van, "If you hurt her, I will kill you." And I had no doubt.

God bless big brothers.

TWENTY-SEVEN

We heard the big wooden door shut and I let out the breath I didn't know I was holding.

"How did that go?" Van asked laying his chin on my shoulder.

"Jesse's going to propose to Julie tonight."

"I'm not all that surprised. Good for him. He's a lucky man."

I nodded. I was really happy that Jesse was moving on with his life. I guess I needed to take a hard look at mine too.

"Can I ask what you guys were doing down here?" Van's words intruded on my thoughts.

"Tough love."

Van's head cocked to the side as he kissed my neck. "Really?"

"Yeah, it was good. I needed it. I think things might be a little easier now on all levels." And I knew Van was the one that had the most to do with that.

He whispered in my ear. "We have a problem."

My heart stopped. "Is this a bad problem? I don't want to deal with a bad problem." Not today.

"This is a good problem." He smirked, "We're out of condoms."

I bit my lip to keep from laughing.

"Are you laughing at me?" He turned me around and kissed me using just enough tongue to remind me what he's capable of.

"Now do you think it's a problem?" Yes. Definite problem.

"Do you have anymore hidden around here?" He asked.

I shook my head no.

"That's a shame, guess we will have to go get some."

I looked at my watch. "Sure, I have a hair appointment in a bit, so you can drop me off and then go buy the condoms, somewhere far, far away." I jumped away from him and ran down the hall before he could catch me.

We were in the SUV headed into Duluth. I asked Van to drive convincing him he needed to learn how to drive in snow. Really I needed him to be in the driver's seat. We were almost to the turn off for the Bong Bridge and Van changed lanes moving into the left turn lane.

I put my hand on his arm, "Go straight."

He looked at me surprised. "Are you going to be okay?"

I nodded and he changed back into the right hand lane and went through the stoplight at the Bong Veteran Historical Center.

Van reached out his hand and laid it gently on my knee. "So tell me, who's this Richard Bong guy? Obviously he has something to do with history around here."

I stared at him.

"Again, I'm from Ireland." And that seemed to be his answer for everything.

"Richard Ira Bong grew up in Poplar, Wisconsin, which is just minutes from here. He attended college in Superior before joining the Air Force. He was an ace pilot in World War II, having shot down over forty Japanese airplanes. He died in 1945 test piloting a new plane for the US government in California. To date, and this may be out of date, he has like 15 different places, streets or bridges named after him." Ugh. I sound like a tour guide. Shoot me now.

"Pretty big stuff coming from such a little place."

I looked over at him under my eyebrow. "We may be little, but we can be loud."

He grinned at me again and squeezed my knee. I knew he was trying to distract me from the bridge approach and I loved him for that. I let him get up towards the crest of the bridge where there was still a breakdown lane, "Pull over here please." I was proud that my voice was steady.

He didn't say a word to me as he slowed the SUV and pulled it over to the side of the bridge putting on the hazards. I tried hard to remain relaxed. It was easier this time. I focused on the spot of warmth that his hand resting on my knee provided. The storm had kept people inside this Saturday and as we sat on the bridge we were nearly alone. I took another deep breath and opened the door.

"Wait." Van stepped out and came around to the passenger side of the SUV giving me a hand over the snow piled on the sidewalk.

I took a deep breath of the fresh air. The storm was long forgotten as the sun glinted off the waves that rippled for eternity. The gulls swooped gliding on the air and dancing amongst and against each other. The harbor was empty. The air was warm, as it always is near the lake in the winter. I stood there looking over the railing at the lake that looked never ending and stretched to depths and to shores far beyond what my eye could see. It was time. I put my hand in my coat pocket and pulled out a necklace made of paper. There were three white origami and one pink one. They were small, all three white doves able to fit in the palm of my hand. I felt Van's hands on my waist as I leaned over the railing to the water below. He was silent, watching, waiting. I held my hand out and the wind took each white dove one at a time and they floated on the breeze to the cold dark water below. Each one landed seconds apart bobbing in the waves for a few seconds before being swallowed up by the cold, dark water. Margie had become my confidant while she was here. It was her nature to see a soul hurting and try to help them. She gave me this necklace before she left and told me that when I was ready I should set them free.

I closed my eyes and I felt Van stir behind me. "You have one left." He whispered in my ear.

It was a simple statement, but so very overwhelming. I pulled the dove off the string and held it in my hand, clutched near my chest so the wind wouldn't take it. Van reached out and put his hand under mine. He stretched his arm and mine out over the railing and the dove sat perfectly in our palms. I could feel the tears as they rolled down my cheeks, but all I could see was this perfectly folded dove that began to flutter in my hand and then slowly, perfectly take off on the breeze. We watched and waited expecting it to fall down into the water with the others, but the wind carried it and it blew onto the land below.

My chest was heaving and Van began to whisper softly, "May the road rise up to meet you. May the wind be always at your back. May the sun shine warm upon your face; the rains fall soft upon your fields and until we meet again, may God hold you in the palm of His hand."

I blinked back more tears watching as the breeze blew the dove like a tumbleweed safe from the water journeying to only the wind knew where. We watched it until we could no longer make it out. Van had wrapped his arms around my waist hugging me tightly against him. I turned away from the railing and looked up at him. His eyes were moist and I reached up and touched his face.

"Now I'm going to be okay." I whispered.

Van had pulled the car down off the bridge and onto the side of the road giving me a moment to collect myself. He held my hand and stared out the window.

Finally he said, "Feel better?"

"I don't know what I feel, but I know that I needed to do that for a long time."

He smiled, "It makes me feel incredibly special that you wanted to share something like that with me." And I already knew that. I saw that on his face on the bridge.

"I honestly believe that if you hadn't come into my life a few days ago that wouldn't have happened."

He turned in his seat, "You don't give yourself enough credit Tula. You have more strength in one finger than most of us have in our whole being. You just have to learn to trust it." He kissed me softly making me feel loved. And it may not be love, but it sure felt like it might be.

"What time is your appointment?" He asked.

I glanced at the clock. "It's at one, so we have a few minutes."

"Good just enough time for you to pick up the raincoats." And he swung the SUV back onto I-35 and headed towards the mall. He pulled into the parking lot at Target and put the SUV in park.

"Well, okay, then you can run in to Target and get them while I keep the car running and warm." I said using my firmest teacher voice.

"Nope. I'm not going to leave you alone. You are going to have to come in with me." He said giving me a grin I had seen before.

"Oh no, mister, I am most certainly not, I can't go walking into Target and buying condoms! It will be all over town in like two seconds." Cue hand failing.

"Is that a bad thing?"

I blew out a breath, "Yes, no, yes." Ugh.

"You had the ones there at the lodge, let's go where you bought those and no one will think twice."

I hung my head low and muttered, "I buy those off Amazon."

"What? I can't hear you when you hang your head like that." I looked up and I knew he heard me. He was smiling like the Cheshire cat.

"I said I order those off Amazon."

He laughed then from the bottom of his soul, "Well okay, that's a good way to avoid any embarrassment, but I don't have time to wait for Amazon." And neither did I.

"You don't understand this do you? Like half of my students work at these places." I lowered my voice, "I mean what are they going to think?"

His eyes sparkled and he was silent for a few beats. "Hooray for Sugar?" And I punched him, hard. He threw his hands up in front of him, "Okay, okay, I'll stop teasing. I'm sure we can do this easily and quickly."

Easy for him to say he didn't know anyone in this town. I threw my hands around in the air, "Fine, whatever, okay, let's go buy the stupid things!" And I was pretty sure he was smiling as he got out of the car. We walked in the store and I grabbed a cart pushing it in front of me.

He leaned over my shoulder, "You need a cart for a box of condoms?"

"Shhhhhh….geez, get a megaphone why don't you!"

I went around picking up all the things that I keep around the lodge for guests, toothbrushes, mouthwash and toothpaste. I came around the next aisle to get the shampoo and lookie here, Irish Spring.

I raised a brow at him. "Body wash, shampoo and deodorant, is that how you manage to always smell like you're fresh out of the shower?" The plethora of Irish Spring spread out before me like a buffet.

He came up behind me and put his hands at my waist, "I noticed you kind of liked the way it smelled on me since you always have your face buried in my shirt. You told me you thought it was spicy and clean."

"And sexy." I said giving him a little back.

"We need to find the condom aisle, quickly." he whispered.

We worked our way to the condom aisle with an even bigger plethora of choices. My eyes glazed over, "Who knew there were so many choices?"

"I did."

I gave him the evil eye. "Magnum? Maybe you should get those." I said pointing.

He came in close again. "Flattery will get you everywhere my dear. If we weren't in public right now I'd show you how far." I gritted my teeth trying not to think about how my body was reacting to his breath against my ear.

"Would you just pick one please?" I was looking around for anyone I might know while I waited for him to throw a box in the cart.

"Sure. Do you want glow in the dark, ribbed, vibrating or heated?" He was enjoying this too much.

"Just pick one!" I said between my teeth.

He stepped forward and grabbed a box off the shelf his shoulders shaking as he tried to control his laughter. "Okay, the contraband is in the cart. Let's make a break for it." I punched him again.

"The value pack?" I guess he had plans.

"Making sure we don't have to do this again for a day or so, babe." He said wrapping his arm around my waist in a way that left nothing to the imagination for anyone watching. I also realized right at that moment that I didn't care if anyone saw him hugging me. Another little piece of that broken heart slipped into place.

I rolled the cart toward the checkout line having thrown a towel over the condoms to keep prying eyes away. I wasn't *that* comfortable with the whole thing yet. I was desperately hoping and praying that no one I knew was checking today, but nope that prayer went unanswered too. The only free line was being manned by one of my former students who was now going to college and married to her dance partner. It would look a little funny to go running to a different aisle and wait in line four people deep, so I was left with little choice. That was the problem with being a midwesterner, being rude was out of the question. Van started unloading the cart and I shifted from foot to foot making small talk with Ginger until he had everything unloaded and pulled the cart forward.

"I'm looking forward to the dance tonight," Ginger said as she checked, "Lewis and I are ready to trip the light fantastic."

Keep her talking. "Good, me too, it's going to be a lot of fun. I'm heading over to Darlene's in a bit for my hair, so I figured I would stop in and stock up on my guest supplies for the holidays."

She finished packing the bags and gave me my total and I could see Van laughing at me out of the corner of my eye as he loaded the bags into the cart. I quickly swiped my credit card, grabbed my receipt, said goodbye and hightailed it out of the store.

Van threw all the bags in the back of the SUV and got in. "I'm hurt. You didn't even introduce me." He didn't look hurt. He looked smug. "That wasn't so hard was it? She didn't even flick an eye when you bought the economy pack." I punched him, hard.

"What?"

"Never mind you don't understand." I said and he sat looking at me like he was prepared to wait me out however long it took for me to make him understand. I threw my hands up in the air, "I know that Duluth seems like a big place, but when you run a business here, one that I dare say, is successful, it's kinda hard to do anything privately. On top of that my profile has been rather high with the foundation and I can pretty much go nowhere without seeing someone I know. There is very little anonymity in a town where you have gone from "the poor girl in that horrible accident" to founder of a nationally recognized foundation. Everybody knows me, everybody, and regardless of what you may think by tomorrow everyone will know I bought an economy pack of condoms!" My hands were flailing around and I was yelling, but I didn't actually care.

"And you care because why?" He had his arms crossed in front of him leaning back against the door. "Does it really matter that much to you what people think? I guess I'm confused about what the real problem is here. Are you really that worried about your reputation? Because I'm pretty sure other Duluth businesswomen have bought condoms before. I don't get it."

"You know what I don't get it either. It's time for my hair appointment." And I didn't want to get into this now in the Target parking lot.

I guess he decided he had pushed me far enough. He pulled me over the console and kissed me thoroughly using more than enough tongue and letting his hands wander places they shouldn't in the Target parking lot before pulling back.

"Maybe that will take their minds off the condoms." And he put the car in drive. God bless tinted windows.

He pulled into the parking lot at Darlene's and put the SUV into park and climbed out.

"Where are you going?" I asked him hands on my hips.

"With you."

"Uhh, no, you can't come in here with me it's a woman's hair salon."

"Well as I said before, I can't leave you alone in there. My job is to protect you, not leave you alone somewhere that could potentially result in you getting kidnapped. Jesse would kill me. Besides I have a lot of other more selfish reasons to keep you safe." And I think I knew what those were. There were thirty-six of them in the back of my SUV.

I blew out a breath, "Alright, I get it, but you better be on your best behavior."

He gave me the who me look and I rolled my eyes, turned my back and stalked to the door still mad about the whole Target debacle. I opened the door to Darlene's and the heat and the smell of ammonia and perm solution hit me full on in the face. After having spent the last five minutes in the parking lot arguing with him my face was cold and I enjoyed the blast of hot air. I shrugged out of my coat and hung it on the coat stand with Van mimicking my motions.

I went over to the receptionist. "Hi, I have a two o'clock with Delci." I said to the receptionist.

"Hi Sugar, she's almost ready for you."

She looked behind me at Van, "And hello to you. What may I help you with?"

She was looking him up and down and had one eyebrow raised like she was inspecting the steak for tonight's dinner. Obviously she didn't realize he was with me. "He's with me." The tone of my voice was much firmer than I had planned it to be and she raised the other eyebrow.

"Well okay then." My point was made and I heard Van snicker.

He stepped up to the counter, "I am sorry to impose upon you, but I was hoping to get a bazzar while Ms. DuBois is having her gruiag fixed." He was pouring on the Irish accent and even I didn't know what the hell he was talking about.

I rolled my eyes at him, "I apologize for my friend, he's fresh off the boat from Ireland."

The receptionist smiled obviously falling for his charm, "I'd be happy to do whatever he asked me to do if I knew what it was."

He was standing there smiling at me smugly like I should be translating for him. "I'm going for the obvious here, but I think he wants a haircut while I'm having my hair done."

He slapped me on the back, "Bang on mi mot." And I made a note to return the condoms.

Delci called me back to the shampoo table and I made small talk with her while she shampooed my hair and brought me back to her chair. Van's presence was turning everyone here into schoolgirls and he was basking in it and laying on the charm.

"So he's with you?" She was combing out my hair and getting it pinned into layers.

"Yeah, he's with me." I sighed.

"You make it sound like a burden." And I remembered that I was supposed to be his host.

"No, no burden, he's a dance instructor here from Ireland to work some routines. Wanted me to take him along for a haircut before tonight. That's all."

"Ireland huh? Is he single?" Yup.

"Yeah I think so, but you know he is from Ireland." Smooth Sugar.

Delci shrugged a shoulder, "You win some you lose some."

Ain't that the truth. She was putting my hair into a French braid and I could feel Van's eyes on me the whole time. It suddenly felt a lot warmer in the room and I got the impression that he would rather I was wearing nothing under the cape Delci had wrapped around me.

"So are you all ready for tonight?" Delci asked.

I jumped, "What?"

"The dinner, tonight?" She looked at me perplexed and my face burned brightly.

"Oh right, the dinner, you betcha. I'm all ready. It's going to be a great time." And I was only half lying. I was starting to look forward to tonight, but then tonight wasn't here yet, so we would see how I felt in a few hours.

Delci clipped the final clip in place and pulled the cape off. "Are you ready to see it?" She twirled my chair around and handed me a mirror so I could see the back. She had done a reverse French braid weaving in an iridescent green ribbon through it and tying it into a small butterfly hair clip on the top. It was elegant and beautiful.

"It's beautiful Delci." I started to laugh then and shook my head.

"What's so funny? Don't you like it?"

"No, I love it, but I was thinking that I hope the ribbon matches my dress. I haven't actually seen it yet!"

She patted my shoulder, "It'll match." That was all she said and then she helped me out of the chair.

Van was done with his "bazzar" and was at the counter with his coat on. I paid for my style and his cut and he held the door open for me.

Delci waved saying, "See you tonight" and I waved back. Van took my hand in his and walked me to the SUV keeping a watchful eye around the parking lot. He loaded me into the passenger side of the SUV and then jumped in the driver's side cranking over the engine and turning the heat on high.

He leaned over the console and whispered, "You are mi daza." And he drug out the za part so it came out sounding incredibly sexy.

"Thanks. Your bazzar was just what you needed."

He nuzzled my neck, "Sorry, I was trying to stay in character ya know, being Irish and all that." Right and all that.

"It was an Emmy wining performance." I said and he kissed me hard on the lips and pointed the car towards home.

TWENTY-EIGHT

The drive home was quiet, the radio being the only noise in the car. The conversation in the car at Target kept replaying in my mind and I knew eventually I would have to explain to him why buying condoms was so difficult for me. I knew exactly why, but trying to explain it to him was going to sound really bad. The thought crossed my mind that telling him as little about Geoff as possible would probably be the best thing all the way around since he still lived in town. I also knew without a doubt that he would get it out of me eventually if he really wanted to know. I sat there listening to Van singing along with Van Morrison to "Brown Eyed Girl". He was jamming in the seat replacing my brown-eyed girl with my blue-eyed girl every time.

I was laughing and joined him on the "do you remember when we used to sing sha la la la la la la."

"He's Irish you know." He said over the sounds on the radio.

"Who?"

"Van Morrison."

"I didn't know that, but I love his version of 'Brown Eyed Girl'."

"Hit single 1967. I believe it's a west coast swing?"

I shook my head, "A little too fast, it works better for an east coast swing. I've seen it done as a rumba and that works too. I actually heard it once at a competition and someone else was singing it. They had sped it up and were doing a mambo to it. It was wrong on so many levels." He was laughing at me.

"I know. I'm a ballroom dork. I can't help it."

"No not a dork, you love what you do. I was thinking about it being a rumba and I can't quite get there with it. Now you want a rumba 'Do You Know' by Enrique, that's a rumba."

"'The Ping Pong Song'! I love that one and 'Save the Last Dance For Me' by Mr. Bublé, love, love that one too."

He was smiling, "You better save the last dance for me tonight, Ms. DuBois. I'm going to need to hold you in my arms by then."

"I promise you the last dance, Mr. Bond, without question." And that would get me through the rest of it.

He reached over and turned down the radio, "Are you ready for tonight, babe?"

"The closer we get to the hour the more nervous I get. I'm worried about if I'm going to be able to hide my emotions from a huge room full of people. It doesn't help that in the back of my mind I know that McElevain is going to show up and that makes me want to throw up."

"I don't want you worrying about if McElevain is going to show up. I'm worrying about if McElevain is going to show up and I'm going to keep you safe if he does. I won't let anyone hurt you tonight, **Tula**. All I want you to do is open up your heart a little and enjoy tonight. Forget about hiding your emotions and just be who you are, even if that means that you cry as much as you laugh."

"I can admit that I'm excited for our family and how that may change tonight. I'm trying to ride on that and let the rest fall into place."

"Good idea. I think you will be surprised to see that just might happen if you give up a little control and be accepting." And I prayed he was right because it seemed like a lot was going to have to fall into place for me to get through tonight.

He pulled down the long drive to the lodge and I powered the garage door up, so he could pull the Sorento in since we had the limo picking us up. He killed the engine and got out pulling his remote out of his pocket and checking it for points of entry. Satisfied that it was all clear he opened the door hauling in all my bags from the store and setting them in the laundry room.

He left me to check through the main lodge for safety sake and I put the stock up items in the storage boxes. But what to do with the condoms? My room? His room? I decided my room and set them on my night stand before crawling onto the bed. Physically I was pretty much ready for tonight except for showering and putting on my dress, but mentally I was still a mess inside. Tonight could be a complete disaster and there was going to be a lot of people there to witness it. I didn't have anything put where it needed to be and I didn't have any answers yet. Throw a madman into the mix and it caused serious heart palpitations. As I sat there I prayed for some peace for my soul and some courage for what lie ahead. I thanked Him for sending me Van and prayed that we would all be safe tonight. I prayed a lot of things and I prayed that He would answer them even though I knew the chances were slim considering my relationship with Him lately.

Van knocked on my door having been in his room checking e-mail and the final layout and instructions for tonight's dinner. "Can I come in?" And he did anyway without waiting for a response.

I was sitting on my bed, feet on the bed rail, elbows on my knees, chin in my hands, looking out my window at the white snow mounds covering the grass. "Sure."

He walked over to the bed and sat down copying my posture with his feet and slipping an arm around my shoulder. "You look deep in thought."

I shrugged my shoulder. "I was saying a few prayers for tonight and I was thinking about throwing in a couple Hail Mary's but I don't know how that goes."

"Hail Mary, full of grace. Our Lord is with thee. **Blessed art thou among women, and blessed is the fruit of your womb, Jesus. Holy Mary, Mother of God, pray for us sinners, now and at the hour of our death.** Amen."

"Amen." I said looking over at him under my brow.

"Sorry I was a good Irish Catholic until **I came to America and you** corrupted me."

"Well, I'm glad you shared it. Now I can say it over and over again in my head in hopes that it will keep me safe tonight."

"I'm going to keep you safe tonight. You have to stop worrying about McElevain, okay?"

I let out a sigh, "Okay. I will try, but I can't promise anything."

I laid my head on his shoulder and sat staring out the window. I knew I should get up and I knew I should go get ready, but I liked being in his arms.

"Whass keepin yeh?" He rubbed my arm **and I stayed silent.** "Listen I'm sorry. I was acting the maggot back there at the store. I should have shown you more respect. I didn't mean to upset you. I know you don't need that tonight. I was trying to figure out what had you so unsettled."

"It's okay, **you were right. I was being way too touchy about the** whole thing. It's just a box of condoms. It wasn't like I was buying drugs or something."

"I'd like to understand if you want to tell me."

"I really wouldn't know where to start."

"I suspect that it **has something to do with the jerk you talked** about last night."

"You are good at this aren't you?"

"I'm a cop, it's my job." And that made me laugh as I thought **about that movie Uncle Buck and the little kid.**

"He said some things to me that have been hard **to forget, things that made an impression on me more than I realized. Hindsight being 20/20 and a lot of** years later, I understand that he probably said them because he wanted to make it my fault that things didn't work out. He **was too much of a coward to** be honest about how he really felt." I rubbed my hands over my face. "Let's forget it, he isn't worth it."

"Well I agree with that, he definitely isn't worth it, but it seems to me **whatever he said must have been brutal for it to stay with you for** donkey's years."

I raised an eyebrow, "Is that a long time?"

He laughed, "A very, very long time."

And he was right, it was brutal and it was the reason I never dated. We sat there looking out the window for a few moments and in his silence he made me want to open my heart up to him and let him fix it all. My earlier resolved wavered and I spoke, "Long story short he told me that I might as well not bother looking for love because not only would nobody want me with my baggage," which I put in quotations with my fingers, "but, I don't know how to even say this."

He was smoothing my hair back and kissed my temple. "Take your time." And he really didn't understand that there was no way to say this.

"That no man would ever want me once he got my pants off and saw what was underneath." It came out on a breath, but those were his exact words and it hung in the air like the aroma of a Friday night fish fry on Saturday morning.

His hands stilled and I felt him stiffen next to me. I got off the bed walking over to the window standing to the side so I could see out, but no one could see in. He was silent for a long time and I felt the tears at the back of my throat, but refused to cry. I stuttered around trying to fill the silence that was deafening, "And, and last night was incredible and you couldn't have made that statement less true," I hesitated.

"But?" I looked back at him still sitting on the bed with his feet on the rail, his jaw moving and his eyes flashing and I turned away again and wrapped my arms around myself. I couldn't come up with anything to say other than the truth, no matter how awful it sounded.

"But buying the condoms felt like I was tempting fate because maybe the next time you made love to me you might decide he was right." And my voice was quiet and sounded shameful. I was embarrassed that I even had the thought, but I did and I couldn't change that. I was glad that I couldn't see what was in his eyes.

I felt him come up behind me his warm breath blowing against the few hairs on the nape of my neck, "Look at me." I was really pretty sure that wasn't a good idea, he sounded angry and I stayed rooted in place. He physically turned me with his hands on my upper arms, "Don't confuse me with some immature Eejit." And I knew this wasn't going to go well.

I held up my hand and wrestled out of his hold going back over to the bed. "Listen, never mind, I don't know why I told you that. Forget I said anything. It's fine. I'm going to go get ready."

I turned towards the bathroom and he stepped in my path putting his hands on my waist and resting his forehead against mine. I felt a tear escape and run down my cheek and I was impressed it was only one.

"I will never be able to forget what you just said to me. That will be something that will stay with me forever."

"Van, don't. It's fine."

"No! It is not fine, quit saying its fine. It's not fine." And his words came out between clenched teeth and I flinched. He took a deep breath and lowered his voice. "It's not fine what he did. It's not fine to say something like that to someone and make something that they have overcome become something humiliating and it's certainly not fine to believe it. Last night was beyond words for me. I have never experienced anything like last night. I have never felt like I felt last night. It never crossed my mind that you were any less of a person, any less of a woman because of the accident. I find your beauty in the things you do and the way you love so many people so unconditionally. What made me want to make love to you last night had nothing to do with your body."

I raised an eyebrow at him.

"Okay, that's a lie. Your body turns me on every time I look at you." That's better. "What I mean is that I wanted to make love to you, all of you, I wanted to make love to your heart and your mind and your body. Does that make sense?"

I nodded. Yeah it made perfect sense.

He lowered his head laying it against my chest listening to my heartbeat like I always do when I dance with him. He was silent and I took a moment to think about what he said. I really liked what he said.

"We got the afternoon. You got this room for two. One thing I've left to do. Discover me, discovering you. One mile to every inch of your skin like porcelain. One pair of candy lips and your bubble gum tongue." He sang in a sultry voice.

"'Your Body Is A Wonderland', John Mayer, rumba." I whispered.

"I really want to make love to you right now." He whispered against my chest. And he stood up and took my hand pressing it against the front of his pants so I could feel just how much.

I sucked in a breath, "It's getting late and we still have to shower."

His eyes glowed green and he backed me up against the bed lifting me with his hands on my hips like I weighed no more than a child. He unhooked my leg throwing it on the bed and pulled off my liner.

"What are you doing?"

"Getting you ready for a shower." And then he stripped his shirt off and mine taking a few moments to work me out of my bra and feather kisses across the tops of both breasts before capturing each nipple in his teeth releasing it quickly, leaving me wanting more. He picked me up and carried me into the bathroom sitting me on my bench. Reaching in he turned on my shower and stripped the rest of his clothes off while he waited for the water to get warm. He knelt down in front of me and unsnapped my pants pulling them out from under me followed by my thong. He transferred me to the shower bench and stepped in front of me taking the brunt of the water. He started soaping me letting the soapy water run down my chest before getting down on his knees so I could soap him. I ran my hands up and down his chest my hands straying lower each time I ran the bar of soap around. His breath caught and his eyes swirled and he leaned in kissing me, putting his finger on just the right spot moving it around and around until my eyes got huge and I clung to him begging for release.

He pulled back his eyes nearly on fire. "Be right back." He stepped out of the shower and left me sitting there turned on as hell and wondering what he was doing. He was back quickly a silver package in his hand.

"Forgot my raincoat." And then he picked me up and sat down on the bench before settling me on his lap.

God bless the economy pack.

TWENTY-NINE

I was standing in front of the mirror taking deep breaths reminding myself that this was nothing I hadn't done before. Go up, give out an award or two, dance a few dances and come home. I can do this, I can do this. I was saying it over and over as I put the finishing touches on my hair. After our "shower" I had to fix a few spots here and there, but considering all that it didn't look too bad. I swiped some dark brown shadow on my eyes and added lash lengthening mascara finishing everything off with coffee bean lipstick. I was wearing the MAMBOS necklace that we had created and sold as a fundraiser last year. It was sterling silver and had two butterflies intwined with vines. I hoped it would work with the dress. I opened the bedroom door to get the dress and stopped short at the doorway. Van was standing there, dressed in his tuxedo pants and shirt, collar unbuttoned, tie in hand. He looked me down and then back up.

"Damn." He threw the tie on the bed and walked towards me. I was wearing nothing but a lace thong. He put one hand on my waist and cupped my breast in the other.

"Have I told you how beautiful you are?"

"Once or twice." I let out a moan as his finger flicked over my nipple.

"How much time do we have?" His voice was husky and I could feel his hardness as he pressed up against me.

"Not nearly enough. I'll have to take a rain check."

He let out an exasperated sigh, bent down and kissed me. He kept rubbing my breast as if in a trance. Give a man a breast and watch their brain shut down. I knew I was going to have to break away even though my body was telling me to give in.

I cleared my throat. "Did you need something?" I waited for my words to wade through the cloud of lust in his eyes.

"Oh sorry, yeah, I need help with my tie." He looked at his hands forgetting that he had tossed it aside like a dirty shirt.

I grabbed my bathrobe and threw it on. No sense tempting fate. I fixed his tie and then pushed him out the door to finish dressing telling him I would meet him in the main room in a few minutes. I sat down on the bed and pulled on my nylons. Julie and Jesse had picked the gown out and had it sent over by messenger last week. They had told me not to

215

open it until tonight. I hope it fits was all I said. Jesse assured me it would and I never peeked. I guess I didn't care then. I care now though and I held my breath as I unzipped the bag and pulled the dress out. It was breathtaking. It was iridescent green with a beaded bodice. The dress had layers that wrapped around me with the edge of each layer being beaded to match the bodice. The dress fell to the floor at the perfect length and had a matching wrap. Delci was right it matched the ribbon in my hair perfectly. It was absolutely amazing. Leave it to Julie.

I stepped into the gown and zipped it up turning each way in the mirror. It fit like a glove. I slipped on a pair of dance slippers. Not very practical for Duluth winter, but I hadn't been planning on having a foot and a half of snow on the ground tonight. I walked to the mirror to take a look. I liked what I saw. It said sophisticated, it said sexy and it said I own this room. It was a good thing I had the dress, I was going to need it to pull off tonight. I heard a knock on the door and I heard Van telling me we were going to be late.

"Come in." I said my back to the door. He opened the door and stopped two strides into the room. I turned to face him and his eyes danced and his lips tipped upwards.

"You take my breath away." He said advancing towards me with his hands reaching for my waist. "I love the dress. It makes you look sexy as hell." Good, so far it was working.

He pulled me too him and locked his arms around my waist, "Now I want to take it off you and make love to you for the rest of the night."

"Tell me how you really feel, don't hold back." I winked at him and he looked at me with hunger in his eyes. He came in and took me for a long kiss and I sighed. Staying home in bed was sounding really good to me, but I couldn't do that to Julie. I stepped back putting a little distance between us.

"You're looking rather dashing yourself Mr. MacNamara or Walsh or Bond, whoever you are."

"Tonight, I'm the luckiest man in Duluth because you are on my arm." He did have a way of building my ego.

We went to the kitchen to get our coats and he went to the fridge and pulled out a container. He opened it and pulled out a wrist corsage. There were three white miniature roses nestled amongst greens. It was delicate and absolutely gorgeous.

He slid it over my wrist and smiled. "Now you're ready."

I looked at him confused, "Is this from Jesse?"

He shook his head. "No. It's from me. I wanted all your special people to be with you tonight." I fought back tears not wanting to ruin my makeup. I looked up at him. His eyes were shining and I liked what I saw.

"Thank you for caring."

He smiled and caressed my cheek. "You are most welcome mi mot, now, your carriage awaits." He held out his arm and led me into the night.

The limo was black, long and elegant. Julie had gotten the local limousine services to give free rides to anyone making a donation of one hundred dollars or more to the foundation. I guess I was a freebie. We sat in the back snuggled into each other enjoying the lights of the city as we began the drive up the hill to Cloquet. We didn't talk, we didn't need to. We approached the high bridge and I felt Van stiffen next to me.

"Okay?" He asked and I snuggled in closer as my answer, concentrating on the lights of Canal Park.

We crossed the bridge and hit I-35 going up the long hill into the dark. Allison, one of our foundation members, works for the Black Bear Convention Center and opened the door for us to come in and speak with the manager about having one of the convention center rooms for the evening. Julie and I met with them several months ago to go over the planning of the event. Unfortunately, I was called out of the meeting urgently as there was an issue at the lodge and Julie had to finish the meeting. When she came out to the lodge later that day she had the use of the convention center for the night, a catered dinner and a DJ free of charge. The woman can get anything done I tell you. I just wish it hadn't been tonight. I noticed Van looking at the big bag I had brought along in the limo. I was waiting to see how long he could last before he asked what was in it. He didn't disappoint.

"What's in the bag?" He motioned at the large duffel bag taking up half the other seat.

"Body parts." I said it with a straight face and smoothed my dress.

"Funny, funny, but I'm serious, what's in the bag."

"I'm serious too, body parts."

He finally reached over and unzipped the bag only to find a body part. He was holding up one of my legs with the dance shoe still attached. He had an eyebrow raised and a full on smile.

"I told you. I always carry a spare with me for big events like this. Sometimes if I don't like how things are feeling with the one foot I can use the other. And if one leg goes down I always have a backup. I've learned that one the hard way."

"Right okay, well let's keep the bag zipped up so no one gets arrested tonight." He put the leg back in the bag and zipped it up crawling back over to the seat next to me. I couldn't tell if he was disturbed by the whole thing or not. He was quiet almost like he regretted asking in the first place.

"So Croquet is where we are going?" He asked butchering the name of the city about as bad as everyone from out of town does.

I stifled a laugh. "No, Cloquet." Putting a heavy emphasis on the "Clo" part. "It was a huge lumber town in the early 1900s and in 1918 there was a huge fire that burned down the city and killed a bunch of people."

He raised a brow, "A bunch of people?" He was laughing at me.

"Yeah a bunch of people, I don't know how many, what do I look like a tour guide?" I was laughing too and it felt good to laugh, really good. "Anyway it has produced a few celebrities in its day. Jessica Lange was born in Cloquet and it is also known for turning out great hockey players including Jamie Langenbrunner."

"From the Dallas Stars!" he shouted.

I patted his knee. "See I knew we would find a tie-in at some point." He winked at me and put his hand over mine. "Part of the city actually lies within the Fond Du Lac Indian Reservation and this is their casino and convention center. They do a lot in the community including running a community college."

The driver's voice came across the speaker in the back telling us we were within minutes of our destination.

Van leaned forward mouth near my temple. "Ready baby?"

"Do you promise to not to leave me tonight? I don't have my gun with me if McElevain shows up. You told me I had to leave it home."

He smiled and brushed back a piece of hair from my face. "You don't need your gun. I'm not going to leave you and if I have to, Jesse will step in. Someone will always be watching you. I can't promise that McElevain won't show up, but he won't hurt you." He looked at me under his eyebrows then and kissed me softly on the lips.

I let out a breath and then sucked one in, for courage. "Okay then I'm as ready as I'll ever be."

"Remember to introduce me as Donavan MacNamara. We need to stay with the story since we will be so public tonight."

I nodded. "I know. I teacher, you student."

"And when we get home I teacher, you student." He wagged his eyebrows at me and the heat returned to my belly.

THIRTY

There were vans from the Duluth News Tribune and the local television stations in the parking area and I was thankful we didn't have to find a spot to park as there wasn't much to choose from. The limo driver brought us to the casino doors inside the parking garage where the door was opened by a tuxedo clad valet attendant. Van stepped out of the car and took my hand helping me out. The casino was busy with people coming and going and I felt a little silly climbing out of this long limo flanked by security. My bag was handed off to a guard with instructions to keep it in an accessible area for me throughout the night.

"Of course, Ms. DuBois." he said leaving the area.

Another attendant escorted us in through the double doors to the convention center. Stepping in, all you heard was the sounds of the machines clanging and the buzzing of voices and the band playing in The Cobalt. Maybe I should go down and sit at the bar and listen to the music, might be easier than going in those convention center doors. The attendants took our coats and I linked my arm in Van's as I heard the first few strains of "Do You Feel The Love Tonight". I had no idea where that was coming from, but I knew there were butterflies in my stomach.

I sat down on one of the benches that lined the convention center. "I can't do this Van. I feel like I'm going to pass out."

He sat down beside me and kissed my temple, "You are not going to pass out. Take a deep breath and remember that everybody inside that room loves you and hey, maybe no one will even notice you come in." I guess that was possible. Simply slip in and sit down.

"Right, okay." I took the deep breath, twice, and stood up and he took my arm walking me to the door that said Otter Creek Ballroom in big letters. There were two more tuxedoed attendants at the doors. It suddenly dawned on me that there was no one else around, "This is weird Van. Where is everyone?"

He stood next to me, his arm through mine holding me steady. "You'll see."

Each attendant pulled open a door to the ballroom and motioned us forward. We took two steps in and my steps slowed and then halted altogether. I looked up at Van in stunned surprise and he had a full on smile.

I heard Jesse say, "Ladies and gentleman, please welcome the guest of honor, Ms. Tula Sugar DuBois." And everyone stood.

Jesse stood at the front of the room on the platform raised stage and I registered his voice in the back of my mind. The room erupted in applause and I was rooted in place. The room was filled with all my friends, students, volunteers from the foundation, community members and what looked to be about half of the greater Duluth area. I saw faces I hadn't seen in years and the faces of those that I love.

Van leaned down and whispered in my ear, "This is how much you are loved." And I was trying to hold myself together, so much for no one noticing me.

"Did you know?" I asked him.

He nodded. Wow. He gave me a moment before leading me up through the room to the platform steps. I stopped short when I saw Justin sitting at a table with his wife Ava and his precious baby girl Amelia. He stood up and placed baby Amelia in my arms.

She was beautiful and so tiny. She looked up at me with so much innocence in her eyes and I knew I had found the reason. It all became very clear to me in that one second when I heard no one and I saw no one but this perfect little baby with chocolate brown eyes that I had seen before. They were the eyes of my best friend who was taken long before he was done living, but in those eyes I saw him telling me to go and be and live. I heard him whisper that he was okay and it was time for me to let him be a memory. I felt my heart lighten and I kissed Amelia softly on the cheek whispering a soft thank you in her ear. She was too little to know what she had done for me, but someday she would. Justin gave me a gentle hug and I put Amelia back in her father's arms.

Van took my arm again and helped me up the stairs to where Jesse and Julie stood in front of a podium. There was a long empty banquet table behind them. Julie pulled me into a hug and we were both pulled into a hug by Jesse.

I felt Van slip away and I whispered in their ears, "What is going on?"

Julie whispered in my ear, "Tonight is all about you and what you have done for all of them." She pulled back and smiled at me brushing the tears away from my eyes and patting my face. "You can do this, Sugar, I know you can."

There were butterflies in my stomach and I searched the room for Van, my eyes finding him standing off to the side hands crossed in front of him. He looked relaxed, but I could tell he was searching the room for anything out of place. He smiled a slow smile at me and my heart rate slowed. The music faded away as everyone settled in and Jesse stepped to the podium.

"We have a great evening planned for you all tonight, but first" he reached under the podium and pulled out a Starbucks coffee cup. "We need to start the night out right." He handed me the cup, "Cinnamon dolce latte gets me out of hot water every time."

The room erupted with laughter and a smile spread across my face. I looked out and saw the waiters bringing coffee to everyone. I couldn't help but laugh. Julie hooked her arm in mine and led me to a seat at the head of the table. She motioned for Van to join me and he settled in next to me taking my hand under the table. The night began with Julie talking about MAMBOS and what the foundation encompasses. She thanked everyone for coming and then introduced several other volunteers that had headed up different fundraisers this year. Each speaker took a spot at the table to the right or left of me. It was great seeing everyone here tonight having fun and laughing. Julie introduced the next guest as one of the seven reasons we were here tonight. A young woman walked out onto the floor and I was on my feet before I even realized it. Van stood quickly steading me. The young woman walked over to where I was and pulled me into a hug.

"Hi Emily." I said through my tears.

She leaned back and smiled. "Hi Sugar. Hope you don't mind I crashed your party."

I laughed shaking my head and she walked to the podium and introduced herself.

"My name is Emily Tarrant and ten years ago tonight I received a new heart. My donor's name was Brent Bowers and he saved my life."

Van handed me a tissue and leaned over, "Finally, happy tears."

Emily told everyone about her journey to find her donor's family and how when she found the MAMBOS website she put it all together. "I didn't know it at the time, but a new family came with this heart and I wouldn't have it any other way. It is my pleasure to introduce you to one of my favorite ladies, my angel's mother, Sharon Knight."

Emily stepped to the side of the podium and Sharon came out from behind the curtain. I was lost. I jumped up and ran around the table pulling her into a hug almost knocking us both over. Jesse grabbed us holding us up. He had a smile a mile wide and tears in his eyes.

"You tricked me!" I was saying it to either one or maybe to both. They each pulled me to them and kissed a cheek.

"Go sit down, Sugar, I have a speech to make and I want to get through it before I cry." Sharon said. I patted her cheek the way I always did when I was little and let her go. "God I missed you." I said.

Jesse led me back to the table and Sharon took the podium hugging Emily on the way by. Emily joined us and Sharon began to speak.

"Ten years ago tonight my life changed. I was working a shift in the trauma room when the call came in that there had been an accident. Multiple fatalities, life threatening injuries the scanner said. I began to prepare the rooms expecting it to be like every other trauma, treat the ones you can and say a prayer for the others. But then my supervisor came over and told me that I needed to wait in the waiting room for Jesse to come. He needed to talk to me. I didn't think too much of it until I saw Jesse walk in the door. I had never seen anyone look so shattered." Sharon paused and gathered herself, "I knew right then that I wouldn't be treating anyone in that accident and that the prayers being said that night would be for our family. I remember sitting together in the waiting room me in my nursing uniform and him in his police uniform thinking that we really had no control over anything. Here were two people who worked every day to help others and we were now the ones who needed help. Finally a doctor came to us and told us that my son was gone, his brain injury too severe for him to recover from, and would I consider donating his organs. He told me that a young girl was dying and if she didn't get a new heart she wouldn't survive the next few days. I knew my son was gone and I knew the pain of losing a child. If I could save one child's life that night and spare another mother that kind of pain then I knew that I had to do it. My decision was made. The Lord needed my son to save seven lives that night and it would bring us together in a way no one would have ever imagined." Sharon talked about personally meeting all the recipients of Brent's organs and how she healed with each meeting. "Tonight we are here to honor the founder of MAMBOS. Ten years ago tonight the Lord needed my son and when I look out around this room I can clearly see why. That night He gave me a daughter, He laid this beautiful, broken girl in my arms and told me to take care of her. I know that I have never been so blessed to have her in my life. If I know Sugar, right now she is overwhelmed and embarrassed to see such an outpouring of support. She likes to be behind the scenes. To quote her, "I just planted the seed" and from what I can see it grew into something that none of us would have dreamed."

I thought back to our conversation last night wondering where she was when I was talking to her. She thanked everyone for coming and then turned the microphone back over to Jesse. She came around the table taking the spot to my left. She hugged me silently and I clung to her like a lifeline.

"I've missed you so much, Mom. I really need you right now." I was trying to get myself under control, but all I wanted to do was hold onto her.

She whispered in my ear, "I've been waiting to hear you call me mom for ten years, Sugar. I told myself that when you called me mom that I had done what the Lord asked me to do." Well if I'd known that was all it would take.

I patted her face and sucked in a breath, "And then some Mom. I love you."

Jesse was speaking, "It's a good thing I got her a double latte because I didn't tell her she was going to make a speech tonight."

The room erupted in laughter at the look of shock on my face. Oh boy, a speech. I looked at Van pretty sure I must have that deer in the headlights look again.

"So without further ado, Ms. Sugar DuBois." Jesse said and Van stood, buttoning his jacket and straightening his lapels giving me time to prepare. He reached over pulled me up guiding me to the podium.

He leaned in and gave me a kiss on the cheek, "Knock 'em dead partner." He winked and returned to his seat. I turned to the podium looking out at the sea of friends that had gathered. I was overwhelmed and now I needed to speak.

Jesse leaned over, "Speak from your heart."

The room quieted and I began, "On the way over here tonight I was thinking about how I was going to get through this. To be honest I had other plans for tonight. They involved hiding under the blankets until it was November eleventh." The audience laughed lightly, that kind of uncomfortable laugh people do when they aren't sure if they are supposed to.

"As you all know it has been ten years since the accident and the last few months have found me looking for the reason why I was left behind that night. It's a question I have struggled with since the accident, but it became so very important for me to answer as this night drew closer. I didn't have it figured out before I got here tonight, but when they opened the doors the answer was right in front of me. It had been there the whole time. Emily, Amy, Justin, Terry, Trisha, John, and Andrew are the reason. Beautiful little Amelia is the reason. Sharon, Jesse and Julie are the reason. Each family that we touch is the reason. Each one of you is the reason. I am humbled by the outpouring of love and support tonight. Each one of you contributed in some way to helping me in my journey to see that answer and I can't thank you enough for your time, talents and donations. It was in Brent's name that I started this and in death he has taught me so much about life. I guess I just needed to pay closer attention. When I started MAMBOS I did it as a way to honor what Brent was in life. As you know Brent and I loved dancing. It was our passion. There wasn't a dance around that Brent didn't love or couldn't do. I, on the other hand, had no time for the mambo. Have you ever seen a short Canadian do the mambo?"

There was a ripple of genuine laughter from the audience and I turned to see the corners of Van's mouth tip upwards.

"So whenever we were at a competition and a little bit nervous Brent would come up behind me and whisper in my ear, "Are you ready? Cause it's time to mambo!" and then he'd do this little shimmy shake and I'd laugh and my nervousness would disappear. So with that in mind MAMBOS or Miracles Are Made By Organ Sharing was born. I was given the opportunity to plant the seed and wait to see if the vine would grow. Last summer when we sat in the garden and watched Emily marry the love of her life, the vine grew. A few weeks ago when I got a phone call from Justin at three in the morning breathless about the beauty of his newborn daughter, the vine grew. Each time one of you tells someone else about what we do the vine grows and it spreads throughout the community and country. Each year there are over one hundred thousand people waiting for a transplant, but we are only doing a little over twenty eight thousand transplants a year. We have a lot of work to do yet, but I want to thank each and every one of you for taking time out of your lives to share Brent's story, our story, and grow the vine. God bless organ donation and the lives it changes."

The room erupted in applause and I turned to Jesse and Sharon giving them my own round of applause. "Now I think it's time to get this party started, but before we do I would like to close with an old Irish blessing that a good friend whispered in my ear today. I say it tonight as a prayer of thanksgiving and in remembrance knowing that we will all meet again."

Suddenly the podium around me filled with the reasons I was here. Jesse, Julie, Sharon, Len, Emily, Justin with little Amelia and Van gathered around me and everyone rose. I was choked up and couldn't speak. Van took my hand and squeezed it starting to speak.

"May the road rise up to meet you," the rest of the room joined in. "May the wind be always at your back. May the sun shine warm upon your face; the rains fall soft upon your fields and until we meet again, may God hold you in the palm of His hand." And the only voice I heard in the room was that of a deep resonating Irishman.

THIRTY-ONE

I stepped behind the curtain to gather myself while the waiters began serving salads. I wasn't prepared for what had happened and I was overwhelmed. I was overwhelmed, in shock, in awe and dumbstruck. I needed a few minutes to get all my emotions under control. I saw the curtain pull back and Julie came through letting the curtain fall behind her. She was beautiful tonight in her long silk sheath gown. It was iridescent green like mine, but simple with spaghetti straps and a scoop neck where her MAMBOS necklace laid. Her hair fell around her face framing it with one corner pulled up by a butterfly clip. At five foot nine inches she could pull off the sheath gown and looked stunning, but she looked very tired, her eyes sunken in their sockets. She also looked nervous. She was playing with her hair that fell near her cheek like she always does when she gets nervous or concentrates.

We stood there looking at each other and she dropped her hands down in front of her. "Everything okay?" Her tone was one I had never heard before, trepidation. "Van's standing guard, but he told me to give you a few minutes."

I nodded, "I need a few minutes to regroup."

Julie motioned her hand towards the curtain and what lay beyond it. "Are you, uh." Her voice wavered and she halted unsure of herself in a way that I have never seen before.

"Upset?" I asked.

She nodded wrapping her arms around herself.

"No, I'm not upset, not at all. I'm stunned, surprised and slightly embarrassed, but I could never be upset."

The relief was visible on her face. "I was thinking we might have gone too far." Her voice was quiet and she was searching my face for any sign that she was right. I walked over to where she stood and tucked the hair back behind her ear that she kept fussing with. There were tears in her eyes and I could see that she was truly worried that she had hurt me somehow.

I grabbed her hands, "You know me better than that, Jules. I have never been so touched than when they opened those doors tonight. Van had to hold me up I was so surprised, but never did the words upset or angry cross my mind. Grateful, joyous and loved yes, but nothing else.

Jesse told me you were good at your job and he was right, but you are better at being my friend."

She winked at me through her tears and tipped her chin up a fraction before letting out a shaky breath and pulling me into a hug. "I'm glad we talked. I needed to make sure you were fine before we went on with the night."

I pulled out of her embrace, "I'm better than fine sweetie. Now I had better get back out there before Jess sends out the mounted patrol." And we both laughed because it was something he would do.

"Tell Jess I'm freshening up and will be back in a few minutes." She said her voice lined with fatigue.

I paused for a minute needing to ask her, but not wanting to offend her, "Jules, you look kind of sick. Are you okay?"

I didn't want to push the issue, but I was really concerned that she wasn't going to make it through the night.

Then I saw fear flash through her eyes before she vehemently denied it. "No, no, I'm fine, I'm a little tired, that's all. Go back out and have dinner I will be right there."

I knew at that moment that I needed to keep an eye on her tonight, something didn't feel right. I assured her I would let Jess know and stepped around the curtain. Van smiled at me and my heart smiled back. He began to escort me back to my seat and halted as I walked past Jesse.

He grabbed my hand question in his eyes and I leaned in and whispered, "Something is very wrong with her."

Jesse started to stand up and I stopped him. "Give her a few minutes, if she isn't back in five I will go find her. She went to the restroom to freshen up, but we need to keep an eye on her, she looks ready to collapse."

He nodded, "Without a doubt."

I gave him a peck on the cheek, "And thank you for tonight. It was exactly what I needed."

He gave me his lopsided little boy smile and I straightened and walked back to my seat. Van pulled out my chair and helped me get settled in. He pressed a kiss to my temple while making it look like he was whispering in my ear. I squeezed his hand under the table. Everyone was eating and I looked down in front of me. There was a salad made with four or five different greens and covered in croutons and onions. Just the way I liked it, no tomatoes, extra onions. I wasn't exactly sure how they knew that though.

Van arched an eyebrow, "No icky tomatoes I see."

"Yeah, how about that." I picked up my fork and dug into the salad, my belly my top priority at the moment. I hadn't taken two bites when waiters filled the wings and a chef in a white coat approached the podium. He seemed familiar, though I could only see the back of him.

He picked up the microphone, "Good evening, I would like to take a moment to introduce myself. My name is Dewey Houston and I'm a good friend of Sugar's." He turned and winked at me and I had one hand over my heart laughing like a fool. I should have known!

He continued, "I hope you enjoy your selections for the evening. In honor of Ms. DuBois you will be feasting on one of her creations. At my restaurant we call it the Sugar Burger." There was whistling and hooting from the around the room. "Ahhh, I see some of you are familiar with it." I clamped my hand over my mouth to keep from laughing even harder. Out of the corner of my eye I saw Julie move back to her seat and sit down. Jess put a protective arm around her.

Dew was still talking. "Those of you who aren't familiar with it need to understand two things about Sugar's cooking. The first is if she had a choice she would make coffee and onions a food group, and the second is when she cooks you will always find one or the other or both in whatever she's serving." And that was 100% accurate. He was bang on as Van would say. "I want to extend a huge thank you to the real chefs and kitchen staff here at the Black Bear. They put up with me leaning over their shoulder all day giving them orders and were quite good natured about it. I wish you a good evening and bon appétit!" The crowd applauded and Dew took a plate from the waiter setting it in front of me with a flourish.

"A Sugar Burger and a side of rings for my girl." He leaned over and kissed me on my forehead.

"I love you Dew, you crazy old man."

He smiled and patted my cheek, "I know, enjoy your night."

He stepped behind the curtain and then reappeared on the floor taking a seat at the table next to his wife, Ivy, who I hadn't even seen! She blew me a kiss and I waved back before focusing my eyes on the sweet smell of onion. I ate with unabashed gusto listening to the room loud with laughter and voices as everyone waited to be served. As everyone began to eat the decibel level lowered until there was little more than the sound of silverware and glasses clinking. I had finished my burger and was leaning back looking out over the room when I heard the soft cry of a baby. My eyes traveled to Justin who had Amelia over one shoulder as he attempted to eat while jiggling her up and down.

I leaned over to Van, "I'll be right back." Letting my eyes travel to the table below and he nodded understanding. I made my way down to their table and pulled out a chair taking Amelia from him.

Justin looked up and smiled. "Thanks."

"No problem, Auntie Sugar needs some of this sweet baby girl." She stopped fussing and looked up at me and I talked to her in that voice that drives everyone but babies nuts. I pulled her up to my shoulder patting her back as she nuzzled my neck cooing.

Justin was watching me, "I think she likes you."

"I sure hope so because I plan to spend a lot of time with this little gal."

Justin looked over at Ava and she gave him a nod. "I'm glad you feel that way. We were going to swing by the lodge and ask you, but now seems like the perfect time. We would like you to be Amelia's godmother." And I was at a loss for words. My eyes traveled to Ava who was smiling at Justin who was looking nervously at me.

"I would be honored, but are you sure?"

"We couldn't be more sure," Ava said, "We want her to know all about the special angel that saved her daddy and you are the perfect person to show her that."

It was ten years ago tonight that Justin got one of Brent's kidneys. He was only seventeen himself that night and he had already been on dialysis for years. He was thinking that his life would end before it started. Ava was his high school sweetheart who came with him to every dialysis appointment and every doctor appointment keeping him company through all of it. She was there the night of the transplant and camped out in his room with him refusing to leave for the first three days. Theirs was a love that really and honestly meant through sickness and in health. Exactly one year after the transplant he asked Ava to marry him and they made a life together in Duluth. They both work as dialysis technicians providing hope to so many of their patients. I let out a little sigh as Amelia squirmed around in my arms and I handed her back to her mother.

"That I can do, my friends, and I think I will get some help from her Uncle Jesse on that one. But I'm teaching her to dance."

Justin grinned, "Well, let's let her walk first." He pulled me into a hug and I assured him it was a deal.

They both looked exhausted the long nights not hidden well on their faces. I motioned for the manager of the convention center to come over. He approached me and I stood excusing myself for a moment. I spoke to the manager for a brief minute and he left assuring me he would take care of things. I returned to the table.

"Did you guys drive in from Duluth?"

Ava nodded.

"Well it's early yet and you guys look exhausted. I don't want either of you driving home. Head out to the front desk when you are ready to call it a night and they will have a room key waiting. Stay here tonight and drive home in the morning. I've taken care of everything and there will be a crib for Amelia waiting in your room. If you need anything call the front desk and they will take care of it. Okay?"

Justin looked relieved. "Thanks Sugar, we were thinking about flipping a coin to see who was going to drive home." We all laughed at the image knowing that it wasn't far from the truth.

"We had to be here tonight, though, we had to see this." Justin motioned around the room.

"Yeah," the word came out on a sigh, "it's really something isn't it?"

I kissed my godbaby on the head and waved goodbye. I took my seat back at the table and Van leaned over, "You're a natural with babies. You had her eating out of the palm of your hand."

"I don't know about that, but she is the sweetest thing ever. Turns out I'm her godmother now, I guess I have some big shoes to fill." He smiled at me and squeezed my hand and I knew it was killing him not to be able to kiss me.

Jess and Julie came over and told me it was time for picture taking, media takes and cake cutting. We posed for pictures for the Duluth News Tribune and I gave a statement regarding organ donation and MAMBOS giving him contact information for the foundation. I also spoke with Courtney from the Northland News Center who were always willing to give the foundation air time. I managed to turn the questions to focus on the foundation and not me. Finally Jesse and Julie grabbed my hand and directed me over to the corner where a large cake sat with the MAMBOS insignia. It said, "May the next ten years be more inspired than the last." They told me time was of the essence so we quickly took pictures of all of us cutting the cake. I understood why as I cut down into it. It was Cold Stone Creamery Coffee Lovers Only ice cream cake and I think some drool escaped my lip.

God Bless Cold Stone Creamery.

THIRTY-TWO

The down time between dinner getting done and them setting up for the dance allowed me time to mill around and visit with some of the volunteers from the foundation and old friends. The mayors of the two port cities were busy making bets about who would win the Packers versus Vikings game the next day and I personally thought Mr. Minnesota was talking a little too much smack considering how the Vikings had been playing. I had fun giving him a little ribbing about it and he freely admitted that it didn't look good, but it did snow in November this year so there was always a little hope for everything. I thanked them for coming and stepped away looking for Van and I found him lounging mere feet away. It didn't seem to matter where I moved to in the room he always found a way to blend in and look relaxed within a few feet of me. I came up beside him.

"Hey."

"Hey yourself."

"I'm going to go freshen up before the dance starts. Do I need an escort?" I already knew the answer. He pushed off the table he was leaning against and put his hand at the small of my back.

"Yeah, you do. Let's find Julie and Sharon too, safety in numbers." he said.

I rolled my eyes, but okay whatever made him happy. We rounded up Julie and Sharon and found the nearest ladies room. Van went in first and cleared it before allowing us in. Thankfully no one else was in there or they would have had the surprise of the night when he looked under the stall. The bathroom was long, spacious and elegant with a full length mirror and a large orange bench in the corner for sitting. I sat down on the bench and readjusted my liner stiffening up my leg with extra socks. God bless thigh highs. Julie and Sharon were fixing their makeup and I was keeping a close eye on Julie. She looked worse now than she did before dinner.

Sharon snapped her purse closed and walked over, sitting beside me. "So who's the hottie?" I smiled surprised she had made it this long without asking.

"Donovan MacNamara. He's a dance instructor from Ireland. He came over to work some routines with me."

Her eyebrow went up, "Really? All the way from Ireland huh? So was he the friend that was with you on the bridge?" She used quotation marks around friend.

"Yeah, he has been a good friend the last few days." He has been my lifeline, but that wasn't going to be shared with Sharon.

I decided to change the subject. "So where were you last night when I called?"

Sharon looked sheepish, "Jesse's."

"I bet you thought it was funny watching the Weather Channel so you could tell me how great the weather was in Florida." I said offhandedly. But her face got serious and her voice lost its teasing tone.

"No I didn't think any part of our conversation was funny. It was killing me to be so close to you and not be able to be there for you. Len and Jess had to hide all the keys so I wouldn't go out in the storm."

I was silent for a beat or two and laid my hand on her lap, "I'm sorry if I worried you. I got through the storm with a little help from a friend and I thought about what you said last night. Once again you were right and when I really took the time to think about it I already knew what the reasons were. I'm still really glad you're here. I've missed you more than I thought possible."

She leaned her cheek against mine, "Me too, sweetie."

My eyes flicked back to Julie. She was leaning against the countertop, her hands the only thing keeping her from falling down and it didn't look like they were going to hold much longer. Her head was hung low and she was gulping in air. She had broken out in a cold sweat and her eyes were teary.

"Jules?"

I jumped up and went over to her putting my arm around her waist. I guided her over to Sharon on the bench and got a cold washcloth to wipe down her forehead as she lay on Sharon's lap gasping for breath.

Sharon was terribly worried and she looked up at me, "Get Jesse."

Terror filled Julie's eyes and she moaned no. And it was then that I knew something was very wrong. I gave her a few moments to see if she would improve before making a scene. Slowly she sat up and gave us a weak smile. She leaned forward putting her head in her hands.

"I'm sorry." And she began crying softly. Oh boy. We were floundering around in the dark on this one.

"Julie, what's wrong honey?" Sharon was rubbing her arm trying to get her to stop crying.

I brought her some tissues and she laughed a sad laugh as I handed them to her. "Nothing's wrong and everything is wrong."

She was getting her color back and I was feeling that at least I wouldn't need to call an ambulance.

"Jules I have been asking you for days if you are sick. I noticed you didn't eat anything tonight and no offense, but you didn't look too good this morning either." Her plate went untouched as did her coffee this morning, but I chalked it up to being busy running the show. Obviously there was a bigger problem. "Maybe you should eat something and you will feel better." I suggested.

She moaned a little and covered her mouth with her hand, "No I don't need any food, please no."

Sharon had her arm around her shoulder trying to keep her calm, "Julie, you are scaring us honey. What do you mean nothing's wrong and everything is wrong?

I sat down in front of her not caring about anything other than my best friend and her pain, "Is it like everything is going so right in one part of your life and so wrong in the other?"

She nodded, "Something like that. Only everything is going so right in one part of my life and so wrong in the same part." And now I'm confused again. "Is this about Jesse? You look so happy when you are together, I don't understand." And I needed to before Jesse did something tonight that he shouldn't.

"Yes, well no, well yes, it's me, not Jesse. Jesse doesn't know."

"Know what Julie?" I asked her softly trying to keep her calm. Her eyes were pleading and begging me not to ask anymore questions.

"I'm going to take a line from your book, Jules. We can't help you if you don't tell us what's wrong. We are here to listen." And she was torn, wanting to tell us and being terribly afraid of whatever this secret was.

She hiccuped softly and said, "I'm pregnant." And with that one single statement my world stopped spinning for a moment.

"Oh my." I said as I heard Sharon suck in a breath and she covered her mouth with her hand.

Julie's voice broke, "I don't know how it happened."

I gave her a shy grin.

"I mean I know how it happened, but it shouldn't have, you know? I don't know how to tell Jess." And I could see terror in her eyes at the thought.

Sharon recovered and asked, "Why honey? He loves you, oh how he loves you, and he will love this baby. He would give you the moon if he thought it would make you happy."

"I know Sharon, but I don't want him to think that I did this on purpose to, you know, trap him or something. I know he loves me." She hiccuped again, "I know he would do anything for me, but..."

"But you are afraid that you are going to lose him because of the baby? I guess I'm confused." I said.

She started breathing fast again and I took her hand to calm her. "Jules, take a deep breath, slow it down. I don't want you passing out on us."

She started to tear up again. "I can't lose him. I can't. I love him too much. I only found out about the baby a few weeks ago, but I already love the little bean too. I didn't do this on purpose. I want you guys to know that," she searched my face, "I didn't. It's just so complicated."

I held her hand rubbing it slowly trying to get her to slow her breathing before she hyperventilated, "Jules, no one is going to think you did this on purpose. We know the kind of person you are and so does Jess, honey. Accidents happen, but you have to tell him."

Sharon asked softly, "How far along are you?"

"Almost twelve weeks." she said embarrassedly.

Wow. "I don't think you are going to be able to hide it much longer sweetie."

I looked up at Sharon and her eyes were shining with tears. I could tell it was taking everything she had not to run out there and tell her son and make it better for this girl. Her words crawled past the shock in my mind, "And why is it complicated? He loves you and you love him and this little baby is a blessing to our family no matter if it was planned or not."

"Paul." I almost didn't hear Sharon utter the name. I looked up at her in surprise. Paul was Jesse's real dad but he hadn't been in the picture for years. He never came to Jesse's graduation or Brent's funeral.

"Forgive me for being obtuse, Mom, but what does Paul have to do with this?"

Sharon leaned in and asked Julie, "Has Jesse told you about Paul?"

Julie nodded wiping her nose, "Oh yeah, he told me everything about him once after he had too much to drink. He has never spoke of him again. He has no time for that man."

Sharon rubbed her back absently, "Jesse only learned how to be the man he is today because of Sugar's dad, but he did learn one lesson from Paul and that was that you don't turn your back on your family. He will not turn his back on his baby and the love of his life. He is nothing like his father you don't have to worry about that. He will do the right thing." And that is what she is afraid of. I saw the look on her face the moment Sharon said it.

"Ahhh, that's what you are afraid of isn't it, Julie? You are afraid that he will do the right thing even if it isn't what he wants."

She flipped her hand ever so slightly, threw her arms around me and sobbed on my shoulder. My heart broke because I knew the exact opposite was true. This man was outside the door right now nervously wondering if she will agree to be his wife. Tears were rolling down Sharon's face and I knew this was killing her.

"Jules look at me." She leaned back and gave me a really pathetic attempt at a smile. "Do you really think that Jess isn't going to want to be with you? Has he ever given you any indication that he isn't happy because this morning in the ballroom when we were alone that was not the impression I got."

She shook her head, "No. He always tells me he fell in love with me years ago and he was just waiting for me to catch up."

I smiled at her softly, "Yeah, now that sounds like Jess. He's a softie at heart. I don't even have to think about this. I automatically know that Jess is going to love this baby as much as you do as soon as you tell him. I know I already do."

She gave me a genuine smile then and nodded. I stood up deciding that we needed a plan of action. "I want you to do something for me okay?"

She sat up straighter, "Okay." And she sounded so defeated that I almost told her about the ring.

"Are you feeling well enough to go out and start the dance?"

"Yeah." And her head was still hung low. She didn't look like she was ready for anything other than a bed, but I gave her credit for trying.

"Good, then we are going to clean you up and we are going to go back out there and we are going to make our way through the rest of this night and then tomorrow we tell Jesse. Sharon and I will be with you if you want or you can tell him alone. However you want to do it, but I think it's time to tell you him, don't you?"

She agreed. "It's getting hard not to, I've been having these spells and passing them off as being overworked, but he's starting to get worried."

"No, he's past worried. He told me he was dragging you to the doctor on Monday whether you liked it or not."

She held up her palms, "Been there, done that."

I helped her up and maneuvered her back to the sink getting her cleaned up and her makeup fixed. In a few minutes she was looking good as new and Sharon and I were standing behind her all three of us reflected in the mirror. I took her hand and smiled at her reflection in the mirror. She still looked scared, but she looked stronger. Almost as if telling someone lifted some of the strain.

Sharon leaned over her shoulder and whispered. "If it matters to you right now, I'm honored to be this baby's grandma."

God bless Kleenex.

THIRTY-THREE

We stepped out the door and were greeted by Van and Jesse, both looking worried. Jess immediately took Julie's arm sensing her weakness.

"You okay?" He asked Julie, but he looked over at me. I tried to look very interested in the handicapped door opener.

"Yeah I'm fine." She patted his arm, but I could tell she was holding on to her composure by a thread. We all walked back towards the ballroom to start the dance and I hung back letting them get a few steps in front of us.

Van leaned in close, "What's going on? I can tell something is wrong."

I smiled at him, a huge "my heart is still trying to believe it" smile, "No just the opposite." I leaned in very close and whispered. "Julie's pregnant."

Van's eyes became the size of saucers, but to his credit he just tossed his eyes to Jess. I shook my head no and his eyebrows went up further. I knew what I had to do and I had an ace in the hole. I waited for everyone to sit down at their tables while I approached the DJ and spoke to him for a minute before taking the microphone.

"Ladies and gentleman, if I could have your attention please." I waited while the room quieted and everyone settled in. I looked around for Jesse and Julie spotting them near the wall, Jess's arm around Julie's waist. She had her head lying on his shoulder and he looked worried and nervous.

I waited for the room to quiet down before I began. "I wanted to take a moment to say a very special thank you to Julie Morris. She was the driving force behind tonight's dinner spending hours and hours getting all of this ready. I was wondering why she didn't let me help more, but I guess now I know." The room chuckled and Jesse smiled shaking his head. "Every year for the past eight years I have had the honor of choosing the volunteer of the year for MAMBOS and every year it is an extremely difficult task. We have so many wonderful volunteers that help us each and every day at the foundation and I would like to take a moment to recognize them all."

I took a few moments to read off the names of the volunteers having them stand at their tables. In all over forty people were standing when I got done and they got a long round of applause. After it settled I continued, "But this year I had no qualms about who would be getting the award tonight. Most of you know her as the go-to lady for anything that needs to get done at the foundation. She has volunteered her time helping me with every aspect of the foundation for the last two years asking for nothing in return. Anything I ask, any crazy idea I come up with, she carries out and has become my sister in arms as we do everything we can to further the cause of organ donation. I would like to introduce you to the MAMBOS Volunteer of the Year, Julie Morris."

I tucked the microphone under my arm and the DJ played Mariah Carey's "Hero" softly as Jesse led Julie onto the floor. She was crying and shaking her head at me. I handed her the MAMBOS Volunteer of the Year plaque and she pulled me into a hug whispering in my ear, "I love you, but I can't speak right now."

"I know, hon, you don't have to." I whispered back.

I turned back to the crowd. "Each year after I pick the volunteer of the year I have something made in their honor that will be sold for the next year as the MAMBOS fundraiser. Last year it was the necklace I see many of you wearing tonight. This year I decided a bracelet would be what was made to honor Julie."

Van stepped forward and handed it to me and I explained it to the crowd, "Each year we try to incorporate a butterfly theme into whatever item is made and this year, more than any year, it was very important to me to have the item reflect every organ donor and their selfless gift. I also wanted it to represent what Julie is in life. She has helped our family through a difficult time, she has helped me through a very difficult time and I'm extremely lucky to call her my friend. As I sat thinking about her and everything she is the design came to me. It's a design that I had carved into Brent's special spot at my home and it was the very first thing that came to mind when I thought of Julie. There are eight butterflies, one large one followed by seven smaller ones entwined on a vine that when clasped around the wrist is a never-ending circle. Julie never got to meet Brent, but I hope that every time she looks at the bracelet she will remember how much she has done in his name for all of us." I stepped over to Julie and fastened the bracelet on her wrist. "I'm not going to ask Jules to give a speech because she wasn't expecting this, but I do ask that you give her a round of applause and thank her for her hours of hard work."

I looked over at Jesse as everyone clapped and his face was filled with the love he felt for her and I knew everything was going to be alright. I pulled Julie into a hug and Jesse pulled the microphone out of my hand. I looked up at him in surprise and he gave me a nervous smile and I knew the time had come. I pulled out of Julie's embrace and whispered "I love you" before taking the plaque out of her hands and stepping off the floor. I joined Van and Sharon at the table.

Jesse began to tell everyone how he had met Julie many years ago through work and how she was a natural when it came to helping people. It's her nature he told us, it's who she is. Everyone in the room was nodding because they knew he was right. I felt Van's arm slide around my shoulder as Jesse continued to talk. He went on to tell everyone how she had been there for him when he needed a friend and how she had helped him see that he could move on with his life without forgetting his brother. That he could honor his brother by living life to the fullest. Julie reached out and took his hand as he choked up.

He cleared his throat, the nervousness getting the better of him for a minute, but he finally continued. "Sugar was right when she said Julie has helped our family through a very difficult time." As he got down on one knee the lights dimmed and the music changed to "Marry Me". He reached into his pocket, pulling out the ring. "And now I am hoping that she will agree to become part of our family. Julie Ann Morris, I have loved you since the first day I met you and I know you have caught up. You are the one who makes my mornings brighter and my nights calmer. Say you will marry me because I need you by my side."

Julie was crying and so was Jesse. Not to mention me, Sharon and Lenny. I saw Sharon, her hand over her heart not sure if what she was witnessing was real. So much was about to be hers and my heart couldn't be fuller. She caught my eye and shook her finger at me having figured out I knew.

I looked back to the floor and we all held our breath waiting for Julie to answer. Tears were flowing down her cheeks and the relief on her face was evident. I was worried she was going to fall down right there. Instead she whispered, "With all my heart, yes." And Jess slipped the ring on her finger. Everyone clapped and whistled as they shared a kiss and we all watched as they danced to the first song of the rest of their lives.

THIRTY-FOUR

I need a break. I had done a foxtrot, two rumbas, a cha-cha, two slow dances with men who were old enough to be my grandfather and group line dance to "Life is a Highway". Thankfully I had no one lined up for another dollar dance. Julie had convinced me about a month ago that a dollar dance type fundraiser would be fun to do tonight. All I had to do was dance with anyone willing to make a ten dollar donation to the foundation. I convinced her to up the ante to fifty bucks hoping that it would keep the numbers down to a minimum. At the time I had no interest in spending the night dancing with every man in Duluth and I also hadn't decided if I was even going. She didn't let me off the hook that easily. She did agree to the fifty dollar donation and then she lined up some other local celebrities that would dance as well. As it turned out fifty dollars was not stopping people from paying for a dance with me. They were keeping me busy and I was smiling because each fifty bucks was more money that we could put towards helping those who really needed it. But I was tired and I needed to adjust my leg before I attempted any more fast songs. Nothing like having your leg fly off and clonk someone on the noggin to ruin the night.

As I worked my way to the edge of the dance floor I was looking around for Van. I always needed an escort to the bathroom because I guess there weren't enough people around to hear me yelling. I rolled my eyes. I understood the "plan" but it was still kind of annoying. I couldn't find him or Jesse in the crowd and I got a funny feeling in the pit of my stomach. The plan was that one of them would always be within ten feet of me on the dance floor. As I got to the corner of the floor I noticed a man in a suit standing with his hands clasped in front of him, legs apart. He walked forward as I entered the shadows at the edge of the dance floor.

He stepped in front of me, "Tula DuBois?" And all the hair on my arms was standing on end. I didn't know him and the way he was looking at me made my stomach roll. He was large, bigger than Van or Jesse, and stocky. He looked like a linebacker for the Green Bay Packers except meaner and uglier. He had a large scar that went like a crescent moon down his face and his eyes were hard. I looked around desperately for Jesse or Van hoping to spot them quickly.

"Don't bother looking for your guys, they're busy. Now you are going to smile and dance with me like you have known me your whole life." He pulled back his suit coat far enough for me to see his gun and that was all I needed. I smiled and he pulled me into the promenade position.

"Very good. Now listen closely. I have a message for you. My boss wants the key and we know you have it."

I wasn't going to let it happen this way. I was not going to be afraid and I was not going to stand here and miss the opportunity to get information. "Maybe I do, maybe I don't, but I won't make any deals until I see for myself that Margie and Nathan are alive." False bravado, but I was angry and I was tired of this whole insanity.

I can't say he smiled, it seemed more like a snarl to me. "My boss figured you would say that." He reached into his pocket and pulled out a picture.

My friends stared back at me. I could tell it was a recent picture because I had been with Margie when she got that haircut. The shot was from the waist up and Nathan had his arm around Margie; she looked hollow, her eyes telling me her story. I strained to memorize the picture in my mind before he put it away.

He tucked it back in his coat pocket. "Now, where's the key."

I rolled my eyes, like I'm going to bring it with me tonight. "It's at the police station in a locked box. Do I look stupid?" I could tell it was not the answer he was looking for.

"I don't believe you. I think you have the key and you and your buddies are trying to find what it belongs to."

"Want to help me with that? I wouldn't mind knowing what it belongs to." I said flippantly.

He laughed like I had told him a smashing good joke, "That's your job to figure out. We don't have a clue, haven't been able to get it out of that bitch of McElevain's." I wanted to heave. He said it like he had tried, hard.

Time to find out what he did know. "Listen, my brother is the detective. The other teacher has nothing to do with this." And I didn't believe for a second that they didn't know who Van was, but I wanted confirmation.

He snorted. "Nice try. We know who Agent Walsh is, you aren't fooling anyone. I've had the rather unpleasant experience of dealing with him before so listen to me now. My boss is angry and when he's angry he sometimes forgets that he isn't supposed to kill people so you might want to let your brother and your lover know that their time is coming. And Margie has a message for you. She told me to tell you that she left her silver ring at the mall and she wants you to get it."

I had no idea what he was talking about. Maybe it was because I was scared to death for my friends, ticked off that he threatened the two most important men in my life and sick for my friend and what she was going through at the hands of these men.

"I have no idea what she is talking about." I finally stammered out.

"You're a smart girl, I'm sure you'll figure out it. And don't worry we will know when you do and then new instructions will follow. If I were you I wouldn't think about it too long though, your friends don't have much time left and neither do you." He dropped my arms and stepped into the shadows.

"Don't follow me or your brother and lover will be dead." He disappeared into the shadows and I stood alone on the dance floor staring after him unable to move.

"Tula!"

"Sugar!"

I hear Van and then Jesse yelling as they each came from a different direction. They both reached me at nearly the same time, Van a few steps ahead of Jesse. He looked at my face and it was enough to tell him that something was very wrong.

I pulled Jesse up to me. "Big guy, scar on his face, said he'd shoot you if you came after him. He went out the side doors toward the parking garage."

He took off running for the door pushing his way through the people. Van took my arm and escorted me off the dance floor taking me out into the hallway for air. I sat down on a padded bench that backed up to the bingo hall. I could hear them calling numbers and the absurdity of life hit me. Tears of anger were breaking loose and Van sat down beside me and put his arm around me.

"Where were you guys?" It came out in a choked, angry voice. "Why couldn't I find you?"

Van pulled me into him and I pushed him away. I wasn't mad at him, I was mad at this whole situation in general. He spun around and knelt down on the floor putting his hands on my knees.

"Dewey came and said a security guard asked him to get us. They said you were ill and that they had taken you to the sick bay to lie down. We couldn't find you on the dance floor and we both took off thinking someone had you. Tell me what happened, Tula."

"I was there, Van! I was in the middle of the line dance. I wouldn't have left without telling you." I was getting hysterical and he knew it.

"It's okay, calm down. Tell me what happened." he said again. I told him everything I could remember about the guy and the picture he showed me of Margie and Nathan.

"Did he threaten you?" Van asked the question quietly, but I could hear the anger in his voice.

"He told me his boss was angry and when he gets angry he forgets he isn't supposed to kill people. He said that Margie, Nathan, me, you and Jesse don't have much time left. He seemed to have a very strong dislike for you."

"Damn it." He ran his fingers through his hair. Jesse came back in the door then and jogged over to the bench. I stiffened, afraid of the look on his face.

"He's gone." No kidding.

Van stood up, "He threatened Tula, told her that none of us have much time left."

Jesse stopped pacing and whipped around staring at me with his mouth hanging open. "Why didn't you follow him, Sugar, or start yelling or do something?" He was angry and I knew he wasn't angry at me. He was angry in general, but it still hurt.

"I don't know, Jesse. I guess I'm not very good at playing cop. He showed me his gun and told me if I followed him you and Van would be dead and he was scary and I believed him."

Van rubbed my arm whispering in my ear. "It's okay, you did good, you did exactly what you were supposed to do." He kissed my temple and I heard Jess let out a breath.

He plopped down on the other side of me, "I'm sorry, Sugar. I'm frustrated as hell with the case and exactly what I was afraid was going to happen is and I can't seem to get a handle on it."

I put my hand over his, "He did say a couple of things that I found interesting. They don't know what the key opens either. He said he couldn't get it out of Margie." That retching feeling came back and I took a deep breath. "He told me that Margie had a message for me. The message was "tell her I left my silver ring at the mall and I need her to go pick it up". Scarface was pretty sure it was a message telling me where to use the key."

"Scarface?" Jesse asked me.

"He's got this huge scar that runs from his ear down to his neck in a crescent shape."

Van stiffened beside me, "I know that guy. I gave him that scar."

Jesse and I both stared at him. "We were doing a raid on a club and he was there. He pulled a knife on me and I got it away from him and took a slash at him before he took off for parts unknown."

"What's his name? We can run him through the database and see if there is anyone connected to him and start to draw the net." Jesse said excitedly.

Van shrugged, "I don't know I always called him Scarface after that." And I started to giggle. Jesse rolled his eyes.

"I have gone through mug shot books looking for him and put his features into the programs we have, but so far I haven't gotten any good hits. He looks too much like every other thug out there. Until we get a mug shot of him with the scar I won't be able to figure out who he is." Van finished.

I thought of the other thing he said, "Oh, and he said they would know when we had the contents and new instructions would follow."

"Well," Jesse stood pulling me back up and running his hands up and down my arms, "nothing we can do right now anyway the mall is closed." I laughed despite myself and he smiled, "So I want you to go back inside and finish out the evening like nothing happened. I want to see that smile on your face I saw earlier and I want to see your feet moving across the dance floor. Tomorrow is soon enough to deal with all the rest. Okay?"

"For you I will."

He kissed my cheek and looked at Van, "Help her get cleaned up and then take her back in. Don't get farther than a few feet from her." I could tell by Van's body language he didn't need to be told that.

"I have to go find Dew and see if he can describe the security guy and then I'm going to go talk to the supervisor about seeing the surveillance video. I don't think it is going to help us much though."

Van shook his head, "Probably not and forget about Dew. He left, said he had to take Ivy home she wasn't feeling well."

Jess hung his head, "Alright, I will stop by the inn tomorrow and talk to him then."

Julie and Sharon came out of the ballroom looking concerned and spotted us by the bingo hall. Jesse gave Van and I the look that said "not a word".

"Jesse, what's going on?" Julie took his arm and they were both looking back and forth waiting for an answer.

I jumped in to save him, "Hi ladies, sorry I started feeling a little dizzy, and so my two knights brought me out for some fresh air. That's all." I could tell that Julie wasn't buying it, but thankfully Sharon was. I would have to let Jess deal with Julie.

Sharon had concern written all over her face. "Are you feeling ill, Sugar? Do you want to go lay down?" And I felt bad lying to her after what happened earlier with Jules. She came over and took my other arm ready to lead me away like a two-year-old to bed.

"No. I'm fine Mom, really." I said planting my feet on the ground.

Jesse whipped around and stared at me slack jawed, "You called her mom." Sharon and I laughed at his reaction.

"Well, that's what she is, Jess." I put my arm around her shoulders and he broke into a huge grin and he pulled us both into a big hug.

"You got that right, Sug. Now, I want you to go freshen up or whatever you ladies do when you spend hours in the bathroom and then come back out and finish the night. I'm going to find Julie a snack." He loped off towards the casino and the three musketeers headed to the ladies room to freshen up while Van stood watch at the door.

"Well, weren't we just here?" I asked and they both laughed. I was hoping to keep them from asking too many questions and thankfully Julie had other things on her mind.

"Did you know Sugar? Did you know he was going to propose?" Julie asked.

"Yeah, he told me this morning at the lodge. He wanted me to know that he was going to make the first good memory for this night. I think he was afraid I wouldn't show up. But he was right in more ways than one. It was all I could do not to tell you earlier. You were breaking my heart."

Julie put her hand on her belly, "I'm going to tell him after the party. I don't want him to be blind sided by it, you know. I don't know how he's going to react to becoming a fiancé and a father in one night."

"After my discussion with him earlier I'm pretty sure he is going to be completely relieved that you aren't dying of a horrible disease and this will seem like a bump in the road once he knows." I said, sitting down on the bench with the premise of adjusting my leg. In reality I was building up my courage to go back out there with a smile on my face and pretend that nothing had happened.

Julie came over and sat down beside me stilling my hand as I adjusted my socks, "Tell me what is going on, please. And don't lie and say nothing, because you saw how that worked for me earlier. It's pretty obvious to me that Van is more than a dance instructor from Ireland."

I heard Sharon snicker from the counter where she was fixing her hair, "All you have to do is catch him looking at her when he thinks no one else is and figure that out. That boy is smitten. And how he calls her Tula, it melts my heart!"

A smile played across my lips because I was pretty sure that wasn't what Julie meant, but at least Sharon was convinced. "He's become special to me the last few days. He protected me from some stuff that otherwise might have hurt me and yeah, I like him, a lot." I moved my eyes to Sharon and back to Julie and mouthed "talk to Jess".

There was a beat or two of silence and she said, "Well, he better be careful because Jess has mentioned a few times how he doesn't like the way he looks at you." And I knew she understood even if she didn't look happy.

"Yeah but Jesse wouldn't like it if Mr. Rogers looked at me cross-eyed. He's a little overprotective."

243

Sharon burst out laughing and was forced to agree with that statement. We left the restroom together and Julie went off to find Jess. I said a prayer they were still engaged when they came back.

THIRTY-FIVE

I spent the next hour doing dollar dances while Van kept the perimeter of the floor covered at all times. I really didn't expect anymore issues tonight. They came and said their piece and now they would wait for us to figure out the message. I wasn't even worried about that anymore, but I was very worried about Julie. She hadn't come back in the room yet and I was praying she wasn't ill again. If she didn't show up soon I was going to have to tell Jess so he could find her. I didn't want to do that, but I didn't know what else to do. I was finishing up a tango with a local author who had made a very generous donation to the foundation when I saw them step in the room. Jess was standing behind her his arms wrapped around her waist, his chin on her shoulder smiling ear to ear. He locked eyes with mine and it was all over.

I thanked the gentleman for the dance and walked off the dance floor before someone else could grab me. I made my way over to them. He had a look of total amazement on his face. He saw me coming and let go of Julie with one arm pulling me into a bear hug.

"I'm gonna be a daddy." His voice held a touch of awe.

"I'm so excited for you, Jess." And once again the tears were there, tears of happiness.

I looked over at Julie and she looked exhausted and sick, but relieved. Jess released me and I took a step back, "Is everything okay? I thought you weren't going to tell him yet."

Jess led us over to an empty table and we sat down. Julie put her hand on the table, "I found him coming back from the security office and refused to let him by until he told me what was going on. He took me to a room and I reminded him that I'm also a cop and can spot one from a mile away. Since he isn't very good at lying to my face I got him to admit who Van was. Then he started telling me what he had done and I started talking loudly."

Jess interrupted. "Yelling, that's her way of saying she was yelling and she got so upset that she almost passed out. I grabbed her as she was going down."

Julie looked embarrassed, "It's been a long night."

245

Concern filled my throat, "I think maybe you should take her home, Jess."

Julie held up her hand, "No, I'm good."

Jess shook his head the way a father does at his kid and rolled his eyes, "She wouldn't let me call an ambulance either, told me it would pass. I laid her down on the floor and told her I was taking her to the hospital and there was this look of fear on her face that made me certain that something was very wrong. I told her that it didn't matter to me what was making her so afraid, she needed to tell me before she made herself any sicker than she already was."

"Then I told him he was going to be a daddy and the whole story came pouring out, but it came out all wrong,"

"And I sat there like a big dumb moose trying to sort it all out." And I'm loving this because they are finishing each other's sentences already. "But finally the light went on and what she was telling me started to sink in."

"And then he started crying and I thought he was that unhappy about the baby."

"When actually I was so relieved that she wasn't sick or dying, but then I thought about a baby and I pretty much lost it. Can you imagine Sugar, a baby!" I was smiling at his disbelief of the whole thing. Jess held up his hand. "Suffice it to say that we are fine. I wish she had told me earlier. I've been so worried about her. I would have made it better."

Things can be so cut and dried for men sometimes. I shrugged my shoulder, "She was scared, Jess. She was afraid you wouldn't want the baby. She was afraid you wouldn't want her. It might not make sense to you, but it was very real for her."

He looked at her then his eyes so full of love, "Yeah, if only I had known. I would have set her straight." And suddenly I wondered what it would feel like to share another life with someone I loved that much. And I knew a week ago that thought would have never crossed my mind.

My eyes drifted toward Van, "I would have warned you she was coming, but I couldn't find you. I figured out pretty quick that you hadn't told her the truth, but I..."

Jess waved a hand, "It's okay. I hadn't told her because I didn't want to add to whatever was causing her so much distress. I'm kicking myself for not picking up on the baby thing earlier."

"You've had a lot on your plate, Jess, and I'm partially to blame for that. I want you to promise me that you will stop worrying so much about me and concentrate on your new family now."

He gave me the father head shake this time, "No, I won't promise that. I worry about you every day, every hour and that's going to continue. But at least I know what's going on with my new fiancée now and I can let out a breath, finish this case and then spend the rest of my life with this beautiful woman and my baby."

Julie stood back up, "Don't worry, I'll beat him later for you." She said winking at me.

I laughed out loud, "Go easy on him, Jules, at least he sent me someone easy on the eyes."

I heard the next song begin and the lights dimmed, the disco ball twirling lazily throwing soft shadows around the floor. I heard the DJ say, "This one goes out to all the lovers out there." And Mr. Bublé started crooning "You'll Never Find Another Love". Jess and Julie headed to the floor and I was about to sit this one out when I felt Van behind me. He grabbed my hand and pulled me onto the dance floor.
He locked me to him and whispered, "I know this one. It's a rumba." And a slow smile spread across my face as he began his Cuban breaks. God bless Michael Bublé.

It was nearly midnight and things were winding down. Van deposited me in a chair next to Lenny and Sharon after our final rumba. He got me a Diet Coke and told me he would be right back and not to move. That wasn't going to be a problem. Tonight was wonderful, but I was exhausted, emotionally and physically. So much had happened I was still having a hard time wrapping my mind around all of it. I understood very deeply that my life had done a complete three sixty, going from complete emptiness to so full that it was bursting at the seams. I had a new man in my life and he may not be here to stay, but he was teaching me so much about how to feel again. I had a new godbaby that was right at the top of my list of people who changed my life and soon I was going to have another little baby to hug and kiss and he or she was going to be a culmination of the two people that I loved so much. On a night that I had lost so much ten years ago I felt like I had come full circle and I was experiencing the joy of all my hard work and the pain I had suffered through. I made a resolution to live the rest of my life remembering this night.

Sharon leaned over, "Len and I are coming back to Wisconsin."

I looked at her with a sudden ill feeling in the pit of my stomach. I didn't want them involved in any of this and having them here was going to complicate matters. "Really?" And I was pretty sure she heard the tremble in my voice.

"We want to be here to help plan the wedding. We already miss everyone too much when we are gone. We've figured out that we aren't great snowbirds. We are going to leave tomorrow and fly to Ohio to be with Melanie and Steve and then we will head back down to Florida to pack up. We should be back by the first of December." And I let out a breath knowing that gave us almost a month to get this all fixed.

Melanie was Len's daughter and she lived in a little town outside Dayton, Ohio, with her husband and twin sons, Charlie and Connor. Melanie was the result of a weekend fling while on tour with the ski team. He didn't marry her mother, but they were still good friends and he raised Melanie with her mother and did a great job. She's a great girl and Len is very proud of her. They spend every Thanksgiving with them enjoying a big fall festival every year. Len and the boys go off to do guy things and Mel and Sharon weave their way through the craft booths.

"What about your place in Florida? You rented that for the whole season. Aren't you going to lose a lot of money?" I asked still not sure about their plan.

She waved her hand at me, "Money, shmoney! This is my grandbaby you are talking about. Besides I called my friend and asked her if her sister still needed a place to stay while her condo was being redone. She was thrilled when I told her our place would be open after December first so it's all arranged. She will take over the lease and we will come back to where we should have never left."

I smiled at her, "That sounds great. I'm glad you will be here for Christmas." I knew I was going to need to be with people who loved me by then because as good as I felt right now I knew that once Van left I would need to use my reserves.

The room suddenly hushed and I noticed the spotlight come on. I looked up wondering why and saw Van on the dance floor holding the microphone. My heart picked up its beat at the sight of him, still dashingly handsome even after so many long hours in his suit in a room with no one he knew. He had stuck close to me the entire night bringing me drinks and pulling me away for rest breaks when he saw me fading. He was gentle and caring and patient and I was trying to convince myself I didn't love him. Infatuation I told myself, that was it, simple infatuation. Then he began to speak.

His accent was heavy as it always is when he is tired. "Good evening. I wanted to take a moment to introduce myself before the final dance. My name is Donavan MacNamara and I came here to Duluth to dance with Ms. Tula DuBois but a few days ago. Her reputation reaches far and wide and when the chance came to work some routines with her it was an opportunity I couldn't turn down. I boarded a plane in Dublin and when I landed in Duluth it was freezing and I was convinced I had landed at the tip of the end of the world." The audience chuckled many nodding their heads. "What I found instead was that the Twin Ports are beautiful amazing towns with amazing people. I have been welcomed everywhere I have gone, though I think it helps to be accompanied by Tula," He winked at me and I could feel the color rising on my cheeks.

"and what I have learned about life in the few short days I have been here is more than what I've learned in my thirty years combined."

I avoided looking at Jesse knowing the look that would be on his face. Sharon leaned over and put her hand on my arm giving me the mother knows all look. I tried to concentrate on Van as he continued.

"The first morning I was here Tula was schooling me on the finer points of American coffee," that got him a round of laughter, "and in the background was this mishmash of music playing and anyone who has spent any time with Tula knows that there is always music playing. So I asked her about her interesting choices in music and do you know what she told me?"

Jesse yelled out, "It's none of your business!" And the crowd went wild. Ugh.

Van was laughing, hard, "Close, it went something like do I have to justify my music choices for you?" He grinned and the audience was still laughing. I dumped my head in my hand and caught sight of Jesse nodding along like he was the funniest guy on the planet.

Van recovered and the audience settled down a little. "But it's what she said next that has captivated me this week. She said "Music is about the rhythm. It's about what my feet want to do when the first few bars start. It's about if it makes me happy, sad, angry or lonely. Music is about what memories it brings back and the memories it makes. If I couldn't dance music would just be notes, but when I dance it becomes my soul." There was a hush in the room as he spoke.

Sharon raised a brow, "Seems like he's been paying attention."

I tipped my chin and saw her smile out of the corner of my eye. Van went on. It was getting a little much if you ask me, but no one did.

"You are all incredibly lucky to have someone like Tula DuBois amongst you and I can see by the gathering of people tonight that you already know that. Jesse told me about the dinner a few days ago and asked me to pick a song for the final dance of the evening. So as I danced with her this week I tossed around the songs that are my soul when I dance. Tula introduced me to a great new song, you might know it," and he began to sing, "'The legend lives on from the Chippewa on down of the big lake they call Gitche Gumee.'" And the crowd went wild, literally. He should know better than to sing these people's theme song if he didn't want a sing along!

He held up his hand, "It's a great song, but it's not what I picked. See I had this conversation with Tula last night and she told me she thought the foxtrot was boring." He hung his head and shook it back and forth as the audience laughed and it even forced a laugh out of me. "I knew exactly what it would be after she told me that. This song for me is my soul when I dance. For some it will bring back memories and for some I hope it makes new ones."

He walked towards me stopping at the edge of the dance floor. "May I have this dance?"

I stood and walked forward entranced by the smile on his face. He bowed and reached out with his hand. I placed my hand in his and he pulled me onto the dance floor. There was whistling and hooting and a few chants of Sugar before the music started. The spotlight was shining down on us and I looked up at Van, his eyes sparkling. He pulled me into the promenade position and I heard Sam Cooke crooning "You Send Me". He led me into the first few box steps of the foxtrot giving me time to regroup.

He whispered into my ear, "This song is all about the lyrics. My feet already knew they wanted to dance with you."

He began to spin me working me through a series of feather steps and turns as we moved around the dance floor. As the music picked up tempo he moved me through weaves and feather steps mixed with chains of open and closed turns. I wasn't sure if my feet were actually touching the floor. I wasn't just moving through the steps, I was dancing. For the first time in a long time, I was dancing. I knew in that moment that he had given me back the ability to really experience something that was at the heart of my soul. He pulled me to him towards the end of the song, adding a few moves that I was pretty sure were not on the list of approved foxtrot steps, ending with a gentle kiss on the final note. The music died off and the crowd clapped and whistled. We stood in the middle of the floor, the spotlight off, the room dark.

"Did I lie?" He asked as he rubbed my back.

"Hardly." The heat was low in my belly and I was ready for this party to end.

THIRTY-SIX

By the time we said goodbye to the last guests it was nearly one a.m. and I needed to sleep. I had experienced every emotion possible tonight, fear, surprise, amazement, joy, love and breathlessness. Julie and I stepped away to thank the convention manager for such a wonderful job and took a few extra minutes to thank the employees who had helped with overseeing that things went smoothly. We rejoined Van and Jesse who were standing near the doors of the hall waiting for us. I could see by their body language that they were both done for the night. They had spun their wheels trying to figure out who Scarface was, as I took to calling him. I was practically holding Julie up and I passed her off to Jess before we both fell down. Both guys had a couple hour old five o'clock shadow and their shoulders were sagging. The long hours were catching up to everyone and I wanted sit down where I was and not move. Van pulled me to him and I laid my head on his shoulder.

"I think we need to get these ladies to their quarters Jess." And I saw Jesse nod.

They led us through the casino towards the main entrance. I assumed that was where the limo was waiting to take us home. Instead they led us past the main entrance to the casino, past the Starbucks and arcade and down a long hallway to the elevators. Van turned to the elevator and punched the up button. Julie was nearly passed out and Jess was half carrying her with his arm around her waist. They herded us into the elevator and Van punched the number two and threw Jesse a card.

"Consider it an early wedding gift from a friend." Jesse smiled snatching the card from the air. I let out a breath relieved to know that they didn't have to drive back home. I looked up at Van and he had his own card in his hand.

He winked at me. "Compliments of the hotel."

The elevator doors opened and Jesse and Julie stepped out. "Make her rest, Jess." I said and he gave a salute and headed down the hall.

Van held the door with his hand, "Meet me at eleven in the manager's office to go over that surveillance video. Or is that too early?" Jesse waved acknowledgement before disappearing into his room and the elevator door slid shut. Van hit the number three button and the elevator pulled us slowly up to the next level.

"So is this really compliments of the hotel?" I never could be sure with him.

"Are you Tula DuBois?" He asked and I rolled my eyes. Really.

"They gave us each a room for the night, but since I knew that mine would sit empty I figured Jess could use it. I kept the whirlpool room for us. I figured you might need if after tonight. You don't mind do you?"

He looked at me hungrily. Nope, don't mind at all. The doors opened and we stepped into the hall, Van looking both ways before letting me step out, his hand at the small of my back propelling me down the hall to our room. He opened the door and flipped on the lights taking a quick look around to make sure nothing was out of order. The room was beautiful. There was a king size bed in the middle covered with pillows and a corner whirlpool tub. Candles surrounded the tub that was already filled with bubbles and there was a bottle of champagne in a bucket of ice with two flutes sitting nearby. The lights dimmed.

"Turn out the light, come take my hand now. We've got tonight babe. Why don't you stay?" His arms came around my waist to do a backwards rumba, "Deep in my soul, I've been so lonely. All of my hopes, fading away. I've longed for love, like everyone else does. We got tonight babe. Why don't we stay?"

I turned and put my arms around his neck, "'We've Got Tonight', Bob Seger. I love that song." And he was kissing me as he slid the zipper down on my dress.

"Me too." he whispered as my dress pooled around my ankles. He reached around and pulled the hair pin and ribbon out of my hair and it slowly fell down around my ears again. He picked me up and set me on the bed pulling off my shoes and tearing my pantyhose away. My thong followed over my hips and then that too was gone. He leaned in and kissed me. "I've been wanting to do that all night."

Me too. "Seems to me that you have too many clothes on Mr. Bond."

I pulled his tie free and he threw his coat onto the bed. I reached for his shirt, but he stilled my hands bending down and releasing my leg before pulling my liner off. He picked me up, kissing me as he walked over to the tub and lowered me into the whirlpool gently until I felt the bottom. I let out a sigh as the warm water wrapped up around me and all the hours of dancing washed away with the gentle water. I probably could have fallen asleep right then, but I was being joined by a man with an obvious plan. I leaned into him and he put his arm around my waist pulling me onto his lap.

"Did you really not know that tonight was all about you?" He asked smoothing my hair back.

"No. I mean why would I? I'd done everything I could think of to block the whole thing out. We do an event like this every year and I expected it to be like every other year. I'm really not as special as everyone made me out to be anyway you know."

He stroked my cheek his eyes softened by the glow of the candles, "I disagree. I happen to know that you are far more special than they made you out to be. I'm really proud of you. You did an amazing job tonight."

"I feel guilty for feeling the way I did about the whole thing now, but it was my only defense against my absolute mind numbing terror that I wouldn't get through it. Turned out that tonight was exactly what I needed." And it was so much more than that.

"I want you to know that tonight changed my life in a way that I never expected. There were so many amazing stories and so much love for such an inspiring family in that room. Honestly some people didn't know that you weren't all related. You function that well together. I have never been part of anything like that before and I couldn't be prouder to call you mi mot even if I couldn't say it out loud. You are so beautiful."

He was so serious and his eyes were soft and peering into mine like he could read my soul. He kissed me then letting his hands gently skim over my body under the water. He pulled away and shifted me back onto the bench reaching for the champagne flutes. He popped the cork on the bubbly and it sprayed into the tub, the coldness of the champagne a stark opposite of the warm water around me. I laughed out loud and threw my hands up to keep it from hitting me. He poured two flutes and set the bottle back into the bucket handing me one.

"Why, if I didn't know better, Mr. Bond, I would think you're trying to get me fluthered and have your way with me." I batted my eyelashes at him and he shook his finger at me.

"No, mi mot I don't need to get you fluthered to have my way with you." And he knew that was the absolute truth.

He pulled me back onto his lap, "I would like to make a toast, to my beautiful mi mot and to a night that I will never forget."

We clinked glasses and I took a drink of the champagne the bubbly tickling my throat as it went down. He took the glass out of my hand setting it back down by the bottle.

He sang into my ear while rubbing my back, "Tonight no one's gonna find us. We'll leave the world behind us. When I make love to you."

"'Tonight I Celebrate My Love', Peabo Bryson, foxtrot."

And then his lips were on mine and he wasn't singing anymore. He was stroking my body, the water gliding across my skin and I could feel that he didn't need any encouragement. I stroked him anyway enjoying how he deepened the kiss with each stroke. He pulled back, his eyes never leaving mine, and he reached around the champagne bucket, pulling out a condom.

I raised an eyebrow, "Compliments of the hotel?"

"No compliments of me." Thank God. And then there was no more talking and he had his way with me.

I laid against his chest my head over his shoulder my legs wrapped around his waist. He was still inside me and I loved how perfectly he fit and how natural it felt. He stirred under me and I moaned, from fatigue and the feeling of being well loved.

"I'm not sure how I'm going to get out of here." I whispered in his neck.

"I'm not sure I want to." His voice tickled my cheek and I had to agree.

He reluctantly moved me to the bench next to him and climbed down the stairs to grab some towels. The light reflected off his water slick skin revealing a scar that ran from his hip down to the back of his knee. It was barely visible and I hadn't noticed it before, but it was there tonight reflected in the candle light. He came out of the bathroom with a towel and robe for me. He lifted me out of the tub drying me before slipping the robe around me. He slid me under the sheets and went back to the tub blowing out the candles.

He climbed in next to me and pulled me into him spoon style. "I know you are exhausted. Sleep now mi mot." He had one arm thrown over my waist the other above his head and his breath was warm against my ear. I grabbed his hand and pulled it up around my chest hugging it to me.

"What does mi mot mean?" I asked sleepily. He had used it so many times the last few days and even as I was falling asleep I had to know.

He whispered softly into my ear, "It means my girl." And I drifted off into a peaceful sleep.

THIRTY-SEVEN

Someone was knocking. I rolled over and elbowed Van, "Someone's knocking."

He was at the door with his gun in his hand before I saw him move off the bed. The wall was blocking my view of the door and since I didn't know who it was I wasn't going to venture to the end to take a look.

"Who is it?"

"Room service."

I rolled my eyes. "This hotel doesn't have room service."

Van materialized from around the wall carrying a tray filled with food and coffee in one hand and a paper bag in the other.

"They do if you're Sugar DuBois." He looked at me with his I'm trying not to laugh at you grin on and he set the tray at the end of the bed.

I had my hands up in the air and my face pointed at the ceiling, "I'm so embarrassed." I didn't look down until I felt him climb back onto the bed.

"Why does all of this embarrass you so much? It's obvious that people really like you and appreciate what you do. I don't know if that's such a bad thing."

"No it's not and don't get me wrong I'm very grateful for everything that everyone has done for me, but I don't know, I just," my voice trailed off and I could see that it wasn't going to be a good enough answer for him. New tactic.

"Why do you get so embarrassed when someone starts praising you about what you have done for Lillie?"

He shrugged. "Because taking care of Lillie wasn't a chore to me, in the beginning I was doing it because it was the right thing to do and I was all she had, but the reality was that within a few days of having her with me she was my life and I needed her as much as she needed me."

And I could tell that wasn't an easy thing for him to admit.

"So in a way Lillie helped you because you had a purpose for getting up every day."

"Yeah something like that." And I could see that he was beginning to understand.

"When I started MAMBOS I told myself I was doing it because it was the right thing to do. I had all this money that I was never going to need and I knew that there were a lot of people who did need it, so the idea of MAMBOS began to form and suddenly I had a purpose. I had something I believed in deeply and it saved me from god knows what. I knew that I would never marry and have children and I was searching for a way to surround myself with people without investing too much emotionally. It didn't work. Now I'm just emotionally attached to half the people in Duluth and Superior." He laughed then and I motioned around the room. "So I'm embarrassed about all of this because the truth is that I needed all of these people in my life more than they needed me." And that was the first time I had ever said that out loud. Once again he was getting me to open up in ways that I never thought possible.

He still had his hand in mine and his head cocked to the side. "So how did you know that you would never get married? You were awfully young when you started MAMBOS."

Out of all of that this is what he gleans from it? Men have unique brains. "For a lot of men I'd be a lot to take on. I come with my own set of differences that maybe aren't..." I paused and blew some bangs out of my eyes, "you know what? We've been over this before. Let's forget it and eat." I eyed the tray and hoped that he would let it go, but he didn't.

"No, I don't want to forget it. We need to work on your self esteem. This is the side of you that you always try to hide. Your outward personality portrays this successful and fiercely independent woman who has the world by the tail and knows exactly what she wants out of it, but that isn't the case at all is it?" I was assuming that was a rhetorical question. "The truth is that somewhere deep inside you feel that you aren't worthy of being loved and that you deserve to be alone." And there you have it, the truth in a nutshell. It was pathetic, but true.

"For a long time I believed that, Van, but something in me is starting to change ever so much. You've made me feel over the last few days like maybe I'm not as huge of a burden to everyone as I think."

His jaw worked like it always did when he was trying not to say something he shouldn't. "This Geoff guy will be a lucky langer if I never meet him I swear to God. You would be a lot to take on for a man and you do have your own set of differences" he twined his fingers in mine, "but not in the way you picture it in your mind." He leaned over me pushing me down to the bed kissing me, hands twined in mine above my head. He pulled up resting on his elbows and said, "I can name at least a dozen men right off the top of my head who would love to have just one date with you." And now he was lying to make me feel better.

I rolled my eyes. "I don't know about a dozen men. I'm only worried about one."

He leaned in kissing me thoroughly and I knew that it was true and I knew that it was impossible to keep him.

"You have nothing to worry about mi mot, I like taking you on." I could tell his mind was wandering away from the tray of breakfast as his hand was wandering to places under my robe. I broke off the kiss and motioned to the tray. "It's going to get cold. We don't want that to happen."

He let out a groan and sat up shaking his head, "No I guess we don't want that." He pulled the covers from the plates and poured coffee in the cups. There was fruit, eggs, bacon, breakfast potatoes, rolls, oatmeal and muffins.

I grabbed a mug of coffee bringing it to my lips. It was fresh and I was in need. After the first couple of gulps I slowed and looked over at Van.

He gave his head a sad shake, "Like an addict getting her fix." I playfully punched him and he grabbed his arm acting hurt.

I offered to kiss it for him, but he passed citing hunger. We finished off the tray quickly, filling our bellies being the only thing on our minds.

He moved the tray to the small table and climbed back on the bed. "I have to meet Jess in a bit, do you want to come?"

"Yeah," I wanted to look at the video too, "I might notice something that I forgot to tell you, but there is one problem. The only extra clothes I have in my bag are underclothes. Will it look strange to show up in my gown?" He held up one finger and grabbed the paper sack on the floor.

"Your friend Melissa sent this up." He handed me the bag and inside was a pair of jeans and a Black Bear Casino T-shirt for each of us. I laughed at the craziness of the whole thing.

"Looks like we're covered."

He took the bag from my hands. "Looks like we're walking billboards, but I guess it's better than wearing that monkey suit again."

He laid the bag on the floor and turned me around rubbing my shoulders. It felt good to relax for a few moments knowing that today would likely be crazier than the last three combined. I leaned my head back against his shoulder.

"Have you had any revelations about Margie's message?" Van kept rubbing my shoulders.

"No, but I'm working on it. I've decided that after we are done with Jesse we'll pick up my car and go to the mall. Maybe if I just walk around it will come to me."

"I was going to suggest that. The Sorento is in the parking lot already, I had one of the off duty guys bring it out. Once we are done we can head right to the mall."

I sighed.

"What did that mean?" He stopped rubbing my shoulders and turned me back to face him.

"Something else the guy said has been bothering me. He said that he was sure I would figure out what the message means and when I do they would know. They knew about the key so if we can narrow down who was told that the key was found then we should be one step closer to the inside guy. I know Jesse changed over all the security on my house, but I'm still a little nervous that I'm vulnerable and we are missing something important."

Van looked pained. "Leave it to you to have to think so much." He stroked my face with his thumb. "Jesse and I had a chat about that last night. We are no longer sure who can be trusted other than the chief. Tomorrow Jesse is going to change the surveillance again to all Superior PD guys and tell them as little as possible."

"It kind of ticks me off that whoever it is, is putting all of us at risk for money." I said.

Van nodded. "Unfortunately, that's human nature. It could be that whoever it is in debt or needs money for a family member or even is being blackmailed by McElevain. All I know is that from here forward we need to be a lot more careful about what we do and who we talk to." He slipped his hand inside my bathrobe, cupping my breast.

"Are you trying to distract me Mr. Bond?" I moaned softly and he leaned in and kissed me tasting like sweet fruit and nutty coffee. He was kissing my neck and I knew where this was leading.

"Is it working?"

My response was a soft moan.

"You are so damn alluring I can't get enough of you." He said kissing my neck.

"We can't do this now. We only have a few minutes until we meet Jesse." I said it only half believing it.

"This will only take a few minutes." He kept kissing me and I lost track of any thought other than how good it felt to be in his arms.

It was eleven ten when we met Jesse and Julie in the hallway. Turns out we needed more than a few minutes. We were all dressed in jeans and casino t-shirts and we couldn't help but laugh at how ridiculous we all looked. Julie looked good and I told her so.

"It's because I spent the night telling her how much I loved her and she was finally able to sleep." Jess said his arm around her waist. And I didn't doubt that one bit.

We took the elevator to the first floor and found the security office. Jess flashed his badge and the security manager came out for us. We trailed behind him to his office where he had the video cued up.

"I don't know how much help it will be," he said, "that part of the ballroom was in the shadows."

Jesse assured him that he wanted to see it anyway, so he played it and I could see myself walking towards the corner of the ballroom. I stopped abruptly and I knew that was when he asked me my name. I gave an involuntary shiver and Julie slipped her arm around my shoulders. Jesse and Van were intently watching the tape waiting to get a glimpse of the man. He pulled me to him and I smiled and we began dancing. He seemed to know where the camera was because he kept himself turned from the camera at all times. I could describe his face and we had at least height and weight from the video. We watched as he fell back into the shadows and I stood on the dance floor alone. The security officer paused the video there and Jesse and Van rocked back on their heels turning to me.

"Anything you think of while watching that you forgot about last night?" Jesse asked.

"He did speak with a southern accent, but otherwise no. He obviously didn't think anyone would know who he was since he didn't disguise himself."

"Or he doesn't care." Jesse and Van said at the same time.

"But something is bothering me about the picture he showed me of Margie and Nathan. It was familiar to me."

Jess's eyebrows scrunched, "What do you mean?"

"Where the picture was taken, the background, it's familiar to me. There is no doubt in my mind that it's a current picture, but the backdrop is someplace I've been before. Give me some time and I might come up with it."

Jess asked the security manager for a copy of the tape and he already had it in hand. We thanked him, reminding him once again about confidentiality. He agreed and offered to help in any way with the investigation. We left the office regrouping in the lobby.

Jesse put his arm around Julie and nodded to the parking lot, "I saw the Sorento in the parking lot, so I assume you guys have a plan?"

Van nodded, "We are going to head over to the mall. Tula thinks she might be able to figure out Margie's message if we wander."

Jesse agreed with our plan and told Van to call him if we find anything or need any help. He and Julie were going to head back themselves and stop at the station for a few minutes. Van grabbed our coats and escorted me to the Sorento that was parked under the portico thanks to the valet service. He was still keeping a close eye on the surrounding area as we walked even though we only had to go several feet. He helped me into the SUV and he went around and got in the driver's side. He cranked the heat up on the dial even though I thought the car was already toasty warm. Then he sat there his eye in the rearview window.

"What's the matter?" I asked because he looked perturbed.

"I'm trying to figure out how I'm going to be able to drive this car through downtown Superior without picking up a tail with that huge sign telling everyone it's you."

I used my Sorento for parades and other dance related events. On each back window I had a large couple dancing and it said, Sugar's Ballroom Dance, wrapped around them. It was a great rolling billboard and I wrote off every trip I made in it. I was smiling because it obviously annoyed him. He had pulled forward out of the portico and was rolling down the length of the hotel to the exit lane.

"You know they come off, right?"

I changed the radio station to easy listening being very nonchalant. I felt the car jerk as he stomped on the brake and pulled up next to the curb.

"No I didn't know that, you could have shared." I looked over at him. I guess I was supposed to know he didn't want them on there.

I shrugged my shoulder. "I didn't know it was a problem." It was his turn to roll his eyes at me and he climbed down out of the driver's seat and opened the back hatch. I leaned over the back of the front seat.

"You see that flat, empty Rubbermaid container?"

He nodded.

"Take them off and lay 'em flat in there. They're just window clings. That's where I put them when I want to be incognito."

I flipped back around and put my sunglasses back on. I could here him in the back moaning and groaning about women and their big ideas. I laughed softly and waited for him to finish.

God bless patience.

THIRTY-EIGHT

He pulled down the long drive to the highway and I got him going east towards Duluth on I-35.

"Tell me what's in this mall we are going to." He had his sunglasses over his eyes again and I couldn't read his face.

"Not much. The Mariner Mall is pretty dead now. There's a Sears, an Embers, a few little shops, and a Younkers. Oh -- and a movie theater."

"So why do you think that she may have hidden something there?"

"Well we already established they didn't feel comfortable driving around Duluth alone. They didn't like all the hills, they were certain they were going to slide down backwards or drive the wrong way on a one way street."

I shook my head at the memory of those two backing up, hands waving in front of them when I suggested they take a trip in to Duluth themselves. They lived in a huge city, but couldn't handle Duluth in the summertime. I could see the corners of his lips tipping up and I'm pretty sure he was thinking he didn't like doing it either.

"When they went out alone they stayed in Superior. Since there is only one mall in Superior that pretty much narrows it down."

"But you can't be sure they didn't go into Duluth on their own someday without your knowledge?" He asked.

I blew out a sigh. "Nope, that's the discouraging part. I can be pretty sure, but not completely sure. That being said, the reason we are going there first is there is a dance studio in the mall. It's run by a friend of mine."

"And you think she may have left the stuff there why?" He was trying to work with me.

"All I have is a gut feeling, Van. She never had a silver ring that I ever saw. The dance studio's name is Sterling Silver Studio. I think it's a play on words. Tell Sugar that I left my silver ring at the mall and I want her to pick it up. That was the message. It's the only thing I can think of." I looked over at Van his mouth was hanging open ever so slightly.

"So you think the key opens something at this Sterling Silver Studio?"

"Right, it's a dance studio and they have a locker room for students. My guess is that the key opens a locker and we will find the information inside." I crossed my arms over my chest feeling quite pleased with myself that I had possibly figured it out.

He looked over at me his sunglasses pushed down on his nose, "I'm impressed, really I am. Most people would have wandered around looking for a jewelry store. That's what I would have done. Way to think it out."

I was smiling ear to ear happy to hear his praise. "Well we don't have the stuff in our hands yet, but I think it is the best place to start." I threw in so I didn't look too big for my britches.

"What time do they open?"

Well that's the problem. I looked over at him and grimaced. "They aren't." I said.

"They aren't open?" He slowed the Sorento taking the Wisconsin exit to the Bong Bridge, merging into traffic.

"They're closed Saturday and Sunday, but I have a plan."

"Please tell me it doesn't involve breaking and entering?" I refrained from punching him by mocking him instead.

"No it doesn't involve breaking and entering. If we get there and no one is around I will call Sara and have her come over. She owns the studio and I'm hoping that if I give her a story about forgetting something in one of the lockers she will come in and open it up for me. It's worth a shot."

He looked pained and confused, "So do you actually go to this dance studio to dance? That seems odd since you have your own."

"They teach different dances than I do. I take several classes there including belly dancing and hula."

Van arched an eyebrow, "Belly dancing? That I would love to see." His eyes were smoky again and I knew I had better move on quickly.

"Sara and I often send each other students. If I get someone more interested in jazz or Zumba, I send them to her and if she gets someone more interested in ballroom, she sends them to me. It works for us. If she's not there I will call her from my cell and we'll wait for her to come over and open up."

Seemed like a great plan to me. He pulled the Sorento down into Superior stopping at the lights by Northwest Outlet.

"I need a Target or a Walmart. Where do I go?" he asked.

I wasn't sure why, but by the look on his face decided not to ask. I told him to turn right and go straight. As we headed down Tower Avenue he saw the Target on the right hand side of the street. He pulled the SUV into the parking lot and shut off the car.

He turned toward me, "We need to go pick up a few things before we go to the mall. Stick with me and don't disappear I don't want anyone getting a second chance at you."

I nodded tersely remembering last nights' encounter and waited for him to come around and take my hand. To the outside world we probably looked like any other couple running into Target for some necessity, but I felt so far away from any other couple and I had no idea what we were there to get. He pulled me towards ladies handbags weaving in and out of aisles until he found a large purse big enough to hold a small child. He handed it to me and pulled me towards the electronics department. He grabbed a cheap nine dollar TracFone and some air time and pulled me back to the checkouts at the front of the store. Every time I opened my mouth to ask a question he gave me the don't bother asking look so I closed my mouth and bit my tongue. We paid for our purchases with cash making no small talk with the cashier and walked back to the SUV. I refused to be dragged out of the store so I dug my feet in making him slow down. He frowned at me, letting go of my hand and coming up next to me putting an arm around my shoulder. He propelled me into the Sorento faster than he was dragging me and I was even less happy about that. He threw the bag at my feet and cranked the engine over snapping his seatbelt on and pulled out of the parking lot. He was driving like a maniac weaving up and down side streets. Jaw tight refusing to talk and watching the rearview mirror.

After a long ten minutes his jaw relaxed and he said, "We had a tail. I was trying to lose him before he could grab you or figure out what we were doing."

"You could have said something you know. You don't have to act all Neanderthal on me."

He smiled and I'm pretty sure he was laughing at me. "Sorry babe. I didn't want to take a chance you would start throwing your arms around and hollering, making a scene."

I couldn't help it this time. I punched him, hard. "I don't make scenes!" I shouldn't yell either.

"Yes, you do, but that's okay. You are incredibly cute while making them." His eyes twinkled at me and I sat on my hands to keep them from flailing around.

"Are you going to tell me what the little shopping expedition was about?" I think I had it figured out, but wanted confirmation.

"You can't go to a dance studio to pick something up without a bag. Since your big body part bag isn't going to be very maneuverable I wanted a bag that could pass as a purse, but if the paperwork is there would hold it all."

He pulled over to the side of the road next to an old abandoned building and reached down to grab the bag. He pulled the paper out of the purse and pulled the tag off the bag before handing it to me. He took the TracFone out of the bag and got it all set up adding the airtime and minutes and handed it to me.

"I have a cell phone." I said.

"I'm aware of that, but I don't want you using it for anything other than lodge business and even then give no identifying information like where you will be at what time, etc. We know that McElevain is aware of our movements somehow. I don't know if your phone is being traced, but better safe than sorry. This phone is untraceable and if we have to ditch it we don't have to worry about it being traced back to you. Use it as much as possible for as much business as you can until this is over."

I gave him a short salute, "Yes sir 007, will it self destruct too?"

He looked at me under his eyebrows. "This is serious, Sugar, I'm doing my job here. I'm trying to keep you safe."

"I know it's just getting creepy that's all."

He reached over and pulled me into a hug kissing my temple. "I will take care of you as long as you listen to me okay?"

I nodded and he chucked me under the chin. "Lead me to the mall madam." He said putting the SUV in gear and I wound him back out to Belknap Street following it down to the lights at Hill Avenue. He turned right and we headed down towards the mall turning onto a service road that ran behind it.

"It's right over there next to the Guadalajara Mexican place and the theaters." I pointed with my finger and he pulled the Sorento up towards the studio driving by slowly, but not stopping. He went back out to the service road driving around like he was lost.

"It looked locked up tight with no lights. Call her."

I pulled the cell phone out that he had bought at Target and punched in her cell phone number that I had saved in my own phone. It rang four times before it picked up and I was afraid it was going to be her voicemail. There was a pause, "Hello." She sounded hurried, but it was her at least and not the voicemail.

"Hi Sara, it's Sugar."

"Hey girl, long time no see." Yeah a whole twelve hours. "Great party last night! I just got up it was so great." Amen sister.

"I hate to ask Sara, but could you meet me at your studio. I've lost one of my liners and I think it might be in a locker at the studio. I really need to look for it. I hate it when I have to call Trey and tell him I've lost another one!"

"Oh yeah, we don't want that, no problem, I was thinking about heading over and doing some book work anyway. Give me twenty minutes and I'll come let you in." I told her we would be waiting and hung up the phone tossing it back in my purse.

"Who is Trey and do you have to call him often to tell you lost a liner?" He was drumming his fingers on the steering wheel keeping his eyes pressed to the rearview mirror as he drove.

"Nope. I never lose liners -- they cost nearly a thousand dollars a piece."

I saw his eyebrows go up in surprise like they always do even when he's trying to act cool.

"A thousand dollars? Are you touched?!"

"Touched?"

He pointed to his head making the "cuckoo" sign.

"I told you it wasn't cheap, it's the technology that goes into them that you're paying for."

"So I'm afraid to ask how much the whole set up is if one liner is a grand." he said.

"Well, that depends on the foot. If you have a dynamic response foot like mine the whole setup can be easily fifteen to twenty thousand, more if you have a more specialized foot. Things like the Cheetah feet that the athletes use can cost thousands more."

"I knew they were expensive, but..." he motioned with his hand in the air.

"But they are worth every penny right?" I said taking his hand and lowering it to the seat of the car.

He grimaced realizing how he must sound. "I was coming off thick there wasn't I? It surprised me that's all, especially since I know you have like three or four feet."

"I do, but luckily I hooked up with Trey and he got me involved with some companies testing out new foot designs. I wear the foot and give them my opinion on how to market the foot to different types of patients. I get to keep the foot when I'm done and that helps me build up my inventory."

"A leg for every day of the week?" He laughed at the absurdity of it.

"So to speak." And I was telling him all of this so he understood that I do come with my own set of differences. "The technology is what we are paying for and without that I wouldn't dance, so I don't complain. I would pay twice that if I had to."

He shrugged his shoulder, "Yeah, I guess if I was in that situation I would probably feel the same way." He fell silent for minute and then looked over at me. "I'm proud of you by the way."

"Why?"

"Because you can tell one hell of a fib."

I laughed at that one. I was pretty sure my mother would be horrified. He pulled into the Presbyterian Church parking lot a ways down from the mall and backed in between two large SUVs.

I looked around, "What are you doing? I don't think now is the time to start going to church."

He rolled his eyes over at me, "I'm hiding for the next twenty minutes. The mall parking lot is empty and I'm tired of watching for bad guys. Hopefully they won't spot us here."

Made sense to me and hopefully he was right. I noticed he didn't turn off the engine.

He turned in his seat and looked at me. "Ever tried this little baby's backseat out?" I couldn't be sure if he was kidding.

"You are kidding, right?"

He stared at me with those eyes that said he wasn't.

I looked around horrified, "We are in a church parking lot! For the love of everything holy do you want to be struck down for real?"

"Good point. I guess it probably wouldn't be too good of an idea to be caught with my pants down in the back of your SUV by a Superior cop, huh?"

"Nope, Jesse would have a bird."

"An absolute canary." He said leaning over and hitting the door locks with his left hand with his right hand he pulled me into him. He started kissing me then, his hand working its way up my parka and under my shirt and I forgot about the fact that we were in a church parking lot for those minutes that he had me under his spell. The bell tower began to toll the hour and we both jumped apart, our hearts racing, nervously laughing when we realized what it was.

God bless perfect timing.

THIRTY-NINE

We drove back through the parking lot and it was completely empty. There was going to be no way to hide the Sorento and I could tell that was causing him stress. He drove around again and I spotted an empty loading bay.

"Can we park in there?" I asked pointing with my finger.

He whipped the SUV down between the long white concrete guards on each side. "Official police business, I say yes."

Since it was Sunday it was probably pretty safe that no huge semi-truck was going to come and smush my SUV into obliteration. We walked around the concrete girders and stepped over the snow piled up against the curb, making our way into the movie theater doors. We stood off to the side keeping an eye out for Sara while hopefully not being spotted by anyone more unsavory. Van had his arms wrapped around my waist and was kissing my neck and leaning in for a longer kiss when someone went by. He was going for the two lovers embracing look when I actually knew he was surveying the whole area at all times. I saw Sara's Kia Sportage pull into the lot and park in front of the studio door.

"She's here," I said against his lips.

Van looked up and raised a brow, "Do you think your friend gave her a deal too?"

"Probably, since she's married to him."

He shook his head and released me telling me to wait while he checked for god knows who, the bogeyman, the grim reaper, Charlie Manson or more likely McElevain. He motioned me out the door and we walked hand in hand quickly past the Guadalajara and to the studio door as Sara was unlocking it.

"Hi Sara, thanks for coming over." I said acting a little too happy.

She turned from the door, "No problem Sugar, you are looking great." She eyed Van up and down and I knew what she was thinking, she came right out and told me what she wanted to do to him last night. She's married, but I couldn't stop her from looking. She let us in the door and I tried to keep my steps slow and even as we headed to the locker room. Thankfully Sara left us to our own accord and didn't follow us in. I waited until we got into the locker room before digging inside the underside of my bra for the key.

"If I'd known that's where it was I would have gotten it for you." He whispered. His were smoky green and I had to look away before I lost track of the reason we were there.

"That's why I didn't tell you." I tossed back at him as I turned the key over in my hand. Since it had no markings on it I was going in blind trying to figure out which locker the key would belong to. I blew out a sigh.

"There's a lot of lockers here, aren't there?" He was reading my mind again.

"Yeah, about a hundred." I walked around the lockers, but quickly realized that most of them had combination locks on them.

"Crap." I felt my lungs deflate disappointed that I may be completely off on this one.

"What's the matter?"

"All of these have combination locks on them, not padlocks that need a key." I knew that he had already picked up on this, but was trying to keep me focused.

"Don't give up, walk around and tell me what you see." Okay, worth a try. I walked around each layer of lockers in numerical order to make sure I hadn't missed any.

"Anything?" I heard Van's voice from several locker aisles away as he stood guard near the door. I was standing in front of the last set of lockers and one padlock was different.

"Tula?"

"Sorry, yeah, I'm here. I just found something."

My heart was beating faster and my palms were getting sweaty. It was the top locker and there was no way I was going to be able to reach it without a chair. I looked around but didn't see anything.

"I need you to come back here and help me. I can't reach the locker."

He stepped around the locker and I got that rush of feeling that almost overwhelms me at times when I see him. I suspected that it was love, but I didn't want to go there.

He looked up at the top row of lockers. "Hmmm, sucks to be short doesn't it." And there went that feeling.

I punched him playfully and he took the key from me. We both took a deep breath and he put the key into the padlock. We let out the breath when the key turned and the padlock opened. Van hooked the padlock on his back pocket and looked into the locker. Inside was a metal box and he pulled it out.

He raised an eyebrow at me and handed me the box. "You found the key, you figured out the message, you open the box."

I took the box, my hand shaking, and flipped the latch open. I slowly opened the top of the box and knew we had found it. Inside were pictures, accounting records, cell phone logs and other paperwork. "It's all here, just like you thought." I blew out a breath ruffling my bangs.

Van took the box and looked inside confirming that the information inside was what Margie had shown him. He shut the lid on the box and snapped the latch closed putting it inside my purse and pulling out the liner.

He smiled at me and put his arm around my waist whispering in my ear. "You did it, now we can make this end." And all I could do was nod because I didn't trust my voice not to break.

We left the locker room and Sara looked up from her paperwork. "Did you find it?"

"Yup." I said holding up the liner to show her before tucking it into the bag.

She did the brow wiping sign and gave me the thumbs up, "Glad you didn't have to call Trey. I'll walk you out and lock up behind you."

I thanked her again for coming in and gave her a quick hug when Van went to get the car. We stood inside the door off to the side and I'm pretty sure that Sara wondered why all the secrecy, but to her credit she didn't ask. Van came around the SUV, put the bag between us, and helped me into the car. He waved at Sara and climbed back into his seat. I slid the bag down next to my feet and Van put the car into gear. I no sooner had my seatbelt on and my phone rang. Van motioned for me to answer it with the SUV's hands-free mobile.

"Hello." I willed my voice to stay steady, not revealing to the caller any emotion.

"Did you find what we are looking for?" It was him. Van looked over at me and mouthed McElevain and I nodded.

"I don't know what you're talking about. I was picking up some dance gear." I shrugged my shoulders at Van holding my palms up. Van nodded to just keep going.

"Listen, I know you picked up what I've been looking for. I would suggest you hand it over and then you can walk away with your life and your lodge." I sucked in a breath, now he was threatening the lodge and now he was really ticking me off.

"No, YOU listen, I don't know what you think I have, but your ultimatums are starting to really tick me off."

"Fine, don't say I didn't warn you. I will get the information that's in that bag at your feet. You can count on that, one way or the other."

The phone went dead and I reached forward punching it off. I laid my head against the headrest and blew out a breath. Van already had the SUV moving maneuvering up and down side streets watching for a tail.

"He knew where the bag was." And I was officially freaked out.

Van's jaw clenched. "Yeah, I knew they would be watching. Listen we need to get this bag to Jesse and let him deal with McElevain while I concentrate on keeping you safe. Use the new phone and call Jess and tell him we need to meet up, but don't sit up, bend down low so no one from street level can see you." I wasn't really sure how that mattered at this point since they seemed to know everything I did before I did it. I grabbed the new phone and punched in Jesse's number. I waited through eight long rings before his voicemail clicked on.

"Jesse, it's Sugar. Can you call me at 218-590-1999? I left my other phone at the hotel. I need you." I quickly hung up the phone before I said anything more and I stayed in that position unable to make myself sit up.

Van was rubbing my back, "It's okay, he'll call back, give him a minute."

"This sucks." I couldn't conjure up any feeling other than fear and anger.

"I know, you're worried about your friends and the lodge, but I promise you that it will all work out." And what he left out was that I was worried about what happens when it does.

He punched on the radio and Uncle Kracker was singing about how someone made him "Smile". I normally loved that song, but my heart wasn't into it. "You make me smile like the sun, fall outta bed, sing like a bird, dizzy in my head, spin like a record crazy on a Sunday night. You make me dance like a fool, forget how to breathe, shine like gold, buzz like a bee, just the thought of you can drive me wild, oh you make me smile."

I heard Van singing along with the radio and I honestly had to work hard not to smile. His voice always made it happen though. I realized the car had stopped while I was down communing with my shoes trying to figure out the best way to sit back up and face the rest of my life. He had pulled over into the McDonald's parking lot and had parked behind the building next to the dumpster.

He reached over and pulled me across the console, "Don't know how I lived without you cuz every time that I get around you I see the best of me inside your eyes. You make me smile." And then he was kissing me softly. "I love your smile."

He looked like he was about to say something else when the phone rang and we both jumped. I fumbled around on the floor hitting the answer button on the fifth ring. Van turned down the radio.

"It's Jess. Did you need me?" And I knew that if someone was listening to my phone they could be listening to his.

"Hey, sorry to interrupt your first day as a newly engaged man, but I wanted you to know I found your cheesehead and put it in the back of Don's closet for the game tonight, in case you want to drive through and pick it up before you go for burgers with the gang."

I heard him hesitate trying to figure out the message, "Okay" and he drug out the "k" for a few seconds, "right, I will be by in a bit." He clicked off and I put the phone back in my real purse.

"Your cheesehead in the back of Don's closet?" he said, laughing. Like he could do better.

"I was afraid that his phone might be traced too so I tried to give him a little code. You know cheeseburger, back of Donald's closet, back of McDonald's and drivethrough for a burger with the gang. You know the Ronald McDonald Gang." I thought it was pretty good actually.

"Do you think he understood?" He had his hand over his mouth and I could tell he was trying not to laugh at me.

"We shall see, shan't we?" Then I punched him, but only kinda hard.

"The good news is no one is following us." I looked out at the parking lot and all the cars coming through the drivethrough.

"How can you tell?"

"Because I lost them back at the mall when I got out at the light and he didn't. Then I drove around every side street and kept off the main road. I haven't seen that vehicle since we pulled out of the parking lot. They are regrouping somewhere, so I hope Jesse doesn't take too long because he could pick us up at anytime." Van was smiling at me, but it was strained and I could see that he wasn't nearly as comfortable with all of this as he was letting on. "I won't let them, you know." He said taking my hand rubbing it between his warm hands.

"Let them what?"

"Hurt you." I nodded a catch in my throat. I knew he would do everything he could, but McElevain wasn't interested in how many people he hurt, that much was obvious.

"I don't care what he does to me. What I can't stand is the thought of the lodge not being there. That hits me somewhere that no one can imagine. It is all I have left of my parents. It's all I have left of my family. I..." my lip trembled and I was ticked that I was letting this jerk make me this upset.

He started to say something and I held my hand up, "I'm fine." I wasn't, but if he said anything I would completely fall apart. I took a drink of water from the bottle in the console and got myself back under control.

His voice was quiet, but brought me back to where we were, "I want you to reach down and take the box out of the bag keeping low. Look inside and see if there is an envelope in there that we can stuff everything into. I would rather slip Jess an envelope than a heavy bag in case someone is watching."

I bent down and unzipped the bag not even taking the box out of the bag. I flipped the latch on the box and opened it once again. Inside was paper work, discs and pictures, but no envelope.

"No envelope." I sat up thinking quickly, my eyes roving the SUV. I opened the console and struck gold.

"Fair play!" Van said, appreciation in his eyes.

I always carry several folders with information about the dance studio, MAMBOS, and the lodge with me in the SUV. I grabbed one for MAMBOS and pulled out the contents throwing it back in the console. Van helped me get all the papers from the box into the folder.

"Now when you get out I want you to keep it inside your coat. Pull Jess into a hug and slip it into his coat nice and easy."

Right, got it, James Bond.

He reached over and took my hand, stroking my scar up and down like he always does when he is lost in thought, but this time his eyes never left the parking lot or the cars swinging through the drivethrough. We both saw Jesse pull in at the same time. I let out a breath, glad that he was here and flashed my I told you so smile at Van.

"You two are like a fine tuned machine." He said shaking his head. I patted the envelope inside my coat as Jess backed in next to my side of the SUV. I waited for him to get out before I opened my door.

I pulled him into a hug and whispered into his ear, "It's all there, everything we need to put him away. Be careful they've been tailing us and we think they are listening in on the phone. Come to the lodge when you think it's safe, but don't call."

I unzipped his parka and slipped the folder in. We were blocked by the dumpster on one side and the SUV on the other.

He pulled back, "Give me an hour."

I nodded and climbed back into the SUV. We waited while Jesse pulled out around the drivethrough and he turned out onto Second Street headed back towards Duluth. I let out a breath.

"You did great, mi mot. We are going to get Margie and Nathan back and we are going to stop McElevain."

"I hope it's soon because I don't think Margie and Nathan have much time left." And neither did I, I could sense that plainer than my own heartbeat. I laid my head back against the headrest, "Take me home, Bond."

Van put the SUV into gear and pulled up to the drivethrough.

"Welcome to McDonald's, can I take your order."

"I need two large café mochas please, extra whipped cream." He smiled at me and I laughed out loud.

"I think you earned it." he said.

God bless McDonald's.

FORTY

Van and I were in the ballroom trying to pretend that we weren't hungrily eating up every last second that we had together. We both knew that the time was coming that we would no longer dance together. We had gotten home from McDonald's without incident and the lodge was locked up tight and unscathed. While we were waiting for Jess to come and tell us what the plan was, we went to the ballroom. I had my head on Van's shoulder and we were slow dancing to "Bless the Broken Road". And this time I was listening to the lyrics and I was feeling that God did bless the broken road that let me to him. The very, very broken road and I was enjoying the feel of his hands in my back pockets and his warm breath on my cheek.

"This much I know is true. That God blessed the broken road that led me straight to you. And now I'm just rolling home into my lovers arms."

His lips gently came down on mine and I kissed him softly praying that if the only prayer He ever answers it be the one that Van stays with me so I can keep breathing.

The music ended and it was just us locked in an embrace still dancing to music that was no longer there. I felt Van still and then the hair on the back of my neck stood up. Before I knew what was happening, the door to the ballroom flew open and a man dressed in black with a very real gun was in the room. Van pushed me out of the way yelling at me to run. As he grabbed his gun out of his shoulder holster the gunman crouched and got off a shot. Van rolled out of the way and the bullet hit the mirror, shattering it. I was working my way towards the relative safety of the large cherry planter when the gunman turned towards me. He aimed his gun and I felt the bullet hit me as I went down. I felt no pain, and realized too late that the socket of my leg was shattered and I went down hard on my side, my breath whooshing out of me. I struggled to get back on my hands and knees, but I knew I wasn't going to make it. I knew he would gun me down long before I could make it to safety. My mind kept yelling at me to move. I flipped over to see where the gunman was and saw him taking aim again. I screamed for Van to help me and he jumped the gunman from the side, tagging him with his stun gun. The gun went off as they went down and I felt burning heat and then pain along my side. I heard the mirror behind me shatter into a million pieces and sprinkle down on the floor. I grabbed my side and looked down at my hand. Blood was oozing out between my fingers and my shirt was turning crimson. All I could hear was Van yelling at me to hold on, hold on. I laid there my hand over my side watching him quickly secure the gunman. He kicked his gun out of the way and scrambled over to me.

"Tula, look at me."

My nose was running and I didn't feel well. My stomach was lurching. The room was very dark with lots of bright stars and I couldn't get a deep breath.

"I think I'm going to be sick." And Van pulled me down on his lap and lay me over on my side.

"Breathe in and out through your nose." And I did this until my stomach settled and the stars disappeared. I heard him yelling into his radio for backup as he pulled my hand off my side. He swore quietly tearing away the rest of my sweater and wadding it up quickly clamping it back over the wound again.

"Are you still with me, love?"

I nodded. "It's a little better." Actually I wasn't sure if I wanted to vomit or pass out.

"Are you hit anywhere else?" His voice was tightly controlled.

"My leg." He pulled up the leg of my pants and the socket was smashed. He released the pin lock and laid it out of the way. He felt around the knee and I flinched.

"Pull the liner off." I told him in a shaky breath, but he shook his head.

"No, it doesn't look like the bullet penetrated, but we will have them check it at the hospital."

He was yelling again into his radio and was reaching for his phone when the room filled with people. Half were dressed in camo and the other in black DPD t-shirts and cargo pants. Jesse bolted into the room and stopped dead.

I gave him a little finger wave. "Hey Jess, fancy meeting you here." He came over and bent down next to me. The torture in his eyes was more than I could handle, so I closed mine. I heard his voice low and angry address Van.

"What the hell happened? You were supposed to protect her not get her shot!"

I felt Van tense under me. I opened my eyes and reached out and grabbed Jesse. "Stop. Don't do this now. This wasn't his fault."

Jesse ran a hand down his face. He looked at Van and unspoken words were exchanged. "Jess we need to get her to a hospital." Van said it softly, "Now."

I tried to sit up, "No!" The movement threw stars in front of my eyes again and my stomach rolled.

I laid there taking shallow breaths. "I can't go to the ER here."

"Tula," Van said between clenched teeth, "You've been shot."

Yeah I knew that. Better to work on Jesse.

"Please Jess. You know this will be a nightmare if you take me in. If we pull everyone off to be at the hospital it leaves the lodge vulnerable. If I stay here then it won't hit the news and we won't give them another chance at us." The pain was a dull burning ache and I knew the blood was slowing. "Please." I pleaded with him as I felt a new wave of nausea hit.

"Oh god." The nausea took me off into some other place as I tried to calm my stomach.

I heard Jess in the background, "Julie? Listen, I need help."

I laid there on Van's leg and bits and pieces of his conversation floated on the air. I could feel Van stroking my hair and talking to me. He kept telling me it was going to be okay. To my ears it sounded like he was trying to convince himself.

I had a hold of his shirt. "Don't leave me alone. Please, I don't want to be alone." My eyes were going closed and I felt him pick me up being careful of my side. He carried me quickly down the hall and that was the last thing I remembered.

FORTY-ONE

"Tula, I need you to wake up." Van was talking to me. I struggled to open my eyes and looked up into his face.

"I don't feel well."

He smiled a tight smile at me. "I know, baby. I know." His eyes were flat. No color reflected in them, all I saw was fear and anger. I knew that anger was directed at himself. I tried to shift, but the pain in my rib stopped me dead. He put his hand on my shoulder. "We've got some people on the way to help you. I want you to talk to me. I want you to stay with me."

He rubbed my shoulder talking to me softly about taking Lillie to Ireland and how much fun he had showing her where he grew up. He had promised her he would take her there if she stayed out of trouble and did well in school. We heard footsteps in the hall and Dr. Mueller walked into the room. He has been my doctor for as long as I can remember and I trusted no one more. He smiled at me coming around the side of the bed. Van got up and gave him the chair.

"What happened, Sugar? Julie said you were hurt and needed me."

"I was in the wrong place at the wrong time." I said as he pulled the sweater off the wound and frowned.

"You know I have to report all gunshot wounds to the police." He glared at Van and Jesse standing at the door.

"Consider it reported." Jesse said in a controlled voice.

Dr. Mueller inspected the gash closer pushing around the edges until he hit my rib. I cried out and tears rushed to my eyes. Van was on the other side of the bed in one stride. He took my hand and squeezed it.

"The bullet dug deep and I'm pretty sure she broke a rib, but I think this is something we can take care of here." Well that explained the intense pain with any movement. Dr. Mueller looked at Jesse then Van. "I'm going to need a little help, either of you good at playing nurse?"

I grimaced. I didn't want either of them to be witness to this. Jesse held up his hand giving us the hang on sign and left the room at a slow trot. He returned thirty seconds later with Julie. I gave her a weak wave and she came over to the bed looking as tired as Jesse. Dr. Mueller and Julie were left to attend to me and I knew that Van and Jesse would regroup. If I knew my brother, he was going to pick a fight with Van. Not much I could do about it now, but later I would have to try to fix whatever damage was done between them.

Julie got me undressed so Dr. Mueller could get down to the business at hand. He gave me a shot of morphine and I floated in and out after that. I registered that Dr. Mueller was talking to me and I snapped my eyes open. "Do you hurt anywhere else, Sugar?"

I pointed in the direction of my leg. "It hurts, but I don't think it's broken."

Dr. Mueller stood and pulled the blanket back off my leg. He took my liner off and felt along the knee and down the two bones to where they ended just below my knee. It hurt, but not as much as before, which I took as good news.

"What happened?" Dr. Mueller stood at the end of the bed one had on my leg, one on his hip.

I gave him a weak smile. "Turns out carbon fiber will deflect a bullet."

He hung his head, but recovered quickly and snapped off his gloves, "I don't think anything is broken, but I don't want you walking on it until the bruising and swelling goes down. Your side is going to smart for a while. At the very least the rib is cracked, but it's more likely that it's broken. There wasn't much I could do with the flesh wound. I cleaned it out and packed it heavy, but there wasn't enough skin to suture. It will have to heal from the inside out. That means you need to keep it packed and bound the way I have it. It will help with the pain in the rib and keep the wound from bleeding. You need to stay in bed for a few days and then take it easy until you come in to see me in a week. Okay?" Jesse came in the room as he finished.

"Doing okay?" He asked and I nodded. He looked like hell. This whole case was taking a toll on him and I felt bad that I was adding to the stress.

"I was outlining for Sugar her do's and don'ts. Do rest, don't get into anymore trouble." Dr. Mueller said in a tone of voice I was sure he reserved for young boys who broke bones while doing stupid stunts.

Jesse's jaw worked and he caught sight of my leg. He sucked in a breath, "Cripes, Sugar, what happened?"

"The first bullet grazed my socket and threw me backwards. It shattered the carbon fiber, but it was enough to deflect it and keep it from going all the way through." I said trying to make it sound like no big deal.

His eyes flashed with anger and his hand came back up into his hair as it always did when he was angry or upset. Julie came around the bed and put her arm around him. I could see him lean into her a little bit, drawing off her strength. Dr. Mueller put a bottle of pain pills and a bottle of antibiotics on the bedside table. Jesse called Van in and Dr. Mueller showed him how to check the bandage and told him he needed to bring me in if he had to change it more than once tonight. Van nodded understanding and Dr. Mueller closed up his bag. He leaned over and kissed my forehead, like he used to do when I was five.

"Call me if you need anything, Sugar, anything. I'm your guy." I thanked him for coming. He gave Van one last angry look and quietly left the room. God bless Dr. Mueller. Jesse and Julie had stepped out of the room and I was worried about him.

Van sat on the edge of the bed. "Julie's with him." He was reading my mind.

I nodded. "He's blaming himself for this and I'm pretty sure no one is going to convince him otherwise."

Van was crouched next to the bed smoothing my hair back looking into my eyes and rubbing my leg until Jesse and Julie came back in. I looked up at Jesse, searching his face. His eyes were red and his voice was taut.

"Van, I need you to come and help me secure the rest of the lodge down so I can head down to the station to interrogate the gunman. I need to be there for that."

Van nodded and stood up. "I'm leaving Tula in your capable hands, Julie, and there will be a guard at the door." Van bent down and kissed me gently on the lips then he and Jesse left together. Julie came around the side of the bed.

"Thanks for helping today, Julie. I hate that you have to be involved in all of this."

She smiled at me. "You know I would do anything for you. It's the least I can do after last night."

I let out a shaky sigh. "Is Jesse okay?"

Julie gave a quiet laugh. "No, no he's not. He's so far from okay with this. He blames himself."

"It wasn't his fault."

Julie patted my shoulder. "Don't worry about Jess. I'll set him straight." And I had no doubt. Julie sat down in the chair next to the bed. "We've been worried about you for months. We've sat here and watched you spiral down into yourself, but I didn't want to stick my nose in where it didn't belong, no matter how many times Jess asked me to. I was with Sharon the other night when you called and she told me about the nightmares. She was physically ill she was so worried about you, Sugar. That is why we came over here yesterday. We had to see for ourselves that you could handle the dinner. I told Jesse we had to let you try and you rallied and you amazed us all, but that's over now and I still think you need to talk about how you are feeling. If you don't want to talk to me about it, Sugar, I completely understand, but I think you need to talk to someone."

"I haven't had a nightmare now in a few nights and I don't think they are going to come back. What I said last night was true. I finally found the reason why I'm here. You can report back to them that the nightmares are gone and I'm working through the bad stuff by focusing on the good stuff."

"Anyone in particular helping with that?" she asked.

I looked at her smiling, but I knew in my heart that a new nightmare would begin when he left.

She leaned forward in her seat, looking towards the door and her voice dropped an octave. "He loves you. You know that right? Everyone can see it."

I nodded. "I know, Julie. Tell him I'm good. I don't want Jesse worrying about me anymore than he already does. It's a little smothering. Besides he has other things to concentrate on now."

She laid her hand on her belly. "Yeah, but I wasn't talking about Jesse."

Oh. Her sentence hung in the air. I couldn't stop the grin from overtaking my face. "He's mi daza, but it's complicated."

Julie frowned. "Mi daza?"

"It means excellent, brilliant, fantastic." And I knew she understood.

"Why is it complicated?" Oh, I don't know, let me count the ways. "The biggest one would be that he doesn't even live here, Jules."

She straightened my blankets adjusting the ice pack on my leg deep in thought. "Remember last night when I was freaking out in the bathroom because I was so worried about tomorrow?"

I nodded.

"In the end did any of that worrying do any good?"

I shook my head no.

"Right so the most important lesson I learned was to live today and tomorrow will work itself out."

I blew out a breath. "I hope you're right, Jules."

We started talking about wedding planning and baby names and I slowly drifted off to sleep. Images of my parents, Brent, Jesse, Sharon and Van floated through my mind. Days I spent with my dad on the lake and riding in the Mustang singing to the radio mixed with dancing with Brent and the hours I spent with my mother watching old movies and baking in the kitchen. The accident roared into view and I cried out. I couldn't stop it, but it wasn't as terrifying as before. I felt Julie's hand on my shoulder and then it was gone, like that, replaced by the memory of Van standing on my front porch and then him making love to me.

I felt a new hand take mine. It was Jesse. "No one is going to hurt you again, Sugar. I promise you that."

I squeezed his hand letting him know that I was alright. He gave me a squeeze back and stalked out of the room. I heard Van slip in as he left, like a dance between two people, one person always watching me. The last thought I had before slipping into a deeper sleep was that someone was going to hurt me again. Van leaving would hurt much longer and much harder than the damage the bullet did to my flesh.

FORTY-TWO

I woke up confused and nauseous. I looked over at Van slung back in the hard backed chair next to his bed and it all came back to me.

"Hey," I said.

"Hey yourself." He looked exhausted fatigue leaving lines near his eyes and his hair was mussed. He leaned forward.

"How you feeling?"

I smiled at him, "Better now that you are here."

He took my hand and we sat quietly like that for awhile as I tried to clear my head. He brought me a cold cloth for my head and the nausea slowly faded. I pulled the blanket back and asked Van to take the ice pack off. I pulled my leg up and did my own assessment, happy that the swelling had gone down and it didn't hurt as much.

"Doc Mueller says it's not broken, so I can be up again quickly." I said weakly.

Van set his jaw. "No, Dr. Mueller said you needed to stay off it for a couple days, which is okay because you have to get a new socket made anyway." He brushed the hair off my forehead.

"I have more than one leg, Van, this isn't my first rodeo."

He sighed, shaking his head. "Listen, are you going to make this hard on me? I have strict orders to make sure you don't walk on that leg until the swelling goes down and I'm honestly a little afraid of the guy that gave me those orders."

"Well, we don't have to tell Dr. Mueller, it can be our little secret."

"It wasn't Dr. Mueller that gave him the order." I looked up to the doorway and saw Trey standing there. Trey was a great friend and he was also the guy that kept me dancing. I threw Van a disgusted look.

"Jeez, what did you do call everyone I know?"

Trey laughed and pushed himself off the doorjamb. "As a matter of fact, Jesse called me because he knew you would be hollering about your dancing foot being down. I picked it up and will have a new one ready in a few days. After I saw all the blood I decided to come see for myself that you were okay. I can take one look at that leg and know you can't walk on it for a few days. That is, of course, unless you want to really damage something and be off it for longer." I rolled my eyes at him.

"Honestly, Sugar, you do make me work for my dollar." he said, shaking his head.

"Fine." I said in a resigned voice. I know he was trying to be helpful, but I was at the end of my patience for the day. "I won't walk on it, but you get that socket done and back to me fast, mister, time off my feet is not convenient right now." Trey gave me a salute and that got him a weak laugh.

"Hey Trey." He stopped and turned back. "When you do the socket this time can you use the studio's logo?" The swirl of green in Van's eyes the first day I met him came to my mind. "And make the background shades of swirling green for MAMBOS." Trey's eyebrows went up in surprise.

"Really?"

I shook my head. "Yeah, I think it's time to have a little fun."

He winked at me, "I agree. I'll call ya when it's ready."

Van stood up quickly stepping over to the door, "We need to keep all of this between us." Van stuck his hand out and Trey took it looking him square in the eyes.

"Take care of her." He said taking Van's hand and then he turned and left.

"You have an amazing group of friends, Tula." Van said, walking back over to the bed.

"I'm unbelievably lucky to have so many people I can count on and I know that."

He bent down and kissed me softly. I looked up at the clock it was nine o'clock. I wanted to take a shower and get in my own bed. I told Van the same.

"No can do. Doc said to keep those bandages dry." They had attempted to clean me up before they worked on me, but I could feel dried blood on my back and hip.

"I really need to get cleaned up."

Van gave a resigned sigh and carefully picked me up and carried me into my bathroom. He deposited me on the dressing bench. "I'll be right back." He darted out of the room and I gingerly pulled my nightshirt and panties off. My sweater had been soaked in blood and had found its way to the garbage can. After they had bound my rib Julie had helped me into the nightshirt cleaning me up the best she could. I grabbed my robe and held it in front of me until Van came back. He was carrying saran wrap and masking tape. He covered the dressing with the saran wrap around and around and taped the edges so that I could shower without getting it wet.

"Parenting experience?" I asked and he laughed and nodded. Hey whatever worked, right now I needed to feel that water on my sore bones. He reached in and turned the shower on letting it get warm. He transferred me to the bench and pulled the curtain closed.

"I'm staying right here in case you need me."

I showered letting the hot water run over my body and soothe away the aches. The water running down the drain was red and I stayed in it until it ran clear. He helped me out of the shower and dried me with a towel slipping a big, soft flannel nightshirt over my head and carrying me back to my bed having already pulled back the covers. He laid me gently on the bed and I put my hand on his chest.

"Can you get in my dresser and get the short nylon stocking, it looks like thigh high for a little person."

He rummaged around in the dresser and pulled it out, "This it?"

"Yeah, thanks."

He handed it to me, "What is this?"

"It's a stump shrinker. You put it on the end of your limb and it keeps the swelling down and shapes the limb. I don't use it much anymore, but if I get an injury I try to wear it for a few days so my leg doesn't swell."

I took the stocking stretching it out getting ready to put it on, but the pain in my side as I tried to bend down to do it and the pain in my knee as I tried to bring it up to me left me exhausted, broken out in a cold sweat and panting for breath. The nausea was back with full force and I could feel the saliva building in my mouth. "I'm going to be sick."

And he was gone and back with the garbage pail before I finished the sentence. He laid me over on my good side and held the pail as I heaved. The pain was excruciating as the movement in my side made it feel like I was being stabbed. I was struggling against heaving again and the searing pain that would come with it. Van was talking to me quietly trying to soothe me and then the stars came and everything faded to black.

Someone was slapping my face, "Tula, come on baby. I'm going to call the ambulance if you don't come back to me."

I dragged my sluggish eyes open and he was smiling at me. "You're a jerk." But he was my jerk.

"I know, but you're scaring me and I am calling the ambulance." He took the garbage pail back to the bathroom and got a cold washcloth for my face. He laid it on my forehead and picked up his phone to call.

I stopped him with my hand, "Please don't, please. I'm okay now."

His face showed how torn he was, "Are you done being stupid?"

"I'm not being stupid." And I would have emphasized that with some hand flailing, but that would hurt too much.

He laughed like I had said the funniest thing in the world. He sat down on the bed and laid his hand on my good leg, "Just for one day, hell just for an hour, could you try to be a little less independent? Could you let someone help you and could you accept that it's not a bad thing?"

"It's not a bad thing Van, but it's something I'm not used to." And something I don't want to get used to, because once he left and I was on my own again I would have to build those walls back up and that would be exhausting work.

"Then it's time to get used to it, because whether you believe it or not I like taking care of you." He picked up the stocking. "Now how in the love do I put this on?"

I showed him how to stretch it and told him to try and do it in one fluid motion then I leaned my head back against the pillow and took a couple of shallow breaths. I knew this was going to be like a shot, hurts like hell while it's happening, but in the long run it's the best thing for you.

"Okay, go."

In the blink of an eye he had it up over my knee and I took a couple more breaths as he adjusted it and then I felt his hand rest on my good leg.

"Good?"

"Yeah, more than good."

He pulled the comforter up over me. The room was quiet except for the soft strains of George Winston. He had plugged my iPod into the dock and once again his thoughtfulness brought tears to my eyes. The song that was playing was "Cast Your Fate to the Wind". It seemed so ironic.

I reached up and stroked his face. "Thank you."

Concern pulled the corners of his mouth into a tight line and he knelt down next to the bed and tucked my hair behind my ear.

"I need to go clean up. Are you going to be okay here by yourself for a few minutes? There's an officer outside your window, but I don't think they are going to try anything again tonight." For the first time I noticed that his shirt was covered in blood.

"Are you coming back?"

He leaned in and kissed me gently on the lips. "You couldn't keep me away."

He got up and promised to be back in a few minutes. My side was aching and I could feel tears pooling behind my eyes. I shook them away, refusing to cry. I closed my eyes and tried to think about happy things like if I was going to have a niece or a nephew. The phone rang and I popped my eyes open. It was late. I looked at the caller ID and saw it was the police station. Jesse.

"Hello." I said, my voice anxious.

"Hi Sugar, it's Julie." Julie had left me a few hours earlier to go check on Jesse at the station.

"Julie, what's the matter, where's Jess?"

"Nothing's the matter and Jess is fine. I was calling to check on you. I wanted to make sure you were okay before we headed home for the night."

"I'm fine Julie. Really. Van is here and there are about forty guys walking around my property thanks to your fiancé." Forty might have been an exaggeration, but not by much.

"How is Jesse holding up? I was a little afraid for the guy he was going to question." And she hesitated long enough for me to know the answer.

"How bad, Julie?"

"He's in the holding room right now getting himself together. They had to pull him off the guy they dragged out of your house before he put him in the hospital."

"Damn." There was silence on the line. "Can you get him out of there for the night?"

"The chief has already clocked him out and I'm about to go collect him. I wanted to be able to tell him I talked to you. I figured it might be the only way to get him to come with me." We both laughed. He was hardheaded and stubborn as any man could be, but when he was working a case he had a one-track mind.

"Tell Van Jesse will be at the lodge sometime after noon to fill him in on the interrogation."

I told her I would pass the message along and we said goodbye. I reached over to put the phone on the night stand and groaned. The ache was now a sharp stabbing pain as the shot of morphine was wearing off.

"Who was on the phone?" Van walked into my room dressed in a t-shirt and long running pants.

"Julie. She was checking to be sure I was okay before she took Jesse home."

Van stopped at the night stand. "Took him home? I figured he would refuse to leave for days now." I filled him in on the interrogation of the gunman and that the chief had relieved him of duty.

"He loves you."

"Yeah. He loves me." Van disappeared into the bathroom and came back out with a glass of water and a white pill.

I raised my eyes at him. "What's that?"

"A happy pill." He smiled and waggled his eyebrows at me.

"Not interested, but thanks." He set it down on my night stand and went around the other side of the bed and climbed in under the covers. It wasn't lost on me that he put his gun on the night stand next to him.

"I think you should take the pill." He tried to pull me towards him and I flinched. He arched one eyebrow at me.

"Okay, I'll take it." He reached across me and picked up the glass and pill. I swallowed it quickly and prayed it would work fast.

He stacked the pillows up against the headboard and carefully pulled me up to him and nestled me in being careful to position me on my left side. He buried his face in my hair and stroked my arm. I could feel myself relaxing. The smell of his fresh Irish Spring almost overpowered me yet I burrowed closer, never wanting to forget the smell of it on him.

"I need to say something." Van's voice was quiet, but serious. Oh boy. Here it comes. I looked up into his face and held my hand up to him.

"You don't have to say it. I know that you aren't planning to stick around the tip of the end of the world once this case is over. I understand this is temporary for you." Too bad it's not for me. I let my hand fall back onto his chest. I was too tired to persuade him to stay. He tipped my chin back up so I could see his face.

"Don't put words in my mouth. I don't like that." I didn't know what to say to that. He looked serious and it was scaring me.

"I've been a cop for a long time now, Tula. I've been trained to put my emotions aside and get the job done. But today..." His voice trailed off and his eyes strayed to the fire so I couldn't see what he was hiding. "I've had a lot of bad days in my life, but today was different. Today I didn't know if I was going to make it past that second when I saw you go down. When I saw him coming at you and then heard the shot. I lost all ability to think or breathe." His breathing was ragged and I saw tears in his eyes. It was killing me to watch him beat himself up about this. He swiped at his eyes, irritated that his emotions were getting the better of him, "Rage overtook me and I had no control over what I was doing. My only thought was getting to you. I had to get to you and I had to make it better for you. I let you down today, Tula, dangerously so." His jaw worked as he tried to control his emotions.

"Van, I meant what I said to Jess. You saved my life today. He had me dead to rights. If you hadn't jumped him when you did he would have killed me. Don't walk down that road. There is nothing good at the end of it."

He was stroking my face with his knuckles running them back and forth like if he stopped I would disappear. "It's going to take a long time for me to get the image of you on the floor bleeding out of my head when I know I could have stopped it."

I sighed. He needed to work through it on his own. I could feel the muscles in his chest contract under my hand as he struggled. I didn't know what to say. I knew what I wanted to say, but I couldn't risk what was left of my heart.

His voice was soft, but controlled again when he spoke, "I was sitting there today watching you sleep and even after being shot you were smiling in your sleep. It was a beautiful thing to see, you were just laying there smiling. I feel like in the past few days every emotion possible has played through my soul. Intrigue when you opened the door and I saw the most beautiful woman staring back at me, heartbreak when I realized how much you have lost in your short life and then joy to realize that you used it to make the world a better place for so many people. And last night when I watched you hold little Amelia in your arms it made me want to put a baby in your arms, my baby. And when you danced with me it was all I could do not to pick you up and take you somewhere safe for the rest of your life." I pulled his hand up to my chest and the only part I heard was "a baby in your arms, my baby".

He leaned down and kissed me, "I love your smile. I love your laugh. I love your tenacity and your ability to pick yourself back up and keep going. When I dance with you I feel like the luckiest man alive and I can't help but never want the song to end. I had no idea when I got on that plane a few days ago how much my life was going to be changed by this beautiful, amazing woman" he leaned down and kissed me gently on the lips "and I love you." He whispered it almost like saying it too loud meant he couldn't take it back.

Tears rushed to my eyes and I blinked them back. "I think I'm hallucinating from all the drugs."

"No, you heard me right. I love you, Tula DuBois. I knew you were special the first time I laid eyes on you, I fell in love the first time I held you, and in that one instant today I was never more sure of anything in my life."

I was trying to keep myself focused on him, but my mind was buzzing and I was starting to feel like I was flying. His face was going in and out of focus and that was the last thing I remembered before dropping into dreamless sleep.

FORTY-THREE

I woke up slowly feeling stiff and sore. I started to roll over and then remembered why that wasn't a good idea. Van had woken me up in the night to give me another pain pill and I dropped back off to sleep in his arms. I looked around me and the sun was streaming in the window. God bless pain pills. I realized I was alone in bed. I played the night backwards and remembered that Van had told me he loved me. I groaned. I had I fallen asleep on him! I looked over at the clock -- ten forty five.

"Tula?" I looked up and saw Van in the doorway.

"I heard you groan, you okay?" He looked concerned.

"I feel like a truck hit me." I grimaced as I tried to sit up.

He nodded. "The morning after is always the worst." He said it like he had experience and my mind conjured up the vision of the scar on his leg.

"Here let me help." He gently pulled me up being careful of my side. He sat me on the edge of the bed and bent down in front of me.

"You must be starving." I was. There was something gnawing in the pit of my stomach.

"I could use some coffee."

He gave a bark of laughter. "Tula is back."

He stroked my face, leaned in and kissed me gently. "I swear I will never let anything happen to you ever again." He was kneeling by my bed resting on the balls of his feet.

I cleared my throat. "About last night, umm...I think I fell asleep during something important."

"You mean when I told you I loved you and then you started snoring?" He bounced slightly on his feet looking nervous.

"I don't snore!" I looked down, "I wasn't sure if I heard you right."

"You heard me right."

I could feel the tears coming to the back of my eyes and felt the clog at the back of my throat. I kept my head down and tried to push the tears back. He got up and sat on the edge of the bed next to me being careful not to jostle me. He gently turned my chin so I was looking at him.

"Why are you crying?" He was looking at me concern in his eyes.

"Because I love you." He put his lips on mine and kissed me gently.

"Why does that make you cry?" He asked rubbing my arm.

"Because I never thought it was possible to know this kind of love. I never thought I would ever feel like this, but I'm so afraid."

"You don't have to be afraid. I know I let you down yesterday, but no one's going to hurt you again."

I shook my head "You don't understand. What I'm afraid of is you leaving. Once you leave I don't know how I am going to put my life back together again." The tears were streaming down my face and I felt like an idiot.

He put his lips on mine. "Shhhhhh.... Let's talk about all that later. Right now I just want to make sure you aren't hurting."

He kissed me gently his lips lingering. Julie's words came back to me about living for today and letting tomorrow work itself out. He wiped my eyes and pulled me carefully to him holding me for a long time whispering all the ways he loved me in my ear. I was smiling by the time he pulled away. He does wondrous things for a girl's ego. He stood up getting ready to pick me up. I stopped him with my hand on his chest.

"You know you can't carry me everywhere. You will get a hernia." He shook his head.

"I think I can handle all one hundred pounds of you." I had to hide the smile. If that's what he wanted to think....

"Okay, where are your crutches?" I stared at him. I held up my arm and the light bulb went on. Not thinking crutches were going to be a lot of help here.

"Crutches are prohibitive. I have a chair in the garage. It's under the blue fabric tarp next to the Mustang.

"A wheelchair, right, didn't know you had one. I'll be right back."

He strode out of the room and I stared out the window at the happy sun shining down on the bright white snow. I could hear the joy of the snowmobilers that the snow came so early as the motors ran in the woods behind the house. It would be this way now until late March when the trails no longer had enough snow to run on. I gave my side a tentative test and was happy that I could at least move my arm around without getting jolts of pain. Van came back riding in my chair and spun it around to face me. He snapped on the brakes and leaned forward hands on my knees. He was giving me the stare that makes me feel like I committed a crime.

"This is an incredible chair, fast and maneuverable. Tell me, what have you been doing the last few days when it was hidden in the garage?" He asked it nonchalantly, but I could hear the pointedness of the question. "Did you hide it out there on purpose?"

I didn't respond.

"I can tell by your silence what the answer is. Why did you hide it from me?"

I turned my gaze back to the window looking out at the lake and he sat quietly in the chair obviously having much practice with patience.

289

"Are you ashamed or are you afraid to look weak?" He asked it in his soft questioning tone that always made me want to spill my guts.

I turned back to him holding his gaze refusing to look away and he sat there in the chair waiting for me to answer. I could tell he was prepared to wait all day if he had to. He was used to interrogations and the long silences. I wasn't sure how to explain to him why I hid it. I could explain it to myself, but chances are once I said it out loud it wouldn't sound nearly as sane.

"See for me this," I motioned to the house and my leg and the chair "is normal, **but to the** rest of the world it's not. The rest of the world doesn't take their leg off at the end of the day. In the beginning, when I first knew you were coming, I wanted to be on equal footing without you considering me unable to take care of myself. I can take care of myself. I've done it everyday for the last ten years."

"And I have never said that you couldn't." He had his head cocked obviously trying to figure out the underlying message.

"I have wonderful people who are passionate about their work and who care enough to make sure I can do everything that I want to do everyday, but without them this is what's left. When my equipment fails, this is what's left. This is the downside of being an amputee." I gave him the palms up. "I'm not ashamed of who I am. I am who I am because of the accident and I'm proud that despite all of that I was able to carry on with my life the way I wanted to, but no, I don't like to look weak. I don't know anyone who does."

Considering I was sitting on the edge of my bed unable to sit up by myself or move around I obviously wasn't succeeding at that right this moment. I gave him the palms up again before laying my hands in my lap. He sat quietly studying me. Maybe he was thinking about what I said or maybe he was thinking about the consequences of sharing a life with someone with limitations.

"I love the fact there are two sides to you, Tula. I love the fact that when you wake up in the morning you're my captive audience for those first few minutes. I love the fact that twenty minutes later you are practically running around this place barking orders and dancing around the kitchen. I love the fact that an hour after that I can waltz with you or walk through the mall holding your hand. But, most of all I love the feel of you in my arms when I get to carry you and the way you lay your head on my shoulder. I understand that this," he made the same motion at the house and the chair and my leg as I did, "is your normal. I get that, but," I sat quietly waiting for him to finish not sure what the but was going to be. "I want you to promise that you won't hide from me. Don't hide when you're angry, don't hide your pain because you don't want to look weak and don't hide what makes you, you."

He got up out of the chair and I stood up on one leg, leaning into him being careful of my rib.

"You always have a way of getting everything out of me, you know that?" He rubbed my back and kissed my temple.

"I'm a cop, it's my job." He held me carefully for a few minutes and then released me grabbing the handles of the chair holding it steady.

"Your chariot awaits."

I carefully pivoted into the seat, loving the way it felt under me. My old chair had been around for the last nine years and was nearly worn out. I had gotten this chair a few months ago, a Quickie Q7, the color of pumpkin and it was lightweight and fast. It had a black sling backrest that I had embroidered with two dancers silhouetted against a moon.

Van leaned in over my shoulder. "This chair makes a statement. It says "out of my way I'm coming through!" I started laughing, hard enough to grab my side and grit my teeth. I saw him flinch as he realized his mistake.

"Promise not to make me laugh for a couple of days, okay?"

He brushed my temple with his lips and promised. He helped me into the bathroom before heading in to make some fresh coffee in the kitchen. I looked longingly at the shower, but was too sore to go through the motions. I carefully changed into a big fleece sweatshirt and a pair of black capris. It hurt too much to fix my hair, so I put in a headband and called it styled. I tried putting on my liner over my leg, but it was too swollen and sore. I admitted defeat, guess I was stuck in the chair for a few days. I didn't have any lessons until next week anyway. I climbed back into the chair and wheeled myself out to the bedroom. I followed the scent of coffee to the kitchen.

"You found the Juhla." I said as I rolled in.

He looked at me blank-faced.

"The coffee. It's called Juhla, it's from Finland." He carried a cup over to the table for me shaking his head.

"I've never met anyone who can name a coffee by the smell. It all smells the same to me." And he has so much to learn. He brought me toast with peanut butter and jelly to the table. "I wondered why I couldn't read the package when I took it out of the cupboard." He gave me a grin and I almost choked trying not to laugh.

We sat together, me eating, him staring at me. I looked up and gave him a shy smile.

"You are so beautiful." He said and I rolled my eyes at him.

"Not bad for having just been shot?" He reached out and took my hand the look in his eyes answering the question.

"What's that sound?" I laid the toast back on the plate. It was coming from the ballroom.

"I called your friend and had him come out this morning to clean the ballroom floor. I also have a glass place repairing the mirrors that shattered."

"Thank you." My heart felt full and I could feel the tears again. I wasn't used to not having to do everything myself and my emotions were still in crazy overdrive.

He reached up and brushed a tear away. I pushed the rest of the toast away. My stomach was still unhappy and what seemed like a good idea earlier no longer did. It wasn't lost on Van.

"Maybe you should go back to bed for awhile and rest." He came around the table to grab my chair.

"No. I need to make some phone calls."

He shook his head. "It's already done. I notified the media that Sugar's would be closed until further notice."

"What?" I could feel my blood start to boil.

"Tula, don't get mad. Just listen to me okay." The only emotion I was feeling now was anger.

I crossed my arms over my chest. "Fine. I'm listening."

Van rolled his eyes and sat back down. "I know you don't want to admit this, but I think your body needs to recover. Even if Trey gets the socket back to you tomorrow are you really going to want to dance on that leg? Dr. Mueller said that you shouldn't do anything strenuous until you see him in a week." I did vaguely recall that. "I don't want to put any of your students in danger either. Imagine if you had a class going on yesterday when the gunman broke in." A chill ran down my spine. I didn't even want to think about that.

I let out a sigh, "Alright, it makes sense I guess. I'm actually relieved that I don't have to put on a happy face and pretend everything is okay when I feel like nothing is."

Van came around and took the handles of my chair pushing me into the main room. He helped me onto the couch and started the fireplace. He sat down on the couch and leaned back against the arm pulling me in between his legs with my head resting on his chest.

"I want you to feel like everything is okay. I want you to be as happy as you were Saturday night." I twined my fingers in his.

"We both know that won't happen until we get this case resolved and even then..."

I let my words be open-ended since neither of us knew what then. We laid together, fingers entwined and quietly waited for tomorrow to work itself out.

FORTY-FOUR

Van and Jesse were planning out a new strategy now that we had the information in our hands. We knew that McElevain would contact us soon and we needed a "go plan" as soon as he did. I was trying to read, but my mind kept floating away. I was holding the book on my lap and had read the same page three times. In such a short time my life had changed so much. I no longer felt paralyzed and unable to move forward and, even though Van was going to leave I knew that I had the strength within me to deal with it. Other people have long distance relationships right? I could too. I could fly to Texas in the winter and spend time there when it wasn't so busy at the lodge and he could come here when he had vacation or for a weekend break. We could work it out. But for how long? The little voice in the back of my mind was at it again. I ignored it, not willing to let it derail my planning. I needed something to hold on to right now and this was all I could come up with. I heard footsteps in the hall and Jesse and Van appeared in the doorway. I set the book aside and smiled up at Jess.

"Hey, you and James Bond done with your planning session?" I asked.

A look of horror filled Jess's face. "What now *he's* Bond? I used to be Bond."

I laughed grabbing my side before it did too much damage. I was happy to see that Jesse was more himself this morning. He looked like a man on a mission, which was better than the way he looked yesterday.

"I guess I have been replaced." But he had a smile on his face when he said it and I knew it was his way of telling me it was okay.

He bent over and kissed my cheek and I grabbed his hand and whispered in his ear. "No one can replace you." He gave a nod and straightened.

"Van will fill you in on the plan as it is and I am going to head back to the station to put things in motion." He slipped out the door and I heard the motor on his truck start up in a few moments.

Van came over to the bed and sat picking up my book. "*The Bone House*?" He looked puzzled.

"Brian Freeman, great author. He writes mysteries that take place in and about Duluth and the North Shore. I'm a little behind in my reading with the busy summer."

"Do you read a lot?" Van had marked my page, **put it on the night stand and stretched out on the bed next to me.**

"Yup. There isn't a lot to do during the long dark nights of winter around here you know. It's a good way to pass the time."

He had his hand on my belly and was rubbing slow circles. "I can think of a lot of things to do on long dark nights of winter." There was a gleam in his eye and I fluttered my lashes at him.

"Oh, you like to read too?"

He groaned and leaned in. "No, I wouldn't have time to read if I lived here. I'd be much, much too busy."

He kissed me then his hand working its way up my shirt until he came to the bandage on my side. He stopped and pulled back. He was breathing heavy and his eyes were all pupil. He hung his head and took a couple of deep breaths.

"I forgot." He said it almost to himself. It was my turn to pull his chin up to look at me.

"I need you to show me how much you love me. I don't need you to beat yourself up about," I indicated my side, "this."

"I don't deserve you." And I felt the same way about him, but I wasn't going to give him back.

"Just kiss me." He sat up and pulled off his shirt and pants, climbing between the sheets. Then he made love to me gently as if I would break under his hands.

I ran my finger up the scar on the back of his leg. He tensed and my hand stilled.

"What happened?"

He was silent. I didn't push him. He rolled over onto his back and put his arm across his forehead. "I was chasing a **drug dealer trying to** catch him before he jumped a fence. I didn't want him to get away. I had **been after him for months, so I was stupid and tried to go over a fence** after him. It was barbed wire. It wasn't meant to be gotten over without damage."

"Ouch."

He nodded, "Yeah, that's a good word for it. The good news is he didn't get away. He got more chewed up than I did and we both ended up in the hospital. I spent four days there and got thirty-eight stitches in my leg." I grimaced. "That part didn't bother me. What bothered me was when they brought Lillie over to see me. She was only about seven and I could tell she was scared to death. I knew then that I had to find a less dangerous job. I was all she had." He blew out a breath and sat up, "So I transferred to the drug task force and even though I still had people shooting at me once in a while it was still safer than walking the property line, so to speak."

"She's all grown up now. You can do whatever you want." I said.

"Yeah, but I like working for the task force. It gives me a sense of accomplishment when I can shut down a big operation or save someone else's sister from a life of drugs."

He was up and putting his pants and shirt back on. "I'm going to check messages. Do you need any help?"

I told him no and he kissed me quickly before heading out the door to his room. I got in my chair and rolled into the bathroom looking for my liner. I quickly found it and rolled it over my knee. I got it on and it didn't hurt, which was a huge step in the right direction. I rolled into my bedroom and opened my closet door grabbing one of my extra legs and snapping the pin into it. I stood, testing the joint without putting all my weight on it. It felt solid and there was only a twinge or two of pain in the joint as I took a few tentative steps. I grabbed the chair from behind using it like a crutch and made my way to the kitchen for a cup of coffee. Van's door was shut and I wondered what he was doing, but knew that there were certain things he wasn't going to tell me about all of this. I limped into the kitchen and fired up the Keurig, sitting in the chair staring out the doors waiting for the brew to be done. I grabbed my travel mug and limped towards my office.

I flipped on the lights to my cozy space, my indoor place I went to when I needed to think. I left the chair in the hallway and limped my way inside using the chairs and desk as handholds. My knee was getting sore now that I was up on it and I regretted having pushed things. I plopped down in my chair and leaned back rocking gently, my head leaning back against the chair. I tried to let my mind wander back to Saturday night. I tried to block out the revulsion I felt for Scarface as he forced me to dance with him and concentrate on the picture and what it was I felt certain I recognized. Maybe part of me didn't want to remember because the longer it took to find them and bring this case to a close the longer Van would stay, but I knew I had to try to do something to avoid more bloodshed.

And so I sat drinking my coffee that turned my stomach and I rocked and I thought some more. The idea began to take shape in the back of my mind and I slowly began to see the picture clearer. Not focusing on their faces, but rather the background and what it was that was around them. It was dark with only a small amount of daylight coming in from above. The room was steel and it was cold and McElevain's words came back to me "hope they don't get cold now that it snowed". And I probably knew where my friends were. I had a strong feeling anyway and knew I needed to call Jesse. I also knew that as soon as I set that wheel in motion so would roll the wheel of losing Van. Maybe I wouldn't lose him, but as soon as life got back to normal and he wasn't here everyday the reality of loving someone all the way across the country with my circumstances might be too much for him. I knew that I could spend time in Texas and I knew he would visit, but this was my home. This was all I had left of my family. I knew he wasn't happy with where he was, but who knows where he might go. Chances are it probably wouldn't be to the tip of the end of the world. That little voice in my head that used to mock me was now a cheerleader telling me that Wisconsin in the spring is beautiful and the summer is lush and green like the hills of Ireland. It was telling me to do the right thing now and let tomorrow work itself out.

I blew out a breath and stood gingerly from behind my desk. I walked slowly to the door and turned off the lights. Then I walked out to call Jesse praying that little voice was right.

Van met me in the entrance to the main room, his hands on his hips, lips in a tight line. "What are you doing?"

"Coming to find you."

He rolled his eyes and motioned at my leg, "I mean why are you walking?"

"I'm being careful."

"You're being stupid." And he was right, but I wasn't going to admit that. Right now my side was screaming at me and I was inches from falling down. I don't know what look was on my face, but his shoulders slumped as he came over and put his arm around my waist and I leaned heavily on him as he helped me to the couch. "Do you think you might be pushing it?" He settled me onto the couch propping pillows behind me and gently releasing my leg and pulling off the liner putting a pillow under my knee. "You don't have to be wonder woman."

I leaned my head back my eyes closed. "I'm hurting."

Physically, mentally, emotionally, every way a person could hurt I was hurting. He kissed my forehead and whispered he understood. He whispered he was hurting for me. He whispered that he wished things were different. He whispered he would take the pain away if he could. He whispered that he loved me. And with each whisper I felt a little better and a little stronger.

"Can you get me some pain medication? I need to call Jesse, but I need to be able to breathe better before I do that." He left my side and I heard him in the kitchen opening the fridge and I heard him pop the top of a can of soda open. In short order he was back in the living room and I was swallowing the pill.

"I really need to call Jesse. I think I know where McElevain has Margie and Nathan."

His eyebrows went up. "This whole investigation would have gotten no where if it weren't for you. You know that, right?" And I don't remember much more because I fell asleep.

"Baby, you gotta wake up. You have company." I heard Van's voice in my ear.

But I was awake. I had been laying awake for the last ten minutes listening to them talk, them being Jesse and Van. I had been listening to Van ask my brother permission to love me. It sounded weird to me and I guess to Jess too since he asked him what on earth he meant by that. Van explained that Jess has been my protector for so many years and was he going to be able to deal with someone else taking over that role. Jess hit him back with if he was planning on protecting me like he did yesterday then no he couldn't deal with that. Van had been rubbing my belly softly and his hand stilled. I struggled to get my eyes open, but the lids were heavy from the pain pill. I heard Van tell him that I wouldn't have needed to be protected if he hadn't brought me into this in the first place. Things were getting tense and I tried to clear the cobwebs in my mind.

"Listen," Jess said, "I'm sorry. The whole last month has become surreal to me and I'm at that stage where my brain isn't always filtering what I say. You're right. If I hadn't done what I did this summer then we wouldn't be here today, but you also wouldn't have this woman in your life. If there is one thing I've learned is that we really have very little control over anything. Look at me. I thought I was doing everything right and I've managed to screw up just about every part of my life. I've lost my two key witnesses, I've put my sister in danger and I didn't even see that the woman I love is carrying my baby. So, no, I will always be her protector, but I gladly accept the help you offer and, yes, you have my permission to love her. Just don't hurt her. She isn't going to do well with that."

His hand began rubbing my belly again, "She's stronger than you think, Jess, and I don't think she has even tapped into half what she's got."

"See here's what you don't understand Van, I know how strong she is. I have spent the last ten years watching her fight back from losing everything in her life, her parents, her partner and her dreams of becoming a champion dancer. She has fought back from mind numbing grief and horrific pain and I pray someday that my daughter is half the woman she is. I also watched one man destroy her emotionally and I won't watch that again. She built walls around herself that I never thought anyone would bring down, but you did. So yes she is strong, but she is still vulnerable and you would do well to remember that."

I turned my head and opened my eyes pretending that I had just awoken.

"Hi Sugar." Jesse was sitting across from me in the big chair, "I heard you pulled a classic Sugar, pushing yourself too far."

I shrugged my shoulder, the sleepiness gone.

"What are you doing here?" I asked to change the subject.

Van was sitting on the floor next to the couch one leg outstretched in front of him the other foot touching his thigh and his left arm slung over the couch resting on my belly, it was loving and protective at the same time. "I called him," He said. "You said you had to talk to him."

I shifted into a more comfortable position. "How's Julie? Is she doing any better?"

Jess did the hand back and forth bit, but he looked less worried. "I took her to the doctor this morning and he didn't like what he was hearing. He did some tests."

My heart contracted and I'm sure it showed on my face.

He held up his hand, "She's okay and so is the baby. I got to hear the heartbeat and I nearly bit through my lip trying not to cry. It was amazing, Sugar. He called us when the tests came back and it turns out she is anemic, which is why she keeps having these spells. He's giving her iron and making her rest for a few weeks."

"Good I think she needs it. If I had known I would never have let this get so far out of control." And that was the truth, but I didn't notice, which made me feel that much worse.

"Don't beat yourself up about it, Sugar. I held her in my arms every night and I didn't know it either. You can't make someone do something they aren't ready to do."

That sounded a lot like my anthem. I stole a glance at Van and he had his head low and his hand rubbed slowly back and forth on my belly.

"She's packing right now under armed guard and moving to my house tonight. I don't want her alone and I can't stand to be without her."

He had a house he had bought near his childhood home and spent the last few years fixing it up and making it his. There were only two bedrooms and I smiled at the thought of how quickly his man cave was going to become a nursery. I also knew he didn't mind.

"Armed guard?" I raised a brow at him.

"Yeah, I know she's a cop and can probably take care of herself, but now she's also my baby's mother and soon to be my wife and I'm not taking any chances. McElevain will use whatever device he can to get what he wants." And a chill ran down my spine.

It was time to tell him what I knew. I blew out a breath and Van's hand stilled on my belly and he picked up my hand gently letting it rest in his.

"I was thinking about the picture that Scarface showed me. I was trying to concentrate on what was around them, not their faces and how scared they looked. Slowly the picture began to develop in my mind and I realized it was somewhere I had been before or someplace like it."

Jess was leaning forward both his elbows on his knees. "Okay, give me a starting point."

"You know when you go tour the *William A. Irvin* and you go into the different quarters. First it's the staterooms up in the front of the boat that have all the wood paneling and electric fireplaces and a couple nice normal sized windows."

Jess nodded, "Yeah there are like four of them or something?"

"Right, but then you go further and you see the crew's quarters with a couple bunks and,"

"Yeah and then the two portals way high up." He motioned above his head.

"What's the *William A. Irvin*?" Van had one eye scrunched as he listened and Jess and I just looked at him.

"What? I'm from Ireland." And that got a laugh because it had become the joke between us.

"It's that boat I showed you down in Canal Park the other day. Remember, the haunted boat."

He smiled at me, "Oh yeah, I vaguely recall that. I was kind of preoccupied that day, looking at you."

Jess rolled his eyes. "So you think that they are being kept on the Irvin?" And he looked confused.

"No, we know that's not possible. I do think they are being kept on a boat, though. The picture was dark but I could see the industrial-type making of the walls and I didn't actually see the portal, but I saw part of one side and that's all I can think it could be. At first I was thinking it could be a train, but there is no way McElevain could keep them in a car at the rail yard. The cars are not accessible once the train shuts down for the season and they would be cold, very cold. I also don't think that McElevain would want to grease too many palms when the chance of them being discovered would be too great there. A big ship, on the other hand, already in dock for a long period would be worth the palm greasing. There isn't a chance that someone is going to happen upon them in the bowels of a thousand footer. We need to check and see if there are any boats in harbor right now. If one is waiting for repairs or getting parts then we need to check that out. If not, then we need to see if there were any ships that left the harbor around the time Margie and Nathan disappeared. It could be that they are taking a long trip somewhere while McElevain figures this out. I know it's a nightmare to think about because the boats are so big, but I have a gut feeling about this. If we don't find them soon we may never see them again."

Jess stood up and walked over to me, kneeling down beside me.

"I need to give you a job at the station as a clairvoyant or something." He kissed my cheek. "If you are right about this you have almost single-handedly figured out this case. You found the key, figured out the message and, God willing, I will find Margie and Nathan soon, but I will take it from here. There is no we anymore, there is only me now."

I opened my mouth to protest and the look on his face made me close it quickly seeing this wasn't a battle that I was going to win.

"Please, promise me you will rest now and let me handle things from here."

"Not like I'm much good in this shape to help anyway." I said sarcastically.

He turned to Van, "We still don't know who the inside man is. The information is still getting to McElevain quickly even though I changed to all Superior guys. I've swept the place for bugs again and found nothing. I guess if we can hide in the woods and not be seen so can McElevain's guy."

Van didn't look overly happy, "So now we have to worry about more leaks with the Superior guys. Pretty soon the ship is going to be so full of leaks we will sink." Nice metaphor.

Jess shook his head, "No, I didn't go into details with anyone other than the chief. The officers have no idea why they are out here. All they know is that they need to report any suspicious activity back to headquarters. For all I know they probably think Sugar's running drugs out of here." And I smacked my forehead with the heel of my hand. Great, just great, that's gonna help business. Van was trying hard not to grin at my reaction and Jess wasn't looking at me. "I really didn't have much choice, guys. I can't risk that what happened yesterday happens again. Your radio is still connected to them and they know that you are an inside man. So if you need anything yell for backup and they will respond."

"This is starting to feel like it's out of control." Van said, his hand running through his hair, his face slack. He put his hand on his hip, "What's your plan for luring out McElevain's guy? Did the gunman give you a positive ID?"

Jess snorted, "The only thing he gave me was a bad attitude and good counsel. I haven't gotten anything out of him no matter what deal we offer. I'm sure he knows that getting out of jail is a one way ticket to the bottom of the lake as far as McElevain is concerned so he clammed right up. I don't have high hopes for him. My only hope is that the inside guy does something to tip his hand and that's why I'm keeping the gunman in the general population at the jail. I'm hoping that the officer working for McElevain attempts to free him or shows his hand some other way. Now that I have pulled everyone and the guys are all back at the station that will give him a good chance. If not, then I will have to take each and every one of them apart limb by limb until we find the guy. I will make him pay for threatening the investigation and for what they did to Sugar." And there was no doubt in my mind by the way his fists clenched that he would do exactly that.

"When it comes time for the limb tearing, I want in." Van said and he and Jess did that cop communication thing again.

I hadn't figured it out, but it was like they had teleprompters in each other's eyes. Or maybe men aren't as far from Mars as we women think.

Jess set his jaw, "Okay, I need to go make some calls about this ship thing. I'm pretty certain if there is a ship in harbor there is only going to be one, two max, and that will make things easier. I will have to put together a task force to get on the boat since a thousand foot boat is not going to be easy to do recon on. In the meantime I need you here," Jess said to Van, "Trust no one and keep everything locked down. Don't go out, don't let anyone in. Once I put this in motion I expect them to try to cause a diversion in order to lure us away from the boat. I would prefer to put you guys in a safe house, but I know Sugar would never leave." And he was right. If the lodge was going down so was I with it.

"This is all I have Jess, I can't leave it." I said and Van laid a hand on my leg.

"I've done this before Jess, I have it under control." he said. "Watch your back and don't worry about us."

Jess shook his hand, "I'm counting on you man. I'm somewhat attached to that woman right there and you've met my mother, right?"

Van smirked, "Yeah I understand ya totally, buddy. I'm a little afraid of her too. Call me on the secondary cell from a secure line once you figure out if Tula is onto something with the ships. I want to know how you are going to approach things once you have the target so I know when to expect things to heat up."

Jess gave me a gentle hug and turned to leave.

Van walked him to the door, "What's your ultimate goal? How do you want this to go down?"

Jess tried a laugh, but it came out sounding defeated. "Ultimately I want to get McElevain and shut down the operation, but I would be happy if I got Margie and Nathan back safely, got a few of the smaller guys under McElevain and we all walk away with our lives. I don't expect McElevain is going to be on the boat even if Margie and Nathan are. He's not that stupid. All we are going to get are a few of his flunkies and muscle. But if we can secure Margie and Nathan then we have them and the information that he wants and it might be easier to lure him out."

"Remember he's not above going higher on the chain of command to get what he wants. I wish I could be out there with you. I want McElevain as much as you do."

Jess stuck his hands in his pockets, "I know you do and I can promise you that I will let you in on the interrogation, but for now I really need you to take care of Sugar, that's your only job, Bond." And that little voice inside me was yelling that I could take care of myself even though we all knew that under these circumstances I couldn't. Jess said goodbye and Van walked him to the door. I heard low voices on the porch and then Van reappeared locking down the doors, closing the shades on the windows and checking the door to the ballroom.

He looked like a man with a plan, "Do you have any plywood anywhere?"

My mind went through the lodge, "I think there are some big sheets in the basement leaning up against the work table that I use for extra tables when I need them. There are probably a dozen of them."

"Nails and hammer?"

"On the work bench."

He nodded, "Okay I am going to put the plywood over the windows on the front of the house. That is the most vulnerable part of the lodge since someone could sit on the lake and lob anything they wanted through the windows. I need two upstairs, two down here in the main room and one for each bedroom down here."

I looked at him skeptically, "Do you really think that's necessary? I don't really want the whole lodge boarded up. It seems a little drastic."

"I will take drastic over something happening to you or the lodge and me having to deal with Jess's wrath." Point taken.

"Okay, I guess it can't hurt, wood can come down, but windows have to be replaced."

"Glad you can see it my way, darling."

He grabbed his radio and informed them that he would be outside doing some work and he was given the go ahead. I heard him pounding as he put up the wood and I laid my head back on the couch and prayed.

FORTY-FIVE

I had dozed off. With the pain pills it didn't take much. My body was done and my mind was exhausted. Van was sitting by the couch again and I smiled at him.

"Hi, all done?"

He nodded, "Yeah, the windows are secure. I couldn't get the plywood up on the outside of the upstairs windows, so I had to do it from the inside. So we might risk a broken window if they aim something at them, but at least the wood should stop it from damaging the inside."

"Van, be honest, what are you worried about here?" I asked him softly.

"I'm worried about you." Nice try.

I leveled a gaze at him, "I heard you and Jess whispering."

He waved his hand at me, "He was telling me once again how I had better watch my Ps and Qs with you." I rolled my eyes and he stood up.

"Let me take you to your bed." He picked me up under my knees and carefully around my back.

"I have a chair right there." He stood up and smiled at me, "I know, but then I don't get to feel you in my arms."

He proceeded to feather kisses against my forehead as I lay on his shoulder. He settled me on my bed and popped on the fireplace before crawling up onto the bed.

"I'm not used to sitting around waiting." I said.

"I know, but you are safer here. Besides I like taking care of you." Oh boy, turbulent water ahead. "About that."

He pressed a kiss to the top of my head, "I love you."

"I love you too." My voice was choked and the tears were close. I really loved him, a lot, but I didn't have the strength to pretend today. Jesse's words came back to me and I knew he was right. I had fought back from a lot, but I was feeling like this might be something I couldn't overcome.

He sighed and I knew why. His mind was going down the same road mine was. "I want you to rest while we wait for Jess to call. I want you to be strong enough to see Margie and Nathan when they are rescued." And I prayed that would be so. I sighed and snuggled in a little closer. I guess he didn't like the sigh.

"What's the matter? You still hurting?"

I shook my head, "The only thing that's still hurting is the part I can't dull. I don't have it in me to act like everything is going to be okay. I just don't. I know that what I told Jesse could save my friends and bring **them back alive, but it is also the last step in watching you walk out my** door."

He took a deep breath, "You don't have to pretend you aren't torn. I am too right now. We've been through a lot and so much has changed in a short period of time. I wish I had more answers." He absently rubbed my arm, "I don't know how this is going to work, I really don't, **but** I know that it has to. I know that I can't walk away from here and never see you again. I know that I can't walk around and live my life if you aren't **in it. I will figure out a way for us to be together. I promise you that right now, right here. I need to hear you tell me that you trust me. I need to** hear you say that no matter what happens you trust me."

I laid my hand across his chest and I felt his heartbeat jumping. I shifted until my ear was over his chest because it was where I felt safe. "I do trust you. I've trusted you since the day I laid eyes on you standing on my front porch, but I can't explain it."

He started singing softly, "You had me from hello. I felt love start **to grow. The moment I looked into your eyes you won me. It was over from the start you completely stole my heart. And now you won't let go. I** never even had a chance you know. You had me from hello."

I brushed back a tear, "'**You Had Me From Hello**', Kenny Chesney, nightclub two step." I can't sing, but I knew the rest of the **song was more** about me than him and I softly whispered the words. "Inside I built a wall. **So high around my heart, I thought I'd never fall. One touch, you brought it down. The bricks of my defenses scattered on the ground. And I swore to me I wasn't going to love again. The last time was the last time I'd let** someone in, but you had me from hello." And then I stopped and I clung **to him and I let him sing to me until I relaxed and felt peaceful again. I fell asleep as he finished the last few bars of "If Tomorrow Never Comes".**

I heard voices and opened one eye. It was Jay Leno. I had fallen asleep and slept for hours. I felt better, much better, but I realized I was alone and I remembered that Van was with me when I fell asleep. The house was silent. Maybe he went to bed in his room so he didn't disturb me, but I knew that wasn't likely. He wouldn't sleep until this was over and he wouldn't leave me alone in bed. My chair was sitting next to my bed so I climbed in it to find him. He was in the kitchen making coffee and putting together a couple of sandwiches.

"Hey it's sleeping beauty." He kissed me, letting his lips linger. "Feeling better?"

"I am. Did Jesse call?"

He nodded, but wouldn't look at me focusing on anything but my face.

"And?"

"And they found a ship, the *American Spirit*, which had been in harbor since October twenty-third having work done on the engine. They did a recon on it and felt with as much certainty as you can get the hostages were on the boat."

"The hostages?"

"Sorry, Margie and Nathan. Last I heard from him he was putting together a task force to go in and get them. That was a couple of hours ago."

"And you should have heard back from him by now. That's what you aren't saying, right?"

"No, I'm only telling you what I know. These things take time and we have to let them play out." he said firmly.

I cocked my head, "I don't believe you. I can tell that you are worried."

He let out a sigh and put the sandwiches at the table, "I've done this job for a lot years, Tula. My gut tells me this is a trap. I think they wanted us to figure out where they were. Margie and Nathan are good pawns, but McElevain would give them up in a heartbeat to get one of ours. Having an officer as a hostage would be like having an ace in the hole. I'm sure he sees it as a one way to ticket out of town. He would be on the run, but a guy with that much money could disappear into a whole new world and we would never find him. If we can't find him, we can't prosecute him. He would enjoy being able to toy with us. I also know that Margie and Nathan won't be safe if he isn't behind bars. He would make sure that they paid in the end, too."

He pushed me over to the table, but I wasn't hungry, he had killed any appetite I had.

"I'll be right back."

I wheeled into the living room where my liner and leg laid and grabbed them rolling the liner on and connecting the leg. I took a couple of practice steps and the leg was good. It didn't feel too bad. I wouldn't be running races, but even if I could walk instead of pushing the chair that would help. I parked the chair in the hallway to Van's disapproving glare.

"It's good. I need a break from the chair it's hurting my side. I'm not planning to dance or anything, just walk. Can you deal with that?"

He huffed, "Fine, but be careful please. Now we need to address the fact that you haven't eaten in over a day. If a sandwich doesn't do it for you, how about some soup?"

Soup actually sounded kind of good and I went to the pantry next to the fridge to grab a can when the sound of glass breaking filled the room. Van yelled for me to get down. I couldn't get down so I wrapped myself inside the door of the pantry and looked around the corner of it. The patio door was shattered into a thousand pieces and there was a rock lying in the middle of the floor.

Van was screaming into the radio for back up when a voice crackled over the radio, "Officer down! Officer down!"

My heart was pounding out of my chest and I was sweating. My side was on fire and I was trying to take shallow breaths, but it wasn't working. There was nothing but silence now. The kind that leaves you certain that another explosion is coming or another window would break in the distance, but there was nothing. I slowly stepped out from behind the pantry and started to walk towards the rock. Van was holding his arm out telling me to stay put and not move. He was talking to the other officer on the radio. The downed officer was coming around after having been tased with 50,000 volts, rendering him unconscious. I could hear him over the radio saying that the guy had tagged him from behind and he didn't see him. Van promised a squad would bring him to the hospital then requested help with the door.

He turned to me, "You okay?"

I nodded, not trusting my voice. He walked over to the door and picked up the rock, turning it over. I saw a million emotions run across his face at whatever was taped to the back of the rock. I could see he was trying to do the cop face thing, but it wasn't working with me. I walked over to him, the glass crunching under my feet.

"Van, what it is?" I asked it softly, but it sounded like I was shouting the room was so quiet. My heart was skipping beats and I knew down deep that his worst fear had come true. They had one of our guys.

"Van, tell me, now."

His voice was low and tight, "Tula, I want you to turn around and go back to your room."

"Van no, you need to tell me what is on that rock. Tell me right now!" And the yelling took too much breath and I winced.

He stared at me the look of pity in his eyes was enough for my heart to know. There was no question in my mind that a madman had my brother. He set the rock back down and stepped forward around the glass putting his hands on my shoulders and guiding me down the hallway.

His lips were tight, "I need to clean this mess up and then I will come in and we will talk. I need some time before I can talk to you about this." And I could see in his eyes the truth.

I felt the tears at the back of my throat and I nodded. He turned and went back to the door where the officer was standing and together they boarded up the door. I turned then and went to his room sitting on the bed as I listened to him clean up the glass. It probably wasn't more than five minutes before I heard his footfalls in the hallway, but it felt like a lifetime. I heard the squad come in and pick up the injured officer and drop off several more. I wasn't really feeling anything anymore and my mind was numb. I came out of his bedroom door and saw him walking towards me his hands in front of him one on top of the other and I could see blood, lots of it.

"I need to clean up." That was all he said and he went into his bathroom and closed the door.

I opened it again and he was standing in front of the sink, his head hung low and his face pinched as the water running over his hands turned the sink red from his blood. He didn't look good, but I didn't think it was the physical pain that was causing him the most anguish. I pushed the desk chair into the bathroom and slid it under him putting my hand on his shoulder and pushing him down. I grabbed bandages and ointment from the bathroom credenza as the water ran over his hands and he rested his head on the edge of the sink. I shut the water off and inspected the wounds, pulling out pieces of glass with the tweezer and throwing them in the sink.

"What the hell, Van? Why didn't you stop?" I demanded.

"I should have boarded up the doors, but since the guys were right out there and the doors faced the back I wanted to have easy access out if we needed it."

"I understand that, but what does that have to do with the fact that you have more glass in your hands than the garbage pail?"

He put his head back down on the sink, maybe he didn't know.

"I think the palm ones need a couple stitches."

He shook his head, "No stitches."

I let out a sigh and did the best I could to close them up with butterfly strips and bandages. In all he had two deep gashes on his palms and several smaller ones on his thumbs and fingers. By the time I was done he had bandages on every finger and two butterfly strips holding each palm gash closed. He wasn't going to be doing anything with his hands for a few days and I told him so. He lifted his head and tested out his hands, wincing as he tried to make fists.

"Thanks." he whispered.

"Tell me what is going on."

He got up out of the chair and put his arm around me walking me to the room and pulling me onto the bed. He pulled a picture out of his back pocket.

"I want you to know that I don't want to show you this. If I had my choice I would take you somewhere and make you believe that this wasn't happening, but I can't do that. I'm sorry."

He handed me the picture and my stomach turned. Staring back at me was Jesse. He was handcuffed and gagged, no shoes, no coat and standing on a dock somewhere along the shore of Lake Superior. The bottom said, "I'll be in touch." And I started to retch then, my stomach in my throat, but the pain in my side brought me back to where I was. I hung my head and took a couple of deep breaths.

"You were right." I said my head still hung low.

"I'm sorry, baby. I never dreamed it would be Jess." He took my hand and held it as I stared at the picture of the only family I had left and I got angry. The fear was gone or maybe the anger was being fueled by the fear, I don't know, but I wasn't going to let him down.

I looked up at Van and he nodded, "Use the anger. It's what I'm doing."

"Have you talked to the chief?" I asked him.

"No, that's my next call, but until we hear from McElevain there isn't much we can do."

He was wrong there. There was a lot we could do and that was be prepared for whatever he threw at us as quickly as possible.

"Julie." I said her name coming out in a whoosh.

Van flinched, "She's safe."

"Does she know? No, I know she doesn't because she would have called me already. Damn it!" I covered my mouth with my hand and closed my eyes.

"Tula?"

I opened my eyes, "I have to be the one to tell her. Here's the plan..." I started to say, but his eyebrows went up and he shook his head.

"Uh, no, I'm the cop. I'm making the plan."

I patted his hand like he was a small child. "Wrong. I'm tired of this disgusting excuse for a human being thinking that he can run our lives. This is going to end. I'm going to change my clothes and we are going to Julie. We will take the Mustang since no one will be expecting us to drive it. We will leave my cell phone open for McElevain to call on. You call the chief on the secondary line now and tell him to meet us at Jesse's. Make sure word does not get to her before I do. I know that we can't trust anyone in the department right now, but we can trust the chief, he's been part of the family for years. Get him on the line and let him make the decisions about who to bring in. Once we know what McElevain's demands are then we can move quickly. Do you know if they got Margie and Nathan out?"

The secondary cell phone rang at that moment and Van looked at the read out. "The chief."

He answered the phone and listened answering with short yes and no answers. He gave him a quick run down of how we wanted to proceed and he agreed to meet us at Jesse's in an hour with the members on the team that went in to get Margie and Nathan. He was confident that they were clean. He pushed the off button and stuck it in his shirt pocket.

"We have Margie and Nathan."

I let out a breath, "Just like you said would happen. Now he's got what he really wants and he's ready to deal."

"Chief has Margie and Nathan in a safe house and they will not be released until we get this mess straightened out." I stood up carefully and went to the door looking over my shoulder. "Meet you at the garage in five minutes."

FORTY-SIX

I went in my room and dug around the back of my armoire until I found my favorite foot. It was energy absorbing with a vertical shock and I knew if I was going to be on my feet, it was the only one that would allow me to walk and keep my knee from giving out. I was able to get my leg down in it by using the liner alone and grabbed a bag throwing in socks and an extra change of clothes. I threw on my rugged jeans that I keep for snowshoeing and a warm sweatshirt. I grabbed the bag and limped down to the mudroom, where I grabbed my boots, hat and mittens and threw them all in my bag, zipping it closed. I forgot my gun. I went back to my room and opened the drawer on my night stand. I pulled out my Glock, grabbing the extra magazines and checking the safety. I tucked it back in the holster and snugged that behind my back. I turned back to the door and Van was standing there watching me.

He motioned at my back, "I'm not comfortable with that."

"I'm not comfortable without it." I had no idea what would happen next, but I knew I could trust this gun. I knew how it felt in my hands and it was dead accurate.

He stepped in the door and pulled me to him being careful of my side, "How are you going to do this? You aren't even supposed to be out of bed." He was rubbing my back and I was trying not to relax because that would be my downfall.

"I just have to. I'm going to do whatever has to be done in order to get Jess back and then I will heal. I suspect that he's going to demand I play out the rest of his game with him."

"Oh no, that's not going to happen, Tula! You can forget that right now or I'm not taking you anywhere!" Van was visibly shaking.

"Listen to me. Jess and Julie have been here for me for the last ten years and now it's my turn to be there for them. You will take me to Julie right now and quit wasting my time telling me I can't when I know I can!" And I tried not to flinch at the pain in my side from yelling.

He pulled me up to within inches of his face. "If I think for even one second that you are going down I will take that leg and I will toss it in the lake. Do you understand me?" His voice was tight with anger.

"You can't toss it in the lake! This is a seven thousand dollar foot!"

He smiled then looking relieved. "Good, then I bet you'll be on your best behavior."

He handed me a cane to use for "support" and I climbed in the Mustang. I had made him crawl under the car and look for friendly and unfriendly GPS devices before we left the garage. He found two, one friendly, one unfriendly and they were sitting on my garage floor. He was driving the Mustang much harder and much faster than I wanted him to, but I knew we had to get there quickly. I hoped that taking the Mustang would give us an element of surprise on McElevain's man who was watching the lodge. I knew it would fit in Jesse's garage and the SUV wouldn't. I didn't want my car parked in front of his house. My side was aching and every bump was torture, but I refused to show it. I had started coughing halfway there and that was adding to the pain. Something told me that the only place I should be going was to the hospital, but I pushed that from my mind. We turned onto his street and I called Julie, waiting for her to pick up the phone.

"Hello?" She didn't recognize the number of the secondary cell phone.

"Julie, its Sugar. I'm outside the house can you power open Jesse's garage door so I can pull in?"

"Why?"

"Because I don't want the Mustang in the driveway." I heard the line go dead.

"She knows something's up. I don't drive the Mustang after the first snowfall." I said.

Van's lips were still in a tight line and we watched the door go up and Julie was silhouetted against the light in the kitchen. Van pulled the car in and killed the engine and Julie sent the door back down. Van got out of the car and came around to my side. He opened the door and helped me swing out being careful not to stress my side.

"Sugar," I heard Julie's voice tremble, "what's going on?"

My heart broke because I knew that I had to go tell my best friend that the man that she loved, the father of her baby, was in the hands of a crazy man.

"Let's go inside, Julie." Van helped me up the stairs and I stepped inside Jesse's house. I tried to not think about him not being here. Van stepped to the front door to wait for the chief while Julie and I sat down on the couch.

"It's Jess isn't it?" she asked, clutching my hand.

I looked down at my hands then back up at her face. She had her cop face on, but her eyes gave her away. Her eyes didn't have a cop face.

"Yeah, it's Jess." She sucked in a deep breath and her lower lip trembled.

"He's alive." And that was all I could say because I didn't know if he was okay.

"Where is he? I want to see him." She was up off the couch and I held onto her hand pulling her back down.

"Sit down, Julie."

She sat back down on the couch hard and crossed her arms over her belly.

"I called Jess earlier today because I thought I had figured out where they had Margie and Nathan. The picture Scarface showed me revealed enough for me to think they were being kept on a freighter. I asked Jess to find out if any were in harbor being repaired. I felt strongly that might be where McElevain was keeping them. He found the *American Spirit* was in port being repaired and had been there for over a month, more than enough time for McElevain to stash Margie and Nathan there. He put together a team and went in. They were able to rescue Margie and Nathan, but somehow, one of McElevain's guys took Jess while the others were busy rescuing Margie and Nathan. Van is certain that kidnapping Margie and Nathan was just a ploy to get one of ours."

A tear trekked down her cheek, "So how do you know he's alive?"

"Earlier tonight someone airmailed a rock through my sliding glass doors in the kitchen. They had taped a picture of Jess on it with a note that said 'I'll be in touch'. The message was pretty damn clear, he wants the information we have in exchange for Jess. Van thinks it was what he wanted the whole time and now he's going to balance the scale."

"I want to see the picture." Julie said her head down.

I shook my head, "No." And there wasn't a chance in hell I was showing her the picture.

"Sugar..."

"No Julie. He's alive and he wasn't hurt. That's all you need to know."

She got up and went to the door where Van stood and held her hand out. He flicked his eyes to me and I shook my head no. He took her hand and held it for a minute. She pleaded with him and he told her that Jess was okay and that seeing the picture wasn't going to tell her anything more than that.

She turned quickly and stalked away from him, her steps picking up speed and she disappeared down the hall to the bathroom. I heard the door slam shut. I struggled to stand up and follow her, afraid that she was going to pass out. I knocked on the door and called her name softly. There was no response, but I could hear the sound of retching and crying.

I opened the door and stepped in clicking the door closed behind me and sat on the tub opposite where she knelt with her head over the toilet. I rubbed her back and whispered for her to take some deep breaths and slow down her breathing so she didn't pass out and hurt herself or the baby. It seemed like mention of the baby snapped her back to reality and she slowly got herself under control. She stepped over to the sink, washing her face and drying it on the towel. I looked at her reflection in the mirror. She was past tired and she was past sick. She looked done to me, like I had never seen done before. She came over and put the lid down on the toilet almost falling down onto it.

"I'm living every cop's worst nightmare, Sugar. I'm experiencing firsthand what some of the people I counsel were feeling. The problem is I'm a cop and I know all too well how this is going to turn out."

"You don't know that, Julie." I said vehemently, "You don't know how this is going to turn out because it's not over yet and I know Jesse. He is going to do everything in his power to get back here to you and this baby."

She looked at me shaking her head like she didn't believe me. "Show me the picture. I need to see the picture."

My resolved wavered a little bit. I had no experience with all of this cop stuff and what was right and what was wrong, but I remembered back to the day in the hospital when I had to see Brent and I knew that I wouldn't make it to the next minute until I did.

"I want you to remember that no matter how bad this looks, he is alive." I reached into my pocket and pulled it out unfolding it. She took it, her hands shaking, and looked at the man she loved handcuffed and gagged and she sobbed softly.

"We are waiting for the chief. Once McElevain calls we'll know how we are to proceed to get him back here. We will get him back, Julie. Everyone's in agreement. Our only goal is to get Jess and to hell with everything else. The rest isn't important."

She was stony silent for minutes staring at the picture. "Have you called Mom?"

I shook my head, "No and I don't plan to unless I have to. The less people involved the better, right?"

She had the glazed look in her eyes people have when they don't want to feel, just want to make it through and she nodded. "How do you think he's going to be in touch?" she asked me, still holding the picture.

"He has my cell phone number. He enjoys calling it to mess with me. I fully expect him to call me and set up an exchange. From there I don't know, but he's decided he is going to use me to get what he wants. He thinks I have more pull than I do."

"No," she shook her head, "it's common knowledge Jesse would do anything to protect you and you are the best card to hold with him. It wouldn't take but five minutes of asking the right questions to anyone in the Twin Ports to figure out what you are to him. Believe me it's no secret. I don't know how it could be."

It was then that I began to catch on to what she was saying. She was saying that I meant more to Jess than she did, than her and their baby.

"I'm sorry, Julie." I said softly, standing up from the tub.

"For what?" She wouldn't look at me.

"For falling apart, for making him feel like he needed to keep an eye on me and this was a good way to do it. If I had admitted I had a problem and asked for help he wouldn't have put Margie and Nathan at my place and he would be here with us right now."

She was silent and that was enough for me to know what she really thought. She really did blame me for this whole thing and as much as I wanted to her to say, "no, Sugar that's not true", I probably deserved it. I blew out a breath, "I'm going to make you some tea." And I walked out of the bathroom quickly before she could see the tears falling.

I walked to the kitchen in a trance her words echoing in my ears. I stood staring at the stove and couldn't remember why I was there. I was tired and my side ached and burned in a way that I had never experienced in my life -- and I've experienced a lot of pain. I was having a hard time catching a breath and I was cold. The cold reminded me why I was there and I busied myself with the water, putting the teakettle on to heat and getting some mugs down. I heard Van come in the room and I didn't turn because I didn't want him to see me crying. He didn't know my best friend thinks I'm the reason my brother is in the hands of a madman.

"Hey pretty lady, can I help with anything?" he asked, coming up behind me.

I shook my head slightly and focused on the teakettle through my tears.

"Is Julie sick?" I could tell by the tone of his voice that he suspected there was a problem.

"Yeah." And that was all I could get out around the lump in my throat.

"Tula, what happened?" He laid his hand on my shoulder and I turned to him. I couldn't throw my arms around him because I hurt too much so I leaned into him and let the tears fall free.

"She's convinced it's my fault that they took Jess. She said everyone in the whole world knows I'm the most important thing to him and that's why they are going to use me as a pawn." I was struggling to cry and breathe at the same time.

"She's just upset." he said, rubbing my back.

"I know, but the worst part is she actually believes it and that's killing me inside." And I couldn't stop my shoulders from shaking as a sob escaped.

He slid his arms around my waist and hugged me carefully. "It's not your fault. Jess is a big boy and makes his own decisions."

"If he hadn't felt the need to protect me then this might not have happened and Julie wouldn't be in there right now wondering if her baby will ever meet its' daddy."

He took my chin in his hand, "Don't do this now. You have to keep it together and be strong for Julie when she can't be. Do you hear me?"

I nodded as the teakettle started to perk and I jumped at the sound. He turned the burner off and poured two cups of water not trusting me to do it myself. I heard music and hot coffee and cool conversation and I looked up at him fumbling for my phone in my pocket.

I pulled it out and answered it my hand trembling, "Hello."

"Ms. DuBois, it's been too long, but the pleasure is all mine once again." My stomach turned and I mouthed McElevain to Van and imitated writing. I sat down at the kitchen table and he brought me a pen and paper.

"I can't say the same." And that was all I said.

"I'm hurt. You should think about being nice since I have your brother and he's a real pain in the ass. It wouldn't take much to convince me to dump him and cut my losses."

I clenched my teeth, "What do you want?" I wasn't about to feed into his scare tactics.

"I want the information that you have and I want my freedom. If I get those two things you get your brother, alive. If I don't, you get him dead. It's your choice really."

"I don't know why you think I have that kind of authority. I'm not a cop."

"Well, that's very true, Ms. DuBois, but since you are sleeping with one I'm sure you can use your feminine wiles to get what you want. You have ten minutes and I will call you back with my list of demands. Make sure you have an answer."

The line went dead and I set the phone down on the table.

"What did he say?" Van was sitting opposite me and had his hands steepled in front of him.

"He told me that Jesse was a pain in the ass and he wouldn't think twice about dumping him and cutting his losses, so we need to do this exactly the way he wants if we want to get him back. He made that very clear."

"What does he want?" Van asked.

"He wants all the information we have on him and his freedom. He says if he gets both he will let Jesse go alive. If he doesn't, he will let him go dead. I told him I don't have that kind of power. He told me since I'm sleeping with a cop he was sure I could work it out in his favor."

Van shook his head throwing his hand around, "You know he needs to get outta that garden! It wouldn't make a damn bit of difference if you were sleeping with me or not, he's going to get what he wants because that's how it works and he knows it. He's messing with you trying to make it look wrong that we have a relationship. Don't let him get under your skin, that's what he wants. I want you to focus on Jesse. Next time he calls tell him you want to talk to Jess before you make any deals. Then agree to whatever he wants and we will make sure it gets done. We will get him back and we will not stop until we do, don't ever forget that."

The chief walked in the door at that moment, "Agreed. Whatever he wants give him. We have made copies of the information that you found and he knows that, but I have all the originals with me. We will let him walk because there is always tomorrow for him, but not for Jesse. Be sure he gives us enough time so we aren't scrambling and making promises we can't keep."

I nodded, "Thanks Chief."

His phone rang and he stepped out of the room as Julie appeared in the doorway. She had her hand on the frame like it was the only thing holding her up and she had aged ten years in the ten minutes I had been in the kitchen.

"I didn't mean that." She pointed back to the bathroom as explanation.

"I deserved it. Just forget about it." I said remorsefully.

Van looked at me eyes wide and face slack. "You didn't deserve anything Tula, you aren't at fault here." And he didn't understand that I was already with inches of losing my brother and my best friend and that I was going to tell her whatever she wanted to hear if it meant I held on to them for a little while longer.

"Van, I'm cold, can you get me a blanket?" I asked my teeth chattering.

He sighed as he got up and brushed past Julie as she stepped in.

"He's right," she said.

I really wasn't feeling well. I was cold and had chills and my stomach was nauseated. I had never gotten that sandwich and I had gone a good twenty four hours without food.

I held my hand out to her and she took it. "I really need something to eat. Do you have any crackers?"

She looked at me funny, but went to the cupboard and got down some saltines and grabbed a cup of tea. Van came back in and wrapped the blanket around my shoulders asking how many minutes we had. I looked at my phone and told him five more minutes. He excused himself to get the chief and Julie set the food in front of me. I was feeling very funky, cold and sweaty, and nauseated. I tried to tell myself I was hungry and I ate a couple crackers and sipped the tea, but it wasn't helping.

Julie bent down in front of me on the floor and took my hand, "Why are you so hot?" She stood up and felt my forehead and looked back at the door dropping her voice, "Sugar, you are burning up."

I had already figured that out. I felt like I did the last time I had the flu, only I suspected it had more to do with the wound on my side than an actual illness.

Her voice was low, "Didn't you take the antibiotics Dr. Mueller gave you?"

I shook my head, "I couldn't eat anything and they made me throw up. That made the pain worse and the whole cycle started over again. So I took one, but that was all." And I could see now that was pretty stupid.

"You really need to go to the hospital. I'm getting Van." and she got up to leave.

"Not on your life, Julie. There is no way anyone is answering this phone but me and there is no way I'm going anywhere until Jess is back home safe with you." I said through clenched teeth. We heard voices coming towards us. "Give me some Tylenol. That will bring the fever down and then Van won't notice."

She rolled her eyes at me, her way of saying as if, but went to the cupboard and grabbed the bottle. She dumped two in my hand seconds before the two men stepped in the room and I quickly swallowed them down with the tea. Julie sat down next to me at the table and Van and Chief sat opposite us. I looked at my phone it had been eleven minutes. We waited four more.

The chief raised his brow, "He's trying to make us sweat so that we give him what he wants, just be patient."

I nodded, but I was not feeling well and the Tylenol wasn't helping. The pain in my side was getting worse and sitting upright was becoming a challenge. I tried leaning over towards that side on the table, but Van's lips were in a tight line and I suspected he knew I was ill. I tried not to look at him. Sixteen, seventeen, eighteen minutes passed and finally the phone rang. I answered it on the first ring.

"Did I give you enough time to get your answer?" He was laughing and it was pissing me off and getting on my last nerve.

"More than, we will give you want you want, but I want to talk to Jess."

He laughed some more, "I figured you would say that. He seems to want to talk to you too." I heard scuffling and motioned for Julie to lean in to listen.

"Hi Sugar." It was Jess and he was doing his cool as a cucumber routine, but I knew otherwise.

"Hi Jess" Julie and I said in unison. I heard Jess suck in a breath as he recognized Julie's voice.

"I'm fine, having a fine time here with the Peanut Gang. Listen to me, Sugar, I don't want you involved any more than you are. Let an expert deal with this, I don't want you getting hurt."

His voice changed then and he whispered, "Julie, baby, I love you and I will be home in a few hours. I missed dinner, so make sure you have a pizza ready when I get there. I'm just at work, I'll be home soon, remember that. Take care of my baby." Julie told him she loved him and then put her head on the table sobbing softly. One of Julie's friends from the station came in the kitchen and sat next to her, putting her arm around her.

I pulled the phone back to my ear and tried to ignore what Jess had told me. I heard scuffling again and McElevain was back.

"There now, let's get down to business." I picked up the pen and started writing.

His list of demands was not long. He wanted all the information we had on him in a satchel with keys to a float plane that was gassed and waiting for him with an approved FAA flight plan clearing him passage to San Antonio, Texas. I suspected he wouldn't make it any further than the middle of Lake Superior before he would land the plane and be picked up by a chartered boat that would spirit him off to some undisclosed airport where he would board a plane to Cabo San Lucas or some other far away destination. I didn't really care. As long as I got Jess back then he could do whatever the hell he wanted. He wanted me to be on the road in front of the airport at Park Point at exactly three a.m. and alone. Any cops, he said, and your brother's dead. Any weapons and your brother is dead. I was to be on foot. I told him that was a problem since his flunky had so kindly shot me and I wasn't getting around too good, so he agreed to an ATV if I left it at the access point to the beach road. I didn't know if I could even make it that far, but I agreed anyway not wanting to anger him. The conversation took a total of ten minutes and when I hung up I handed the list over to Van and the chief.

As soon as he saw the part about me delivering the information he started shaking his head and saying, "No, no, no, no, no, you are not doing this. My god, Jess will literally take me apart if he sees you out there. No, not going to happen. There isn't a chance in hell I'm sending you out there in the shape you are in." I stared at him. I knew he loved me and he was trying to keep me safe, but this was how McElevain wanted it and he was going to get what he wanted.

The chief stood up, "Listen while you guys figure this out I'm going to get the ball in motion. We only have a few hours until he wants to meet and I need to get the flight plan approved. Notify me when you have a decision."

He strode out of the room with the piece of paper in his hand and Julie stood up and without a word left too. I tried to put everything in the back of my mind and convince the man I love this was a good idea.

"He told me it has to be me or the deal is off." I whispered.

"I don't care what he told you. It isn't going to happen." He threw back.

"Since when did you become my keeper?" I demanded my eyes blurry from the fever and anger.

His eyes flashed green. "I became your keeper when Jess brought me here to keep you safe. I became your keeper when I fell in love with you and became your lover and I become your keeper when I see you doing something stupid like you are right now!"

His voice was low, but angry. I stood up slowly because that was the only way I could move right now. Every movement was an effort and I wasn't about to let him see that he was right. "I need to go to the bathroom."

I turned and walked out of the room as dignified as I could while clutching my side and limping on a leg that had seen better days.

God bless determination.

FORTY-SEVEN

I locked myself in the bathroom and held a wash rag under the cold water. I held it over my face trying to calm my flushed cheeks. I had been holding in a coughing fit for the last ten minutes and finally let it out. I felt something wet on my hand and looked down. It was blood. I quickly scrubbed it off my hand not wanting to waver from my plan. I lay down on the bathroom rug and tried to make my brain put all my scattered thoughts in order. I had to get this job done. I coughed again and more blood came up, but then the coughing settled and I decided it was old blood from the rib breaking yesterday.

I about had myself convinced when I heard a knock on the door followed by a tentative, "Tula?" It was Van. I struggled to sit up and used the tub to pull myself to a standing position with great effort. I unlocked the door, but didn't open it. I went back and sat down on the toilet, the cold wash rag over my face. I heard the door click open and then click closed behind him.

There was a litany going on inside my head of all the reasons why I needed to do this. I was telling myself I was not going to cry, lean on him or let him talk me out of it. That all changed of course the second he pulled the rag down and looked into my eyes. I saw so much love there along with anger and pity. He was kneeling in front of the toilet and I leaned over onto his shoulder. His face brushed mine and he held me that way for a long time before pulling back and putting a hand on my forehead.

"You're sick baby, you gotta go to the hospital." His eyes were tortured.

No sense denying it. "I promise as soon as we get him back I will let you take me to the hospital personally, but I have to do this." He leaned back on the bathtub and propped his forearms on his thighs.

"Why? McElevain isn't going to care if it's you or not as long as he gets what he wants. He likes the fact that he can toy with Jesse by making him think he's putting you in danger." Nice try at reverse psychology I had to give him that.

I cocked my head, "I can't count the number of times that Jesse and Julie have been here for me. I have to at least try to repay that. He asked for me and he will get me."

He tossed up a hand, "Tula, don't you get it? They want to be here for you. They are your family, families help each other. That's the way it works. It isn't about keeping score. It's about love and devotion, not about who has done more for who. Don't you see that?"

My teeth started to chatter at that point and I clenched my teeth together to stop them, "I do understand that! He's my brother Van, what the hell do you want me to do? Leave him hanging out there? What if it was Lillie?"

"No, don't even go there. There is no comparison here! I'm not,"

"What? You're not crippled? Is that what you were going to say?"

"God no, that never crossed my mind. I was going to say that I'm not a dance instructor who has no business playing cop. I have been trained in hostage recovery and situations like this. You can't compare it."

I looked at him stubbornly, "Yes you can. You just said it's about love and devotion. If you weren't a cop and Lillie was in trouble you would be doing the exact same thing I am and you know it!" And I was panting for breath my head hanging low because it was taking a lot of effort to keep yelling at him.

He rubbed my back and helped me slow my breathing down until I could talk again. "For the first year after the accident I was a sore ass to be around, as my dad always said. I wasn't trying to be, but it was my only defense against what I was feeling inside. I didn't eat, I didn't sleep and spent every hour of every day walking around like my whole life hadn't been wiped out in a single breath. It didn't work. I collapsed at school one day and never got up. I spent a week in the hospital and two months in physical rehab and do you know who was there every night? Do you know who would sit and rub my leg and keep the muscles loose? Do you know who gave up friends and girls and good times at the bar to come in and dance the same stupid patterns over and over again until I'm sure he wanted to puke? Do you know who didn't call me a stupid ungrateful kid and leave me to deal with all of it by myself?"

"I'm going out on a limb here and saying Jesse." He said giving me a one sided smile.

I tried to laugh, but coughed instead. I tasted blood and swallowed it back down before he could see. "Yeah, Jesse. Jesse and Sharon. They cried for me and they cried with me and they showed me what devotion is. So I know it's not about keeping score or paying anyone back. It's about being there and doing everything I can to make sure he gets back here to his baby and his wife." I put my head down and panted for air.

He reached out and took my hand, running his thumb along my scar. "Alright, this is how it's going to work and you will do all of the above or you won't do it, do you understand me?"

I nodded.

He stood up. "I'm going to change the bandage on your side and you are going to take some more fever relievers and lay down until it is time to go."

He looked at his watch, "It's one now, so you have an hour until we have to leave to get down to Park Point. You will wear a full bullet proof vest and a full neck guard under your parka. He won't know it's there and that will give you added protection. You will drive the ATV as far in as possible and only walk the last few feet, you falling down and not getting back up is not going to help Jesse."

"Okay."

"And if I think for a minute that you aren't going to be able to do this you are done and someone else will. Understood?"

I nodded again.

He pulled me in and hugged me carefully, "I love you and it's killing me to let you do this, but I want you to know I do understand. I don't like it and I want to shake you until your teeth rattle, but I understand. If it was Lillie I would be doing the same thing, as much as I hate to admit you are right."

I pressed my nose into his shirt inhaling the smell of him knowing if things didn't go right I may never know the scent of him again. He pulled back and lifted my shirt. His lips pressed into a thin line.

"Well there's a reaction I never thought I would see on a guy's face when I showed him my breasts." I tried laughing, but coughed instead and bent over at the waist. I swallowed the blood even though I wanted to vomit.

He dropped my shirt and opened the bathroom door calling Julie. "I need to lay her down and get her side redressed. Do you have supplies?"

She didn't ask questions. She told him to take me to Jesse's room and she would be right in. She brought in enough first aid supplies to supply a small hospital and sucked in a breath when she saw my side.

"This is crazy. You are not doing this, Sugar. Van tell her she is not doing this. She needs a hospital and an IV drip."

Van shrugged his shoulder, "Tried that, she won't listen. So she is going to do this and then I'm allowed to personally take her to the hospital."

Van started changing the bandage and I drifted off because the whole thing made me want to be sick. He was being gentle, but everything that touched it caused a blazing fire through my side. I was so cold and I was shivering. Julie brought me some Advil and I swallowed it with a sip of water. She covered me with a quilt.

Van finished taping off the pads and let my shirt fall down over it. "Against my better judgment, you have an hour to prove to me you can do this. I'm leaving Julie here and she's going to make sure you don't pass out and never wake up. I have to make the plan with the team and get everyone in position. I will be back at two to get you dressed."

I nodded only half awake not sure how an hour was going to help and I think he knew it. He wanted me to pass out and not wake up so that I didn't go out there and do something stupid like get shot or killed. I could respect that, but I was going. I drifted off to sleep and the pain subsided a little and I stopped shivering. God bless Advil.

I woke suddenly and Julie put a hand on my shoulder. I looked at the alarm on the side of the bed and it was 1:30. I had only been asleep a few minutes, but I felt a little stronger and I could tell that the Tylenol and Advil had kicked in. My fever was down, but the pain in my side was up and I struggled against it. I started coughing and covered my mouth with my hand remembering too late that Julie was in the room. She handed me a tissue and I took it wiping my hand and my mouth. I looked down and the amount of blood was glaring and even I was getting scared. My breathing was heavy and my chest felt tight. Like someone had blown up a balloon inside my chest and I couldn't exhale. I tried to shove the Kleenex in my jeans pocket before she saw it. "Don't bother. I found the other tissues in the bathroom. How long have you been coughing up blood?"

I put my game face on, "It's old blood from last night."

She leveled a glare at me, "It's bright red and as fresh as it can get and you are going to the hospital."

"Right, as soon as I get Jess."

"No, I will go get Jesse and you will go to the hospital." She said standing up.

"Oh yeah that's a great idea, Julie. Let's send the pregnant woman out there to face a madman. That's an outstanding plan! Like Jesse wouldn't have a bird if he saw you standing out there facing down a gun."

She laughed hysterically, "Like he's not gonna have a bird when you show up? Like he's not gonna take down every single one of us for letting you out there? I think the fever has cooked your brain a little bit, Sugar. You've met Jesse, right?"

I rolled my eyes at her, "I'm family he'll get over it. I couldn't forgive myself if something happened to you or the baby. I'm doing it and that's final. Another hour isn't going to make or break me and then I will gladly submit to any amount of medical care I need, but not until I know he's back with you where he belongs."

"I can end this right now, **Sugar. I can go out there and tell** Van you're coughing up blood and after what he saw changing that bandage I can promise you there would be an ambulance here in thirty seconds."

I let out a sigh. "Julie, **I have gotten the message loud and clear that you blame me for this and that's okay.** I blame myself, but I'm trying to get Jess back here safe, to you and the baby, that's all. McElevain made it very clear what he wants and come hell or high water he's going to get it if **it means you hold my brother in your** arms tonight."

She started crying softly then and collapsed on the bed. I put my hand on her shoulder and whispered, "When Brent and I first started dancing we were little, really little Julie. We were two happy little kids who wanted nothing more than to enjoy our passion together and not care what anyone else thought. Then Paul left and Brent cried, all the time. He wouldn't dance and he wouldn't go to school. He didn't realize what a piece of crap his father was, all he knew was that his life had changed more than he could handle. One night my dad picked me up from the dance studio and I got in the car and I told him, "Daddy you have to help them. You have to make Brent stop crying. I know you can do it Daddy you always make me stop crying when I'm sad." I was seven, I had no idea what divorce was. All I knew was that my friend was sad and my big strong daddy could fix it. He took me for an ice cream that day and then he took me home and talked to my mom. We all got in the car and drove over to Sharon's house. They sent us kids out to play and they talked for what seemed like hours. Jesse sat on the porch glowering like someone had just stolen his bike and I will never ever forget the look on his face. He was twelve, but he looked so old. He sat there defeated, shoulders slumped watching Brent like he would disappear too if he blinked his eyes. Over the next few months the boys would come to the lodge after school when Sharon had to work and my mom would feed them pie and love on them. When Brent and I were at lessons my dad would take Jesse out to his shop and they would work on projects or walk in the woods and talk. Eventually Brent stopped crying and started dancing again and Jesse stopped glowering and smiled again. As he got older he didn't have to come out to the lodge anymore after school, but he did anyway. He came out every night and helped my dad and ate my mom's food and talked about his dreams of becoming a police officer. He drove me and Brent back and forth from school to the dance studio and to competitions. We spent every holiday together and every birthday together and we all became part of the same family. My parents were right there with Sharon the day Jesse graduated from high school and again the day he graduated from the academy. And then the accident happened and you know he acts like I lost so much more than he did, but the reality is that he lost just as much. I know that we aren't a traditional family, Julie, but we are still family. And I know that it's hard for others to understand, but when Jesse looks at me he sees my father and he sees his brother and he wants to make them proud of him. Families fight, families love, and families help each other. And now you are part of our family, Jules, and I couldn't be happier about that. But you are his number one priority and I don't ever want you to think for a minute that I don't know that or want that. His alliance will lie with you and that little precious baby you are carrying right now. I hope that you can accept that he is always going to worry about me a little bit. I gave up on trying to convince him otherwise a long time ago. He's coming home to you. He's coming home to his baby. He's not coming home to me. You are his life now, you know that right?"

I started to cough then swallowing the blood so she wouldn't see it.

She wiped her eyes and put her hand over mine. "I'm having a bad day."

"Yeah" I pulled her into me the best I could, "I know, but I'm going to make tomorrow better if you let me, but you have to let me."

We heard the door click open and Van walked in the room. Julie was still in my arms as he stopped at the end of the bed. I held my breath waiting for her decision. She straightened up and stood busying herself with folding the quilt and helping me up off the bed.

"When you see my fiancé make sure to tell him the pizza's in the oven." She said giving me a weak smile. I let out what little breath I could squeeze out and promised her I would.

To say I felt like the Thanksgiving turkey would be a good analogy. Van had me strapped into more body armor than I could hold up and then added extra for "safety's sake". He had my parka over all of it and surprisingly it still fit. That told me one of two things -- either they make bulletproof vests a lot sleeker these days or I had lost a lot of weight. I knew it was the latter and I promised myself a plate of onion rings and a burger as soon as I could breathe again. I felt like I was at a dress fitting with all the "hold your arms out" and "don't look down" I was getting from Van. He had me set up with an ear piece that was hidden in my hat and went down my back to a radio so he could hear me and I could hear him. He added a scarf to cover the neck protector and dropped my Glock in my front coat pocket.

"It's loaded. It's there for emergencies only. Don't think about drawing it unless you have no other option." he said firmly.

I nodded. I couldn't speak because every time I did I started to cough and I couldn't risk any blood escaping where he would see it. He took me out to the garage where Chief Van Brunswick waited. He told me that the plane was gassed up and waiting. There were several men placed in strategic locations and he assured me no one would see them. I was getting butterflies in my stomach, but I pushed them back focusing my last remaining energy on what I had to remember to get Jesse back here as fast as I could. Chief Van Brunswick handed me the messenger bag with the keys and the paperwork.

"There's no tracking device in here, is there?" I asked stupidly.

He shook his head, "No, I'm playing it by the book with him. He will dump the bag anyway so there is no sense in ticking him off. I want this to go down clean with hostage recovery and nothing else." Hostage recovery. I felt the bile rise and I swallowed it back down.

"We had better go." I said putting the bag over my shoulder, but he reached up and took my arm.

"Sugar, ten years ago I had to take a rookie cop aside and tell him that he had lost half his family. I can't tell that woman in there that she's lost half of hers. Listen to Agent Walsh, do what he tells you to do and don't think twice about shooting the son of a bitch if you get the chance."

"Consider it done, Chief." I whispered.

He ducked into his car and waited for Van to load me in the unmarked Crown Vic. The garage doors opened and Chief Van Brunswick pulled out first. I saw Julie in the doorway to the garage and waved a small wave. I mouthed I love you and she nodded before one of her fellow officers pulled her in the door and closed it.

FORTY-EIGHT

It was getting harder and harder to breathe. I was coughing with little to no provocation and trying to hide the blood from Van. He had taken me through Superior and across the Bong Bridge, getting on 35-E and taking the exit for the DECC. I was concentrating on keeping my breathing slow and even. I was watching him out of the corner of my eye and he would start to say something and then close his mouth. This went on until we made it to the bridge. Van finally broke the silence.

"The ATV will be waiting once we get to the park area."

I nodded as we crossed the lift bridge, no boats in sight the night dark and murky like the water below us. The kind of night that if you walked far enough and long enough it would swallow you up and you would become part of it. The memory of the last time we were here together skittered through my mind and I shivered even though I was roasting like a Thanksgiving turkey. His hand left the wheel and reached across taking mine and squeezing it.

"I'm going to be in your ear the whole time, baby. Hopefully I will be able to hear exactly what he is saying, but I will prompt you if I can't and I need you to try and repeat it for me. If for some reason you don't hear me in your ear just do what he says. We have our guys in the airport and surrounding the beach area."

"He said no cops."

"He won't know they are there. The SEALs aren't seen."

I raised an eyebrow. "SEALs?"

He shrugged his shoulder. "I have a lot of friends and I count Jesse as one of them." And that was all he said.

Minnesota Point was seven miles long and Sky Harbor Airport sat the very end flanked by the beach on one side and the harbor on the other. I guess taking off from the airport provided a spectacular view and was well worth it if you had the chance. I've never had the chance and the way I was feeling I didn't know that I ever would. I started to cough and turned my head, coughing into a tissue which I quickly put in my pocket. It was getting harder and harder to breathe and I was wheezing like a four-pack-a-day smoker. I tried to slow my breathing and leaned back against the seat trying to get comfortable, as comfortable as you could get with a broken rib and four layers of body armor.

"You have to tell me where to go, **Tula**, I don't know where I am." **he said.**

I spoke softly hoping that would keep the coughing at bay, "The only way you can go is straight. If you turn either direction you are in the lake."

He laughed then and the silence was broken for a moment before the car was quiet again. He stopped at the stop sign by the old boarded up ICO station and put the car in park, turning to me.

"If you die out there I'm going to be really, really ticked at you."

I nodded my lower lip trembling, "I have no intention of doing that, Mr. Bond. My first order of business is getting Jess out of that maniac's hands and then I think I'm going to go visit Dr. Mueller. I'm feeling a little funky." I tried to suck in a deeper breath, but failed sounding like a kitten whimpering.

His eyes found mine and he shook his head, "Damn it you are stubborn."

"Yeah, but you still love me." I tried to sound jovial, but it came out sounding feeble.

"Yeah I do love you and against every grain of my being I'm taking you to that park and putting you on an ATV to go save your brother. But I want you to know that I think you're being stupid."

"You've made that exhaustively clear." I whispered.

He put the car in gear and crossed through the stop sign. The entire point was dark, only an occasional street light shining in the distance or from a house where a mother was up with her child. It made the lights from the harbor seem so far away. I loved the harbor at night. The lights beckoned the ships to port after a long journey and the lift bridge welcomed them in and gave them a slow salute of passage as they headed back out. Once Thanksgiving rolled around the Bentleyville light show would start at Bayfront Park and people would flock from all over the country to see the largest display of Christmas lights in the area. I could picture the sight in my mind, the twinkling multicolored lights, the kids pulling at their parent's hands to see Santa and the fire pits glowing with coals to warm your hands. But this year the gales of November blew early and covered the ground with a foot of snow. Everyone who calls Park Point home had rolled up the sidewalks and settled in for their long winters nap. I knew when they all woke up in a few hours they would have no idea what had transpired in their backyard. People don't even think about how the police protect them until an officer goes down and then it's in the headlines for days. If the officer is lucky enough to live, they become a legend; if they aren't, the funeral is covered live on TV and for a week or two everyone thanks a cop for their service. But then the hoopla dies down and people go back to being oblivious. When you have a cop in your family you are never oblivious.

Van pulled the Crown Vic into Park Point Park where the ATV sat unloaded and ready for me. He came around and helped me out of the car. I was so pudgy it reminded me of being a kid all dressed up for playing in the snow, where one wrong move would send you toppling over and leave you unable to get back up. He pulled me into him. I leaned into him and laid my head on his shoulder. I could hardly breathe and I knew I didn't have much time before things really went south. He leaned down and kissed me softly on the lips and I pulled away before he could go further. I didn't want to chance him tasting the blood. He released me and grabbed the satchel walking me to the ATV and draping it across the seat. He helped me onto the machine, being careful of my leg.

"Stay on this as long as you can and when you get off leave it running. I'm going down to the meeting point and when I get there we are going to test your ear piece again to make sure it's dialed in. Don't go anywhere until you hear me in your ear." He looked at his watch. "I need three minutes to get in place and that leaves us ten minutes for you to get to the drop off point."

I heard a sound far off in the distance. It sounded like a helicopter. I looked up in the sky, but couldn't see anything.

"It's the Medivac helicopter." He said. "We can't take the chance the ambulance gets bridged on the way to the hospital. We didn't have time to stop any harbor arrivals so we have the helicopter on standby in case we need to fly someone out of here."

Fly you out of here is what he didn't say.

I nodded, "Okay, I'm ready."

He kissed me again, "Nothing stupid, right? No heroics. Do what he says and leave the rest to the professionals."

"Got it."

"Don't make me regret this." And we both knew he already did. He kissed me then and I tried not to cry. He whispered he loved me and he turned, got in the car and drove away leaving me in the dark, alone.

Funny how long three minutes are in the dark, alone and not sure if you would be able to take another breath. Funny how every last thing you wish you had said to everyone in your life goes through your mind when you know you might not be coming back. Funny how when I woke up this morning the worst possible thing for me was letting Van see me weak and it never occurred to me that life could get so much worse than that.

"Tula, can you hear me?" I heard Van's voice in my ear and he jerked me back to the present. I whispered yes into the microphone because I was scared that the boogyman would hear me.

"Van, I want to say thank you for everything..."

He interrupted me then. "Tula, you can't do this now. I'm not going to be able to get through this if you do this now. We can have this discussion in the car on the way to the hospital. No, we will have this discussion in the car on the way to the hospital. Tell me you love me and that's all I need to hear."

I wiped my nose with my coat sleeve and wheezed heavily. "I love you, you are my life."

The earpiece fell silent for a moment and then I heard him again and he was clearing his throat. "Put the ATV in gear and head towards the point. Go slow and if you don't like something or something doesn't feel right, abort immediately."

I didn't answer as I put the machine in gear and got a feel for it. I had been driving three wheelers, four wheelers and snowmobiles my whole life. Sometimes they were the only way to get around after a big storm dumped two feet of snow in one day. This was a Polaris 4 x 4 that had more bells and whistles than my car. I didn't know what most of them did, but I didn't need to. I needed to know how to stop and go. The closer I got to the beach the more worried I became that I wouldn't get back without passing out. As I got closer to the entrance to the beach parking area I started doubting my sanity with the whole thing. I was sweating under all this gear and that was making it even harder to breathe. I tried to concentrate on Jesse's face in my mind as I drove into the dark the only thing breaking the darkness was the headlights on my ATV and the far off safety lights of the airport.

"You are doing great, baby, keep going as far as you can. When you turn onto the road tell me what you see." Van whispered in my ear.

I turned the ATV due south and the headlights shone past the empty parking stalls that in the summer were filled with parents and kids getting out their lounge chairs and beach balls ready for a day at the beach. The kids would be yelling for their parents to hurry up as they raced ahead up the beach walk to get the first peek of the water. They didn't care that the water they were about to jump into was freezing, they only cared about the fun they were going to have and that it meant time together.

Tonight though it wasn't warm and it wasn't sunny and the lake didn't look welcoming. There was no moon, the sky was murky black, and it blended into the water. You couldn't see anything. I was crawling now and stopped the ATV when the headlights bounced off the hulking body of the float plane on the tarmac.

"I don't see anything. I can see the plane, but he's not out here."

I let out a wheeze and coughed, spitting the blood out instead of swallowing it. I sat on the idling ATV looking around me in all directions. A shadow caught my eye and then the shape formed as he walked up the boardwalk from the beach. He was pulling Jesse along with him a gun to his head. I didn't move frozen by the sight of my brother in the arms of a bastard who didn't even care about his own family much less mine.

"Tula, do you have a visual on McElevain? My men are reporting he's approaching." Van's words snapped me out of my trance.

"Yeah I see him." I whispered out of fear that he would hear me.

"Good, now try to get him talking. The snipers are getting him in range so they can take him down, but you need to keep him talking."

"Van, he's got a gun to Jesse's head." I said between clenched teeth.

He was silent for a heartbeat, "I know, keep him talking."

I held back on the ATV and waited. McElevain pulled Jesse down the beach access that was now covered in snow. Jesse was still not wearing any shoes or coat. He had a gag around his mouth and shackles at his ankles. I couldn't tell by his body language if he was ticked that I was here or if he was relieved. McElevain stopped in the middle of the parking lot and started backing up towards the airport keeping the gun trained on Jesse's head.

He stopped short of the gate to the airport and yelled. "Pleasure to finally meet you, Sugar. You don't mind if I call you that, do you? I feel like I know you so well."

I remained silent. There was no way I could yell and I wasn't about to give him the satisfaction of letting him know that his words revolted me.

"Get off the machine and walk forward ten steps then toss the bag over. Don't make any sudden movements or I will shoot your brother." He said pushing the barrel of the gun harder into Jesse's head.

I put my hands up in the air to show him I was clean and slid off the ATV. I was surprised to find myself still on my feet on the pavement, but I was certain I was not going to have the strength to walk those ten steps. I pulled the bag off and started walking...one, two, three, four, five... my breathing was ragged and there was a strange bubbling sound coming from somewhere.

I heard Van in my ear. "Are you going to make it?" And his voice was strained and it made me scared.

I started counting out loud so he could hear, "...six, seven, eight, nine, ten." I stopped and held the bag at my side.

"Don't throw the bag, get him to talk, we need more time." he whispered in my ear.

McElevain stood with his back to the airport and I knew somewhere in there someone was locking him into target. The headlights of the ATV were the only thing giving us any light and I could see Jesse, he was begging me to throw the bag and leave.

"Toss the key to his handcuffs over here first." I wheezed out.

McElevain looked at me like I was speaking in foreign tongue.

"I'm not throwing the bag until I have the key." I said again.

"I don't think you are holding any of the cards to be calling the shots, Ms. DuBois."

"You really are a son of a bitch." I said my anger getting the better of me.

"Be careful, Sugar, or I might take you too and let my men have at you like they did that slut Margie."

I tried to suck in a breath but failed. "She's your daughter."

"No, she's not. She's my brother's daughter. My wife, her mother, was also a slut. I had the paternity test done and I have the proof. I killed her mother and raised her as my own figuring one day she would come in handy and she did. My brother deserves her now. So you see your little plan to get her father up here to give her away worked. He came."

My mind was spinning. My stomach turned for Margie and what she must have gone through at his hands.

"I don't care about your torrid family affairs, McElevain, I want you to let my brother go and leave for whatever parts unknown you are heading for."

I coughed and doubled over at the waist spitting out blood, the crimson red a harsh contrast against the white snow.

"Well, well, aren't you a fiery little thing? Barely able to walk, but you come all the way out here to save your brother. I'd clap, but my hands are tied up right now."

"You really are a bastard. If you hadn't sent your goon out to take pot shots at me I might be feeling a little more amicable towards you. But instead you're just..." I paused to take a breath and he laughed then. Jesse shifted his eyes back and forth begging me not to push him.

"I might be a bastard, Sugar, but I'm still holding a gun to your brother's head. If you hadn't been so stubborn and had handed over the key in the first place we wouldn't be standing here now, so you can consider yourself responsible for all of this."

I heard Van's voice low in my ear, "Don't listen to him. He's trying to make you angry and do something that will give him a reason to let his finger get twitchy on that trigger. This is not your fault and you know it. You need to throw that bag to him now because I can hear your breathing and it sounds really bad." And bad it was. All I could taste was blood and my stomach turned. I *knew* this wasn't my fault. I learned a hard lesson about that one already and I wasn't about to accept the blame for his bad decisions.

He motioned to the bag with his gun. "Throw that bag over here and tell that cop in your ear that he'd better stand down or your brother won't have a head."

"There's no cop in my ear. It's just you and me out here." I wheezed.

He laughed again and the sound was grating like nails on a chalkboard. "Oh I'm sorry, maybe I should say tell your lover that I'm going to blow your brother's brains all over the tarmac if he even thinks about moving in." He paused then and waved the gun around some more, "You know that makes me wonder, how close are you to Agent Walsh?"

"My relationship with Agent Walsh has nothing to do with where we are right now."

"Oh dear, sweet, misguided Sugar. That's where you are wrong. You see the day will come when I will find him and settle a score or two. We've crossed paths before and he's never been able to shut me down for long, but he's been annoying enough to cost me a lot of time and money. I was planning on taking his sister to my private hideaway and showing her what it's like to be with a real man, but I might come back for you. You're sexy as hell and it is common knowledge that I can make you my captive audience with very little effort."

What happened next was like the stuff you see in movies. There was a splash from behind them near the airport and McElevain turned his head long enough for me to reach for my gun. Jesse elbowed him in the ribs and ducked out of his head hold as McElevain got off a shot towards me. I watched Jesse roll out onto the ground kicking McElevain's feet out from under him with his shackles as McElevain swung his arm around and fired again. I aimed at McElevain and got off a shot right before his bullet slammed into me and knocked me backwards onto the ground and my head hit the pavement.

There was silence and then I heard feet pounding and Jess yelling for backup around his gag. I coughed and blood spewed from my mouth. I couldn't breathe. My lungs felt like lead and there was no air moving through them. I couldn't roll over so I laid there coughing and listening to the blood bubbling and I prayed. I prayed the kind of prayer that leaves you shaking your fists and screaming at the Lord. The kind of prayer that says I'm not ready to end it here and how dare you take me now after everything you've put me through. The kind of prayer that leaves you exhausted because you just said all the things that you have wanted to say to Him for the last ten years, but never would because you were afraid to let Him know just how mad you were. I never actually muttered a word, the screaming and the yelling and the fist shaking was only in my head, but I was sobbing and half choking on the blood that kept coming up. I heard Van screaming my name over and over thinking he was in my ear, but he was already there ripping at my jacket and screaming for the paramedics. I heard the wail of sirens and the whoop whoop of chopper blades. Van had my coat off and was tearing off the Velcro on the bullet proof vest. I coughed and choked on the blood and he rolled me over and I vomited more blood all over Jesse's jeans who had crawled over to me. Every part of me hurt. I swiped at my mouth with my hand and Van lifted me up, reclining me on his lap trying to keep me from choking more.

Jesse was leaning over me shouting my name and I pulled him into me. "Did I get him?" My words were slurred.

"Yeah, you got him Sis."

I knew I had to tell him it was all okay. "Go home Jess, the pizza's in the oven." And I hoped he heard me.

Everything was becoming distant now the sounds not as loud and the lights not as bright. Van was slapping my face and yelling my name over and over, "Damn it Tula, stay with me! Do not go to sleep! Come on Tula, I love you, stay here with me. Take a breath damn it!"

I reached up and touched his face struggling to speak with the last of the air in my body, "Thanks for the long slow beautiful dance my love."

"Rascal Flatts and don't think for a minute I'm done with that dance. I'm just giving you a breather." He was crying and now my lungs weren't the only thing hurting.

The paramedics swarmed around me and Jesse pulled Van away trying to give the paramedics room to work and then I was on a stretcher and they were running me towards the chopper. They stopped at the chopper door and Van appeared at my side.

He leaned down next to me kissing my temple, "I will see you at the hospital. I love you."

He let my hand drop to the stretcher as the EMTs loaded me into the helicopter and all I can remember thinking is I was getting my chance to fly out of Sky Harbor and I was going to miss that spectacular view.

FORTY-NINE

I felt pain. My whole body ached and I moaned, but I could breathe again. I rolled my head from side to side trying to shake the cobwebs loose. I had an oxygen mask over my face and felt a hand on my shoulder.

"Sugar, honey, it's Sharon." I opened one eye because it was all I could get open and she stood there with a look on her face I had seen before. I raised my hand and she took it holding it carefully.

"Hi Mom." Only it sounded like "hi non" through the filtered mask.

She reached up and grabbed something bringing it down over my face and I realized it was the cannula for the oxygen. She unhooked the mask and hooked the cannula up so I could talk.

"What time is it?" My voice was raspy and my throat hurt.

"It's six in the morning." she said quietly.

"How can that be?" I croaked.

"Sugar, its Thursday at six a.m." That meant that I had lost too many days.

"Where am I?"

"St. Mary's, honey." She said patting my arm.

"I remember now." The whole thing came crashing back on me and my lip trembled. I cleared my throat, "Jesse?"

"He's in the waiting room with Julie." She said.

I didn't want to ask the next question but there was no way I couldn't. "Van?"

"I'm right here." My eyes drifted to the door where he stood holding a cup of coffee. He hadn't shaved in days and he wore scrubs that made him look like a sexy doctor on ER. He was still here.

Sharon leaned down and hugged me, gently whispering in my ear. "He's been here the whole time." And she left to go tell the nurse I was awake.

"Hi." I said as he sat down beside me in a chair. He looked worried, angry and tired. His hands were wrapped in white gauze like he was a mummy.

"What happened to your hands?" I asked my voice barely audible.

He held up his hands then for me to see. "Stitches."

I smiled against my better judgement. "Why am I not surprised. I tried to tell you."

He looked at me then and his eyes lost some of the dullness and started to come back to life a little bit. "My hands were bleeding all over the place and they finally told me I was a biohazard and took me to the ER."

I started laughing or tried, but broke into a coughing jag that took my breath away and reminded me why I was there. Van stood up and rubbed my chest looking for the nurse call button, but I stopped him. It was fading a little and I coughed a few more times and it passed. He kept rubbing my chest. I leaned back into the pillows and closed my eyes as he rubbed away the pain.

I opened an eye and I knew I had to ask. "Tell me why I'm here. What happened?"

"What happened? Well let's see, you went out to play Tula the cop with a punctured lung and a horrific infection raging through your bloodstream. That's what happened. While you were trying to play hero, your lung and chest were filling up with blood and cutting off your ability to breathe. When McElevain's bullet hit your vest, it crushed what was left of the rib and it went the rest of the way through your lung collapsing it and you nearly died in my arms. The EMTs had to put in a chest tube in the field and airlift you off the Point. By the time you got here you needed three units of blood and your rib was so shattered they had to take it out in pieces so they could reinflate your lung. On top of that you are on massive amounts of antibiotics to kill the infection from the first bullet. You got out of the ICU this morning. I guess two bullets in two days is too many. That's what happened." Yeah, he was angry.

I felt the tears at the back of my eyes, "I didn't think it was that bad."

"You didn't think it was that bad? You thought coughing up blood was not that bad? You thought having a fever of one hundred and five was not that bad? Well I did and I should have stopped it when I took that bandage off. I should have," both of his hands were gripping the blanket and he released it flinching and taking a calming breath, "Julie told me she knew you were bleeding. She almost lost her mind when she heard that you went down and they airlifted you out of there."

I grimaced.

"Yeah, so, yeah." The last yeah came out defeated.

"Is McElevain..."

"Dead?" he asked and I nodded.

"Yes."

I blew out air relieved to feel that I could again. "Are you mad at me?" It was a stupid question. Of course he was mad at me. The last few sentences were enough to tell me that.

He looked down at his hands and then back up at my face. "I was mad at you the whole time you were out there and for about three seconds after the shots were fired, but then I heard you in my ear as I ran and I could hear bubbling like you were inside an aquarium and I was terrified. When I saw you laying there with the snow cherry red all around you I lost it. I mean I went off the deep end. I was watching the woman I love die in my arms and I had no way to help you. I was screaming at you and I was screaming at the EMTs and I was screaming at God. Jess pulled me off of you while the EMTs did their job and I started screaming at him and he stood there and took it because I'm pretty sure he thought he deserved it. Those twenty minutes it took to get to the hospital were the longest twenty minutes of my life and I swore that if you pulled through this I would shake the stubbornness out of you the next time you decided to do something half as stupid as what you just did. But then after hours of waiting and surgery and touch and go and too much time to think they let me see you and the only thing I felt was how undeniably lucky I was that you are as stubborn as you are. All I could see when I looked at you was love that was unimaginable to me two weeks ago."

He reached up and wiped away the tear from my cheek. We sat quietly, him holding my hand, me afraid to breathe. He kept massaging the scar on my arm and I began to relax again allowing myself to take a little deeper breath each time.

"What happens next?" I asked, afraid to know the answer.

"My chief wants me back in Texas ASAP. I was supposed to have left already, but I had to see you first."

I tipped my chin up refusing to cry. I knew this day was coming and now I had to be a big girl.

"The whole case is a big mess and I'm in hot water for how things went down."

"But it wasn't your fault. You were just a wingman, so to speak."

He shook his head. "It was my investigation to start with and I convinced the chief this was the best way to get McElevain and his organization."

"And you did." I said.

He nodded, "Yeah, but the guy is dead so now he wants me back to answer the Feds questions and dot every I and cross every T."

"Are you coming back?" I shouldn't have asked it, but my brain wasn't firing on all cylinders.

His eyes fixed on mine and all he said was, "It's going to be complicated for awhile, Tula. They are saying at least a month before your lung is healed and you can do anything. I'm going to be so busy I might not get a break for months, so I can't really answer that question very well. But I do know we have to trust things will work out like they are supposed to."

I nodded again quickly and took another deep breath to keep from crying.

"I love you, **Tula**, and I don't want to leave, but I don't want to end up on the wrong side of the court either." he said.

"I understand. It's your job and you have to do it." And I realized after I said it and saw his shoulders sag it was the wrong thing to say.

"Van, it's okay. When you came here a week ago it wasn't like you didn't have a whole other life somewhere else. I understand that. I love you and I don't want you in trouble for something that I did. Go back to Texas and take care of what needs taking care of. I'm obviously not going anywhere for awhile."

He stood up and leaned down and kissed me softly.

"It hurts to move my arms." I whispered.

"I know." he said.

"Can you put your arms around me one more time so I can watch you leave without falling apart?" I asked, trying to keep the tears at bay.

There were tubes going everywhere, but he kicked his shoes off and slid in next to me on the bed being careful of the chest tube and wrapped one around me the other he rested his head on. He kissed my ear and my temple and leaned his forehead against my hair.

He began to sing softly, "Standing beside her the stars shined even brighter, and for a moment all the world was still. I knew we belonged together the moment my eyes met yours and I thought nothing lasts forever, but maybe this one will. A deep breath and baby steps, that's how the whole thing starts. It's a long slow beautiful dance to the beat of our hearts." And there was something about that song that was haunting when it was sung by an Irishman who was about to leave you. The only sounds in the room was the beeping on the monitor and the sound of me crying.

"This is killing me." He said as he kissed the tears from my face. "I love you, Tula." And he got off the bed and walked out the door.

"I love you too." I whispered.

FIFTY

My nurse came in the room minutes after Van left. It was another familiar face. Jenny was a good friend of mine.

"Hey Sugar, looks like you hit a rough patch." Jenny came over and stood by the bed. I held up my palms. Jenny had gotten married at the lodge several years ago and still came to the parties with her husband on Friday nights.

"Hey Jenny. Fancy meeting you here." I tried to crack a joke, but it came out sounding lame.

"Shaun called me from the chopper when he picked you up off the Point."

I tried to think back, but I couldn't remember anything after the gunshots. It was like my memory had been wiped clean. "I don't remember seeing Shaun." I said weakly.

She patted my hand. "That's okay, he said you were in pretty rough shape and he was hoping you wouldn't remember much because I guess it was pretty touch and go for a while there."

She checked the monitors and my chest tube and busied herself in the room. I knew she was giving me some time to get myself together. She asked me to take some deep breaths, but there was nothing I wanted to do less and I didn't hide that fact from her. She helped me understand that deep breathing was going to get me out of there faster so I gave it my best shot trying to ignore the pain in my side where the bullet impacted. I laid my head back on the pillow when I was done and did some shallower panting to kill the pain. Jenny asked if there was anything she could get me, but I was pretty certain that what I wanted she had no control over. I thanked her anyway, she gave me the call button, and told me she would be back in a bit.

I turned my head towards the window and watched the sunrise welcoming in a new day. It was a little after seven and the day lay before me. I promised myself that the only thing I had to do today was breathe and I tried not to think about Van back at the lodge packing his stuff, getting on a plane and leaving. Selfishly I was glad I didn't have to watch.

"Sugar?" It was Sharon. I turned my head back to the door. I waved because it was easier than talking. She walked over to the bed and took the chair that Van had vacated. She took my hand then and held it quietly like she did many years ago during another time in my life when she was the only thing I had.

"Sorry I ruined your Thanksgiving."

She squeezed my hand. I could see the pain and the hurt in her eyes and I needed her to understand. I needed her to understand that I couldn't be responsible for her losing another son. "I couldn't tell you that you had lost another son, Mom. No matter how scared I was I knew that I couldn't look you in the eye and tell you that I had the chance to save him and I didn't. I knew you'd be mad and I knew Jess would be mad, but I won't apologize for doing what I thought was the right thing at the right time."

"Don't." She held up her hand and I closed my eyes.

I had no more tears. The tears were gone. My heart ached, but I had nothing more to give. My body was worn out, my mind was worn out, and I didn't have the reserves to try to make people understand. I opened my eyes when my fuzzy brain grasped the sound I was hearing was the woman who had been my strength all these years breaking down, her composure slipping away, leaving only her raw pain.

"Mom," I said reaching for her, but she got up and walked out. I tried to suck in a breath, but it turned to a sob. The two people I love the most had just walked out on me. Turns out I still had tears because they were falling and my face was wet. I turned back to the window the sunshine mocking me trying to pretend like it wasn't hell in this room right now.

I heard a rustling at the door and thought it was Jenny back to check on me. I didn't turn, too exhausted and ashamed of the tears that were still falling down my face. I didn't want to turn back to the door hoping that whoever it was would go away. When I looked back again Jess stood at the end of the bed.

"Heavy traffic in here this morning?" He said it as much like a statement as a question and I nodded.

"Mind if I park my tired butt in that chair?"

"Spot looks empty."

He came around and sat down in the chair. I was beginning to wonder if it was the chair, everyone that sat in it disappeared out of my life.

I motioned at the door. "Mom? Sharon?" Not sure what to call her anymore.

"She's with Jules."

I nodded again my lips tight so they wouldn't quiver. He couldn't look me in the eye and there was stillness to the room like everything had stopped spinning.

"You okay?" I asked it like I wasn't the one laying in the hospital bed.

He gave me the so-so sign.

"Did he hurt you?"

"Not physically, Sugar." And I knew what that meant.

"You broke your promise to me." he said, looking towards me but not at me.

"What promise?" I couldn't remember any promise, but then I was on a lot of drugs.

"The one where you promised not to end up in the hospital." And that was only a week ago, but it seemed like an eternity.

I tried to look him in the eye. "I decided I had just cause to break that promise."

He took a ragged breath and I saw his shoulder go up almost into a shrug, but not quite.

"Van told me McElevain's dead."

"Yeah." And that was all he said.

"I saw where I hit him. I remember that very vividly, probably will for the rest of my life."

"You have always been dead on with that Glock."

"Is this common knowledge?"

"They are listing his death as a gunshot wound. They will let the public assume it was the police."

"Do you think it would have ended any other way?" I asked quietly.

Jess shook his head. "No, he would have died by a sniper bullet if not yours. The only difference was how many other people were going to go down with him. I already knew he had no intention of letting either of us live. He intended to get the information, put a bullet in both of us and then double back to the boat he had on the beach."

"Then why did he demand a plane?"

"He wanted to make everyone believe he was flying out of there. He actually had a boat already chartered and waiting. All he needed to do was get the information and get out."

"But he didn't know that Van had the SEALs on the beach."

"No and by the time we had made it halfway down the beach walk, the SEALs already had all the guys in the boat taken down and the boat disabled. He wouldn't have gotten anywhere. He was a desperate man and desperate men don't always think straight. I know you aren't going to like what I have to say next, but I want you to hear me out."

I nodded.

"You will have to give a statement to the police. I don't want you to lie and I don't want you to act like the shooting didn't happen. Give the statement to the best of your knowledge. They will not press any charges so don't worry about admitting guilt to the shooting. As far as the department is concerned you deserve a gold star, but they have to be unhappy about a citizen carrying around a gun."

"I have a permit!" And that hurt. Note to self, don't yell and don't jump around.

Jess held up his hand. "I know. I want you to understand that the statement is a formality so we can finish things up. There were enough police there to corroborate it, so tell the truth."

"No problem." I had no reason to lie.

"And after you give the statement I want you to talk to Julie." I rolled my eyes at him.

"Sugar, I'm not kidding this time. I know that Julie is your best friend, but her job is to take people who have been put in situations like these and walk them through their emotions so that they aren't haunted for the rest of their lives. You will have to deal with happened and as you like to say 'put it where it needs to be'. Even cops who are trained to do what you did need to talk to someone in the aftermath of a shooting."

He rubbed my arm. "You did the right thing, Sugar, and I don't ever want you to second guess that. I want you to be at peace with what happened." And he still wasn't looking at me.

"I'm not so sure anymore, Jess. I thought I was doing the right thing, but the fact is the man I love just left to take the blame for something I did, the woman I consider my mother walked out on me, my best friend can't talk to me and you can't look me in the eye. So far I'm 0 for 4."

"I can't speak for anyone else, Sugar, but I can't look you in the eye because I don't want to see your father staring back at me asking me why I almost got his daughter killed. He trusted me with you and I failed him."

"My father isn't in my eyes, Jess, and you certainly didn't fail him. Every decision you made over the last six months has been out of love, nothing else. I made the decision to go out there and, right or wrong, it was my decision. When I saw the picture of you on that rock every day of the last ten years played through my mind. All the times you sat with me in a hospital room, all the times you made me laugh and all the times you let me be a jerk and never told me to grow up. And then I went over to your house and I saw Julie, my best friend, the love of your life and I had to show her that same picture. And I know what she said was out of fear for her baby, but it broke my heart to think she thought you would put me above her, so I was determined to show her otherwise. I knew it was stupid from the minute I agreed to it, but it didn't matter to me. What mattered to me was that you got back to her."

Jess didn't speak for a long time. "And she sees that now, but she feels like it's too late."

"You are kidding, right?" I was astounded that she thought she was to blame for this.

"I wish I was. They didn't tell Julie what happened. They told her I was okay and coming home. I got out of the squad and I was covered in blood, your blood. I was crying and she knew. I couldn't even comfort her I was so angry. I walked past her into the bathroom and locked the door and took a shower. When I came back out I told her I was going to the hospital because you weren't dead, yet, and then I got back in the squad car and left. I left her standing there alone. I reinforced right there for her that she wasn't the most important thing in my life."

A tear was running down my cheek and I swore softly. "Jess, she had to know that you weren't even thinking at that point. You had been through a lot."

"I don't think she did. I think she went into counselor mode so she could shut down and not feel anything. She drove to the hospital herself and she got us coffee and she made us eat and she called Mom and told her to come home. When the doctors told us you were going to be okay she left and no one could find her. Mom walked up to me and she punched me, hard, and told me I was being an asshole."

My brows went up in surprise remembering not to move too quickly. "Whoa ho, Mom doesn't cuss!"

He laughed. "I guess she saves it for the big stuff. She was right though. I was being an asshole and it was because I was having a hard time dealing with what happened and I was having a hard time trying to figure out how not to be angry at you while you fought for your life and at Julie for not stopping the whole thing. I had already taken Bond down at the knees about it and he was refusing to talk to me. I even talked back to Mom if you can believe it."

"Not good, Jess." I shook my head remembering the last time he had done that, when he was twelve.

"The fact of the matter was that the reason we were all standing in this hospital was because of me and I didn't know how to deal with that, but I knew I couldn't lose Julie and the baby. So I started looking for her and she wouldn't answer her cell phone or pages over the intercom and I got really scared. Scared like I have never been before and I've been scared a lot lately." And that wasn't easy for him to admit.

"I sat down in a chair somewhere, I don't even know where I was, and a chaplain came up to me and asked me if I was alright. He recognized me then and did that hand on the shoulder thing that ministers do, you know what I mean?"

I nodded.

"Everything just kind of tumbled out and when I took a breath he said he had heard a woman crying in the chapel and didn't interrupt, but maybe I should. Then he squeezed my shoulder and said "you are already forgiven son, forgive yourself" and he walked away."

Jess's lower lip began to tremble and it was all I could do not to pull him into a hug and tell him it didn't matter, he didn't have to tell me, but it obviously mattered to him. The best I could do was take his hand, holding it the best I could with the tubes jutting out everywhere.

He cleared his throat. "I opened the door to the chapel and there sat the most wonderful thing that has ever happened to me, sobbing. The kind of sobbing that hurts your chest and breaks your heart. She couldn't talk to me or maybe she wouldn't, I don't really know, I just know that my gut told me she was fading out. It was like she was unable to comprehend what was going on around her. Like once she knew you were going to be okay she lost her ability to function. I couldn't get her to tell me if she was alright and then she started vomiting and passed out and I didn't know what to do. I scooped her up and she was so limp against me that I ran with her to the ER certain that I was about to lose her or the baby. I was standing at the door yelling for someone to let me in and they came and took her from my arms and there I was again standing in that ER waiting room like I was ten years ago wondering if when the doctor came through that door if he was going to tell me my whole life was gone again. Then the chaplain came in and he took me to a private room and he sat with me and I told him the whole story. I told him that I hadn't been very good at forgiving God and I needed a miracle now and didn't know how to pray for that or for that matter if I deserved to pray for that. He quietly started saying Psalm 23."

"'The Lord is my Shepherd'. That was my Mom's favorite verse. Do you remember that?"

He nodded. "Yeah, I remembered as soon as he started to say it and I started saying it with him as it came back to me. I closed my eyes and I saw your mom. I was young and I was sitting at the table at the lodge and she was bringing me food and she was telling me that she was there and everything was going to be okay and I knew she was taking care of Julie and you. It was like she was telling me to take a breath because she had it covered. I told the chaplain then about that Psalm and about your mother. I told him how much of a difference she made in my life and then I told him about your dad and you. He got me coffee and we sat together and I learned how to pray again. We sat there together until the doctor came in. Julie's doctor had been called in and he told me that she was alright and so was the baby. The chaplain patted my back and got up and said, "I think you know how to take it from here, Jesse" and he left. I knew exactly where to take it and the doctor took me to Julie. They had given her some fluid and some medicine to help the nausea and she didn't look like death anymore, but she was far from okay. They assured me that she needed rest, that her body couldn't stay awake any longer and that her mind was doing what it was supposed to by making her hit a wall. They showed me the pictures of our baby and told me that everything was fine and I took the pictures and never let them go. I tried to show them to her, but she wouldn't look, she wouldn't talk to me, she wouldn't communicate at all. She just stared off into space and cried.

They wanted to admit her, but she begged me with her eyes to take her home, so I carried her to the car and laid her on the backseat and she curled up in a fetal position and never stopped crying. I could barely see through the tears to drive home it was so horribly heart wrenching to listen to and on top of it I knew I had caused it, but I kept hearing your mom's voice in my ear telling me she had it covered. I carried her in the house and I climbed in the shower with her, holding her up, letting the hot water run over us because she wasn't strong enough to do it herself. I laid her on the bed and climbed in next to her holding her tight to me so she could hear my heartbeat and know that I was there and wasn't going to leave. I had to keep telling her she was okay and that no one blamed her and that I wasn't mad at her and that I was sorry and a million other things as I rocked her back and forth until she finally cried herself to sleep. I held her for hours watching her, touching her face, making sure she was breathing and praying that when she woke up I could explain to her how much I needed her, how much I wanted her." He stopped and took a shaky breath. "When she woke up she still couldn't talk to me, but she wasn't crying. It was like she was dead inside, like nothing mattered anymore."

"God Jess, this awful to listen to, I can't imagine living it." I said wiping away a tear from my cheek.

"You know Julie as well as I do and you know she will never open that locked up place in her heart that holds her childhood. You know that if you want her to talk about her early life it has to involve a lot of alcohol or a lot of anger." And the few times she had too much to drink at the campfires and she would make a comment here or there it usually ended with her in tears in my bathroom. Now that I think about it, it also usually ended in Jesse taking her home. I'm such a dolt.

"Yeah, she can't seem to put that where it needs to be." I said.

"No, she can't and when she feels threatened she immediately shuts down and goes into that mode where she doesn't feel, she just survives."

"I'm sorry Jess, this is my fault. If I had been able to talk to her all those months ago we wouldn't be here. I see that now."

"True, we wouldn't be here right now, but you also wouldn't have Bond in your life and I can see by the way that he looks at you that he was the reason the whole thing happened. He was supposed to be here and he was supposed to be the one that brought you back to us this time." And I had to give him that.

"Only he's not here, Jess. He's gone now and I don't know that I will ever see him again."

"Oh you will see him again. A man doesn't look at a woman like he looks at you and not do everything he can to be with her. I happen to be one of those men who looks at a woman like that and now she's pregnant with my baby and will soon be my wife. You have to let it all play out, Sugar, but he will be back." And now it's time to change the subject.

"So if she's having your baby and she's going to be your wife, **does** that mean everything is okay?"

"Nice use of my words to channel me away from your love life." He gave me a low high five and I smiled because this was the Jesse I wanted in my room. The Jesse that was happy.

"I quit trying to get her to talk. I laid my hand on her belly, which by the way you can feel this little bump now and it blows my mind that my baby is growing in there. It still just blows my mind."

"I hope I get to feel that." And I wasn't sure that I ever would if she couldn't forgive me for almost taking away what she held most dear.

"You will, Sugar. She's not mad at you, she's mad at herself for 'throwing you under the bus' as she put it."

I let out a sigh. "That's not how it was, Jess."

"I think it was, Sugar, at least for her. I sat there with my hand on her belly and I told her about the hours I had spent sitting in a room in the dark with nothing to do but think about my life. All I could picture was her face in my mind. That night at the bowling alley when everyone was long gone and it was only me and her and how she would laugh at my horrible jokes, the first time she told me she loved me and the first time I made love to her. I told her how the vision of slipping that ring on her finger and then her telling me I was going to be a daddy was the only thing that kept me sane. It was the only thing that allowed me to keep my cool because I knew that I had to make the right decisions in order to get back to her. She slowly started to open up and she told me how you had told her about our early years together as kids and that you had tried to explain to her why I'm so protective of you. She said that you tried to get her to see that I was coming back to her and the baby and no one else. And even though she knew it was wrong to send you out there she saw it as a way to show me that you could stand on your own two feet once and for all. The thing is, I already knew that. I had already seen that more times than I can count. The fact that you are laying here talking to me is proof enough of that. The doctors didn't expect you to pull through, but I did. I never doubted it because I've seen it before. I told her that I worry about you because we are family and that it comes along with the job of being a brother and that isn't going to change, but that she is my life now, her and the baby. And then I told her what the chaplain said to me and I reminded her that we are only human and we don't always have to like what happens in our lives, but if we learn from it then it wasn't a mistake."

"Agreed. So is she okay now?"

He did the so-so hand movement again. "We stayed in bed and I let her talk. I learned some things I didn't know about her childhood that tore my heart out, but I was glad that she could finally talk about them a little bit with me. I understand now why she reacts the way she does sometimes, but I told her that she was safe now with us and that no one expected her to be perfect, we just want her to be ours. I spread the ultrasound pictures of our baby out on the bed and she saw them for the first time and then came tears of happiness. We talked about our hopes and dreams for this little one. I told her that he or she was going to have three very special guardian angels to keep watch over their life and that he or she was going to have a grandma and a grandpa and a really special aunt that was going to make sure he or she grew up happy and healthy and that in the end nothing else matters. Then I made her eat telling her that her baby's aunt was gonna be really ticked if she landed herself in the hospital bed next to her."

I swiped at my tears. "Yeah I would be."

"So physically she's okay, but I haven't decided about emotionally yet. That could take some time."

I nodded and had enough experience to know that it would take until she accepted that it wasn't her fault.

"What you did was incredibly stupid. It was reckless and I still can't believe that the chief and Bond went along with it, but thank you for bringing me back to her. The only thing I could think of the whole time I was out there was that I couldn't leave her and never meet my baby. I don't know that things would have gone down the way they had if it hadn't been you. He was already unhinged and I knew things would turn explosive. He went on a rampage about it for an hour before the meeting, how he thought they were going to send some flunky cop in and he would shoot them on sight. I had never been so worried that it would be you and so worried that it wouldn't. As sick as you were you still managed to distract him enough that he let his guard down and that's the only reason we are all still here, some better off than others. I'd offer you a job on my team, but I don't think I can take the heat from Julie and Bond. Not to mention Mom. Good gravy, if looks could kill." He shivered and I laughed weakly, "My heroics would have been wasted?"

"Exactly."

"Well thanks, but I'm really not interested Jess. You can keep the cops and robbers thing I've had all the excitement I can handle for a while."

He stood up, "When you're stronger I will have you give that statement."

"Okay, can it wait until tomorrow? I kind of need to pretend for a day that it didn't happen."

"It can wait until you get released as far as I am concerned." He leaned over and kissed my forehead.

"What about Margie and Nathan?"

"They have been released from the safe house and are taking care of the paperwork that comes along with a relative dying in a different state. It isn't helping that he was also a drug dealer, kidnapper and gun runner. I'm sure they will be by as soon as they are done."

"Jess, was Margie you know, okay?" I asked him, remembering the look on her face in the picture.

He shook his head barely enough for me to notice, "She needed some medical care. The doctors treated the physical wounds, but I think it is going to take a lot of care from Nathan to treat the other wounds."

"Does she know about her paternity?" I needed to know so I didn't say anything I shouldn't.

"I don't know. I have no intention of telling her and since McElevain is dead and the next of kin is his brother the business is hers anyway. Why muddy the waters, you know?"

"I won't say anything either, but she may know. He may have told her."

"Yeah, he may have, that would be typical of his total disregard for human emotion." He was angry and he took a deep breath and tucked the blanket up around me, "Okay, enough talk. Time to get some rest."

I grabbed his hand. "Tell Mom and Julie I'm sorry and I need them."

"No, I won't tell them you are sorry because you don't have anything to be sorry about, but I will tell them you need them."

I started coughing then and couldn't stop. It hurt and I wanted to fade to black to make it stop. It may be good for my lungs, but the incisions and the chest tube hated it. Jess got Jenny and she gave me some medication that made me drop off into a medicated sleep. The kind of sleep that never really made you feel better, but dulled the pain and let you hang in the darkness for hours and try to heal.

God bless oblivion.

FIFTY-ONE

I slept then on and off for what seemed like only minutes. I heard the nurses coming in and out and the shuffle of feet on the floor, but I never opened my eyes. I was in that state of semi-consciousness where you knew that life was going on around you, but you didn't care. They came in to take my vitals and make me cough and breathe deep and I did what they asked, but never opened my eyes or let myself come up out of that darkness. The darkness was safe, but the lights weren't. The darkness was letting me put all the things that happened in the places that they needed to go so that when I did open my eyes I could get up, walk around and live again. In the darkness I could ask God to forgive me for yelling at him. In the darkness I could thank Him for letting us all still be here. In the darkness I was finally able to understand the bigger picture and why He took from me what He took in order to give me all the rest. In the darkness I was able to love Him again. In the darkness I could start to remember why I lived. In the darkness I was riding in the Mustang with my father and then with Van. In the darkness I was at the fire pit and Van had his arm around me and was singing in the voice that filled my heart. My parents and Brent were smiling now.

There were no more nightmares and I was certain they would never return. I felt my hands being picked up and settled against two very different palms, but both palms I knew. I struggled to come awake and it took me a long time, but when I was finally able to pull my lids open, Julie sat next to me on one side and Sharon on the other. They both looked like hell and probably should be in bed. My eyes drifted to the clock and it was after one o'clock. I was surprised that much time had passed.

"Hi." I coughed and it didn't hurt as bad as the last time. At least that was some good news.

Sharon motioned to the tray sitting off to the side. "They thought maybe your mom could get you to eat something, so they sent me in." She looked down at her hands and then back at me.

"Maybe she can. I was dreaming about green Jell-O, you know it's my favorite." I hate green Jell-O and it's the only kind the hospital *ever* had.

Sharon brought the tray over and I had the fine dining selections of chicken broth, coffee, apple juice and yes, green Jell-O. So many choices so little time.

"I think I'll pass on everything but the apple juice, Mom." I saw her shoulders relax and I was glad that she could be here with me again. She stuck a straw in the juice and brought it over and I took a few sips. I always marvel at how when you take the first few sips after being without water it's always impossible to stop. You want to guzzle the whole thing even though you know it will make you sick. I quickly handed what was left to Sharon so I wouldn't suck it all down. Vomiting right now would be painful.

"The doctor said you've lost over ten pounds, Sugar." Sharon said it in her best mother voice.

"Well, I've been getting a lot of exercise lately." I said sheepishly.

Julie snorted and tried to hide the smile that I was relieved to see on her face even if it was only for a second.

Sharon leveled an eye at me and I rolled mine. "Okay, fine, give me a day and then I promise to eat whatever you bring me, but green Jell-O is not passing these lips. You can start with some decent coffee and then work your way up to a burger and rings, okay?"

She smiled then and I patted her cheek. Julie still wasn't making eye contact and I called her name. She looked up at me and she had big crocodile tears in her eyes, the kind that you see in a little one's eyes when they can't find their favorite stuffed animal or when they lose their best friend.

"How you doing, Jules? I heard you pulled a classic Sugar and pushed yourself too far."

She shrugged her shoulder as a response. Guess she probably learned that from me too.

"I don't know what that means, Julie."

"It means it's been a rough few weeks." she muttered.

Amen to that sister. "Sorta feels like a roller coaster, doesn't it?" She nodded, but she still wasn't looking at me.

"Julie, look at me, please. My heart can't take watching you sit there beating yourself up about something beyond your control."

She snapped her head up. "I had control, Sugar. I held all the control in my hand and I didn't do anything with it. I just sent you out to get butchered."

"Julie, you didn't send me out to get butchered!" Ow, ow, don't yell Sugar. "I went out there on my own free will." I whispered.

"Sugar, you said that Jesse's first priority was me and the baby. You said that he was coming back to me and you were right, but I was scared. I was scared, but that doesn't explain my behavior or excuse it. My words were cruel and you didn't do anything to deserve them."

"Jules, you don't have to explain it. I understand."

"Yes I do and I don't know how you could understand the things I said and did that night. You needed me more at that moment then you ever have and I failed you. I've never had a family. I went from one foster home to another until I was finally old enough to take care of myself. I don't even know who my parents are. I never knew the love of a mother until Sharon came into my life and Lenny, he's exactly what I pictured a dad would be like. He's funny and he's loving and he's understanding. I had no idea how to be a sister until I met you and you made it seem so natural. It felt right and I started to understand a little bit why other people thought families were so great. I mean I always understood the concept of family, but I never experienced it until I started spending time with all of you.

When I first met Jesse he said I was like a skittish dog that would always hover on the outskirts of the fire, but never come close enough to be touched. So he backed off and let me come to him. He gained my trust by introducing me to you, knowing that fundamentally as a person you would somehow teach me how to trust people. He knew you would teach me how to experience family because that is who you are. He was right -- you and I really hit it off. Pretty soon you had me eating out of the palm of your hand, so to speak, because I knew that I could trust you and that you would always be there for me. Slowly Jesse was able to get me to trust him and then to love him. We have only been dating for nine months, Sugar, but I've loved him for years. I was just too afraid to do anything about it. And then in the blink of an eye we were together and things were amazing, I was happy for the first time in my life and I felt like I had a chance at the family life that was always beyond my grasp. But then the day came that I was holding up that positive pregnancy test and my world fell apart. I slipped back into that self-preservation mode and I was too petrified to even tell you, even though there was this little voice in my head that told you would help." I understood that voice. I have a love/hate relationship with that voice. "Fear was the reason I didn't or couldn't tell Jess about the baby and it was the reason I didn't stop you from going out there. All I could see was my own chance at a real family, me and Jesse and the baby, and I wasn't going to let anyone take that away from me, not even you."

She stopped then and I thought she was finished. I was about to say something when Sharon laid her hand on my arm and gave her head a gentle shake. Julie was angry now, at herself, and her shoulders squared and her face took on a look of forcefulness.

"I hated myself for thinking that and I hated myself for every crappy thing that ever happened to me. I've done enough victim counseling to know that none of it was my fault, but I've also done enough to know that doesn't matter. Funny that I spend my days helping other people walk through their demons and I can't even face mine. I wanted to scream at the top of my lungs for someone to call an ambulance the whole time Van was strapping that damn vest on you. I wanted to beg you not to go out there and die and leave me here alone, but in the end I couldn't do any of those things. I froze and sold you down the river so that I wouldn't lose the one thing I couldn't live without. I have spent my entire life alone, but I never felt as alone as I did standing on that step watching them drive you away. I never want to feel that again, Sugar, ever. I want you to understand that I see it all now, not that I expect that fact to make things better, but I learned a very hard and very fast lesson in family and once again it was you who taught me. I see now exactly what I should have done and I can never change what happened or make it different. I deserve Jesse's anger and I deserve Sharon's disappointment and I deserve however you are feeling about me right now. I hope that I didn't screw things up so badly that we can't heal as a family and move on. You guys are the only family I have and I can't be without that anymore." She laid her hand on my leg and Sharon grabbed it.

"Jesse's not angry at you, Jules." I said. "He never was. He was mad at himself for bringing this all down on us, even though he did it with best intentions. He knows he screwed up and he hopes that you forgive him. I'm pretty sure he is going to spend the rest of his life proving to you that you are all he wants."

Sharon spoke softly then and I had to strain to hear her. "I'm not disappointed in you, Julie. If I've implied that in some way it was not intentional and I don't ever want you to think that. You two girls fill my heart with nothing but pride and love. I haven't been able to breathe for the last few days because I wasn't here and look what happened. I wasn't here and I didn't do my job as a mother. A few hours ago I walked away from my daughter who needed me because I didn't want her to see me fall apart. I didn't want her to know that for the last few days I doubted I would ever talk to her again. I couldn't tell her how grateful I was to her for being the strongest one of all of us during her weakest moment, but when Jesse came out and told me that she needed me, that she needed us, it became obvious that love keeps going. It doesn't stop because we make a mistake, it doesn't care about the mistake. It just keeps moving us forward and I prayed that she would understand that. I hope you do too."

Sharon wiped away a tear from my cheek and I started coughing holding my side and wishing it would stop. Sharon got me some water and settled me back on my pillows and I tried taking a few deep breaths before speaking.

"Mom's right, Julie. Love keeps going. I love you more now than ever, but you are right about one thing. You do deserve how I am feeling right now."

She hung her head and nodded and I refused to look at Sharon knowing the angry look that would be on her face. "I'm feeling heartbreak that you even think that you somehow caused all of this and I'm feeling lucky that you are going to be my sister and the mother of my niece or nephew. I have no intention of cutting you out of my life. I need my sister right now. I mean I really need you. You have to forgive yourself for whatever mistakes you think you made. I will tell you what a wise woman once told me, I can't forgive you for something I don't blame you for."

Sharon smiled and Julie let out a wobbly laugh. "I've heard that a couple times over the last few days."

"Then it must be true."

She nodded, "It must be."

"Julie, I want you to go home and I want you to lay down with Jesse and I want you to sleep for hours and then I want you to eat, a lot, and then I want you to sleep some more and I don't want to see you or Jesse back here until tomorrow afternoon at the earliest."

Julie was about to object and I held up my hand. "Mom will call if there are any problems, but there won't be. I'm fine and I'm pretty boring right now so use this time to let yourself just be. I'm really concerned about you, no offense, but you don't look very strong right now. Go home and let Jess hold you and soak up being newly engaged and experience Jesse's wonder at that baby growing inside you."

She stood and was unsteady for a minute holding onto the bed for support. She leaned in and gave me a hug whispering that she loved me and thanking me for sticking by her hormone raging body. I told her I loved her too and that raging hormones might even stand up in a court of law. Hearing her laugh did more than all the medicine they had given me so far.

"Julie?"

She was turning to go, but turned back to the bed, "Yeah Sugar?"

I patted the bed and she sat. I reached out with my hand, "Can I?"

She nodded putting my hand on her belly and covering it with her own. I closed my eyes then and said hello to the newest member of the family.

God bless babies.

FIFTY-TWO

The next few days were spent sleeping and breathing and having chest x-rays and physical therapy. Trey showed up at the door Friday morning with my new socket. I was finishing breakfast when I heard a knock on the door and looked up.

"Hey Trey." He stepped in the door and had my leg wrapped in a garbage sack with a bow on it. "Whatcha got?" I asked him, laughing because my shoe was still attached from when he picked it up off the ballroom floor.

"A present." He said taking a seat in the chair by my bed.

"I'm excited to see it, show me." I said swinging my legs off the bed thankful I had throw on a pair of capris and a t-shirt instead of a clean hospital gown after my shower. He handed me the leg and I pulled the bag off the socket and was stunned silent. It was like nothing I had ever seen before and as familiar as home.

"Trey..." Was all I could say because beautiful didn't begin to cover it. The socket was MAMBOS green and the designs started at the top of the socket and went down like the stumps around the fire pit in my backyard. When I looked down I saw two dancers under a sunset with three eagles flying past, I saw a '65 Mustang, the MAMBOS insignia and at the bottom was the most amazing part of all. I saw all our names going around in a circle, James, Bonny, Sugar, Brent, Jesse and Sharon and each one had a butterfly worked into their name and the tip of the J touched the bottom of the N and it went around in a never ending circle. As I turned the socket I saw on the back there was a very small tree, a crann as I was certain it was, with a V & T 4-ever carved into it. That brought tears to my eyes and I concentrated on the leg until I got them under control. It was amazing and I knew from a distance you would see a swirling design, but every time I looked down at it I would feel them with me.

"How did you? I mean, these are my carvings! How did you get it transferred to the socket?" I stammered.

"I had a little help from a friend." He said.

"Tell me Trey, I really want to know."

"Your Irish friend asked me before you woke up that day if I would make you a new socket that was more, what's the word he used, deadly." And I started to laugh. "He took me out to the fire pit and showed me the carvings. I had no idea you had that kind of talent, Sugar. I was impressed."

"It's just some doodling I do at the fire pit." I said.

He rolled his eyes, "Yeah he said you would say that. Anyway, he told me his ideas and I kind of balked at him because that socket is so far from anything I would ever know you to want. He patted my back and assured me that he knew what he was doing and to trust him. He took digital pictures of the carvings and somehow he created the name band. I had it transferred over to the green material and sewed it into the carbon fiber before finishing the socket. I think it turned out incredible."

"Absolutely Trey, its mi daza as Van would say." And my friend knew me better than I did. Trey helped me get it on making adjustments until it fit like a glove again.

"You look beautiful as always, Sugar. I hope you show this leg off, it's worth letting other people see how much he loves you." I looked up at him and he laughed. "It wasn't rocket science to see how much he loves you, Sugar. I can tell he's going to take good care of you and I couldn't be happier."

"He's gone, Trey. Back to his other life now that the investigation is over." I said staring intently at my leg.

"Maybe he's gone right now, but he won't be gone for long."

Then he kissed my cheek and told me to take it easy because he was going on vacation for a week and wouldn't be around to fix anything for me. I thanked him and then shooed him out the door laughing at his insistence that I kept him in business. The leg was amazing and it was definitely worth showing off. I grabbed my cell phone and sent Van a text that read.

"It's mi daza. Thank you for caring so much that you knew what was in my heart better than I did. I love you. Stay safe."

And it was killing me that I couldn't call him, but I had no idea where he was and I suspected he was probably taking the heat for how badly things went down. My phone vibrated and I saw a text come in.

"I'm glad you like it. I can't wait to see it. I miss you already."

I had just finished reading it when Sharon, Jesse and Julie came in the door and pulled up short at the sight of me standing there on my new leg, two different shoes and tears in my eyes. No one spoke, but Julie crept forward getting down close looking at the socket from opposite me. I motioned for her to stand behind me and she stood behind my shoulder and I rolled it back and forth so she could see it. She was joined by Jesse and Sharon and there was silence.

Jesse finally said, "How do you feel about that?"

"It makes me want to wear shorts in November." I said.

He nodded, "Something tells me Bond's a leg man."

"Fair play!" And I gave him a high five because he was bang on.

355

I was finishing lunch and thinking about a nap before more therapy. I really wanted to get the chest tube out so I could go home, but the doctor was telling me tube out tomorrow and home on Sunday. I guess I could deal with that. Everyone here was wonderful, but it wasn't home and that was where I wanted to be in. In my own bed on my own pillow that might still smell like the man I love. I was lounging back in the chair smiling to myself when I heard a knock on the door and looked up. Margie and Nathan were standing in the doorway with a big bouquet of flowers. Margie looked haunted and Nathan had his arm protectively around her shoulder.

"Hi guys!" I said, pushing the foot down on the recliner as they stepped in the door. Their faces broke into smiles. Margie came over and hugged me while Nathan sat the flowers next to the other thirty some bouquets I had gotten from friends and students as they heard what happened.

Nathan laughed. "Sugar, I think you could start your own floral shop!"

"I know it's crazy, I don't know where to even put them anymore, but, thank you, they are lovely."

"They aren't from us, we found them sitting by the door." He handed me the card.

I took a closer look and I was pretty sure I knew who they were from. There were white tea roses, pink tea roses, trumpet lilies and green carnations. I flipped open the card and read it quickly. All it said was, **"I'm always thinking about you."** I smiled and tucked it next to me for safe keeping.

"This is from us." Margie said handing me a thin wrapped box. "It's our way of saying thanks for everything this summer."

I tore open the package and was taken by complete surprise to find what was underneath. "Are you kidding me? An iPad?"

"We know you've been wanting one, but couldn't justify it with all your other equipment, so we decided that if it's a gift you can't say no!"

"Yeah," Nathan said, "And besides we loaded it up with all kinds of apps that you can use for the studio, so now it's totally legal." And loaded it up they had. There were new playlists, Ebooks and face-to-face calling.

"I have everything set up so we can use that to stay in touch. I have a project in the works and I might need some ideas from you, so I will be able to stay in contact. The other great part is if you flip the pad around you can use the camera on the back to show whoever you are video conferencing with anything you want them to see. I thought that might come in really handy for the foundation." Margie said.

"I'm really touched, guys. This means more to me than you know right now. I'm kinda of hanging out here with nothing to do, so now I won't be so lonely." And tears were in my eyes at their thoughtfulness.

"I had Mike put all your music on it too, so you can sit here and at least have that. There might be a new playlist on there too." She said winking at me and I had already noticed one that said Tula's songs. Only one person calls me that.

Margie laid her hand on my leg and contacted the hardness of the socket. She pulled my pants leg up a little higher. "Omigod Sugar! That is a work of art! When did you get that?" They both had their heads twisted around trying to look at it upside down and I told them to stand behind me.

"Trey brought it over today. My other socket was broken so he had to make me a new one."

"These are some of the carvings from the fire pit and by the looks of it a few new ones." Margie said as she looked at them from the right angle.

"Yeah, a friend of mine sent him digital pictures of the designs and Trey did the rest. It's really pretty neat." I trailed off.

Nathan snickered. "A friend? You mean the kind of friend that sends bouquets of flowers like that one?" He jerked his finger to the roses behind me.

"Yeah, that kind of friend. He was involved in the investigation and he's gone now, but I will always have this to remember him by."

Margie started laughing, very hard. "Sugar, really! We know all about you and Agent Walsh! Before he left we spoke with him and he hinted that if I saw you I should remember everything you said and he mentioned a few times if I wanted to take a picture or two he wouldn't mind that either. I got the impression pretty quickly that he's more than a friend. He looked like he lost his best friend he was so depressed." And that made me a little bit happy to hear.

"So when you are guys heading back to Texas?" I asked as an opener to feel the waters.

"Later this afternoon, we have a flight out at four to Temple and then we have to meet with investigators for a few days before flying home. But don't worry we will be back. We hear there's a wedding being planned around here and we already got our informal invite. You can bet we will be here, I wouldn't miss that wedding for the world." she said, taking Nathan's hand.

"They are great together, aren't they?" I said my heart a little lighter thinking about them and what they were giving us.

"They are, Sugar. We all saw that this summer, everyone but you, seemed like you either couldn't or wouldn't see it. I called Jesse on it one night and he made me promise that I would never say a word to you about them. I tried to convince him that maybe it would help you to know he was happy, but I guess maybe he knew best." She looked down at her hands.

"I was really struggling this summer Margie. I can't deny that. I was going downhill fast and if it weren't for you guys I probably wouldn't have made it as long as I did. I want you to know that you got me through this summer. Looking back I still can't believe you guys put up with me."

"You were in a lot of pain, Sugar, and even though you thought you were doing a great job of hiding it, everyone could see it. The day I had to get in that cab and leave was one of the hardest things I've had to do in a long time. Nathan had to keep telling me that Jesse was taking care of you and that you would be fine. I'm glad Agent Walsh came to stay with you."

"Yeah I'm awfully glad he came to stay with me too. He really helped me see what I was missing in this world."

I was intent on keeping the conversation light because I didn't know what to say about what happened on the Point. I sat there staring at my friends and nothing I could ask them would avoid the topics I wanted to avoid. I killed the man that raised her and I didn't even know if she knew that.

"I really missed you guys." And it sounded lame to my ears too.

Nathan took Margie's hand. "Jesse and Agent Walsh told us exactly what happened, Sugar. I'm not sure if you know that."

"No I don't know a lot right now. I know the basics. I think they are trying to protect me and not get me worked up. I'm sorry Margie." I said softly.

She laughed harshly. "Don't be sorry and don't for one second feel guilty about taking that piece of crap off this earth, Sugar. You saved more people's lives than you know that night." Nathan put his arm around her shoulder.

"I'm still sorry about what happened, Margie. I'm sorry for you and for your family. You didn't deserve to go through what you went through because you wanted to stop something so wrong." And I was sorry for her. The rest I didn't care about.

"I will be fine, Sugar. I need some time and some distance from this place. I got my own revenge already, so you don't need to worry about me." She said.

I raised a brow. "That really doesn't sound like you at all, Margie." I said carefully.

She shrugged and shook her head. "What I mean is that when they brought him into the hospital he was still breathing, but there was no brainwave activity. He wouldn't survive the night. They asked me if I would donate his organs and I told them absolutely, if you have a chance to make up for some of his wrongs then you go for it. He was hell-bent on destroying everyone's life **but** in the end he saved seven. I'm pretty sure **that would not have made him happy, but it gave me a little bit of peace** that at least some families weren't being torn apart that night."

"Wow. No one told me." I said.

"**I hope that it makes up in some way for all the pain he caused** everyone here."

"Margie, those **families are getting a second chance with their loved ones now and that is the best gift** you could have given them. I will make sure he is added to the list of donors for the foundation."

"I really would rather you didn't, Sugar. My father doesn't deserve that honor." **she said sharply.**

I patted her hand. "Okay, whatever you want, Margie." And I was going to leave it at that. She obviously didn't know he wasn't her father and I wasn't going to tread into those waters.

"Before you leave, **Margie, the wedding video and pictures are on my desk in my office. Have Sharon let you in so you can take them back to** show the rest of your family. I know they are anxious to see them. You **look so beautiful in your gown and Nathan you are so handsome in your tuxedo. They turned out really good and your uncle looked so proud to be** there with you. He's really a great guy, Margie."

Nathan squeezed her shoulder and nodded at her.

"Yeah, **he is a great guy and I was very relieved to hear that he was not involved in what my father, I mean Edward was doing. He has been cleared of any charges and is running the plantation for us right now until we can get a new manager hired and get this mess straightened** out." she said.

"Edward?" I asked hesitantly.

Margie was looking at me funny. "I think you already know what I'm talking about, **Sugar.**"

Oh boy. I was pretty sure the look on my face resembled that deer in the headlights again.

"It's okay, Sugar. I know that Edward wasn't my real father. He **took great pleasure in torturing me with that while he held me captive. I always wondered how I could be his daughter because we were so** different. I'm not okay with what he did, but I'm okay with knowing that my father didn't do all those horrible things to people. My father is a good **man who** works hard and deserves me as his daughter." **she said smiling.**

"Amen to that, **Margie. Does your uncle, well your father, your** uncle know?" I asked.

She laughed. "What to call him, right? No, he doesn't know yet. I can't wait to tell him when we get back. I'**m going to show him the wedding pictures and tell him that it turns out my father did walk me** down the aisle. I'm pretty sure that it's something he already suspects, **but could never prove. It will be the first memory as father and daughter and I hope to** make many more now that Edward is out of our lives."

I looked over at Nathan, "Promise you will take care of her. She's really something special and I'm going to miss you both."

Nathan stood and kissed my cheek. "She is the best thing in my life and you can bet your life she will never suffer like that again. I have fought with jealousy that I didn't get to kill him with my own two hands. I love you, Sugar."

I hugged him back and told him I loved him too. Margie stood up and grabbed the iPad. "Okay, now, hang on," She went in the hallway and grabbed a nurse, "group shot!"

I stood up and Nathan held on to me on one side and Margie pulled up my pants leg on the other and we smiled at the camera. I prayed it captured the look in my eye. I hope it said thank you.

Margie leaned over and whispered in my ear. "His email is saved in there under 'The man I love'."

God bless priceless moments.

FIFTY-THREE

I was sitting in Jesse's office after giving them my statement. I had been released from the hospital yesterday morning, but he refused to let me leave the house until today. Sharon brought me down today to get it over with so they could begin to wrap everything up in a neat little bow, but there was one piece of the puzzle that I hadn't seen yet. Every time I asked Jess he changed the subject. When the officer taking my statement asked me if I was going to press charges I was shocked to find out who the inside man was. I had managed to get away with an "I need to think about it" so I could find Jesse and beat the hell out of him for not telling me.

"Hi Sug, all done in the hot seat?" he asked me, putting his hand on my shoulder. I shrugged it off.

"It was fine. Nothing I didn't expect. I told them to call me if they needed anything else."

"Good, now go home and rest some more. I don't want you back in the hospital." And that was his way of dismissing me.

"I'm fine Jess, but I need to talk to you." And I stayed rooted in place.

"Okay," he said sitting in the chair next to me, "shoot."

"Did you find out who the inside man was?" I asked, not letting on that I already knew.

"Sugar, listen," Jess started into his attempt at putting me off.

"No, you listen Jess, I want to know who it was. Is it someone I know?"

He leaned forward putting his elbows on his knees and folding his hands nodding.

"Dew." he said, barely audible.

"Dew? As in Dewey, my Dew?" I watched his face.

He nodded again reaching out and taking my hand, but I shook him off.

"Why didn't you tell me? Why did I have to hear it from Ernie? Didn't you think I deserved to know?" And I was angry, but I needed to stop yelling since my lung was still not in perfect form.

"Sugar, take it down a notch or I'm hauling you out of here." He reached over and shut the door to his office.

"He needed money." Jess said simply.

361

"He runs an extremely high volume business, Jess. He's got money!"

Jess let out a sigh. "It's Ivy."

"What do you mean 'it's Ivy'?" And my heart was picking up its pace.

"She has MS and the medical bills are bleeding them dry. He needed the money to pay for her treatment. She needed a procedure and he doesn't have insurance." Jess was angry.

"Where is he?" I asked gripping the arm of the chair.

"Where is who?" he asked.

"Dew."

"In jail. He's being held on a hundred thousand dollar bail. He's being charged with conspiracy to commit a crime." Jess finished quietly.

"What can you prove, Jess? Do you have proof he was working for McElevain?" I asked him firmly.

"Sugar…"

"Damn it Jess, I deserve to know this, do you have proof?" I demanded.

"All we have is the fact that his medical bills were paid in cash. We also have proof that he put the GPS on your cars and watched your property from a tree stand on his. I guess when they asked him to throw the rock through your door, he took down the guy and came straight here to the station to report it. It was too late by then, though, the damage was done."

"So you can't prove that he took any money, but you can prove he put GPS on my cars."

He took a breath. "The DA has to decide the burden of proof not me, Sugar."

"Take me to him." I stood carefully remembering not to move too quickly.

"No, Sugar, I can't do that." He stood up and steadied me with one hand.

"Yes you can, now." I said quietly.

His shoulders slumped. "He's in the Douglas County Jail, he isn't here."

"Fine, take me there then." I opened my cell phone and called Sharon.

"Hi Mom, you can head back to the lodge Jess is going to bring me back, looks like I will be a little longer than expected." I assured her that everything was fine and I would be home in a bit and she hung up hesitantly after making me put Jess on the line to talk to her.

"Now," I said, "let's go."

He led me to the garage and he helped me into his Blazer. "Sugar, what the hell do you think you are going to do when you get there?"

"I'm going to talk to him, Jess. I'm going to ask him why he did it."

Jess shook his head, "He's not going to tell you that! He's not talking except through a lawyer. Are you that naïve to think he's going to admit to you that he was involved with a drug lord?"

I decided I wasn't going to talk to him anymore and looked out the window as we crossed the high bridge. The memory of crossing it with Van hit me square in the face and I let the tears fall because it hurt my lungs too much to hold them in. He pulled into the parking lot at the police station and gave me a minute to get myself together. He picked up his cell phone and called Julie asking her to meet us at the back door. She opened the door and motioned. Jess helped me out of the car and put his arm around me, but I pushed him away. I saw Julie raise a brow, but I didn't care.

"Hi Sugar. How you feeling?" she asked me as I stepped in the door.

"I've been better, Julie." I saw Jesse give her that annoying cop look that everyone around here but me understands and he took me to a holding room. I sat there in the chair looking at my hands trying to decide what I was going to say to a man, who according to everyone I trusted, had done horrible things to me. What do you say to the person who nearly got you killed? The door opened and Dew came in handcuffed looking a thousand times older than he did a week ago. I stood up and pulled him into a careful hug, so I didn't knock him over.

Jess held the door open, "We are watching from the other room." That was all he said and he was gone.

"Sugar, I'm sorry." Dew started and I held up my hand.

"Tell me what's wrong with Ivy. She looked fine at the dinner." I said.

"She has multiple sclerosis. Some days are better than others. Some days she has problems doing just about everything and then some days she's a little better, but she has trouble eating. She has a tube that feeds her now because she can't swallow." His voice broke and I reached out taking his hand with mine.

"Who's with her right now, Dew?" I asked him gently.

"Her sister, but she can't stay for long. I will have to find a place to put her while I'm in here." He wasn't looking at me, his head down and his eyes trained at his feet.

"Dew, why didn't you come to me? I have money. I have more money than I can spend and you know that. Why didn't you come to me? I would have helped you." And he was silent.

"I never intended for it to go this far, Sugar."

"Dew, don't say anything more please. I can't promise they aren't listening." And I didn't want him to say something he couldn't take back.

"I don't care anymore, Sugar. I'm so tired. I miss Ivy so bad and I worry about her every second. I can't afford bail and the business is not going to run itself. I need to explain what happened in case they might take mercy on an old man." he said softly. "I was supposed to make sure he knew when his daughter and her husband left the lodge and he would take care of Ivy's bills. I had a bug planted in the house and when I heard them tell you goodbye I called him. That was all I did Sugar, I swear on my life. He held good to his promise too and paid Ivy's bills, but he knew he had me then and he threatened to expose me if I didn't keep helping him. I didn't know what to do. I couldn't leave Ivy alone and he knew that. I wanted to come to you, but by then I knew I would be arrested. When I put the GPS things on your cars I thought it was a bug, I didn't know it was a tracking device, Sugar, I swear!"

"Did you come in my garage and do that, Dew?" I asked him angrily.

He shook his head, "No, I put the one on the Mustang the day you came to the bar and I put the one on the Sorento when it was parked in Superior one day. I wouldn't have let them hurt you, Sugar."

I looked at him and threw up a hand. "They were shooting at me and I nearly died, Dew!"

He didn't respond he just kept looking at his shoes.

"Did you lure Van and Jess away at the dance so that McElevain's goon could talk to me?"

He looked up and nodded. "But I knew you would be safe because they only wanted to talk to you and there were enough people around. I'm sorry Sugar. I know it's too late for that, but I want you to know that when he came to me and asked me throw that rock through your window I refused. As soon as I saw Jess on that rock I knew things had gone too far. I cold-cocked the goon and dragged him out of the bar and then took off as fast as I could to the station. I was in such a panic I didn't even take the rock with me. I'm such an idiot."

"You're not an idiot, Dew," I said, "but that might have helped your case."

"I lied to them and told them they offered to pay me to do it, but that I refused. I should have told them the whole story I think it would have been better."

I leaned on the table. "Dew, look at me."

He finally looked up and there were tears in his eyes. "Tell me what you are going to do when you get out of this place."

He looked at me quizzically. "I'm going to go home and I'm going to gather Ivy up in my arms and I'm going to tell her that I love her and that I screwed up and beg her to forgive me. That's if I ever get out of here. They are going to charge me with conspiracy, Sugar, that's a felony, and stalking and endangering a police officer and I don't even remember what else. I could be behind bars for the rest of my life. I don't know how to take care of Ivy from here."

He started crying softly then. I sat there trying to take it all in and from what I was hearing there wasn't much that they could make stick without looking like heartless eejits.

"Dew, I will take care of Ivy. I want you to tell them exactly what happened. I don't want you to leave out a thing. I don't care how bad you think it sounds I want you to tell them everything he made you do and everything he told you was going to happen if you didn't. Do you understand me?"

He nodded and I stood up. "I love you, Dew, and even though I don't like what you did, I do understand."

He kept his head hung low and I hugged him gently and walked out. Jesse met me at the door as I came out and he put his arm around me and I leaned into him.

"He's ready to confess." I said and Jess stopped dead in his tracks.

"What do you mean he's ready to confess?" He turned and held me at arms length.

"He's ready to tell you everything. He's scared and all he needed was someone to talk to. Maybe you should have thought about that, Jess. Call me when his bond is reset and I will pay it."

"Sugar, if he confesses his bail could be revoked or it could go up, substantially." Jesse said.

"I'm aware of that. Call me after you have treated him like a human being and you are ready to respect my choices."

He sighed and I left. I found Julie leaning up against the wall by the back door. I held my hand up the other wrapped around my side.

"I'm calling for a ride." I said my voice sounding breathy.

"Sugar, I'm taking you home." Julie said pushing the door open and taking my elbow guiding me to Jesse's Blazer. I collapsed into the seat and laid my head back against the headrest. She started the car and turned on the heat.

"I think I ticked off your fiancé." I said almost gasping for air.

"He deserves it. He's being a, what does Van call it, a pain in the arse?"

I nodded, but I was too short of breath to speak.

"Do I need to take you to the hospital, you don't look good." Julie said her voice full of concern.

I rolled my head towards her on the headrest. "No, I need to go home and rest. Seems my lungs aren't cut out for yelling." And she put the SUV in gear and took me home.

Julie had helped me into the house and into my bed stripping off my shoes and my coat and helping Sharon tuck me in. She made me promise to sleep and then left telling me she would be back to "talk" in a few days. In other words, counsel me about the shooting. That was fine with me -- it could wait more than a few days. I had already put that where it needed to be. Sharon sat by my bed and scolded me for not taking it easy and then kissed my forehead and went to make lunch. I pulled Van's pillow up next to me and buried my face in it. Sharon had discreetly laid it on my bed and I found it when I got home. The smell of his Irish Spring still lingered and when I lay with it I could sleep as peacefully as I did when he was here. It was hard in the morning to get up and leave it on the bed, but I figured they might commit me if I walked around with it like a security blanket. I slept through lunch and I slept through dinner too and didn't wake up until Wednesday morning when I smelled coffee.

I opened my eyes and felt halfway human for the first time in weeks. I carefully sat up testing my side and the ache was better and the breathing was free. I took a shower and dressed in my best lay around the house and do nothing clothes. When I stepped back into my bedroom I heard voices. I knew that Sharon was no longer alone. We had a visitor and I was in no big hurry to go visit, but the lure of the coffee won out.

I stepped into the kitchen and Sharon was there fixing eggs and Jesse sat at the table under the chandelier like he had so many mornings of my life.

Sharon came over and took stock of me. "You look really good today, Sugar. I think you needed all that sleep."

"Morning Mom, I feel good. I'm even ready to help with the Thanksgiving dinner tomorrow. I'll make the pies." She laughed then and handed me a cup of coffee shooing me to the table to sit.

"She's right, you look really good Sis. I like seeing the pink in your cheeks." Jess said fiddling with the place mat.

"Hi Jess." And that was all I felt like saying right now.

Sharon sat two plates of eggs down on the table and excused herself telling me she needed to call Lenny. Sure.

I reached for my fork, but really wasn't hungry. I didn't like being angry with him. I didn't like walking away from someone angry. You never know if that'll be the last time you'll see them.

"I took Dew's statement personally." he said.

I shrugged my shoulder, "So how much does he need for bail? My accountant is ready to transfer the money as soon as he's notified. He needs to be home with Ivy at least for the holidays." I said still not willing to forgive him.

"He's been released on his own recognizance," Jess said playing with his fork, "and I have strongly recommended to the DA that he drop the charges siting extenuating circumstances."

I reached over and stopped his fork fiddling. "You did?" I asked. "What made you change your mind?"

"I sat in there listening to him tell me about Ivy and how sick she was and how badly she needed the surgery or she wouldn't have made it and I pictured myself a few weeks ago so deathly afraid that Julie was really sick, or worse. Even though I don't condone for one minute what he did I began to understand why he did it. I honestly believe that he didn't have any idea how bad McElevain was. I honestly believe he thought he'd found a way to hold onto his pride and take care of his wife. He helped himself by coming to the station that night, but I don't know what the DA is going to do. I told the DA that you were waiting to pay his bail and were not going to press charges. That will weigh heavily in his decision I'm sure." And I nodded reaching for my cup and took a sip, the hot liquid soothing my throat. "So anyway he is home with Ivy and I should know more in a few days about if he will be charged and with what."

"Thanks, Jesse, it means a lot to me that you at least tried. I don't like what he did either, but I also don't believe he felt he had any other choice for whatever reason."

"So am I still invited to Thanksgiving dinner?" he asked.

I stood up and so did he and I let him pull me into a hug. "Of course you are, you were never not invited. I just hadn't decided if I was going to talk to you." He laughed a little at that one. "I can't stay mad at you very long you know that. I'm happy that we are all here to celebrate it this year."

And we weren't all here, one person was missing, but that was something I couldn't do anything about.

FIFTY-FOUR

The kitchen smelled like pumpkin pie, sweet potatoes, roasting turkey and onion sage dressing. The oven was keeping the kitchen toasty warm and I sat in my MAMBOS t-shirt and capris taking a break from the cooking to enjoy the company. My feet were stuffed in my bunny slippers and I was nursing a mocha nut coffee at the table. I could hear the TV in the great room and Jess and Len talking about the game that was going "to be on as soon as this stupid parade is done". They were bantering about who was going to get the Thanksgiving classic turkey leg award and the discussion was getting heated.

Julie and Sharon were at the table with me paging through wedding catalogs and nursery furnishings. Julie was leaning towards berry red for the dresses and blue for the nursery. Sharon was leaning towards cranberry for the dresses and pink for the nursery. Sharon had been staying in my now-empty spare room and fussing over me like a mother hen no matter how much I insisted that I was fine. It has been great having her here. She filled the void in the house that Van left and she has been doing most of the work for today. I was letting Sharon take the reins and did what I could with preparations and recipe advice.

My side was feeling better today than yesterday even and only certain movements caused pain now. My leg was back to dancing, but my lung wasn't so I hadn't spent much time in the ballroom since I got home. I had to cancel all my group classes, but next week I would start letting my couples come back in for practice so I could stay on top of their routines. My heart wasn't in it, though, and I was glad the Thanksgiving holiday meant I could be closed guilt-free for five days. I was grateful to have Sharon and Lenny here for the holidays. They, along with baby Bowers, were helping my heart heal.

"Earth to Sugar." Sharon was waving her hand in front of my face and my mouth tipped up as the memory of Van doing that at Dew's not that long ago came to mind.

"What?"

Julie and Sharon were both smiling at me, their eyes laughing.

Julie said, "I just told you I was going to wear a diaper dress and you said 'make it blue'."

Oops. "Sorry guys my mind was wandering." I said.

Sharon rolled her eyes, "Never would have guessed."

Julie laid the catalog down. "So do you have any plans for New Year's Eve?"

"Nope." I know, I know, pathetic.

"So you aren't having a party in the ballroom or anything?"

"Noooooo, why?" Was she trying to rub it in?

"Jess and I thought that maybe we could get married here in the ballroom on New Year's Eve. I really want to get married before I turn into a two-ton Tilly."

Yeah like that was going to happen. Even nine months pregnant Julie wouldn't look like a two-ton Tilly. My prediction was that she would have this little basketball sticking out and the rest of her would look exactly the same.

"I would love for you to get married in my ballroom on New Year's Eve! But are you sure? The ballroom isn't exactly very traditional."

"I think it's perfect. We haven't exactly done things traditionally up to this point so why start now. We don't really want a big wedding. It will be us and about a hundred or so of the Twin Ports finest."

"It sounds perfect to me, Julie." And it did because it gave me something to focus on over the holidays.

"Good, but we have one condition." She paused and I waited learning early on in my career never to push a bride.

"You aren't allowed to do any of the work that night." She said firmly. I raised an eyebrow, but she held up a hand. "The only way we will have the wedding here is if you let us cater it out and we hire the DJ that works for you in the summer."

"Why? I don't mind doing the cooking and I can hire my servers for the night..."

Julie put her hand over mine, "Because the only thing I want you to worry about that night is being my maid of honor. Will you do that for me, Sugar?"

My eyes teared up and emotion clogged my throat. "Yeah, I'll do that for you, sweetie." I got up and hugged her tight to me feeling the little baby bump sticking out and I cried harder. Jess came into the kitchen just then for two more beers.

"Let me guess, she said yes." he said, laughing at our tears.

"Yeah, you big coot, I said yes." We sat back down at the table and I asked him, "So who's the best man?"

Jess came over and kissed the top of my head. "Haven't decided yet." And he took his beers and left.

"Has he really not decided?" I asked Julie, surprised.

"He says he has some "feelers" out whatever that means. He has a few close friends at work, but no one that feels like a brother to him. He'll figure it out I'm sure."

"So I went to the doctor yesterday." Julie said between bites of turkey, her appetite having returned with gusto. We were gathered around the big kitchen table that was covered in every imaginable Thanksgiving fare available -- turkey, stuffing, sweet potatoes, corn, biscuits and cranberries. The pumpkin pies sat in the pie safe waiting to be cut. I had gotten up to get more turkey and brought the platter back to the table as Julie made her announcement.

"Wait a minute. I thought you didn't have to go again for a couple of weeks. Is something wrong?" I asked her, laying my hand on her shoulder. Then I noticed Jess was smiling like the cat that ate the canary and I wondered what was up. He didn't look worried.

"No everything is wonderful," Julie said, "better than wonderful actually. The doctor called me because he got one of those new 3D ultrasound machines and he needed some test dummies to come in and help his sonographers dial everything in."

I laughed, "Well isn't it nice to know that your name comes to mind when someone thinks test dummy." Jess playfully swatted at me.

"Hey, I didn't care it was a chance to finally get to see baby Bowers and get an exact due date, since you know we weren't really very sure." And she still blushed every time that came up.

Jess piped in, "Turns out she is already at sixteen weeks, which is a few weeks farther along than we thought."

"The ultrasound estimated my due date as May eleventh." And the room was silent. I saw Sharon stop dead and goose bumps went up my arms. It kind of felt like the air had been sucked out of the room and all you heard was the ticking of the clock on the stove.

I finally said, "That's Brent's birthday." And Jess said, "Yeah, pretty cool huh?" And it was cool, really cool.

Julie got up from the table and grabbed her purse pulling out an envelope. "They gave me a video of the ultrasound we can watch later, but I can't wait any longer to introduce you to baby Bowers."
She pulled out the still shots from the ultrasound and we all gathered around her begging for the first glance. Usually when someone pulls out ultrasound pictures I do the whole "Oh how cute" and the "look at those little feet" because frankly I never have a clue what I'm looking at. The pictures always looked like a distorted kidney bean or an alien. But not these, these were amazing. This was the most perfect little baby ever. Sleepy eyes, pixie nose, perfect lips and tiny little toes. We were handing the pictures back and forth oohing and ahhing at the newest addition to the family hardly believing that we could see such perfect images of him when he weighed less than a candy bar.

Jess slid a picture on top of the one I was looking at. I was stumped on this one. I didn't have a clue what it was. I turned my head one way and then the other my brain finally realizing it was two legs, make that two legs and a very little tiny third one. I saw the printing at the bottom. It said, "**James Brenton Bowers, 16 weeks**". And my hand came up over my mouth and pretty soon the tears were over the lashes and Jess slipped his arm around me.

"Tell them what it says, Sugar." Jess prodded.

Sharon was looking worried and Lenny had his arm around her. Julie was smiling through her tears and I cleared my throat making a couple of false starts before I could finally say the words.

"It says, James Brenton Bowers, sixteen weeks."

I turned the picture around and handed it to Sharon who took it with shaking hands and pressed it to her chest not even looking at it.

"This little boy is going to remind us everyday that they live on in us." Jess planted a kiss on my cheek.

"Dad would be touched." I whispered, **the tears falling down**.

He took my hand, "Yeah he would. I can see him and Brent right now giving each other a high five." And I laughed at the image, but he was right. They were looking down right now and this little baby was going to be a constant reminder that God is good.

We all wiped our tears and finished lunch, stuffing ourselves until we didn't even have room for pie. We talked about the holidays, the wedding, the nursery and the Bulldogs, but we never talked about what happened a few weeks ago. I checked my phone every five minutes for a text, but there wasn't one. I really wanted to **tell him about bab**y James. I really wanted to hear his voice. I really wanted to feel his arms around me again, but I wasn't sure if I should do any of the above. Jesse saw me checking my **phone for the fourth time in ten minutes.**

"He's coming back, **Sugar**." Everyone ducked their heads **acting** like he hadn't spoken.

"No I mean it. He's coming back. I've said it before and I will say it again a man doesn't look at a woman the way he looked at you and stay away. It's okay though, I won't force you to say I was **right when he shows** up at the door."

"Pretty damn sure of yourself aren't you, Officer Know It All?" That got a snicker out of Julie.

"Yup." And that was all he said.

I looked around the table and everyone was leaning back in their chair like they were drunk on food, so I sent them all into the great room to beach themselves like whales while I cleaned up. I needed some quiet time anyway. I started the dishwasher and took a cup of coffee to the patio doors looking out.

The doors had been replaced while I was in the hospital and had been upgraded from sliding doors to French doors with easy pull down handles. There was a ramp added to the door leading out to the deck and it was pretty obvious that Van saw the one part of the lodge that still hadn't been made handicapped accessible. It was late afternoon and the sun was starting to set. It was beautiful as it filtered through the trees, casting shadows on the deck. They weren't scary shadows anymore and I was thankful that I didn't have to be afraid to stand here now. I was thankful for so much, but my heart still hurt. I felt my phone vibrate and my breathing quickened as I read the words.

"I love you. I miss you. I want you. I need you. I wish I was there today."

I felt the exact same way so I texted him back.

"I love you. I miss you. I want you. I need you. I wish I was there today."

I closed my phone and sat staring out the window as the sun went down and the woods settled into a quiet hum. I knew I had made it through another day. My phone vibrated again and there was another text. I opened it with a shaky hand and read what it said.

"Lillie came home for a surprise visit. We had Sugar Burgers and rings. She says hi. She also says we are worth fighting for. I say she's right and I love you."

And this felt like dangerous territory.

"Tell her I love her and tell her thank you for being there. I'm fighting every day to make it to the next. I don't want you to feel pressured to make any choices that you aren't ready to make, but tomorrow when the sun comes up I'll be thinking of you and I hope you understand that I'm giving you space not because I want to, but because I love you." And I hoped he understood that it was for the best.

"Sugar." I turned around and Jess was in the kitchen doorway holding a single pink rose.

"This just came for you." I walked over setting my coffee cup on the counter, my heart rate speeding up knowing exactly who it was from.

"Really? On Thanksgiving?"

He shrugged his shoulder and I took it from him. There was a small card attached and I knew what it would be. I took it out of the envelope and read it, "'Drop everything now. Meet me in the pouring rain. Kiss me on the sidewalk. Take away the pain. 'Cause I see sparks fly whenever you smile.'"

"Bond?" Jess asked.

"Yeah." I said wistfully. I pulled out my phone, texting him back quickly.

"'Get me with those green eyes, baby, as the lights go down. Give me something that'll haunt me when you're not around. 'Cause I see sparks fly whenever you smile.' Taylor Swift, 'Sparks Fly', I'm not dancing. I love you."

As I was typing Jess was talking. "He's coming back you know. I wasn't kidding at lunch. I may not have liked the way he looked at you, but he was a man in love and I respect that." He plunked a kiss on my forehead and grabbed a beer. I didn't want to focus too closely on what might be. I was going to let my heart be happy for a while.

I laid the rose down on the table and held up my hand to Jess asking him to wait. I went over to my drawer that held all my spare keys and took one out, wrapping my fingers around it. I had been waiting for the right time to do this and now was the time. I walked back over to him and took his hand, pressing the key into it and wrapping his fingers up over it.

"Dad would want you to have it." I said.

His eyes were quizzical as he opened his hand and saw the silver key with the galloping mustang on it. His eyes got big and he shook his head no.

"No Sugar. No, no, no. I'm not taking the Mustang. No, that is your car. That's you and your dad's song. No." And he tried to put the key back in my hand, but I put them behind my back.

I was smiling at his insistence. "That car is our car, Jess. That car is the family car. That car needs some memories made in it instead of sitting in the garage for most of the year. That car needs a little one in it again. A little one who can hear the stories about dad and keep the memories alive."

He pulled me into a hug. "He's coming back, Sugar. He's coming back and then you can make your own memories in that car."

"Jess, I want you to have the car. I know that you will love it and take care of it the same way my dad did and I know that baby James is going to love riding in it with his dad, like we did with ours."

Jess pulled back and stared at the key not saying anything for a long time. His lower lip trembled a bit and he hung his head to hide the tears in his eyes. He tossed the key up in the air and caught it again holding it up between his two fingers. "You're right, Sugar, the car is the family car, but it's also part of this lodge and part of you and I'm touched you trust me with her. I will make you a deal. She's already locked up tight for the winter so I think we need to keep her here until it's time to bring baby James home from the hospital. I think we should make that her maiden voyage for the spring. I will keep the spare key and when I want to drive her I know where she is, but she's not leaving her home. Deal?"

He pulled me into a hug and I told him it was a deal.

God bless compromise.

FIFTY-FIVE

It was only the first week in December and it was snowing, again. It had snowed on and off practically every day since Thanksgiving. Today's snow was light and airy. It's the kind of snow that when it lands on your car you can blow it away with a gentle puff. It's the kind of snow that is so light that it dances around on the breeze and never really lands, continually being bounced back up and moved down the way. It's the kind of snow that makes you think about Christmas shopping, caroling and Santa Claus, but today those were the last things on my mind. I was sitting in the Sorento, having just left St. Mary's Financial Department and my head was spinning. Jess had asked me to get a final total of my charges for the police department to turn into their insurance carrier. Turns out they would be paying my hospital bills because I was a civilian engaged in official police business. I was never more relieved to hear that because helicopter rides off the Point are pricey. Like it was any other day, I went in and asked for an itemized bill only to be told several long minutes later my bill had been paid in full and there was nothing to take care of. I spoke with the head of the department who told me my bill had been paid in cash several days after I was released. It gave me that feeling in the pit of my stomach, the kind of feeling that said either you had too much coffee or drug money just paid your hospital bill. I had to call Jesse and I dialed his number, putting the phone up to my ear.

"Hi Sugar." he said, his voice warming my heart.

"Hi Jesse, hey can I ask you something?"

"Sure."

"Did the department already pay my hospital bill?" I asked it like you would ask what the score of the Packer game was.

"Of course not, Sugar, I'm still waiting for the bill. Did you get it?" And I let out that breath that said, 'no I didn't get it and I'm frustrated because I can't figure this out'.

"What, something happen?" I heard his voice change from light to concerned and I explained the whole thing to him.

"So what's got you so twitterpated about this?" he asked.

"Seriously Jess? What's got me so twitterpated? Who pays a huge hospital bill in cash?" And he didn't know this, but there had been a large deposit into the foundation's petty cash fund right after Thanksgiving that I was also trying to sort out.

"Did you guys ever find the money Margie said was missing?" Margie had told the police that there was over a million dollars unaccounted for when she got back to the plantation and looked at his "books". He had told her it was his "stash" for getting out of the country, but so far there had been no sign of it.

"Nope, we haven't and it's not likely we will, Sugar. How about if you walk away from this and not worry about how it got paid? How about if you say thank you to the wind and get on with your life because I'm not going to chase rainbows. I'm pretty certain that the department is going to be ecstatic they don't have to pay it and aren't going to delve too deeply into it either." And he was right, but it didn't make me feel any better. "Maybe you should call Margie and ask her if you are that hung up about it." he finally said.

"I did that, Jesse, when I found a half a million dollars in the petty cash fund for the foundation a few weeks ago, deposited from a dead man's account." I said it off hand and was rewarded with a breath on his end being blown out.

"And what did she say?" he recovered quickly.

"She said she didn't know what I was talking about, but I know her well enough to see on her face that she was lying."

"Sugar, we never had this conversation. I have no idea how your bill got paid, must have been someone that cares about you. End of story. I love you and good bye."

The line went dead and I knew he was right, but it didn't change how I felt. I guess I was going to have to get over it. My phone rang again and I looked down at the caller ID, it was Jesse again.

"Yes?" I said laughing at his sigh.

"I forgot to tell you that I talked to the DA." He hesitated and my heart stopped beating while I waited.

"He is dropping all charges against Dew citing lack of burden of proof and extenuating circumstances. As long as you aren't pressing charges Dew will remain out of jail." My heart started beating again.

"Thanks for telling me Jess, I appreciate it."

"I heard what you did, Sugar. Dew doesn't deserve you." Jesse said quietly. I told him I loved him and good bye, hanging up and shifting the car into gear.

If there was one thing the last few months has taught me is that hurt and anger are emotions not worth carrying around. I was hurt by what Dew did, but I wasn't angry with him. I just couldn't figure out how to get rid of the hurt, so a few days ago I went to Dew's house and talked to him and Ivy about their situation and how I could help. McElevain's money may have settled a few bills, but it wasn't going to settle all the future ones. When I left the hurt was gone and I was three-quarter share owner in a small restaurant off Moccasin Mike Road. I had my accountant invest the money so Dew will have the money he needs to take care of Ivy and still be able to keep the restaurant. My only stipulation was that the Sugar Burgers and rings are on the house when I stop in. He thought that was more than fair.

I swung through Starbucks, grabbed a couple of coffees, and drove over to my financial advisors office, dreading the monthly MAMBOS financial meeting. This usually consisted of me and him drinking coffee and going over the portfolio, but I knew today would not be a usual meeting. He would have the final numbers from the foundation dinner and with any luck he would have tracked down where that huge sum of money had come from. I had found the deposit when I was reconciling receipts to the account after the foundation dinner and had called him immediately. I went directly to the bank and talked to the manager who walked me through the transaction. It had come from a recently deceased man's account who was a ward of the state. As far as he was concerned it was a typical deposit other than the size of it, but the money had cleared through and the account was viable. I asked Robyn to look into it a little more and hopefully he had some better answers for me.

I met him as he was coming out of his office headed for the coffee machine. I handed him a Starbucks and we went to his office for full disclosure. He closed the door and sat down behind his desk.

"So, how are you feeling?" He asked like maybe he needed to know before he told me what he had found out.

"I'm great, Robyn, fit as a fiddle, well fit as a fiddle for someone recovering from surgery, but almost good as new." And that was physically, because emotionally I had a ways to go.

"Good because I have a lot of information here for you and some you are really going to like and some you are really not going to like, so tell me -- do you want the good news or the bad news?"

And I told him the bad news because sometimes it makes you appreciate the good news more. What he told me next was not going to help my heartburn. I politely listened to what he had to tell me, took the thick folder of information, and told him I would be in touch when I knew where I wanted to go next. Then I escaped back to my car and put it in drive, letting it take me by autopilot to the McDonald's drivethrough for a coffee and a little bit of balm for my soul.

It helped when my phone beeped and I saw, **"How is my blue eyed girl? I miss you and I long to hold you. Wish things were different."**

I wished things were different too, but I also knew that I needed to let him make the decisions. I was already onboard with spending the rest of my life with him. I texted him back.

"I'm breathing and I miss you too. I pray someday you will hold me again, but I understand that things are different now."

I put the phone back in my pocket and shifted the car into gear. He had been gone over three weeks and I hadn't talked to him other than by text or email. He had gotten the pictures of my new socket and emailed me back saying it was beautiful, but it was nothing compared to the woman wearing it. He kept me updated about the case as best as he could, but otherwise never delved into anything more personal. I had a new friend on my Facebook page, Lillie Walsh, but his page was silent. No posts, no communication with Lillie, nothing. I didn't know how long this would go on, but every time I heard from him I knew he was still thinking about me and that gave me hope that things would work out. I tried to tell myself I needed to trust in time, but the fact of the matter was giving him up was not going to be something that came easy to me. Giving him up was going to be the most difficult thing I would ever have to do and I've done a lot of difficult things in my life.

Somehow I found my way back home and saw Julie's car sitting in the parking area of the lodge when I got there. I suspected I knew why she was here. We still hadn't had our little chat about what happened on the Point. I didn't see any need for it, but I guess Jesse still did. I powered up my garage door, slipping the SUV inside closing the door. I opened the mudroom door and went inside, hanging my coat on the rack and changing into my slippers.

"Jules?" I yelled from the mudroom.

"In the kitchen, Sugar." I opened the door and found Julie holding open the coffee cupboard shaking her head.

"It's time for therapy, hon." And I remembered the last time someone stood in front of my coffee cupboard shaking their head.

"I'm past therapy. I'm hopeless." I said holding up my coffee cup. She agreed and then I politely asked her to step out of the way so I could make the coffee. I brewed up a pot of decaf in deference to my new nephew who probably wouldn't appreciate the caffeine jolt and brought her a mug to the kitchen table. Julie was looking nervous and I asked her what was up.

"Jesse asked me to come over and do the official counselor to counselee thing. He said it's been long enough."

"And what do you think?" I asked her, sitting down at the table.

She looked at me then and cocked her head. "I think that you don't have a thing to say about it because you have already put it where it needs to be." And she nails it!

I sipped my coffee and thought about how I was going to tell her that I was okay with killing a man. "Julie, this is going to sound really coldhearted but I want you to hear me out."

She nodded and sat back in her chair.

"I took a man's life there is no denying that, I did and I can't change that. I also know that I've already been forgiven by the people that matter. Margie and Nathan did not want to see anyone else hurt or anyone else's family torn apart and they understand **and forgive me for what I did. Hell, Nathan flat out thanked me. I asked God to forgive me** because taking someone's life, even if you don't intend to, is still **fundamentally against everything I believe in. I believe in life and I believe that everyone has some good in them. I struggled with that when it came** to McElevain because there wasn't much good that could be found, but **then Margie walked into my hospital room and told me he saved seven** people's lives that night **and then I had my answer. I found the good in him even if it was in death and I heard the Lord tell me that I was forgiven. Maybe my thinking is flawed and I will never know that for sure until I** face my creator, but I have peace about what happened and it doesn't **haunt me. I know that what I did was the right thing at the right time at** least for some people involved." I trailed off and she nodded.

"Well that pretty much covers it then doesn't it, **Sugar. I guess my** work here is done."

We both laughed because for once I wasn't in tears. Julie **fiddled with her coffee cup.** "Now that we have that out of the way, **I want to ask** your opinion about something."

"Okay, shoot." I said taking a drink of my coffee needing the **warmth to hit me and warm me from the cold.**

"I've been thinking about quitting my **job and staying home once** the baby is born, but I'm not sure what Jess will say."

"Have you talked to him about it?" I asked her, **already knowing** what his answer would be.

She shook her head. "No, I haven't. I just don't know that I want **to be away from the baby all the time. You know my job, I get called at all** different times of the day and night and I know I won't want to leave him. I don't know if we can afford to have only one of us working."

"Julie, really, you know the money is there to take care **of your kids whether you choose to work or stay home with them. Jesse took care** of that years ago, so what is the real problem?"

"I don't want to work. I want to stay home and be with my son **and be there when Jess is there. You know our schedules can be crazy and** sometimes we don't even see each other for days. I don't want that." she said quickly.

"So I'm still not seeing a problem."

"It's not that I don't want to work." she said slowly.

Aha. "So the real problem is that you think people are going to think that you don't want to work."

"Something like that, I guess."

Well lucky for me I had the perfect solution for that problem. "I think that's rubbish and you know it too. I remember how hard my mom worked everyday and she never left the house. I'm pretty **sure that Jess will be thrilled to have you at home taking care of his son. I really do. He** loves you and wants you to be happy, but I can understand how you feel too. I might be able to help with both of those factors."

"How so?" she looked perplexed.

I started to tell her about my day, "I talked to Robyn today and it turns out that the foundation dinner brought in over fifty thousand dollars."

Julie's eyebrows shot up, "No way! I hadn't seen the final numbers yet what with everything that has happened. That's fantastic!"

"It is and is so much more than we had hoped for. Robyn is going to invest it so that we can use the interest on the money and not even touch the principal for years to come."

"That's going to make our job a lot easier, Sugar."

"That's very true, but I'm not done. There was a half million dollar deposit made into the petty cash account about two weeks ago and no one knows where it came from."

And the look on her face told me that she knew nothing about it. I was really starting to believe that even if the money was from McElevain's stolen millions, it wasn't by either her or Jess's hand.

"What?" Her voice was subdued and she leaned into the table. "That can't be possible Sugar. Who drops a half million dollars into someone else's account?"

"I honestly don't know. I have spent the last two weeks trying every way from Sunday to trace back the deposit. It came from a recently deceased man's account and he was a ward of the state, so there is no family to contact. I didn't know what to think. I asked Robyn to look into it for me and he told me today that it's all legal."

"So you think it's a dead end then? We could help a lot of people with that money."

"You're right about that, Jules, and as far as it being a dead end, I Skyped Margie."

"And?" she asked, drawing it out.

"And she says she doesn't know anything about it either, but the look on her face told me otherwise."

"What does that mean?"

"It means that I'm pretty sure that money was drug money, but I can't prove it."

We were silent then both of us sipping our coffee. Julie was the first to speak. "Ultimately, Sugar, you are the founder of the foundation and it's your decision to decide what you want to do with it. Did you talk to the attorney?"

"Yup, I did. He feels that the money was transferred from a legal account of a real person so there is nothing illegal about keeping it as long as we claim it as a gift."

"That money could keep the foundation going for a very long time." she said slowly.

"Yeah it could and since I can't prove it, and there doesn't seem to be any paper trail, I will keep the money, but I am going to invest it in such a way that if we have to return it we have only been using the interest off the money and not the principal. Robyn told me there is a statue of limitations on it and once that time is up, then it's ours regardless. Once we have waited out that limitation time period then we can decide what to do with it from there."

"I agree. That sounds like the safest way to play the cards and still be able to benefit from the money. I guess you have been busy today." she said smiling.

"I'm still not done." And I laughed at the look on her face.

Julie shook her head at me. "I don't know if I can take much more."

"It's been a busy couple of weeks. What I'm about to tell you next is where you staying home with James comes into play." And that got her attention.

"The main reason I Skyped in with Margie was because I got this package in the mail the other day. When I opened it I found a jar of peanut butter."

Julie literally laughed out loud, "A jar of peanut butter?"

"It was an early birthday present." I said smirking.

"One of the strangest you have ever gotten?" she asked.

"You could say that, but then I took a closer look at the jar." I held my finger up and went to the cupboard. I got the jar down, bringing it over to her.

She took the jar from my hand and looked at the label reading it out loud. "'Journey Peanut Butter'," she raised an eyebrow.

"Keep reading." I motioned with my hand.

"Made from organic Mexican peanuts and Wisconsin-produced honey. All proceeds from the sale of this product will be donated to the MAMBOS Foundation in memory and honor of all the families touched by organ donation and transplantation. Life is a journey, savor every mile." At the bottom was the MAMBOS butterfly and green ribbon.

Jules looked up at me, "Wow."

"That's pretty much what I said. She is going to be donating the profits from all sales in the Midwest to MAMBOS. She is also selling it in other parts of the country and will be donating the proceeds to local organ donation chapters in those areas. She is using local producers for the honey from each part of the country to support local agriculture. Her plan is to eventually have a plant in each region of the country that will employ the underserved and the mentally and physically challenged. She has big dreams and I know that she will achieve every one of them."

"That's really amazing, Sugar." Julie was as stunned as I was.

"Because of the money we will get on a steady basis from the sales I've made a decision."

"Okay, bad or good?" She looked worried and I wasn't sure why.

"Good. I think. With the influx of all of this money, **Robyn is going to invest it so that we can afford to pay someone full time to keep the foundation running** for years to come." I watched her face, but she didn't say anything as she fiddled with her cup.

"So are you stepping out of MAMBOS?" she didn't make eye contact.

"Noooo, but I can see that it's too much for us to handle on a part time basis anymore and in the summer you are doing all the work yourself since I am so busy here. I will still stay on and help as much as I can, but I know how hard it was on you this past year trying to do it all yourself and work full time and I didn't even know half of what was going on." And I was still mad at myself about that.

"Sugar, stop, don't even go there." She held her hand up and I sighed.

"All I'm saying is that even though you didn't think I saw what was going on, I did. I knew it was getting to be too much to handle and it was first on my agenda for this winter. You know I have really wanted to have a place once a week where anyone whose life has been touched by organ donation can come in and talk to each other, to a counselor or a nurse and get advice, have a shoulder to cry on or have a cup of coffee and remember a loved one. I have been offered the use of a room free of charge once a week and I want to put some couches in and make it a nice comfortable place for anyone to come and visit. I don't want it to be a support group type situation. I envision it to be a relaxing place where questions can get answered, volunteers can come and sign up and families can just be together. Nothing structured, nothing planned, nothing more than an open door, coffee in the pot, and ears that will listen."

"I think that's a great idea. I get asked all the time if we have something like that. I always direct people to the organ transplant support groups, but sometimes that's not what they need. We have talked about this before and you know I would support it."

"Good. Well I have the couches and a couple of nurses."

"You do?" she asked, surprised.

"I talked to Mom and Lenny about it and since they aren't working in the field anymore they have been looking for something to do. So I convinced them to come in and try to help answer those medical questions that we can't and help navigate families through the system before and after transplants. Mom is going to finish the courses to become a nurse navigator like Lenny is. They are really excited about it."

She smiled, "They will be good at that."

"Yes, they will, so all I need now is a counselor and someone to run the foundation full time. I am hoping to find one person to do both jobs."

"Okay, do you want me to put an ad together and get it out on the website?"

Pregnancy must be affecting her brain. I sat looking at her hoping the light bulb would go on, but apparently the switch was dead.

"No, Julie, I want you. I want you to be the administrator and counselor." I said softly.

She was stunned silent for a moment finally coming out with, "Really? I don't know that's not really my specialty, Sug."

"Your specialty is helping people."

"I'm not so sure about that. I haven't done a very good job of helping you lately."

I sighed then. "Julie, it's really hard to help someone who can't admit that they have a problem. The fact that you stuck by me through the whole cruddy summer and did all the work yourself helped me. The fact that you didn't push me or force me to be something I couldn't be at the time helped me. I knew I was a mess, Julie, I knew it every night when I laid down to sleep and I woke up sobbing. I knew it every time I tried to get excited about something but couldn't. I knew it every time I tried to think about next year, but couldn't see past November tenth. I so badly wanted help, but I didn't think I deserved to ask for it. I didn't know how to say to you, I'm dying inside and I need help. I was afraid to look weak and I certainly didn't want to end up back at the hospital, so I smiled and pretended that I wasn't falling apart." My voice cracked and I took a minute to get myself under control, my voice dropping lower. "But it wasn't all okay. I almost didn't make it, but in the end you fixed it for me. You got me to November eleventh by what you did on November tenth."

"I want to see you happy again. I'm sorry things have been so hard." she said, shrugging her shoulder.

"I'm trying to focus on the things that need focusing on and right now that's you and Jesse and that little baby and MAMBOS. Here is what I want and I will understand if you say no. Don't feel that you can't say no. No pressure, okay?" I raised a brow at her and she nodded again.

"I was hoping that one day a week we open the MAMBOS doors to anyone who wants to come in. I will take care of the baby while you and Mom are there. That way I get time with my new little nephew and you get some time that doesn't involve spit up, drool and diapers." She was tearing up, but she was smiling and I put my hand on hers.

"The rest of the time you can work from home and be with James and I will pay you a salary. It probably won't be what you are making now, but it will be a good supplement to Jesse's income and you won't need to pay daycare. If you are worried about not being prepared to take the counselor role I have found several classes you can take in the coming months to help prepare you and, of course, the foundation will pay for it. I want you to think about it. I know you are the person for the job and it's yours if you want it."

Julie started crying then, serious waterworks, "I'm honored that you think I have done a good enough job the last few years to do it full time."

I laughed, "Good enough job? You raised fifty thousand dollars in one night, Julie!"

Her tears turned to laughter, "Yeah, but you must have earned at least twenty five of it dancing with all those guys!" And it was a lot of dancing, but it was worth every step.

Julie wiped her eyes. "It sounds perfect to me, an answer to my prayer really. I'm going to talk to Jesse about it, but I'm pretty sure that he will be as excited as I am."

"I think so too. He wants you to be happy that much I know."

"He wants you to be happy too, Sugar." And here we go again. Now I say, "but I am happy" and she says, "no you're not, you're miserable". Ugh.

"I am happy. I have everything I could ever want. Not only will you be my best friend, but now you will actually be my sister and you are giving us a little boy who is going to keep us on our toes. Life is good."

"You don't have everything you could ever want and you might as well stop trying to pretend like everything is the same as it was a month ago. It's not and it will never be again. Too much has changed." She said emphasizing the 'much'.

I crossed my arms over my chest, "So, what, now you feel the need to point out how my life sucks because yours doesn't?" And I didn't mean for it to come out that way. I hung my head, "I'm sorry, Julie, that was uncalled for."

And I could feel tears and I was mad and I was sad and I was tired of pretending that I wasn't. She stood up and set her cup in the kitchen sink. I stood up feeling bad that I upset her and not wanting her to go away mad.

"Julie…"

She came over and took my hand, "It's time to talk. Let's go somewhere more comfortable." She dragged me to the living room and sat me down on the couch. "I just meant that it's okay to admit that you want love. You have spent the last eight years denying that you are even a woman much less one who has feelings about men. Your biggest goal was to fade into the background and be the person that everyone knows is there and always counts on, but never approaches. You were *hands off* there was no question about that."

"That wasn't my intention." Yes it was. Who was I kidding?

"Yes it was and I'm not saying that it wasn't what you needed at the time, but times change and it's okay to admit that. You have gone through so much and Jess and I were actually relieved to know that Van was here with you because we didn't know how to help you anymore. Most people who have gone through what you have gone through never make it this far," she held up her hands and motioned around the lodge, "they fade to black and can't deal with what happened. You fought back all those years ago, which told me that you thought life was still worth living. Jess was so upset with himself for adding the stress of the investigation to it that I wasn't sure that he was going to make it through either. He was so afraid we were going to lose you this time. He went through bottles and bottles of Tums and I had to remind him on a daily basis that you are a fighter. I had to promise him that I would step in and risk our friendship if I thought that you were going down, but I didn't have to because your guardian angel brought Van here. He came in here and brought down all those walls that you had built up and he got in there and fixed the parts of you that we couldn't and we are forever grateful to him for healing you and bringing you back to us." Julie patted my hand.

"Van showed me that it was okay to feel again and that it was okay to need someone and that it was okay to accept help. He didn't give me a choice really. I can admit that things have changed Julie, but I don't know what's going to happen now." Julie wiped away a tear from my cheek. "He made me see that I am beautiful and that even with my past I'm still worth being with. He made me feel sexy and he made me feel loved and I didn't realize how badly I needed that."

"You are beautiful and you are sexy and you would have a line out your door if word got out that you were on the market, but you aren't, are you?" She asked.

I shook my head no.

"Because you already gave him your heart, right?"

I nodded.

"But you aren't sure that he gave you his?"

"He tells me he loves me and he knows I love him, but we haven't figured out any of the rest." I said.

"Maybe you should call him or maybe you should use that new iPad and video call him." she said in her best counselor voice.

I flinched. "I don't know if that's a good idea. I know he's busy finishing up the case and I don't want to interfere with that."
Julie blew out a breath, "So how long are you going to sit here and play it safe?"

And it was my turn to blow out a breath, "You don't understand, Julie. My only date before the accident was Brent and you couldn't even call that a date. After the accident it was never easy for me. In the back of my mind I always knew that if things got too serious and I had to, you know," I motioned to my leg, "reveal myself, that I was opening myself up for heartache again. This time I don't have to worry about that. Everything I am is already out there, but if he wants to be with me I want it to be because he chooses me, not because he feels guilty."

Julie had one eyebrow raised like I was speaking Spanish, "I don't follow you, Sugar."

"While he was here it was wonderful. He was so loving and made me feel like the only woman for him, but I'm not the only woman, **Jules.** There are a lot of women out there that are whole and don't have the," I struggled for the word, "issues I have and will have as I get older. If he comes to me I want it to be because he wants to be with me, not because he feels that I pressured him into doing it. Calling him and trying to video call him isn't going to give him the space he needs to decide what he wants. Does that make sense?"

She rolled her eyes. "Oh yes, it makes total sense to me now. Your self esteem sucks, that's what makes sense to me. I mean it's totally in the toilet. You honestly think that if you call him that he's going to think that you're pressuring him? Maybe he will think, "Oh she loves me and she misses me." Have you ever thought of that? Maybe he will want to figure out a way to get back here and hold you in his arms if he actually hears your voice instead of reading some stupid text message." Her hands were flailing around and she was talking loudly. Wow. Pregnancy was really affecting her brain. The little voice in my head whispered that she was probably right, but I told it to shut up.

I took a deep breath, "I'm letting him set the tone. He has my phone number and it works both ways, Julie. It's the way it has to be."

"No, it's the way you think it has to be! For the love of Pete girl! Okay, fine if that's the way you want it." She flopped back down on the couch. I stared at her not sure I wanted to open my mouth. Pregnancy seemed to be causing her some emotional upheaval.

"I'm going to go home and talk to Jess about MAMBOS." She pulled me into a hug and I felt her soften a little bit as she hugged me. "Think about what I said, okay? Maybe you would feel better if you heard his voice. I'm sure he's not at the station at midnight." And she was right, but I was chicken. I nodded anyway.

She stood up and I reluctantly joined her. "Jess and I will pick you up at six for your birthday." I held up my hand to object, but she refused to have any of it. "It's just a burger and a beer at the Brewhouse with us and Sharon and Lenny. No big deal I promise."

"Alright that I can handle. Call me and tell me what Jess says about the foundation job. I want to get rolling on it as soon as I can." She assured me she would and she left out the front door leaving me with nothing but the sound of my own thoughts. I flipped on the stereo and Enrique filled the room.

God bless music.

FIFTY-SIX

The rest of the day was spent digging out my Christmas decorations from the basement so I could get a feel for what I had and what I needed to pick up. Every year the ballroom and lodge were decorated to the hilt and ready for all the parties and fun that happened during December. This year I wasn't in the mood for Christmas. I wasn't in the mood for the parties and I had canceled the usual Friday night parties for the month. I claimed that I needed more time to heal before I could do it and promised a full month of parties in January and everyone understood, or at least they said they did. I also knew that I needed to have the ballroom decorated for a wedding and not having to take down Christmas to put up a wedding would make things simpler. That was my excuse anyway, but I knew the real reason why. My phone rang and I checked the caller ID, not willing to admit that I was disappointed to see Jess's number.

"Hey, how's my favorite brother?" I asked, **stepping off the stool I was on trying to reach the rest of the boxes.**

"I'm your only brother."

"And that makes you my favorite."

"Well your favorite brother is calling to talk."

"About?" I asked him cautiously.

"Your MAMBOS offer."

"It was just an offer, Jess. I will understand if it isn't something you guys want to commit to."

"Not something we want to commit to? Sugar, I couldn't be happier! I wasn't sure how I was going to approach the whole I don't want **you to work once the baby comes topic without getting her dander up and making her dig her heels in more."** And I could see him shaking his head.

I laughed. "You guys gotta communicate better."

"I know, but she's been a little, what's the word?" **he paused.**

"Touchy?" I threw out there.

He chuckled. "Well that's a good start. I wanted her to make the decision on her own and come to me instead of the other way around."

"I can understand that. So is the answer yes?" I finally asked.

"Yes, yes, yes! That's a yes from every one of us here. Once again **you always find a way to take care of everyone you love, Sis."**

"I was being a little selfish, **Jess. I need her to keep MAMBOS** running smoothly, she's the only one I trust. I'm really excited that she's gonna be here for me, I mean the foundation, and in the process it helps you guys. That makes it a win-win for all of us."

"Julie is here for you anytime you need her, Sis." Darn, he caught my slip up.

"I know." I said softly.

"She's napping or I would let you talk to her now."

"No, she needs the rest and I'm good. Tell her I love her."

"I will. I love you too, Sis, you know that right?"

"Yeah, I know that." I told him I loved him and we hung up.

I showered and heated up a TV dinner. I wasn't hungry, but there was something about the order of how your day was supposed to go that made me do it. After a bite or two I dumped it in the garbage pail and went to my office to check email. I had checked my phone a thousand more times, but there was no message. I wanted to pick up the phone and call him, but I was afraid to. It was that simple. If I heard his voice would I be able to keep going on like this? I had all but made my decision that I was going to fly down to Texas on Monday.

I had nothing pressing until closer to the holidays and that would leave me two weeks to be with him before coming back here for Christmas and the wedding. That was as far as I could look into the future right now. Maybe what we needed was some time in his environment to see if we could make it work someplace other than here. And maybe I was making a mistake, but then again maybe Julie was right and it was what he needed. Maybe he needed to see that I would meet him halfway. If he needed to see that I was willing to give up the lodge to be with him then that is what I would show him. I went out to the porch swing in my parka and sat down not minding the biting cold and the brisk wind. It was late, almost ten, but I wasn't tired. I needed to hear his voice. I picked up my phone and dialed waiting for him to answer.

His voicemail picked up and I heard, "You have reached the voicemail of Donovan Walsh. I will be unavailable until December fifth. Please leave a message and I will get back to you as soon as possible. P.S. If this is Sugar, I still love you."

I heard a beep and said, "'**Austin**', Blake Shelton, I'm not dancing right now. Call me when you get this. I'm leaving for Texas on Monday the fifth. I need to be with you, no matter where that is. I don't know if you are feeling the same way, but all I know is that I love you and I can hardly breathe without you. Okay, well, bye." And I hung up, took a deep breath and I knew that I had made the right decision.

God bless best friends.

FIFTY-SEVEN

And then again maybe I didn't make the right decision. I hadn't heard back from him at all today. No usual text, no flowers, no phone call, nothing. I didn't buy my tickets deciding that last minute was as good as planning it. What if he wasn't available? I didn't want to show up when he was still tied up with the case. Better to let him call me. Chicken, the little voice said. I took another drink of my coffee until it faded out. It was five o'clock on my birthday and Jess and Julie would be here soon. My heart hurt. I tried to convince myself that he was "unavailable" because of the case and he would text me soon or call or something. But if that didn't happen my backup plan for the night was to get drunk and then come home and pass out. Mature it wasn't, but I was going with it. It was better than feeling the way I felt all day. Of course it didn't take much to get me drunk, a glass or two of wine, a couple of beers or one mixed drink and I'd be stumbling around. But I was determined to tie one on so I couldn't think tonight and tomorrow I would be too miserable to care.

I looked at my watch. Jess and Julie would be here in a few minutes and I was looking pretty hot in my new low-cut scoop neck sweater I had gotten from Sharon earlier today. It accentuated my now ample bosom, thanks to my Miracle Bra. It flared at the waist where it met my black pencil skirt with a slit up the side. My leg was dressed up in its fabulousness and my feet were stuffed into a pair of Danskin jazz shoes with open toes. It might be December and it might be cold, but I was going full out tonight. It's my birthday and it's my party. I took a couple of steps to test out my legs, but quickly plunked back down in the chair wondering how I was going to get to the car without falling over. Maybe I could lean on Jess, he wouldn't mind. I heard the car pull up in the driveway and I slammed back the rest of the coffee, set the mug on the table, grabbed my coat and stumbled to the front door. I threw the door open before they had a chance to knock.

"Hi guys." Only it sounded like, "Hi githssss."

I saw Julie give Jess an eyebrow and they stepped in the door, backing me up. I nearly fell over backwards.

"Whoopsies, careful there, cowboy, my leg's a little wobbly tonight."

Jess was smirking and Julie was shaking her head.

389

"What?" I was trying to get my coat on and kept missing the sleeve the damn thing dancing out from behind me at every turn.

"Um, Sugar," Jess paused long enough to grab my sleeve and help me stuff my arm in it. "I don't think it's just your leg that's wobbly. How much have you had to drink?"

I gave him 'who me' hands. "A couple of Gitche Gumee Gobblers. What took you guys so long to get here?"

Julie shot Jess another look and he said, "We're early and what the hell is a Gitche Gumee Gobbler?"

I rolled my eyes at him. Doesn't everyone know what a Gitche Gumee Gobbler is? "Really? Haven't you ever had one? Oh you gotta have one! Come on I'll make you one." I tried to drag him into the kitchen with me, but he stood his ground and I nearly toppled over.

"I don't want one, I want to know what it is." he said, a sparkle dancing through his eye.

"It's Fitger's Crème Liqueur coffee with a shot of Irish cream and a shot of Kahlua and whipped cream on the top. The good kind that comes out of the can all spirally." I made the motion with my hand. Now that I was thinking about it I wanted another one.

Julie was biting her lip and Jess was shaking his head. "So basically it's coffee with a bunch of booze, why is it called a gobbler?"

Men, you must explain everything in detail. "Because you want to gobble it up its so good, silly pants."

And I fell backwards and grabbed the couch before I landed on my butt. The coffee was supposed to keep you sober while the alcohol made you buzzed, but it didn't seem to be working out that way.

"I think it's time to go." Jess said.

"Me too, let's get this party started." I took a couple cha-cha steps towards the door. "You're driving right?" I asked him over my shoulder.

Jess laughed, "Uh yeah."

I leaned on him, heavily, as we went down the stairs and piled into his Blazer. He took Second Street into Superior stopping at McDonald's for a large coffee and a cheeseburger.

He handed it back to me, "Eat this and then drink that."

"But Jess we are going for dinner and you don't want to spoil my appetite. Mom would get mad." I pouted in the back seat refusing to take the coffee.

"Sugar, Mom's gonna kick my arse if I bring you to dinner drunk. Now eat the damn burger!"

"Jeez, what's got your cacks in a wad? And I am not drunk! I had a couple of drinks for my birthday. Is that against the law now, Officer Jesse?"

"Cacks in a wad?" he asked, rather put out.

"Yeah, cacks in a wad, knickers in a twist, undies in a bundle, pants..."

"I get it!" he snapped.

Julie's shoulders were shaking and I could hear her laughing. I know she thought she was being so cool, but I could still hear her.

"I hear you laughing at me, Jules. And I'm not drunk!"

Jess leveled an eye at me and I started to giggle. "Okay, maybe I'm a little drunk. But that's okay, right? It's my birthday! I can get drunk on my birthday, that's like the birthday rule isn't it? It's okay to get drunk on your birthday." I was sure I had read that somewhere.

That cheeseburger was smelling really good and Jess was still holding it over the seat. I took it from his hands. "That smells really good, just a couple bites won't hurt, but don't tell Mom cause she will be all 'Sugar, why aren't you hungry? You need to eat!'"

And I took a bite of the cheeseburger and it was so good. It tasted like heaven. So then of course I had to wash it down with the coffee cause you can't eat a whole cheeseburger without drinking something, it just isn't possible. Then I realized that we weren't moving.

"Jess."

"Yes, Sugar?"

"Why aren't we moving?" I looked out the window and, yep, we were still sitting in McDonald's parking lot.

"Because I want you to be able to walk into the restaurant without falling down, so I'm waiting until the coffee and the cheeseburger hit your gut and you sober up."

I crossed my arms and harrumphed at him, "Man, you go and get engaged and you start acting like Officer No Fun."

He rolled his eyes.

"I saw that. I can see you in the mirror you know."

Julie excused herself to use the bathroom at that point running into McDonald's before her pregnant bladder exploded, which made me start to giggle at the image. Jess turned on the radio to fill the silence or maybe so he didn't have to talk to me and I jammed to Guns n' Roses in the backseat. It seemed like forever before Julie rolled back in, but she had a shake and handed it back so I forgave her for holding up the show.

"Thanks, you're so sweet." And I took a couple of sucks off the straw and got an ice cream headache. Jess put the car back into gear and drove slowly, like serious 'grandpa can't see over the dashboard and it's a blizzard out' slow, to Fitger's. By the time we got there I was starting to feel less fuzzy and was unhappily able to remember why I had started drinking to begin with.

"This sucks." I said.

Julie flipped around. "Excuse me?"

"I said this sucks."

She rolled her eyes, "I heard what you said. I want to know why you said it."

"Because now that I'm sober again I remember why I started drinking and I think I want a beer. No a whiskey sour, no I don't like whiskey. How about a tequila sunrise or wait, no, sloe gin. Yeah, sloe gin and Diet Coke, let me out, Henry, I need a drink." Jess hit the door locks and looked in the rearview mirror.

"Sugar, I don't know if we can use the word sober yet to describe you. Why did you start drinking, we never established that. You don't normally drink, so I'm sure you had a perfectly good reason." And I did.

"Because your wife told me to call a certain someone," I put emphasis on that word and looked at Julie, "and I did and I haven't heard from him since I acted the maggot and left a message telling him I was coming to Texas tomorrow." Stupid, that's what it was, stupid.

I saw Jess mouth "acted the maggot" to Julie.

"Yeah acting the maggot. Haven't you ever heard that before Jess? It means being stupid, you know acting the maggot, jeez."

Julie piped in. "I'm not his wife yet."

I waved my hand, "Whatever, semantics my friend."

"You know just because you haven't heard from him doesn't mean that he's acting the maggot." He gave Julie a high five and grinned.

"Funny. Very funny, glad you are enjoying my unhappiness on my birthday, Jess." I crossed my arms over my chest and refused to look at him.

"Oh come on, Tula. Promise me you will go in there and have a good attitude? We are going to have a lot of fun and we want you sober so you can remember it." He gave me his award winning I'm the best brother in the world smile.

Tula. Nice. Fine, I'd sneak some shots when he wasn't looking. I huffed out a breath. "Fine, yeah whatever. Let's go get this over with."

Jess grinned at Julie and unlocked the doors. We tumbled out into the night and I fell flat on my keister. I knew it was gonna be a long night.

God bless sloe gin.

FIFTY-EIGHT

We stepped inside the front door of Fitger's and went up the ramp to the Brewhouse. Patrick was seating guests tonight and I waved as we approached.

"Hey Patrick!" He came over and gave me a birthday hug and I asked him where my birthday beer was.

"Sugar!" Jess said sharply.

"What?" I was laughing though and so was he. Patrick assured me there was plenty of birthday beer, but there was no place to sit in the restaurant. I looked around him through the door at the three people eating a burger. It looked like a ghost town.

"Umm, Patrick there is no one in there."

"True, not right now anyway, but we are closed for a private party, so...."

"So...... I really wanted a fish wrap." I said.

Patrick looked back at the restaurant and then at Jess. He held up his finger. "You know what, it's Sunday so the Red Star is closed to the public. Why don't you guys grab a booth and I will let you eat over there, but don't tell the brew master. He gets all uptight about that." He winked at me then.

I pretended to zip my lip. "Not a word, I promise."

Patrick grabbed the key and we walked across the hall to the Red Star. You wouldn't actually know that this club was here. It just looked like part of the wall that ran the length of the hallway. That is, of course, unless you were here on a Saturday night then there would be no question. He pulled open the door and ushered me in, the thought that we needed some light barely entering my mind before they snapped on and about a fifty of my friends jumped out and yelled surprise. I was standing there in utter shock not having suspected a thing.

"Are you kidding me with this? What happened to a burger and a beer?" I was laughing because Sharon and Lenny were there and had on those dumb party hats with the little sparkles that bounce around on the top and they looked like total dorks. I took three more steps in and lookie there, the bar. It spread out before with a plethora of poisons to choose from. There had to be at least twenty shelves of the best poison in town.

393

"She's looking for her birthday beer Martin!" Patrick yelled, "Give her a good one!"

I love that guy. I looked over at Jesse and Julie and they were looking sheepish. "What the hell! Let's party!" I yelled and the crowd cheered and the music started.

"Hey Martin, how about skipping that beer and giving me a long slow comfortable screw up against the wall."

Martin's eyes popped out of his head. "Excuse me, Sugar?!"

I leaned over and whispered, "The drink Martin, the drink. Only skip the cherry. I want Officer Prohibition over there to think its orange juice." I winked at him.

He laughed out loud then and made the drink keeping an eye out on who was watching him doing the pouring. He handed me the glass and I gave him a kiss on the cheek, thanked him and told him to keep 'em coming.

I saw Sharon making her way over and she pulled me into a hug. "Hi birthday girl, thought you were never going to get here."
I laughed, "Well I'm here so all is well."

Sharon whispered in my ear, "Come over to the table. I have something for you." She had already given me my birthday present, so I couldn't imagine what it could be.

We walked to the table and there was a box sitting there. I opened it and found a wrist corsage with three white tea roses mixed with greens. I took it out and slipped it on my wrist. There was a card that said, "May be surrounded by a million people I still feel all alone. I just wanna go home. Oh, I miss you, you know."

"Michael Bublé, 'Home'." I whispered.

"Is it from him?" Sharon asked shyly.

"If I know him this is his way of making sure all the special people in my life are with me tonight. Except him." My heart didn't feel so heavy anymore and I felt like I didn't blow it completely with the phone call. I literally let out a breath I didn't know I was holding.

Jess and Julie came up and Jess slipped an arm around me whispering in my ear, "Looks like you got drunk for nothing."

I punched him then, hard, but he just grabbed his arm and laughed at me. The four of them led me out of the bar area and through the doorway where the DJ sat in his booth. The Red Star was long and narrow and the back of the club was covered in long booth-type seating, black leather seats and various animal prints on the backrests, leopard, lion you name it and they wrapped around making each one a booth like area to sit and well, drink. The walls were old brick and stone and the overall feeling was that you were in the basement of an old speakeasy and you expected a gangster like Al Capone to come walking through the door. The DJ sat in a booth so high up you had to climb a ladder to reach him or jump really high while trying to talk to him.

We took the booth in the middle of the room and I heard the DJ break in as the song finished. "I see that the birthday girl has arrived. This ones for you, Ms. Sugar." I looked up and realized that the DJ was Dan, one of my former students who was now a junior at UMD. He also did DJ work for me in the summer. The music started and it was Hot Chelle Rae with "Tonight, Tonight". Jess pulled me up and hauled me over to the dance floor where we did a very odd version of the swing, joining the group with "Just don't stop let's keep the beat pumping, Keep the beat up, lets drop the beat down. It's my party dance if I want to. We can get crazy let it all out." And that's exactly how I felt. It was my party and I could get as crazy as I wanted to except that my side started to hurt before the song finished and I made my way back to the table.

"You okay?" Sharon asked as I sat down.

"Yeah, I'm a little out of shape after, you know, everything. Dr. Mueller said it might take a couple months to get back to full speed. I think I better try a slower song."

And I wasn't lying, but I also really wasn't in the mood to dance. I reached for my glass and it was empty, bummer. Well that was solved easy enough.

I leaned over, "Hey I'll be right back." And I went to the bar. Martin was filling my glass before I got there sliding it across the table.

"Put it on my tab." I yelled.

He shook his head, "Nope I'm putting it on Jesse's!" I gave him a thumbs up because that was perfect. Annie Lennox was "Walking On Broken Glass" as I walked back onto the dance floor and I did a cha-cha to the booth before sitting down and watching my students trip the light fantastic. Patrick personally brought in my fish wrap and it smelled so good. What isn't good about trout, wild rice and cheese wrapped up in a hot garlic tortilla? Oh yeah, I remember, the icky tomatoes. I waited for him to leave and then picked them out while Sharon shook her head at me.

"What? It's my birthday!" And I wasn't eating tomatoes. There were onion rings and beer battered fries to go along with it and my stomach was feeling funky. Every time I tried to get up, the floor met me. Time to find some coffee.

Jess leaned over, "What's in that orange juice?"

I gave him my I don't know what you are talking about look. "Pulp?"

"Nice try, Sugar. Martin ratted you out. He was getting a little concerned that you were going to fall down on his watch and smash your head on the concrete. I'm cutting you off."

Just what I needed -- another father. "Fine, whatever, Daddy. I already decided I'd had enough for your information. I can't decide if I want to barf or pass out." And I was leaning towards barfing, on him.

He smiled at me and magically a cup of very strong, very black, very yummy smelling Fitger's coffee appeared in front of me.

I raised a brow at him, "Nope, sorry, it's straight." I belted it back and he was right, bummer. "You always were a cheap drunk." I punched him, hard.

"Falling For You" came on and I saw Becca and Aaron head for the dance floor. I started hooting and chanting "Becca, Becca" and she was totally embarrassed. And as usual as soon as they began to dance everyone fell away and we all watched as they told their story to us in dance. I was cheering and whistling at the end as Aaron dipped her and I jumped up to tell them they rocked but had to grab Jesse's shoulder to keep from tipping over. When I finally made it over to them I had to ask them what the heck they were doing in a bar. They pointed at their moms in the corner and I waved going over to say hi for a few minutes and to apologize for the few cancelled lessons, but it didn't look like it mattered much to the kids. They had the routine nailed.

I heard the first few bars of "I'll Be" said goodbye to them and went back over to the booth, but Jess grabbed my hand. "Come waltz with me." he said.

"I don't know if I can, Jess, I'm not in very good shape yet." He looked at me under a brow, "Sugar, it's me, I know three moves, you'll be fine."

He pulled me out and I discovered that it was a little difficult to do the Viennese waltz in the Red Star, not much room to get any momentum going before you ran into a booth or the wall. Jess led me back to the table and pulled Julie up for a slow dance. I sat there watching my students and old friends dancing to the music. Julie and Jess were slow dancing to "Bridge Over Troubled Water", the original version with Garfunkel and then as I sobered up I realized that I had heard "Walking On Broken Glass", "Open Arms", "Just The Way You Are", "Falling For You" and "'65 Mustang". I excused myself and made my way to the DJ booth, opening the door and hauling my half sober hiney up the metal ladder, so glad no one was paying attention.

Dan leaned over and I yelled "Hey Dan, how's it going?"

"Great, Ms. Sugar, how about yourself? Enjoying your birthday?" He had his headphones down around his neck.

"Yeah, it's been great. Hey Dan, who's picking the music tonight?"

"What?" He asked cupping his ear.

"I said, who's picking the music?" I was trying not to yell too loud and I knew he could hear me.

"Oh the music? It's a combination of requests, fan favorites and recent hits!"

"Really?" Bridge Over Troubled Water" is a fan favorite?" I yelled.

"I guess so -- it was on the sign up sheet!" He gave me thumbs up and put his headphones back up over his ears doing his DJ thing.

I rolled my eyes and half jumped half fell back down the ladder to the floor. I was starting to feel like the coffee was making quick work of the sloe gin and vodka and I wasn't feeling half bad by the time the next song come on. It was "Hot Coffee". For the love of God, really? That song is decades old. But the next couple of songs really did me in. Dan hit me with Michael Bublé's "Lost" and then "Hold On" and I was up and out the doors at the first few bars of "Good Morning Beautiful". I couldn't take much more.

I sat down on the bench around the corner of the club trying to take a deep breath, but the food sat like lead in my belly and my head spun around like a little kid's top. Even the usual sunny yellow brightness on the walls didn't make my heart feel any lighter. I was not only a heartsick birthday girl, but I was a drunk heartsick birthday girl and there is nothing more pathetic than that. I needed to call a cab and go home because I wasn't going back in the club for more torture. I was about to go get my phone when I heard Gordon Lightfoot singing about the wreck of the Edmund Fitzgerald. I jumped up off the bench and ran up the ramp to the bathroom where I didn't have to hear the music, nearly tipping over the railing on the way up.

The bathroom was empty, thank God for small favors, and I sat in a stall and sucked in air to ward off puking. I had done enough of that in the last few weeks and didn't care to do it again. The little voice in my head was telling me to get on a plane and find him and it was the first time I felt like listening to it in a very long time. I gave it ample time for the song to be over and then I went to the bathroom mirror, washing my face and hands, fixing my hair out of habit, and giving myself the pep talk of a lifetime. "You are going to go home and pack a bag and get a flight to Texas. You are going to find him and tell him how you feel and that you are ready to do whatever you have to do to be with him. You will not walk away from him until you know how he feels and you will not cry like a baby if he tells you that he needs more time and you will not fall apart if he tells you he has changed his mind. You are a strong independent woman who doesn't need a man to feel worthwhile. You are a successful business woman who has made it this far in life without a man and can certainly muddle through without him. You are woman."

Yeah right. The only part that was actually going to happen was the me going home and getting a flight to Texas. The rest probably wasn't going to go down like that, but hey, I've surprised myself before. I blew out a breath at the tired looking face in the mirror and spun on my heel leaving the bathroom with a plan.

I walked down the ramp carefully because the tilt of the floor was still not quite level when you took into account all the booze I had drank. I was working my way back to the club for a ride home so I could get my car and leave for the airport. If I couldn't get a flight out then I'd point the car south and start driving. As I came around the corner I heard "You Send Me" and I stood frozen in time as I listened to the words of the song we had danced to that night. The song that made me remember the childish glee that filled his face when he found the *Sam Cooke* album, the song that made me remember him, sexy as hell, as he danced the foxtrot with me and how it wasn't infatuation that night, it was and is love. I instinctively climbed into the window bay that allowed sunshine into the old brewery by day, but by night was black as a shadow. It enveloped me as I sat with my back against the window and put my head in my hands telling myself it was my birthday, I could cry if wanted to.

"Sugar? Sugar?"

I could hear Sharon calling me as she came up the ramp and I let her walk right by as she headed into the bathroom. It didn't take long and she was coming back again looking more worried than the first time she walked by. I put my head back in my hands and sat still hoping that I would blend into the night and she wouldn't see me in my current state of affliction.

"Sugar?" I looked up and Sharon was blocking out what little light was left from the hallway. What is it about mothers? It's like they have a sixth sense or something when it comes to their kids.

I smiled a sad smile and tossed my hands palms up in the air. "Hi Mom." My voice broke and she knelt on the window ledge.

"Sugar, honey, what is going on? Why are you so upset?" Sharon looked very worried and her eyes were darting around like she was expecting a serial killer at any moment.

"I'm a mess, Mom. I have to go home. I need a ride." I was hiccup talking and didn't know that I was making a lot of sense.

"Of course, honey." She handed me a tissue. "Did something happen to upset you?" And those simple words from the most important woman in my life had me sobbing like a four year old who fell off her bike.

"Yeah something happened alright, Mom. I fell in love with a man who lives over a thousand miles away from me."

Sharon pulled me to her rubbing my back and whispering it was going to be okay, even though she didn't now that it was. "I thought you were having a good time. You seemed like it anyway, other than the fact that you had too much to drink." Sharon said a bit disapprovingly.

"You noticed?" I hiccuped again.

Sharon laughed really hard, "Sugar, you couldn't walk in a straight line and the whole "my legs not adjusted right" wasn't working for you. I've seen you walk better with your leg on backwards." And that got her a smile.

"I really can't deal with the not knowing anymore, Mom. I have to get on a plane and fly to Texas or drive all night long if that is what I have to do, but I have to do this."

"And then what?" she asked quietly.

"I don't know then what. I need to know if he still wants to be with me, Mom, because I want to be with him and as much as I hate to admit it I can't even breathe I need him so bad."

"I have no doubt in my mind that he still wants to be with you." She said, smoothing my hair out of my face.

"Well I'm glad you're so sure. I wish I was." I dropped my hands into my lap and Sharon put an arm around me pulling me out towards the ledge putting my feet down on the floor and pulling me up.

"It'll all work out, Sugar. Just trust in time."

The hallway was quiet and I was praying that meant the DJ was taking a break so I could sneak in and say goodbye. Sharon and I started walking down the ramp when I heard Dan say, "This one goes out to Julie." And Uncle Kracker broke into "Smile".

I whipped around going back to the window and climbing in pinning Sharon with a glare. "What is going on, Mom? This is insane! Every song I've heard since we got here is somehow tied to the time I spent with him."

"Sugar, it's always that way when you are missing someone you love, every song reminds you of them." She said in her best mother tone, but she looked nervous to me or guilty.

I shook my head. "No, Mom, I mean literally every song has a direct relation to a memory for me." Sharon looked skeptical.

"No, I'm serious. "Walking on Broken Glass"? "Open Arms"? "You Send Me"? "Bridge Over Troubled Water"? I mean who even knows those songs anymore?" I motioned out at the bar, "And this song! Van sang this song to me in the car the day after the foundation dinner right before my whole world blew up." My voice dropped and I took a breath letting my hands drop.

Sharon twisted her hands together. "I'm sure it's just coincidence, Sugar."

"Sure it's a coincidence. Let's see... the next song that plays ought to be what, "Bless the Broken Road". I swear to God if I hear that I'm pulling the plug." And now I was angry.

She glanced nervously towards the door. "Come on, it's your birthday and you haven't even cut the cake yet."

"No," I held up my hand, "I can't do this anymore. I need to go home. Can you take me home? If you can't take me home I'll call a cab."

Sharon shook her head soothing me, "Okay, Sugar, okay, I will take you home, but will you stay long enough to cut the cake? Please?"

"Yeah, please?" It was Jess and he was walking up the ramp towards us. "Hey birthday girl, was wondering where you got off to. Are you okay?" He looked about as guilty as Sharon.

I nodded, "Yeah I'm okay, but I'm going home." I told him what I had told Sharon, but that I would be back in a week to finish the wedding plans.

"This is something I have to do." I said, ending my speech.

"We understand, Sugar. It's cool, really, but first let's cut the cake and then we can distract the crowd with it while you leave. Deal?"

I shrugged, "Deal."

I stood up. They each took an arm and we walked back down the brick ramp, pulling open the doors to the club. Jesse went off to find Patrick and I made a halfhearted attempt to visit with a couple more friends from a different dance studio, declining their offer to buy me a drink telling them I was getting ready to call it a night. Thankfully at that moment Patrick came in carrying a beautifully decorated butterfly shaped cake with twenty-eight lit candles.

I took a deep breath, made a wish and blew out the candles as the crowd began to sing, "Happy birthday to you, happy birthday to you, happy birthday dear, Sugar, happy birthday to you." And I froze because the hair was standing up on the back of my neck and the temperature in the room had gone up a few degrees.

I heard a deep baritone sing, "Happy birthday Mi Mot, happy birthday Mi Mot, happy birthday, happy birthday, happy birthday Mi Mot." And his arms came around my waist and he whispered in my ear, "Hey baby, sorry I'm late."

My legs ceased to hold me up at that point. He pulled me up, turned me around, and kissed me and it was like he had never been gone. The crowd clapped and hooted and I clung to him like he was a mirage, certain I was dreaming or in a drunken coma. I was touching his face and I knew he was real and suddenly I realized that everyone was in on this. I looked over at Sharon and Jess and they were smiling ear to ear and Jules was crying, sobbing actually, and I started laughing at her because she was soooo pregnant! Suddenly everyone was around us, hugging us and slapping Van on the back, welcoming him home. I liked the sound of that word.

"This song goes out to the birthday girl from the man who found the right road." Dan hit the lights down and Rascal Flatts began singing "Bless The Broken Road" and I started laughing almost uncontrollably.

Van led me to the dance floor and pulled me into him. "I heard you weren't dancing, so I had to come back and find out why." He whispered in my ear.

"Don't ever leave me again." I said crying again.

"I'm sorry baby, I'm sorry. Never again." He pulled me into him and he stuck his hands in my back pockets and kissed me, thoroughly.

"I've missed you." he said his voice husky, "You fill my dreams and I wake up in pain for you. When this song is over I'm taking you home and making love to you for the rest of the night."

"Are you really here?" I asked him reaching up and trailing a finger down his cheekbone.

He leaned in and took me for a longer kiss and then started to sing. "Now I'm just rolling home into my lover's arms. This much I know is true. That God blessed the broken road that led me straight to you." And we danced until there was no music. He was really here.

I looked up into his swirling green eyes, "Take me home, Bond."

"Mmmm gladly."

FIFTY-NINE

I woke up slowly stretching and smiling to myself. I rolled over and snuggled in closer to Van who stirred next to me. I wasn't dreaming -- he was here and he was in my bed.

"Good morning beautiful." And it was a good morning. It was an even better last night.

We left the party after making everyone promise to keep partying and to eat my cake, assuring them that I was going to have my cake and eat it too. Van drove me back home to the lodge in his big old Texas truck and I sat next to him my head on his shoulder as he told me about the case. With McElevain dead, they managed to shut down the largest marijuana growing plantation in Mexico and in doing so stopped a massive amount of it from entering the United States. I could tell he was proud to be part of that. Margie and Nathan's testimony put the final nail in the coffin of the other partners and they were all facing prison time. They had cleaned house on the plantation and the States side of things and were working with US Immigration to hire documented immigrants for their factories in the US, as well as a new plantation manager. I had talked to Margie and she was excited about running the operation her way and planned to go back and forth between Mexico and the US to make sure that things were being run the way she wanted. Edward's brother, Margie's real father, had been cleared of any charges and it looked like he was nothing more than a pawn to McElevain too. Margie showed him the papers she found regarding her paternity and he told her he always wondered, but was too afraid to challenge his brother. He was all too happy to turn the plantation over to Margie and to spend the rest of his life being her father. He was going to help her with getting the factories set up in the US for the new peanut butter. I was happy for them. They had been through a lot at the hands of Edward and they deserved to reap the benefits.

Van told me he had been promoted to lead task force detective in the division of drug trafficking, but I didn't ask him any questions. I didn't want to ruin how good the moment felt. I listened to him talk and held onto him, letting his scent wrap around me and his warmth remind me that he was real. He pulled into the lodge and we tumbled out of the truck and into my bedroom. He made love to me then with barely contained passion and then held me and kissed me and told me how much he missed me. Then he took me to the shower and we made love again, and again in bed, and again and again, but we never spoke about the past or the future. We held each other and pretended like it was all okay and that nothing else mattered but what was happening at that exact moment. I looked out the window and the sun was shining and it was Monday morning. I knew that the darkness of the night was gone and with it the ability to keep from saying what had to be said.

"You want some coffee?" I asked him, my face buried in his neck.

"Nope, I just want you." And he rolled over and his eyes were smoky.

"If I didn't know better I'd think you missed me, Mr. Bond."

He pulled back and ran his hand down the length of my face tucking my hair behind my ears. "No I didn't miss you, Ms. DuBois. I ached for you. Everywhere I went and everything I did all I could think about was if you were okay and I wondered if you felt the same way." His lips found mine and he kissed me gently, "I don't ever want to ache like that again."

"Me either." I whispered.

Then his mouth was on my nipple and his thigh was between mine and he was hard, everywhere. His hands were wandering and he easily found his way to that spot, the spot that always left me breathless and begging for him to be in me. This time I didn't have to beg. I reached down and stroked him until his breath caught in his throat and then he stilled and slipped inside me and began a slow dance as my eyes rolled back in my head and I forgot all about the sun and I forgot all about it being Monday and I forgot all about talking. We slowly came back down to earth wrapped in each other's arms and completely exhausted.

"Damn." He swore softly in my ear and lifted his head up pulling out of me and sitting up.

"What?"

He ran a hand through his hair. "You make me forget my mind when you touch me and I forgot a raincoat."

The sentence hung in the air.

"One time isn't a big deal." I stammered.

"Yes, it is a big deal. I don't want...."

"A baby with me?" I scooted up to the headboard and pulled the sheet up around me. "Take my word for it, there won't be a baby, that window is closed for another month." He looked relieved and I looked away.

"Would having a baby with me be that bad?" I tried to say it very matter of fact, but I failed.

He looked over at me and his eyes softened. He crawled back up to me and laid his head on my belly. "No having a baby with you would not be that bad. Having a baby with you would be amazing. Having a baby

403

with you would be a lot of fun." He wagged his eyebrows at me. "I just want to do things right."

I stroked his hair, running my fingers through it absently, "Well if that is what sex is like without a condom after I'm done at the real estate agent's, I'm going to the doctor." He growled and pulled himself up and started to kiss me, but then stopped short and pulled back.

"What do you mean after the real estate agent? Why are you going to a real estate agent?"

"I'm putting the lodge up for sale." In other words I'm going all in.

"What? You aren't serious, are you?" He was up off the bed now looking for his clothes. He pulled on his boxers and then his jeans leaving them hanging open at the waist. He ran his hand through his hair and paced in front of the bed.

"No, I'm dead serious. I'm selling the lodge."

"What are you talking about? Why are you selling?" And I was getting the impression that was not what he wanted me to do.

"Because I'm moving to Texas to be with you?" And it came out more like a question than a statement. He stopped pacing then and his arms hung at his side.

"Tula, what are you talking about? I'm here." He was motioning with his arms up and down his body like I couldn't see that with my own two eyes.

"I can see that Van, but you aren't staying and I need to be where you are. Up until about thirty seconds ago I thought you felt the same way. You told me that you got a big promotion and I know that if we are going to be together then I'm going to have to sell the lodge."

He had a look on his face that was somewhere between disbelief and shock. I swung my legs over the bed and grabbed my clothes from last night pulling them on and rolling my liner and leg on. He was silent and I didn't know what that meant. I came around the bed and put my hand on his chest.

"I know some people down near Dallas that can hook me up with a dance studio and I can teach there. It'll work out. This is just a building." I shrugged my shoulder as way of making that sound true.

"No, it won't work out and this is not just a building. This is Sugar's, this is you. What about Jesse and Julie? What about little baby James who is going to need his Aunt Sugar? What about Sharon? What about MAMBOS?" And now he was going to make me cry.

"I don't know okay!" Cue hand flailing. I fought back the tears. "I don't have all the answers. I don't know how I'm going to leave this town and everybody I love, but I love you more. I don't know how I'm going to sell this house and the memories of my childhood, but if that is what it takes to be with you then I will sign those papers because ultimately without you here it means nothing to me anyway. When you aren't here I don't breathe. I love you more than all of this." I motioned around the house. "So I don't have all the answers okay? I just don't." And my hands fell to my sides and a tear escaped over my eyelash and I stood there more tears rolling down my cheeks.

"God I love you." He pulled me into him then and hugged me and it felt like a good thing. He directed me over to my window where his truck was parked in the driveway.

"I want to show you something. You see that truck?"

I wiped a hand under each eye. "Yup, I see your truck. It's very nice. It's very Walker Texas Ranger."

He laughed. "See what's in the back of the truck?"

I looked and there was a big tarp covering a pile of something, maybe boxes. "Umm, a tarp?"

"Yeah, a tarp... a tarp covering the boxes that hold my life."

He led me back over to the bed and pulled me down. "You aren't selling the lodge, Tula." I opened my mouth to say something and he held up his hand. "Hear me out." I closed my mouth and put my hands in my lap.

"Lillie came home on Thanksgiving break to see me. I had gone into the office on Thanksgiving telling myself I needed to catch up on some more paperwork, but really it was to avoid being home alone. The chief came in and offered me the promotion and all I wanted to do was grab my phone and call you. I left the office and drove home to do just that, but when I got home I found Lillie in the living room, stocking feet up on the coffee table, like I always found her when I would come home from work when she was little. It was like she knew I needed her. I sat down on the couch next to her and her big strong brother started crying and couldn't stop. I'm pretty sure I scared her to death."

That feeling was back in the pit of my stomach. That, I've had too much coffee or I'm about to lose the man I love, feeling and since I hadn't had any coffee today I was pretty sure which one it was.

"She hugged me and made me promise that I wasn't dying of cancer and then she got me a beer and she let me talk. She got me another beer and let me keep talking and then she said probably the most adult thing I've ever heard her say. She said, 'So you love this chick, why is this rocket science?'" And I snorted because I had enough experience with college girls to know that is totally something they would say.

"She didn't understand the implications of living across the country from each other, right?"

He shook his head. "Oh no, she understood completely. What she said next was what I really needed to hear. She said, "You can take that promotion and stay here in Texas, but you'll be miserable Donny Don,"

I raised an eyebrow and he blushed, "That's what she always calls me."

"Okay, sorry, go on Donny Don."

He rolled his eyes. "She told me that home wasn't a place, it's a feeling. It's the place that makes you happy. It's the place where your soul rests. It's the place where when you close your eyes at night that's where you find yourself. She told me that if I wasn't in that place then I was simply existing and not living. Can you believe that? My eighteen year old sister comes up with that and I never did."

I put my arm around his waist. "Sometimes it takes someone not so close to the situation."

"Maybe, but as I sat there it became clear that the place that I go when I close my eyes is here. When I close my eyes I'm holding you. When I close my eyes I'm dancing in the ballroom with you. When I close my eyes I'm carrying you to my bed. You are the place my soul rests. Sugar's is the place that makes me feel happy. So I turned down the promotion, and Lillie helped me pack up the apartment and my truck and I drove her back to Chicago. When I dropped her off at her dorm she gave me a hug and told me to drive straight home." He shrugged his shoulders and his hand rested on my knee. "And then I got your message and I followed the sound of your voice."

I stuttered, "So, so you turned down the promotion?"

"You betcha and I quit my job and let my lease go on my apartment and gave everything that I didn't absolutely need to Goodwill and I got in my truck and I drove and I prayed and I called Julie."

"Why did you call Julie?"

"Because Julie's your best friend and Julie could answer my prayer. I asked her if you were okay and she said, "No, she's not okay. She's depressing the hell out of all of us and only you can fix it." Then she dropped her voice and said, "and you better fix it or else Jesse's gonna make sure you experience Lake Superior firsthand and I'll help." I thunked my forehead, but he was laughing so I guess he wasn't too disturbed.

"And that answered my prayer and I kept driving. And then I called Jesse and told him I was on my way back and we hatched out the birthday surprise."

"So you two were behind the playlist, weren't you?" And suddenly everything made sense.

"Yeah, we were. I was hoping that you would be so enamored by the time I sang happy birthday that you would forgive me for leaving you hanging when you needed me most. Instead it drove you to drink." And I started to laugh, uncontrollably and then the laughter turned to tears and he pulled me into him and held me.

"How much did you have to drink anyway? I think I like inebriated Tula. You get adventurous when you get all liquored up."

I playfully swatted him. "Too much. I didn't even want to go to the stupid party. All I wanted to do was stay in bed with my head under the covers. But then no one told me you were coming. When I heard you singing I was certain that I needed to stop drinking."

He winked at me, "No one was supposed to tell you I **was coming.** That would have ruined your birthday present."

I pulled back out of his arms my voice soft, "So you quit your job?"

He caressed my face, "Yeah, I did. See I know this woman, this **really sexy woman, who has this business and I thought that maybe she** might need some help running it."

"Oh really? Do I know her?" He kissed me pulling my lower lip **through his teeth.**

"You might. Of course there was also that other job offer."

"Job offer?"

"Jesse called me under the ruse of telling me about baby James, but mostly it was to toss out a couple more veiled threats."

"Are you messing with me or was he really threatening you?" Van **looked at me under one eyebrow and I knew Jesse well enough to know the answer.**

"I can't believe those two! I told them I didn't **want you to feel pressured and they go and lean** on you like a casino pit boss!"

"To be honest it actually helped me. I didn't feel good about **leaving you when I did. I choose my job over you and that was wrong on so many levels. You said you understood,** but I really wasn't sure that you did. I know I wouldn't have. I deserved a lot more flack than I got from them."

"I did understand, Van. When you came here you had a whole other life and I didn't expect you to ignore that. But it's funny, Jess kept saying, "He's coming back, Sugar. A man doesn't look at a woman like he looked at you and stay away." I did my best Jesse voice and he laughed.

"He's right about that. He knew the day of the storm when we were sitting in that tree stand and he was pouring his heart out to me. I was getting ready to come back in and he looked at me and thanked me for looking out for you. There must have been something in my eyes because he looked at me and I believe his exact words were, 'My God you're a wolf in sheep's clothing', and he was right. So after he threatened to find me a coffin on The Edmund Fitzgerald he told me he had room on his team for a new task force agent and would I be interested. So, I think I will be gainfully employed any way you look at it. Is that going to work for you?" And this time he wasn't acting the maggot. I looked in his eyes and I saw a touch of fear.

"It's more than going to work for me." And the feeling in my stomach disappeared.

God bless peace.

SIXTY

Christmas Eve meant a lot of things in my family. I meant staying in your jammies until it was time to get dressed for church, it meant cut out cookies in the pie safe and butterhorn rolls in the oven. It meant Bing Crosby on the radio and piles of blankets on the couch. It meant the fireplace never quit burning and the house was never quiet. It meant eggnog and friends and good tidings and the train running around the base of the Christmas tree. This year it meant the start of a new life for me. I was still in my jammies and the cutout cookies were in the pie safe and my mother's butterhorn rolls were in the oven and Bing Crosby was on the radio. There was a pile of blankets on my bed where I spent a lot of time lately being loved by a man who couldn't seem to let me go. The eggnog was chilling in the fridge and the train was running around the base of the Christmas tree. The tree was filled with presents for a certain little baby boy who at this time next year would be trying to pull said tree over. And there was this guy, this really sexy Irishman, who had stepped in and changed it all. Sometimes I had to stop and look around because so much in my life had changed that it almost didn't seem real.

Van had turned down Jesse's offer to be on his team and instead became a consultant to the Superior and Duluth Police Departments in the drug trafficking unit. It allowed him flexibility to help me in the summertime and still kept him involved in something he strongly believed in.

Jess was given a promotion and with it a nice increase in his pay, so Julie quit her day job. She works full time for the foundation now getting the "James and Bonny House of Light" off the ground before the baby comes. The father of one our donors heard about our plans to open a place for families and deeded the foundation a small one-bedroom house. I went to the bank and closed that account. I took the money to renovate the house into something I think would make my dad proud. The inside is being fully redone with a private office for Sharon and Julie. There is going to be that area with couches and a coffeepot where people can come and talk. In the corner there will be a beautiful aviary with all the birds my mother never got to see. I know she sees them now. My father's favorite thing to carve was lighthouses, which was the inspiration for the house, and I was looking forward to displaying many of his carvings once the house was finished. I was currently in the process of designing the sign for the front of the house, the sign that I would carve. Come spring there would be landscaping and new paint. It may not have been my father's dream when he saved the money all those years ago, but I think he would be happy that it was mine. In a few short days Jesse and Julie would be getting married and the last few weeks had been spent getting the ballroom ready and all the last minute preparations that go with a wedding. I was lucky, though, as Julie wasn't too hung up about formalities and that made it easier to plan. I had the caterers and the DJ set to go, now all I needed was for Jesse to tell me who the best man was. That was still a mystery.

I felt a pair of arms go around my waist, "Merry almost Christmas."

I turned. "Same to you, Mr. Bond."

"When are those buns going to be done?" he asked, nodding towards the oven.

"Those aren't for you to eat! Those are for Christmas morning." I told him sternly.

"I know that, I want to know if I have enough time to take you go to my bed and have my way with you." he said kissing my neck.

"No, you don't and besides everyone is going to be here soon! I am not going to get caught in bed with you on Christmas Eve!" I pulled out of his arms and dodged right, but he read me and caught me, flipping me over his shoulder, carrying me fireman style into the living room, depositing me on the couch, and kissing me thoroughly.

"Change your mind yet?" he asked in his sultry voice. Yes.

He grinned at me evilly already knowing the answer and pulled me up off the couch. "Sorry, I'd love to stay, but I have to go pick up your Christmas present." He said leaving me standing there flustered, cheeks red.

"What? Now you're gonna leave? That's not fair, Mr. Bond!" I walked over and brushed up against him and heard him suck in a breath. He pulled me into him then, "Stop doing that or I will be late for your Christmas present."

"You started it," I said against his shirt.

"And I will finish it, later, right now I have to go." he said, planting a kiss on my lips and heading towards the kitchen as I heard the timer go off on the oven. "Is it okay if I take the Sorento? I don't want to get my truck dirty." He said as he threw me a kiss and ran out the door. I wasn't even going to respond to that. Just then I heard him stick his head in the door and say, "And you need to be dressed in something much less provocative when I get back or your Christmas present is going to have to wait."

I set the rolls out to cool and went to my bedroom to get dressed. When I came back out I found Jesse and Julie sitting by the fireplace and Sharon and Lenny were pulling down the drive.

"Hi, I didn't hear you come in." I said.

Julie looked at Jesse smugly. "I told him that we need to start using the doorbell. Never know when we are going to be interrupting something." She said and I gave her a high five. Jess had a stricken look on his face.

"Probably would be a good idea, Jess. You never..."

"Stop! Stop!" he said, throwing his hands over his ears. I gave Julie another high five, only a little lower this time so he wouldn't see us.

Sharon and Lenny came in the back door carrying all kinds of packages -- like there wasn't enough here already! Sharon had the traditional Mogen David wine and I got out the eggnog and glasses for everyone.

"Where's Van?" Sharon asked me as we worked in the kitchen finishing up with the frosting on the rolls and getting the trays of goodies out of the fridge for lunch. It was nearly one o'clock now and he had been gone for almost two hours.

"I have no idea. He told me he was going to get my Christmas present, but that was a couple hours ago. Hope he didn't crash my Sorento." I said only half jokingly.

We heard the garage door roll up as I finished my sentence and I said a little "thank you Jesus" prayer that he was home in one piece.

"Hey Sugar, come here a second." Jess yelled. I told Sharon I'd be right back and went in the living room to see what was up. Jess was bent over the fireplace trying to get the screen put back around it.

"What are you doing?" I asked him.

"I was trying to get the fireplace lit, but the remote wouldn't work." he said.

I adjusted the screen and flipped the switch on the mantle. "Ta da!" I said.

"Smart ass.".

"Jess, you have lived here as long as I have, you know how this works. Maybe you aren't getting enough sleep."

And Julie jumped up and gave me another high five as Van walked in the room.

"Well look at the whole family here." he said, looking a little sheepish.

"Hi, wondered where you got off to, we've been waiting for you to start the party." I said stepping up and giving him a kiss, since he was standing under the mistletoe. I looked up with my eyes and he laughed then, stepping further into the room.

"Sorry I'm late, but I was picking up Tula's Christmas present, well kind of both of our Christmas presents. But it's one of those things that can't wait to be opened so is it okay if I bring it in now?" he asked me with a grin overtaking his whole face.

We all shrugged so he told us to close our eyes and I heard some scuffling around and then he said "open!" When I opened my eyes the final member of the family was there. I ran over pulling her into a hug, "Lillie!" I said, crying already.

"Hi Tula," she said, "it's nice to finally meet you." Van pulled us both into a hug and kissed our temples. "I had to have both my girls here tonight." he said.

I punched him, hard, "You told me she couldn't come home because of school!"

"I lied." he said as the rest of the family crowded in to meet her.

"Jess, were you in on this too? Is that why you dismantled my fireplace?" I asked him, laughing.

He nodded, "Sorry I had to think fast!" And my heart was fuller now than I ever thought it could be.

"Well no wonder you haven't come up with a best man if that's how you think fast!" I laughed back at him.

Van turned then, his arm around Lillie, "He has a best man."

I looked at Jess. "You do? You told me yesterday you were still feeling it out." Which I put in heavy quotations marks.

"And I was, yesterday, but apparently today I'm certain." He said.

I looked back and forth between him and Van and it hit me.

"Bond's your best man!" I said.

"Yeah and you are the maid of honor, see how that works out. You get to dance with him all night and you never know if you get lucky and catch the bouquet maybe you will be the next one to get married." He said tongue in cheek and I hugged him instead of punching him.

Van let go of Lillie and stepped over to Jess doing the man hug thing. "I thought about what you said, Jess, and you were right. It just took me a little while to see that. So I am honored to be your best man and stand beside you as you marry your beautiful lady."

"And it helps that your beautiful lady will be standing next to her?" Jess asked.

"That helps." Van pulled me into him, kissing me hard on the lips.

"Can I ask what you said to him?" Julie asked quietly slipping her arm around Jesse's waist.

Jess shrugged his shoulder. "I asked him if he would stand with me on the most important day of my life because I needed a brother by my side."

Van still had his arm around me. "I didn't think I had much right to be called a brother, but then he said something that got me thinking. He told me that you don't choose your family, God gives them to you. He said flesh and blood doesn't make a family, your heart makes you a family. As I thought back over the last few months I realized he was right. None of us share blood, but I would do anything for any one of you so that makes you my family."

Julie had tears in her eyes and so did I.

"God is good." I said giving Van a gentle kiss and everyone said amen. I let go of Van's hand and grabbed Lillie's pulling her into the kitchen to talk with her in private.

"I'm sorry," I said to her. "I had no idea you were coming! This must be really uncomfortable for you." I got her a glass of eggnog, sans rum, and Sharon and Julie joined me.

"Not at all Tula, I feel like I already know everyone so well from what Van has shared with me. I walked in the door and Sharon had me in a bear hug two seconds after she saw me and was already mothering me!" Sharon winked at her then because that was the truth. "I know that you love my brother and I know he would die for you and the same goes for your brother and Julie. That's all I need to know. I already feel at home and I can't wait to get to know you better so I can finally say I have a sister, wait, actually can I say I have two sisters?"

"As long as I get to say I do too!" Julie said laughing and we sat around the table like we had known each other for fifteen years instead of fifteen minutes. Lillie told us all about school and how she hoped to stay in the Midwest after graduation because she loved snow. I told her she needed to hold the verdict out on that one for more than one snowfall, but she seemed truly happy and I was glad that she felt comfortable here with us.

"How long are you staying, Lillie?" I asked her when there was a break in the conversation.

"I have until the beginning of January. I was hoping for an invite to this big wedding that's coming up. I really want to see my brother in a monkey suit!"

"Consider yourself invited then," Julie said, "I've seen him in a monkey suit and it's worth sticking around for!"

And I punched her, but only a little hard cause she's pregnant. The kitchen filled with men then wanting food and we ate and we talked and we laughed and we sang carols and for the first time in ten years I saw everything I had instead of everything I didn't have.

God bless perspective.

SIXTY-ONE

We laughed and sang and ate and danced and finally around dark we climbed in the car to show Lillie the lights of Duluth. This time of year there were lights everywhere and without question tonight would be an extremely busy night at all the displays. We took two cars with me, Van and Lillie in the Sorento and Jesse, Julie, Sharon, and Lenny in Jesse's Blazer and took the high bridge into Duluth. I could see Lillie with her nose pressed to the glass in the back of the car as we reached the top of the bridge and you could see the lights from Bayfront Park and all the lights of the harbor. From the bridge it looked almost surreal with all the white surrounded by all multicolored lights that twinkled and blinked almost to the rhythm of the lake. I remembered being a kid and having my nose pressed to the glass just like that. Van had his hand on my knee and squeezed it as we approached the bridge, but I was okay. For the first time in a very long time I was okay. We took I-35 and exited to the DECC ready to pile out into the night to see Bentleyville before they closed down for another season, but Van turned left and was going towards Canal Park.

"Van, you missed the turn!" I said, looking behind me to see if Jess was following. He was still following us and was probably wondering what was going on.

"No I didn't. I heard about this other great light show out on Park Point. The Spirit In The Lights. I thought it might be nice to go down by the beach."

And I didn't. I hadn't been out to Park Point since the shooting and was hoping that the next time I went out there it would look nothing like the dark place of death that it was when I left it last and would be filled with sunlight and green leaves and happiness again.

"That's a really nice show Van, but really I think we should stay on this side of the bridge." I tried to sound nonchalant, but he knows me too well and it wasn't likely that would work. I felt Lillie's hand on my shoulder then and I laid my hand over hers. Van turned right into Canal Park and the bridge loomed ahead of me lighting up the night with the lighthouses beaconing in the ships. There were cars pouring off the bridge having been to the Hales home to see the lights and heading back to their homes for the final Christmas preparations. I heard the bells meaning the bridge was going up and we would have to wait.

"I guess we are getting bridged." Van said, **putting the car in park and turning to me.**

"You're starting to sound like native Duluthian." I said.

Lillie was transfixed watching the bridge go up and he leaned over and whispered, "I want to take you back over this bridge and I want you to remember it the way it looks tonight. I want to banish the last memory of you here in my mind and make a new one. Okay?" And I nodded because I knew he was right.

We heard a knock at the window and Jess stood there his hands in his pockets. Van rolled down the window. "What's up, Bond? I thought we were hitting Bentleyville."

"We were, but I decided to take a little trip over the bridge. You guys want to follow?"

Jess shrugged, "We already are." He ran back to his Blazer and Van put up the window as the bridge was on its way back down.

I took a deep breath and he put the SUV in gear and we crossed the bridge. The light show was not far once you got onto the Point and it was standing room only near the Hales house. Forget parking on the street, it wasn't going to happen tonight. Van kept going straight until he got to the stop sign at the boarded up ICO.

"Do you remember what I said to you the last time we were here?" he asked me as he waited for pedestrians to cross.

"Yeah, you told me if I got myself killed you were gonna be really, really ticked." I said it in my fake Irish accent and Lillie broke into a fit of giggles.

He pulled me over the console and kissed me leaving me breathless. "I'm really glad you didn't die out here." He released the brake and rolled forward and I took his hand.

"Where are you going by the way? The light show is way back there." I looked behind us and Jess was following us doing the "what the heck?" hand signs. I did them pointing back and then at Van and rolled my eyes. I saw him and Julie start laughing and knew he understood.

"I'm going to go down here a ways and turn around. Then we can park in the public lot and walk."

And down there a little ways was not where I wanted to go. Down there a ways was okay to stay down there for a few more months as far as I was concerned. He rolled the Sorento towards the airport and as we got closer I tried to stay relaxed and remember that there was nothing scary out there tonight and there was no reason for me to be afraid. He pulled the SUV into a parking space opposite of the beach walk that lead down to the lake. I saw the same hulking bodies of the float planes on the tarmac and the lights twinkling on the runway. The sky wasn't as dark as it was that night, though. The moon shone bright and the stars twinkled in the sky.

I opened the door and heard the waves lapping against the beach. It was quiet and the air was fresh and I sucked in a deep breath remembering that the last time I was here I couldn't do that. It reminded me that life is always changing, but good can come from every experience. Because of this place I had finally found peace and I know who the important people in my life are. I stood there with the door to the Sorento propping me up and Jesse pulled in and parked next to me, opening his door and stepping out. He was facing the harbor and I was facing the beach and he smiled at me.

"Fancy meeting you here." he said softly.

"Yeah, fancy that. You okay with this?" I asked him.

He slammed the door to his Blazer and whispered in my ear, "I am if you are."

And I nodded agreement. He went around to help Julie out and then Sharon and Lenny piled out of the car. Van was standing by the back of the SUV and was holding Lillie's hand.

"I thought maybe we should take a walk down to the beach." He said, his brogue heavy and his eyes sparkling.

"Well I'd be **glad to**, Mr. Bond, as long as you don't mind helping me. Walking in sand covered with snow is still a challenge for me."

And he did one better. He came over and picked me up off my feet, slamming the door with his foot.

"I love helping you." he said, kissing me.

I heard Sharon give a little contented sigh and smiled to myself, she was such a mom. Jess helped Julie and Lillie down the path and Lenny brought up the rear with Sharon. As we broke over the crest and saw the beach it took my breath away. There was a fire going on the sand with the snow cleared off and a ring of cranns surrounding the fire. It looked like my fire pit in the woods and I knew this was where he was all morning.

I nuzzled his neck. "Did you do all this for me?"

"With a little help from a friend." He said and I looked towards Jess, but I could see that he knew nothing about it. Julie, on the other hand, looked guilty.

He set me on my feet near a crann and I looked down. Each one had a V & T 4-ever carved into the top. I sat and everyone else followed, Jesse with Julie, Sharon with Lenny and Lillie sandwiched between Julie and Sharon. There were no cranns left.

"I think you counted wrong, Van, there's no place for you to sit." I said and scooted over so he could share with me.

He shook his head. "I don't need a place to sit."

And he got down on one knee in the sand and pulled out a ring. It was gold with green emeralds surrounding an emerald cut diamond and it was breathtaking. The fire light shone against the diamond making it sparkle and throw shapes against the black of the sand. Time stood still. I registered the sharp intake of breath from my family and the fire crackling, but I was focused on this man who was kneeling before me looking more nervous than I ever thought he could be.

"Tula, I fell for you the first time I saw you. It was like you knew my soul from the first day we met. When I saw you peeking out from behind that door I had no idea that I was about to find out that soulmates really exist. The first time you called me Van was like coming home and when you made me Irish crème cake I lost my heart. When I pulled you into a waltz and you melted in my arms I fell in love. You made my heart ache every time I saw you crying and during the storm, when you cried in my arms, all I wanted to do was wrap my arms around you and protect you from all the bad things that have happened. When I made love to you for the first time I knew that I would never be able to be without you again. I thought I couldn't possibly love you more than I did at that moment, but I was wrong. You continued to amaze me with your tenacity for life and your love for the people in it. I wasn't lying at the foundation dinner when I told everyone how honored I was to be part of that. Experiencing that with you changed me as a person and made me see the bigger picture. Then that horrible day in the ballroom happened and I got a little taste of hell. I had no idea that full blown hell was yet to come and in the blink of an eye I was holding you in my arms here in this very place begging for someone to help you. The fear in your eyes made me want to trade places with you and I would have if the good Lord had let me. I knew then what love was. We have been through so much in such a short time, but the time I spent away from you was enough to tell me that you are my home. This is real. I never thought that it could be this easy to love someone, but I was wrong. It comes natural to me and I love every part of you."

He held the ring up. "My grandmother gave me this ring before she died and told me that I should give it to the woman that I wanted to spend my life with. Lillie got it out on Thanksgiving and handed it to me and told me to tell her what I saw. When I looked at the emeralds I saw Wisconsin as I flew over it for the first time. I saw you standing there at the door peeking out at me not sure if I was an enemy or your savior. I saw you sleeping in my arms in the honeymoon cabin and laying in my arms after we made love. I saw you wearing your stunning green dress and dancing with me to Sam Cooke. But when I looked in the diamond I saw you walking down the aisle to marry me and I saw you holding our baby in your arms and I saw you dancing with me forever in the ballroom in the lodge. In our home. You are the woman I want to spend my life with. So here today in front of all our family I beg you to marry me because I can't be without you ever again."

My heart stopped beating halfway through the speech and my eyes could barely focus past the blurriness of the tears. I sank down onto the sand and took his face in my hands. "You are my life and my love and with everything I have and everything I am, yes, I will marry you."

He slipped the ring on my finger and pulled me into a kiss as our family clapped and hooted and cried.

God bless love...

ABOUT THE AUTHOR

Katie Mettner grew up in Eau Claire, Wisconsin, and moved to the Northwoods as a young adult where she now resides with her husband and three children. Her love affair with Lake Superior began when she met her husband, Dwayne, and he drove her across the bridge one snowy November day with her nose pressed up against the glass. It was in that moment the scene was set for her breakout novel!

Katie doesn't let the detours on the road of life break her stride and, after a long hiatus, she is finally able to waltz again. Her stories are a reflection of her love for family intricately woven with life experience. When the gales of November blow early you can find Katie at the computer with a cup of joe, listening to Michael Bublé and working on Sugar's next adventure.....

Katie would love to hear from you! You can contact her at sugarsdance@gmail.com

Chicago Kraut Dogs

One (1) package Johnsonville Brats or Skin-on hot dogs
One (1) can or bag of sauerkraut
One (1) Gala Apples (or any sweet apple) cored and sliced
Brown Sugar
One (1) 12 ounce can or bottle of Leinenkugel's Beer (If you have the misfortune to live where Leinenkugel's beer is not available then any old beer will do)

Spray Crock-Pot with nonstick cooking spray and layer brats or hot dogs in the bottom. After draining liquid from sauerkraut spread evenly over meat. Lay sliced apples on top of sauerkraut and sprinkle with brown sugar. Finally pour beer over the entire concoction. Simmer on low for 6-8 hours or high for 4 and low for 2. Serve in Chicago style hot dog rolls (Brownberry Select makes a great one!) Pile high with kraut and apples!

Sugar Burgers

1 1/2 pounds lean ground beef
1 cup coffee
1 tablespoon Worcestershire sauce
1/2 teaspoon salt
1/2 teaspoon ground mustard
1/4 teaspoon pepper
1 egg
1/2 cup Bread crumbs (plain)
1 onion, chopped fine (You decide the size☺)
1/2 cup ketchup (Don't be using any of those icky whole tomatoes)

One (1) onion, Large
Butter
More coffee
Onion ciabatta rolls

Mix above ingredients together (make sure to make extra coffee to drink while waiting) and spread mixture in ungreased loaf pan. Do not put ketchup on top of loaf. Bake at 350° F uncovered for 60 to 75 minutes or until internal meat temperature reaches 160° F.

While you wait for the meatloaf to get done and while sipping your coffee take the second onion (or two) and slice in rings. Add to frying pan with butter and more coffee and cook until onions are translucent. Remove from heat.

Place slice of meatloaf on toasted ciabatta roll, top with layer of ketchup and cover in caramelized onions.

Save extra slices of meatloaf and freeze in individual servings and once thawed they can be fried on a griddle and then the whole mouthwatering adventure can begin again.

P.S. If you don't have time to make meatloaf, don't like meatloaf or ran out of coffee (GASP!) you can grill regular hamburger patties and add the onions on the ciabatta roll.

Gitche Gumee Gobblers

Fitger's Crème Liqueur coffee (Can be purchased online, but if you don't have the pleasure of Fitger's coffee any type of black coffee will do)
One (1) shot Kahlúa
One (1) shot Bailey's Irish Cream
Whipped Cream (The good kind that comes out of the can all spirally)
Feel free to adjust alcohol to your liking and remember to drink responsibly.